THE
GHOSTWRITER

Julie Clark is the *New York Times* bestselling author of *The Last Flight*. It has earned starred reviews from *Kirkus*, *Publishers Weekly*, and *Library Journal*, and the *New York Times* has called it 'thoroughly absorbing'. It's been named an Indie Next Pick, a *Library Reads* Pick, and a Best Book of 2020 by Amazon Editors and Apple Books. Her debut, *The Ones We Choose*, was published in 2018 and has been optioned for television by Lionsgate. She lives in Los Angeles with her two sons and a golden doodle with poor impulse control.

THE
GHOSTWRITER

Julie Clark

ZAFFRE

First published in the UK in 2025 by
ZAFFRE
An imprint of Zaffre Publishing Group
A Bonnier Books UK company
4th Floor, Victoria House, Bloomsbury Square, London, WC1B 4DA
Owned by Bonnier Books
Sveavägen 56, Stockholm, Sweden

This is a work of fiction. Names, places, events and
incidents are either the products of the author's
imagination or used fictitiously. Any resemblance to
actual persons, living or dead, or actual
events is purely coincidental.

A CIP catalogue record for this book is
available from the British Library.

ISBN: 978-1-80418-852-1

Also available as an ebook and an audiobook

1 3 5 7 9 10 8 6 4 2

Typeset by IDSUK (Data Connection) Ltd
Printed and bound in Great Britain by 4edge Limited

Zaffre is an imprint of Zaffre Publishing Group
A Bonnier Books UK company
www.bonnierbooks.co.uk

To all the readers who hate it when characters hold their breath: *I did the best I could.*

Foreword

"I know what your dad did."

It was the year I'd turned ten, and one of my classmates had slid onto the bench next to me at school, his voice a hot whisper in my ear.

I set down my bologna sandwich. "He wrote a book." I hadn't been wild about my father's meteoric rise as an author. He talked louder. Drank more than usual—which had been a lot to begin with—and traveled more, leaving me home with his assistant, Melinda, a young woman who now let herself into our house with her own key. Who would tell me my father was too busy to sign my math tests or quiz me for spelling.

My father's success had caught the attention of the literary world—his books were now sitting alongside Stephen King on the shelves and bestseller lists, and in some weeks even outselling him. But it had caught the attention of the rest of Ojai as well, sparking whispers and memories that became loud enough for the kids to notice.

The boy, whose name I no longer remember, had shaken his head, eyes sparkling with glee to be the one to tell me. To shatter my childhood right there in the school cafeteria. "Your dad killed his brother and sister. Murdered them in their own home."

"You're a liar," I'd accused him. "You're just jealous."

But the reaction of the other kids around us stole the certainty from my words. Because there wasn't the scornful skepticism I'd expected, but rather a silent shock that he'd had the guts to say aloud what everyone else already knew.

That's how it started. How I discovered the dark secret that lived at the center of my family.

*   *   *

From there, the murder of Danny and Poppy Taylor became a tale told in hushed whispers at slumber parties alongside Ouija boards and visits from Bloody Mary in the mirror at midnight. Two kids, just like us, stabbed to death in 1975 while the entire town celebrated the official beginning of summer at the annual Ojai Carnival one hundred yards behind their house.

All of my classmates became experts on the story, despite the fact that by the time it began circulating among them, Danny and Poppy had been dead for over fifteen years. How Poppy was supposed to meet her best friend at the Tilt-A-Whirl after making a quick stop at home for a sweater. How she'd been ambushed, murdered in her own bedroom while her older brother, Danny, had been killed in the hallway, just steps away from saving her.

Old newspaper clippings had been dug out of closets and passed around at recess like contraband, kids studying their class photos. Poppy's slight build, wavy hair that looked like it tangled easily, freckles blooming across her cheeks. The way Danny's face glowed with lost potential, his bright smile a promise never fulfilled.

They discussed where Danny had been found, how desperate he must have been to get to his younger sister, to protect her at the expense of his own life. But Danny had failed, Poppy had died, and their names became the property of others, dragged out of the past and into the present. *Don't end up like Danny and Poppy.* Buried inside the rote questions of parents. *Will an adult be home?*

Everything in my childhood suddenly made sense. The low buzz that seemed to follow us wherever we went. That extra space in line at the supermarket. A phone that never rang for play dates or birthday party invitations. I'd always assumed it was because my mother had left when I was five, a shame I carried until a bigger one pushed it away.

Once I knew, it wasn't hard to find the albums tucked in the back of my father's closet.

An early photo, my grandmother's flowery cursive on the back—*Danny age nine, Vince age eight, Poppy age six*—lined up on a brown striped couch, posing with mugs of hot chocolate in their pajamas. Another, a few years later, playing cards around a small Formica kitchen table, their mother a blur in the background, their father's cigarette smoke a gentle swirl rising up from the ashtray at the edge of the frame.

I marked the passage of time as the three siblings aged, the years and days creeping closer to June 13, 1975.

Three years left as they washed the family's station wagon in the driveway—Danny in his OP shorts, holding the hose, my father a shirtless and skinny twelve-year-old, bending over to sponge the hood of the car, and ten-year-old Poppy shrieking as an arc of water hits her back.

Two years left at an academic awards ceremony for Danny, standing tall and handsome in his suit, my grandparents, still unbroken, flanking him on either side.

One year left at my father's fifteenth birthday party, hovering over a homemade birthday cake, glaring at whoever was taking the picture.

Ten months left in Poppy's ninth-grade class picture, her smile revealing a slightly crooked front tooth she probably hated, her long hair pulled back into two barrettes resting just above her ears. I wondered if, on some level, she knew the fate that awaited her at the end of the school year. If she knew that was going to be the last class photograph she ever took. Or if she was simply thinking about whether her hair looked okay or how she would do on a math quiz she might have had later that day.

I read and reread the ten-year retrospective, rehashing the same theories, the same questions that seemed to burn bright in the minds of those who knew Danny. Who'd loved Poppy. They all spoke of Danny's potential, his popularity, his sense of humor. They described Poppy's fierce commitment to equal rights. Her tenacity. Her dream of becoming a filmmaker.

And they spoke of my father as well. The way he'd carry a joke too far, often bordering on cruel. How he'd always strived—and failed—to fit in. At the time, they'd all wondered how awkward Vincent had managed to land that girlfriend.

The one who'd grow up to become my mother.

Their stories uncovered parts of myself that had always been there—my father's intensity. My mother's insecurity. My aunt's fire, and my uncle's charisma.

But as a ghostwriter—a person who listens to other people's stories and spins them into a narrative—I understand now how very hard is to discover what someone has chosen to conceal. And when they die, their secrets get buried in time until there's no one around to remember them.

All that's left now is a fifty-year-old murder that sits at the center of my family, as much a part of my DNA as my brown hair.

4

I've imagined June 13, 1975, a million times. I can see it in my mind, as if from above, watching it unfold like a movie. A young teenage girl running home to grab a sweater, the house just ahead of her. Are the streetlights on yet? The coroner put her time of death at approximately seven in the evening, Danny's shortly after that.

Poppy had no idea what was about to happen to her in that house. The horrific nightmare her final moments would become. No matter how many ways I imagine it, she never had a chance. In the span of one hour, according to the autopsy results, my father had gone from middle child to only child.

Some people say the trauma is what pushed him to grow up to become one of the most prolific horror writers of his generation. Others are not so generous.

My father is a talented novelist—a professional liar by trade and by instinct. I'm not naive enough to think that everything he's told me is the absolute truth. I invite you to judge for yourself, as I've had to do.

Olivia Taylor Dumont
June 13, 2025

Chapter 1

March 2024

I'm washing my coffee mug, hot water tumbling into the deep copper sink, when my phone rings. Wiping my hands on a towel, I cross the room toward the long dining table I bought at a flea market years ago.

I grab the vibrating phone, expecting to see Tom's name and face flashing on the screen. He always calls on his way to the job site and we pass his commute with the never-ending topics we always turn over—why Congress behaves like a bunch of spoiled ten-year-olds. Or what really happened to JonBenét Ramsay. Other times, he'll counsel me through my panic that I haven't been hired for a job in a year. Regardless, ever since we met, we've never stopped talking. I finally understand what other people mean when they reference their *person*. Tom is my person and I'm his.

But it's not Tom calling, it's my literary agent, Nicole. The only person from the publishing world I speak to anymore. At first, my writing friends would check in with me, offering support. Invitations to meet up for coffee or drinks. Sending me links for writing retreats and conferences. But when I continued to pass on them, those invitations turned into supportive texts and emails, then eventually stopped altogether.

A flutter of hope passes through me. Perhaps my exile is finally over.

I glance out the window, across the deck to the wooden structure that serves as my writing studio, and wonder how many months it's been since I entered it. Six? Ten? My mind touches quickly on Tom again, the man who designed it, imagining his delight if I could tell him I finally landed a book.

"I hope you're calling about a job," I say.

It's been over a year since I sat onstage at a major literary conference—the only female writer asked to participate in a panel about ghostwriting in the twenty-first century—and torpedoed my career.

"I am," Nicole says, then hesitates as if she isn't sure how to proceed. "But it's not . . . typical."

I step through the sliding glass doors onto the flagstone patio that overlooks the canyon, and when it's clear, the ocean in the distance. But today the sky is gray, the green trees below me only just beginning to appear as the morning cloud cover starts to burn off. This house, perched high in the hills of Topanga Canyon and purchased with my first big advance—a book about a young female golfer who'd rocketed herself out of foster care and onto the national stage—was the closest I'd come to feeling at home since I left Ojai for the last time at age fourteen.

I love this house, with its stone and plaster walls, sensitive plumbing and quirky corners. Not everyone wants to live up a winding canyon road at least thirty minutes from basic amenities. Not to mention the yearly fires that keep Topanga's residents hyperalert to wind and weather conditions, go bags packed in the trunks of their cars, ready to evacuate at a moment's notice. But I understood the danger. The shadow of it familiar, like a country road leading you home, its twists and turns unwinding like a memory. When you grow up being told your father is a murderer, you learn how to compartmentalize danger in a way that allows you to ignore it most of the time, even though your subconscious is constantly alert. Preparing for it. Waiting for it to surface.

"Just tell me," I say.

"We've been contacted by Vincent Taylor's team. You know, the horror writer? They want you to ghostwrite his next book."

I barely feel the breeze dancing around my ankles and across my bare arms, my mind a swirling mess of confusion at the mention of that name. Vincent Taylor, my father. I haven't spoken to him in at least twenty years, and no one in my current life knows we're related. And yet, he's the dark core I've walled off from the rest of my life.

Nicole hurries to fill my silence. "I know this isn't your usual niche, but it's a job, and they're asking for you."

"I'm not a novelist," I finally say, my voice sounding higher than normal, and I clear my throat to cover my nerves. "There are plenty of people who could do that better than me."

I hear Nicole shuffling things on her desk and imagine the view outside her window in Manhattan, the busy street below clogged with cars and pedestrians. "I know that, but they're telling me he's insisting on you." Her voice drops an octave, curious. "I have to ask, how do you know him?"

I lower myself onto one of the iron chairs surrounding an outdoor table, vines of wisteria crisscrossing overhead. The breeze makes the single lamp suspended above me sway, a sigh of air winding up the canyon. "I don't," I say.

It isn't a lie. I've worked hard to create a life separate from my father, living abroad until I could be certain the American media had forgotten Vincent Taylor ever had a daughter. I moved back in 2005 with dual citizenship and the last name of the man I was married to briefly in my twenties—Dumont. But it's been even longer since I considered Vincent Taylor someone I knew.

After my return, I worked as a journalist, thinking I wanted to write about people like my father, the ones who bent the rules, played the system, and took advantage of their privilege. But I hated it. Always fighting to get the story. Ambushing people at the park, the supermarket, on the phone, trying to get a quote they didn't want to give. Doing the very thing that had been done to me, until I'd managed to change my name and disappear.

I fell into ghostwriting by accident. A former grad-school classmate had become an editor at a major publishing house in New York. She'd reached out to me about a book project she had under contract—a memoir about an iconic film legend of the sixties. The ghostwriter had to drop off the project for undisclosed reasons. My friend was in a bind and needed someone who could hit their deadline. I said yes and discovered I was good at it.

Since then, I've been filling the world with books about strong women. The first Asian-American woman to go into space. Politicians changing the landscape of women's rights. Scientists at the top of their fields. I love the anonymity of ghostwriting, the ability to slip into someone else's skin and inhabit their life just long enough to tell a good story. No one can see who I am or remember who my father is. I'm an invisible hand on the page instead of the name on the cover.

"Well, it's good money," Nicole continues. "He lives in Ojai, so probably not a bad gig either."

"Is there anything else?" I ask, suddenly desperate. A question I've posed too many times to count. In texts, emails, phone calls.

But really what I'm asking is how, after so many years of success, could I have landed here? All I did that day was say out loud what everyone was thinking about the man who sat center stage. John Calder, whose most recent book about a politician-turned-convicted-sex-trafficker, was offensive and misogynistic. "Is it just about the money, John, or is there a line you won't cross? A person you won't elevate, no matter the size of the advance?" I'd asked when it was my turn to talk.

I don't remember what the original question had been, the facilitator an esteemed reviewer from the *New York Times*. But I can still hear the collective inhalation from the audience, the way everyone's head swiveled to where I sat near the end of the stage, my chair a different shade of blue than everyone else's, as if my presence there had been an afterthought. And I knew in that moment I'd made a mistake. The facilitator had cleared his throat and said, "Tell us how you really feel, Ms. Dumont." The crowd had laughed, and the conversation had moved forward, but I'd known in that moment my words had been fatal. To publicly call out a man like John Calder, with his long list of bestsellers and his connections to influential circles ranging from politics to the entertainment industry, regardless of the depraved topics he introduced into public discourse, was an error Nicole couldn't make disappear.

The publisher of the book I'd been promoting asked me to release an apology. Instead, I went on a social media rant about the misogyny in publishing that allowed men like John Calder to profit off depravity. That paid them twice as much as their female counterparts, with larger marketing budgets that exploded their sales numbers. Which, in turn, earned them even bigger advances. I was exhausted by the amount of work it took just to come in second. And angry as well that talent mattered so little to the people on top. The last four posts on that thread sealed my fate:

(7/10) While the rest of us are out here trying to do the hard work of elevating marginalized voices, telling stories that matter to the collective good, John Calder has decided to go a different route.

(8/10) Perhaps like attracts like. You are the company you keep, and John Calder keeps the company of some of the most vile and corrupt individuals in our society.

(9/10) I'm talking about the pedophile politician. The CEO who is also a white supremacist. The judge who gives rape a pass so that it won't "ruin a young man's life."

(10/10) It baffles me that publishers want to support people like this. Who think John Calder is enough of a talent to give him money and a platform to do it.

Because of that, John Calder went on a national media blitz decrying my attempt to cancel him. Then he sued, claiming that he lost out on two book deals because of me, the subjects deciding to go in a less controversial direction. The trial was held in the state where the literary festival had been, and I found myself in front of a judge just itching to put a mouthy woman in her place. He slapped a prohibitive fine on me, $500,000, and advised me to be mindful of my words. To not let myself get so emotional. To *calm down*.

And while people were quietly supportive, that didn't extend to recommending me for ghostwriting jobs. It wasn't as simple as changing my name and writing under an alias. In this genre, you needed a proven track record to get the big books, and mine had been one of the best. Until it wasn't.

"You know I've made every call," Nicole says now. "Tried to cash in on every favor. We just have to wait this out."

To be honest, it's a miracle she hasn't dropped me as a client.

I want to say no to this project. I have to say no—not just because I've worked hard to completely separate myself from my family and the trauma that sits at the center of it, but also because I won't allow myself to be manipulated by my father. Because there's no way this is about a job.

"I thought Vincent Taylor retired a few years ago," I say.

"Men like him love to stage a comeback," Nicole says. "However, I got the sense, talking with his team, that it's not going very well. They've hit some snags, and if this book can be delivered on their timeline, without any more problems, they might be willing to work with us on other projects." She pauses for emphasis. "This could open the door for you again."

I walk to the edge of the patio, where a handmade railing carved from an old oak tree divides my property from the national forest land below it, and stare into the cloudy distance. "What kind of snags?" I ask. "What's the problem?"

"They were light on details. There will be full disclosure once you agree."

A hawk circles overhead, and I feel a sudden wariness, an affinity with the invisible creature it's hunting. "How much?" I finally ask.

"They're starting at two fifty. I can probably get them up since he's asking for you specifically. There's also a royalty split that, if the book earns out—and there's no reason to think that it won't—will be a solid source of income for you." She pauses. "You might not have to sell your house."

The hawk dives and I turn away from the view and back toward my house, remembering the couple who'd toured it just days ago, gliding up the driveway in their silent Tesla, the husband's sockless feet in expensive Italian loafers, the wife clutching her Birkin bag to her chest as they navigated the dirt path winding toward the wooden stairs that led up to the front door. I'd smiled at them on my way out, knowing I didn't want to subject myself to the opinions of potential buyers, but the woman's voice floated down to me from above as I sat in my car with the windows down. "This is a teardown," she'd said, disdain dripping through her words.

And later that evening, when my real estate agent called to tell me they weren't going to make an offer, she'd suggested dropping the price. Again.

"Fine," I tell Nicole now, knowing I'll regret it. Knowing this job will cost me in ways I can't even begin to imagine.

"I'll let them know and circle back with full details."

"How soon does he want to start?" I ask.

"They're in a rush, so I'm thinking it'll move quickly. Plan to head up there by the end of the week."

We disconnect, and I look back toward the canyon, no sign of the hawk or its prey. I try to think about this not just as an opportunity, but a necessity. My father used to always say *No regrets, no looking back*. I make a promise to not let myself get sucked into whatever plan he's got for me. Because this book has to be a ruse; my father has been churning out novels for decades and he certainly doesn't need my help to do it. I will

view it as a necessary evil to move past this phase of my life—
to stave off the overdraft notices arriving almost daily on my
phone. To pay what I owe to both John Calder and my attorney.
And perhaps to also get some closure with a man who has been
virtually unknown to me my entire life.

Regardless, at age forty-four and after nearly a three-decade
absence, I'm finally going back home.

Chapter 2

On Friday, Tom is up to see me off, the early morning light just barely brushing the tops of the trees surrounding my house. I stand on the deck drinking my coffee, looking out over the canyon, an interesting mix of anxiety and nerves swirling through me. When the contract had landed in my in-box on Wednesday, I'd called Nicole to go over the details.

"They don't want to disclose he worked with a ghostwriter, so you're going to need to keep this quiet," she'd said. "They'd suggested an NDA, but I was able to walk them back by reminding them that you're a pro and have worked on projects like this before."

"That's fine," I said. The last thing I wanted was to let anyone know I was ghostwriting a horror novel for a man despised almost as much as John Calder.

Nicole's voice cut through the line, reading from the contract. "'AUTHOR will not reveal collaboration on WORK in conversations, interviews, media,' blah blah," she read. "Obviously, since it's Vincent Taylor, he's going to want his fans to think he wrote it himself. But the publisher will know, and that's all we care about."

"Understood," I told her, not bothering to say that I would take this secret to my grave—happily—if it meant I could get back to work. I tried not to think about what taking this job said about me. How easily I've lowered myself to Calder's level, taking on a project for the size of the advance and not caring who the collaboration was with.

Tom comes up next to me and together we look out into the distance, the sky a silken pink that reminds me of the mountains surrounding Ojai at sunset. But of course I don't mention that.

When I'd told him about the job, he'd had a hundred questions—who, where, how long. I deflected by telling him there was an NDA and that I wasn't able to disclose anything. And while it was technically a lie—I hadn't been asked to sign anything—I rationalized it by reminding myself that I'd worked on many books before where I couldn't disclose I was the ghostwriter, and that this wasn't any different. But I knew he'd be angry if he found out. Tom grew up in a house full of lies— both of his parents were narcissists who cheated and manipulated and lied—and when we first started dating, he was up front about how lying was a nonstarter for him.

But I hadn't known that yet when I gave him the backstory I've given everyone since moving back to the United States—that I was raised by two loving parents and that my father had died suddenly of a heart attack when I was abroad for high school, and that my mother had passed away from uterine cancer while I was in college. In those early days, when we were still sharing the basics about our lives, I never considered telling him the real story. I hadn't told anyone, for years, about who I was related to, or what had happened in my family. So it never felt like a lie I was telling Tom specifically. The truth lives far away, in a distant corner of my past that I have no intention of ever visiting. There was no reason to worry about discovery because there was no way I'd ever have a reason to contact either of my parents. It doesn't impact who I am as a partner to him. It's simply not relevant.

"Are you all packed?" he asks me now.

"Pretty much," I say.

He pulls me into a tight hug and I feel a flare of guilt that this secret I thought was so carefully hidden is suddenly right next to me again. A beating heart, waiting for me to acknowledge it.

He walks me to my car, carrying my bag, and leans down to give me one last kiss through my open window. "Call me when you're settled tonight, okay?"

My eyes lock on his, and in this moment I regret taking the job. I shouldn't be doing this—not just lying to him about the legalities of it, but returning to a place I decided to leave long ago. But the contract is signed, the advance is being processed, and the only thing I can do is hope I can be in and out without incident.

* * *

I take the coast north, cutting east toward Ojai at Ventura, allowing my mind to travel back to my childhood, before I knew about the murders or noticed the cloud of suspicion that trailed after my father. To a time when we lived in a tiny apartment just off of Ojai Avenue. Every Sunday, we'd eat lunch at Nina's Diner, where I'd inhale one of their burgers with the famous red relish and my father would mainline black coffee, trying to regulate whatever hangover he had at the time. He'd entertain me with stories about Lionel Foolhardy—a clumsy and accident-prone boy whose good intentions created disaster wherever he went— pet guinea pigs accidentally set loose in the classroom when Lionel was assigned to clean the cage. A small fire caused by a science experiment gone wrong.

But that was before my father's writing career had exploded. Before his drinking had gotten worse, before he'd spiraled into cocaine as well. It was only as an adult that I'd realized what he was doing—self-medicating to deal with whatever trauma he carried. Drugs, alcohol, women—he was a frequent topic in the tabloids until even the media grew weary of him.

I'm not estranged from my father because I think he killed Danny and Poppy. Despite his many flaws, I don't believe the man I once worshipped could be a murderer. But fame and trauma turned a once loving father into one I barely recognized. Habits became addictions and the father I knew disappeared, replaced by a man who consistently let me down. Who, after my mother abandoned me, decided to do the same. Sent abroad to boarding school at age fourteen, I spent most school holidays rattling around an empty campus or with friends. When he did manage to cobble together a vacation, I spent my time alone because my father always booked last-minute speaking engagements wherever we went, and then he'd spend the rest of his time in the hotel bar. It's hard to know who hurt me more—my mother for leaving and never looking back, or my father, who disappeared before my eyes. Pieces of him vanishing like a parlor trick, until there was no one left but me.

* * *

As I enter the outskirts of Ojai, I note the changes in the landscape. New money flushing the old Ojai out. I pass through downtown, traffic clogging Ojai Avenue as tourists crisscross the two-laned road, people floating by on bikes borrowed from the resort, and memories come flooding back. Of riding on my father's shoulders, eating an ice cream cone. Of holding my mother's hand as we crossed the street, her swishing skirt more vivid in my mind than her face. Of the light in Ojai, this magical golden hue that fades to pink just as the sun sets. The scent of eucalyptus and rosemary on the miles of trails surrounding the town.

And of Jack Randall, the son of Danny's best friend, Mark. Jack, a boy who'd also been raised by someone traumatized by that day in 1975. We'd each learned early on how to live alongside memories never spoken aloud. But together, we searched for answers in secret, whispering our theories behind my closed bedroom door or at the lunch table at school.

Aside from poring over my father's photo albums, we would visit the library, telling the librarian we were working on a report about the history of Ojai. In reality, we spent the time flipping through microfiche news articles from June and July 1975, looking for information on the murders. Those articles offered little more than vague pieces to the puzzle. *An active case being aggressively pursued.* But the ten-year retrospective in the Ojai paper was much more detailed, probably because my father was no longer a minor and people were ready to name names.

The police's working theory from the beginning was that the killer was someone passing through town. Poppy had reportedly hitchhiked into Ventura and back again the weekend before, and they were looking for anyone who'd seen Poppy get out of that car, hoping to lock down a make and model. Track down the man who'd met a young, attractive girl and returned the following weekend because he saw an opportunity. Danny had just been collateral damage. But among the locals, there were rumors. Rumblings of a different story that began to surface. That were later passed between my classmates like that newspaper article. Stories about fights between my father and Danny.

About how my father and Poppy had been seen arguing shortly before the murders. That my father had gotten physical with her.

There is so much to unravel, tangled not just by perspective, but by the passage of time. Nearly fifty years have gone by. Memories have faded. Innuendo and suspicion have calcified into something concrete. Everyone has a theory but no one has any answers. And my father sits at the center, refusing to acknowledge any of it.

One thing he will say to anyone who dares to bring it up is that he had an alibi. He'd been with my mother, Lydia, which was verified by the teacher who'd also been with them, mediating an argument between my parents. *It was good enough for the police. I don't give a shit what anyone else thinks.*

Soon, traffic slows down enough for me to realize none of the familiar landmarks are left – the ice cream parlor with its round globe lights in rainbow colors, the mom-and-pop pharmacy where Jack had once stolen a five-cent piece of Bazooka gum just to prove that he could. But if I stare hard enough, I feel like I might see Jack on his BMX bike, weaving his way through the pedestrians, and me pedaling hard on my old Schwinn, trying to keep up. I know he still lives here, running his family winery, and I wonder if he'd recognize me. Or if his eyes would slide over me, just another tourist passing through.

Chapter 3

My father's street on the east end of town remains mostly unchanged, and as I turn into the long driveway, the years fall away. I consult the small Post-it on my dash, punching in the code sent to me by my father's attorney, and the electronic gates swing open. My tires crunch on the gravel, the foliage on either side thick and green, and I pull into an open carport, parking next to a fountain that used to bubble water but is now dry and cracked.

The house is a two-story Spanish-style hacienda my father bought shortly after his first book sold one million copies. It looks the same at a glance but is showing the years upon closer inspection. Chipped roof tiles, peeling paint around the windows. But the landscapers have been doing their job keeping the space clear of weeds, switching out the roses I remember for drought-resistant plants and hardscape. The steps leading up to the oak front door are swept, the hand-painted tiles still colorful and bright.

I lift my hand to knock, but the door opens as if the person on the other side had been waiting for me.

But it's not my father. It's a small woman wearing a blue track suit, her gray hair in a low bun at the base of her neck. I look beyond her, expecting to see or hear my father, but the space behind her is empty.

She raises her eyebrows, as if expecting me to explain myself. I glance over my shoulder toward the driveway, then say, "I'm Olivia Dumont."

"*Dumont*." She rolls her eyes. "I know who you are." Finally, she steps aside, allowing me to pass through the foyer and into the great room. The same furniture—well-worn leather chairs and couches in the same configuration—greets me. The terracotta floor gives the space a warmth against the white plaster walls. Dark beams high above are free of dust and cobwebs.

Unsure what to do, I stand there waiting. The directions from my father's attorney had been very specific. I was to drive straight to the house, arriving no later than nine in the morning. I was to tell no one in town who I was or why I was there. I would be staying in the guesthouse and working only in the mornings with Mr. Taylor.

"My name is Alma," she says, though she doesn't say who she is to my father—a companion? Some kind of housekeeper? "Can I get you some tea? I was just going to make some for Mr. Taylor."

"I'd love something stronger, if you have it. A gin and tonic?" I give a hollow laugh. "I know it's early but . . ." I'm surprised by how tense I am. Forever that young girl, quivering with nerves at the prospect of a difficult conversation with her father.

She mutters something under her breath about fathers and daughters before gesturing toward the back staircase. "He's in his office. I assume you know the way."

Dismissed, I take the back stairs, a narrow tunnel that drops me just outside my old bedroom. I ease the door open and see it exactly as I remember. My bed shoved into a corner under the window, where I used to lie and stare at the stars peeking through the trees. Dreaming of one day leaving this town. I'd gotten what I wanted, but I never expected I'd get it so soon. Never expected how easy it was for my father to ship me off to Switzerland when I was fourteen and resume his life as if

I'd been a phase. *Fatherhood? I tried that once. It was fun for a little while.*

I keep walking, past my father's closed bedroom door to the end of the hallway, then down three steps to the door of his study, a corner room perched above the garage. I hesitate. The last time I spoke to my father was the night of my college graduation. But that wasn't the last time I saw him; that was at a literary conference in New York about eight years ago. I always make it a habit to check the list of panelists and keynote speakers before attending one. If he's on the schedule, I always pass. But that time, he'd been a late add and I'd missed the announcement. I'd been standing with a group of friends in the lobby of a hotel in Times Square when a commotion in the distance caught our attention. A wave of energy rippled through the crowd and my father appeared, surrounded by adoring acolytes and conference administrators. He'd glanced our way, his eyes landing on me for just a second before sliding away and passing through the revolving door and out onto the street.

"I can't believe he's still relevant," one of my friends had said.

I don't remember what I'd responded, my mind still on that glance. At the lack of recognition, and I felt a complicated mixture of sadness and regret. I'd left the conference that afternoon, citing an emergency at home.

I knock softly on his office door.

"Enter."

He's seated at his enormous desk facing the windows that span one entire wall of the room. The rest is dominated by floor-to-ceiling bookshelves, filled with copies of his own books, printed in what must be more than forty languages. His hair is now completely white, looking slightly unkempt, as if he's been running his hands through it, trying to noodle out a plot problem.

But the computer screen in front of him is dark. The stacks of papers and books littering the desk's surface appear to be arranged rather than the result of a writer at work. He swivels in his chair to face me.

I stand there, unsure of what to say. *Hi, Dad* seems too easy when there is so much more I want to ask. *What's going on? Why am I here?* Surely he doesn't really want me to write a book for him.

"Welcome home," he says. He must notice the expression on my face because then he says, "You look like you have some questions."

"What the hell is going on?" I finally ask.

He gives me a sharp look and says, "I hired you to do a job, Olivia."

Echoes of the past fold over me, my father's commanding tone sending me back to my childhood, and I press my lips together, reminding myself that I'm an adult and I can leave at any point.

"Let me rephrase," I say. "Why have you brought me here? What is it you really want?"

"I thought the terms of the contract were clear."

"I don't write novels," I tell him. "I sure as hell don't write them for people like you."

"And yet, here you are." We stare at each other, a silent stand-off. Then he says, "You really screwed the pooch on that John Calder thing."

Of course, my father would have heard about my massive misstep. Publishing is a small industry and people love to gossip.

"Not even I was canceled like that," he continues, "and they all thought I got away with murder."

"Most people still believe you did," I say, unable to help myself.

He ignores my jab. "I figured a job right now—even a lowly novel—would be appreciated."

"I don't need your help." It's offensive to think that after all these years, the many ways he failed me as a parent—as a human—he thinks he can show up now with a favor and expect all to be forgiven.

"Sit down, Olivia. Looking up at you hurts my neck."

The hardwood creaks under my weight, a familiar sound despite the decades since I heard it last. The quilted chair is still in the corner, the place where I once did my homework.

I sit, allowing myself a moment to really look at him. The first thing I notice is the way his shirt bags around his shoulders, no longer filling it out. His legs look like twigs beneath his usual dark jeans, bony ankles poking out with mismatched socks beneath the hems. It's like looking at a bad portrait of a man I used to know. Familiar landmarks are there—the way his chin juts out, his slightly large ears pushing out from beneath the unruly mop of hair. The bridge of his nose still crooked. But he's diminished. This was a man whose intensity could easily command an audience of hundreds. But now it's as if he's reverted back to the sullen teenager he once was, time circling in on itself.

Before I can say anything, Alma enters, bringing tea for my father and another one for me.

"I thought . . ." I start, but stop when I see the look she's giving me.

"No alcohol in the house," she says. To my father she asks, "Have you told her yet?"

"She's been here two minutes." He sounds annoyed, but his nerves are visible in the way his hands tremble, in the agitated way his gaze jumps from his tea to the window, to the books on the shelves.

Alma stares at him, waiting. They seem locked in some kind of silent argument, until finally my father capitulates and answers her question. "No."

Alma turns to me. "Your father is sick."

I look at him again, wondering what it might be. Cancer? His heart?

But Alma speaks for him. "It's Lewy body dementia." When she sees my confused expression she says, "It's a cross between Alzheimer's and Parkinson's. It's degenerative, though there are things we're doing to slow it down." She gives my father a pointed look and says, "And working on a book with his estranged daughter isn't one of them."

I nod, unable to speak, my mind trying to catch up.

Alma continues, "Your father's disease has progressed enough that it's compromised his written language."

"I'm sorry to interrupt, and I don't mean to be rude," I say to her. "But what exactly is your role here?"

"I am your father's caregiver. He hired me shortly after his diagnosis on the advice of his doctor. I drive him to his appointments. I make sure that he eats and takes his medications on time. I make sure that nothing upsets him." Her lips form a tight line, telling me that my presence here is not something she welcomes. Or perhaps she's judging me for the fact that it's her doing those things for him and not me.

My father interrupts. "I have a completed draft of a book. I'm under contract to finish it, but I can't." He looks down for a second, then up again, Alma a silent sentinel next to me, giving him the space to continue. "When you find yourself in a place like this, you look back on your life. You have regrets."

I wait to see if he'll expand on which of his many regrets he's referring to.

"I don't know if this is something I can do for you," I finally say. "I realize I signed a contract but . . ." I look past him through the windows to the mountains in the distance. My father has the perfect vantage point to see the pink moment Ojai is famous for, when the sunset illuminates the mountains in a magnificent shade of rose.

"I know I've let you down in a thousand different ways," he says. "But I need this, and I think you do too." When I don't respond, he says, "Let's just try it out. If, after a week, it isn't working, you're free to go."

I think again of the money I owe John Calder. Of the $500,000 that I've barely made a dent in. Of my mortgage payment, which had been late again last month, and the call from my attorney's billing department, asking for me to get current on my account, which is edging up towards $200,000. I think of my house that I will surely lose if I don't make this work. I take a sip of my tea, wishing desperately for that gin and tonic, and say, "Okay. A week."

My father slaps his hands on his knees, delighted. "Excellent." To Alma he says, "We have a few more things to discuss. Could you take Olivia's things up to the guesthouse?"

"That won't be necessary," I interject. "I can get myself settled."

"There are clean sheets and fresh towels," Alma says. "Unfortunately I couldn't do anything about the boxes, but hopefully they won't get in your way." She leaves, closing the door softly behind her.

"Any dead hamsters in them?" I joke.

When I was young, my father loved designing treasure hunts for me. He'd leave me notes on the bathroom counter, sending me running to his sock drawer for a shiny silver dollar, or taped to the milk carton, directing me to the broom closet where I'd find a package of my favorite licorice sticks. But when I was eight, I came home from school to find a box sitting in front of our apartment door. That particular hunt had involved boxes of many kinds, growing larger and larger until I'd found the final box tucked underneath the sink in the bathroom.

"That was a mistake," my father snaps, pulling me back to the present. "It could have happened to anyone."

"Not to people with a basic understanding of biology," I tell him. "Everyone knows you need to punch more than two holes in the lid."

I take another sip of tea, waiting for my father's flare of defensiveness to die down. Finally he says, "I'm seven years sober, you know."

"Congratulations," I say, wondering if he's about to make some kind of amends.

"It nearly killed me, so I quit. The irony is that now I'm dying anyway."

I shake off the complicated swell of regret and fear that I might lose a man I've spent years convincing myself I didn't need. "Tell me about the book."

My father swivels in his chair and opens the bottom desk drawer, pulling out a stack of legal pads held together with rubber bands—twenty or thirty of them. Horrified, I realize he's written the entire thing by hand. "There are a few things you need to know." He hesitates, as if unsure how to continue. "First of all, it's not a novel. It's a memoir."

"I don't understand," I say. "I was told it was your next horror novel. Why lie about that?"

"We didn't want anyone to know about the scope of the project in the event you passed on it."

Of course. My father wants me to ghostwrite a memoir about his glorious career. To extol his talent, his many awards and successes. I don't know if I'll be able to do that objectively, but I promised I would try.

"There's certainly a lot of material to work with," I say. "I'll need access to all of your editors, your publicists over the years, your agent of course. And just so you know, I'm not going to gloss over your addiction or your behavior. You wouldn't want me to. Scandal sells books, and you certainly created a lot of it."

"You misunderstand," he says. "The memoir isn't about my career. It's about my childhood. Specifically, it's about my family and the months leading up to the murders of Danny and Poppy."

I sit back in my chair and stare at him, the lie about the novel suddenly making sense. If word got out that my father wanted to write a tell-all about the murders, people would go berserk. My mind shifts again to who I'll need to talk to—Danny and Poppy's friends, anyone who worked on the case in 1975. People who knew my father.

My mother.

I don't know if I'm ready to tackle this project, and yet I feel as if I've been waiting my entire life to write it.

"I'll have to read what you've written so far," I finally say. "But I'll also need your permission to talk to the people who were there. Have you done any of that prep work? Let them know you're writing a book?" I ask, my chest tightening, imagining having to approach people cold. Typically, when someone decides to write a memoir, they tell the people closest to them that I'll be reaching out, and that it's okay to talk to me.

My father shakes his head. "I don't think that'll be necessary. I haven't hired you to write a book; I've hired you to fix the one that already exists."

"But what if I have to rewrite something?"

"I know how to write a book, Olivia."

"You know how to write a novel," I clarify. "This is completely different. A book like this has to hang on facts, not fiction."

"This is a nonnegotiable. No one knows what I know, so they can't help you anyway. And I'd like to remind you that a breach of contract is probably not something you'd like to explore." His gaze is hard and he holds mine, waiting for me to capitulate.

I want to get up and leave. Tell him this isn't how I work. Or that I'm happy to figure out nondisclosure agreements for the people involved if that would make him feel more comfortable, but the idea of approaching them—Poppy's best friend, Margot. Danny's best friend, Mark. My mother—and explaining that my father is writing a book about their shared trauma isn't something I want to do.

He hands me the stack of legal pads. "I apologize for not typing it." He waves in the general direction of the mess that now sits on my lap, the edges of the pages limp, some of them stained. "Everything you need is in there," he says. "All you have to do is transcribe it and clean it up. I thought I could do it myself, but my disease had other plans." He looks defeated. "This should be easy money for you. I estimate four weeks, tops. Then you can be on your way."

My unease at the idea of sitting down with my mother for the first time in nearly forty years melts away as I stare at the stack of ruffled pages. I will admit, I'm intensely curious to see what my father has to say about that time. Those events.

"Why do you want to write this book?" I ask. "What are you hoping to accomplish?"

My father sighs and looks out the window. "I need the money," he admits. His voice is quieter as he continues. "The kind of lifestyle I was leading, it gets expensive."

I think of how many books my father has sold over the course of his career. The size of his advances and film options— seven of his books have made it to the screen. "Are you telling me you're broke?"

He looks at me again and says, "I'm saying that there isn't much left. Certainly not enough to pay for my care, which is only going to get more expensive as my condition worsens."

"What about the house?" I ask. "It's got to be worth several million at this point."

He shakes his head. "It needs a new roof. Updated plumbing and electrical. But aside from that, I pulled most of the equity out and spent it."

"What about other investments? Properties?"

"I never got around to buying any."

I'm numb. I often imagined how I would hear of my father's passing. An obituary in the *New York Times* landing in my in-box? A social media post floating through my feed? I never expected he'd leave me anything, always assuming his money would go to charity. To be honest, I'm not that surprised there's nothing left.

God, what a pair we make.

"I need this to work, Olivia. But aside from the money, it's been decades of speculation. Of rumors and innuendo. I realize I played a part in all of that by refusing to speak about it." He gives me a searching look and says, "No one knew Poppy and Danny the way I did. Not their friends, not even our parents. When I die, they'll die with me, without ever having gotten to live. This is the least I can do for them."

I say nothing, knowing this isn't about my aunt and uncle. It's about money and about manipulating me one last time.

Chapter 4

The first thing I do once I'm settled in the guesthouse is google *Lewy body dementia*. I scan the links until I find a source I can trust.

LBD is a progressive disease with a decline in mental abilities. Affected individuals might have visual hallucinations and changes in attention or their ability to focus. REM disorders are often a precursor. Physical symptoms include loss of smell, dizziness, muscle rigidity and/or tremors, slower movement, and difficulty walking. Life expectancy is typically seven to eight years after symptom onset, although it can be significantly shorter. LBD differs from Alzheimer's in that there are no defined stages, making LBD more challenging to navigate.

I stare at the screen, trying to wrap my mind around the idea that my vibrant, energetic father could be reduced to something like this. He seemed fine when we spoke earlier. Sharp, aware of his surroundings. And yet, he's called me here to do something he should have been able to do for himself.

I look around the guesthouse. If this room is any indication, my father has been declining for some time. After our conversation, I'd crossed the courtyard with my bag and what felt like twenty pounds of legal pads, climbed the steep stairs, and fumbled around for the light switch. When I flipped it, the room illuminated in a dim glow from a single fixture overhead, revealing at least fifty bankers boxes crowding the room. They press in on me now, stacked five or six tall, lining the walls of the small space that can't be more than eight hundred square feet, including an ancient kitchenette that doesn't look safe to use. In some places, the stacks are two and three boxes deep, and I think again of that awful treasure hunt when I was eight.

I remember the way I'd slowed down as I approached the box sitting on our front step, my name written in unfamiliar script on the lid. My mind immediately leapt to my mother, who still haunted the quiet corners of my dreams, the woman I still expected to return for me someday. I'd stared down at the box, imagining her sneaking into town while I was at school, from wherever she'd been hiding, and leaving me something. My heart set loose in an unsteady rhythm that I no longer tried to contain as my mind chased the possibilities—

A silver bangle bracelet that would remind me of her every time it flashed beneath my sleeve.

A book she'd treasured as a child, inscribed to me.

A scarf she'd knit herself.

Tickets to see Madonna.

But when I opened the box and saw the first clue written in my father's handwriting, I was embarrassed by the ridiculous way my mind went to zebras instead of horses. I unlocked our front door and stepped into the dark interior, window shades drawn tight against the warm Ojai afternoon. I dropped my backpack and the empty box by the door and reread the clue.

The place where we can always find an escape. The bookshelves in the living room, which contained another box with another clue.

Cozy hugs can be found here. The top shelf of my father's closet, where he kept his sweaters.

I bounced from room to room, earlier thoughts of my mother long forgotten, focused on the hunt. Not knowing whether I'd find something spectacular at the end of it or something mundane. Not caring either way. My father had a gift for creating fun in a life where money was tight and friends were few. No one's mother allowed them to come over to play after school, since there was never an adult home. The kids in my third grade class seemed too busy to include me in their after-school activities. Except Jack.

I found the last box under the bathroom sink, the dark space warm and dank. It had a couple holes punched in the top and I held my breath as I opened it carefully.

As my eyes adjusted to the dim light, I could see the brown fluff in the corner of the box, the hamster I'd been begging my father to get me for months, half-hidden beneath wood shavings. "Hello, little guy," I said, my voice bouncing off the tile walls of the bathroom and vibrating inside my ears. I stroked his back, so soft I could barely feel it.

The hamster was quiet and I wiggled my fingers underneath him, noticing that he wasn't as warm as our classroom hamster, Nibbles. That I couldn't feel his tiny heartbeat pounding through his chest the way I could when I picked up Nibbles.

I prodded him again with my fingers, panic welling up inside of me, the mirror over the sink reflecting my horror back to me.

I don't remember what happened after that. Did I throw the box away? Run to the neighbor's apartment and wait for my father to get home? It's as if the memory ends with the discovery of a dead hamster in a box.

I pull myself back to the present, then pick up my phone to call Nicole.

"Did you get there okay?" she asks when she answers. "What's he like?"

I look at the stack of legal pads on the desk in front of me, twisting my finger in the oversize rubber band holding them together and say, "Honestly, he's not what I expected."

"In what way?" she asks.

I think about how to answer her, what to say that won't reveal the truth of my connection to him. "I expected the dynamic man we used to see in the public sphere. Here, he's just dimmer. Diminished."

"I guess that's what old age will do."

"He's sick," I tell her, lowering my voice even though there isn't anyone around to hear me.

"Oh wow," she says. "What is it?"

"Lewy body dementia."

She gives a low whistle. "Isn't that what Robin Williams had? No wonder they called you in."

I pull my finger out of the rubber band, letting it snap back against the pages. "There's something else. It's not a novel," I tell her. "It's a memoir about the murders."

"Jesus."

"He's written the whole thing by hand," I say, flipping through the pages on top. "On about thirty legal pads. Black ink. It looks like some kind of serial killer manifesto."

Her voice turns serious. "Do you want me to push for you to get a room at a hotel instead? An Airbnb?"

"It's fine. He's fine," I say. "They've got me in the guesthouse. It's totally separate, with a door that locks. Did you read that email from Neil?"

Neil is the editor assigned to the book, a man notorious for his ruthless red pen. He'd emailed last night, asking that I stay in close contact, reiterating the June deadline.

"I did. Do you need me to intervene? See if we can extend it a bit?"

"Do we have that kind of leverage?" I ask.

"Not sure," she says. "I'm happy to feel him out if you want."

I think about how important it is that the publisher has confidence in my ability to not only work with my father, but to meet my deadline. I need this job to be a success so I can get back to elevating the voices I want to elevate. "No," I tell her. "Let me see what I can do first."

"Just pick a place and begin," she suggests. "And cc me on everything. I'm sure if you can get a draft they're happy with, you can do the copy edits at home."

I imagine returning to Topanga, to the financial troubles that await me there. Of leaving my father to his slow decline, letting Alma deal with the packing up and sale of this house. Finding a care facility for him when he becomes too difficult to manage at home and figuring out how to pay for it. None of those jobs are mine, and yet I feel a stab of guilt for abdicating my role as his daughter. All these years, I've been righteous in my decision to cut him from my life. And now, what I feel most is doubt.

"Some good news," Nicole says, pulling me back. "The first chunk of your advance landed, and we'll get it out to you in a couple days." They'd rushed the contract and payment, and while Nicole had tried to get creative with the advance structure, fighting for me to get as much as possible up front, the publisher had held firm. $100,000 upon signing the contract, another $100,000 upon acceptance of a finished manuscript, and the remainder split between the publication of the hardcover edition and the paperback.

Between what I owe John Calder and my attorney's fees, that first chunk of money will likely spend less than forty-eight hours in my bank account.

"I've got a meeting," Nicole says. "Call if you need anything."

"I will," I say, then disconnect.

I slide off the rubber bands, being careful not to tear any of the pages from the spine, and start to read.

The sharp, jagged edges of my father's handwriting send me back to my days at boarding school, when he'd drop me an occasional card from wherever he was in the world, telling me about this successful talk or that prestigious award, the *f*'s and the *g*'s like spikes striking upward or downward. A handwriting expert would likely have a field day.

But after about twenty minutes, my head begins to ache behind my eyes. What I've read so far isn't the first draft of a book, it's a man rambling about his childhood. The things he loved, the things he hated. His resentment over having to share a room with his older brother while his sister got her own. This is the kind of stuff I usually let a subject blow through in the first few days of a project, never bothering to writing any of it down.

I stand and stretch, then wander over to a stack of boxes and lift the lid off one nearest me, finding a jumble of papers inside. Taking a handful, I pull them out and flip through them. Paid bill stubs for cable, utilities, water and power, dated several years ago. Unused pads of paper, promotions from local real estate agents. I toss it all back inside and lift another lid. Advance reader copies of books sent to my father to endorse, wedged in so tight, I can't squeeze my fingers between them to lift one out. Some titles I recognize, while others are unfamiliar, the publication dates emblazoned on the spines long since passed.

The bed is in the far corner, under a window with a sheer curtain that thankfully looks freshly laundered. I sit on it, noticing the old clock radio flashing the wrong time, and allow myself to finally absorb the fact that I'm back after so many years. Shadows of my younger self dance in the corners, teasing me out, forcing me to remember things I'd long forgotten. The way I used to play hopscotch in the courtyard, my father coming down on his breaks to play with me, the two of us making up ridiculous rhymes as we hopped on one foot. Or the way we'd sit in the living room watching TV—me with a mug of hot chocolate and him with his bottomless glass of whiskey. Those elaborate treasure hunts he'd design for me—sending me racing all over the house and surrounding grounds, never knowing if the final prize would be something big like a new bike, or small like a pencil box in the shape of a dog. Or that dead hamster, suffocated in a box under the bathroom sink. Always exhilarated by the trail of clues, but also cautious about what I might find.

I spent years chasing after my father, hoping the man who showed up would be the version of him that I needed. Occasionally, I got him. A sage piece of advice delivered across the Atlantic on a long-distance phone call. A card with a funny drawing landing in my mailbox for Groundhog Day. But by the time I was seventeen, it had been years since I'd seen that man. He no longer existed. I stayed abroad for college, and by the time I graduated, I knew I needed to cut him out of my life.

"I don't understand why you're moving to Paris," he'd said at my graduation dinner after his fourth whiskey sour. "You should come home."

My roommate's parents shifted in their seats, no doubt surprised to find the famous Vincent Taylor such a disappointment.

"Because you're a train wreck," I'd said. "You could live anywhere, and yet you've never moved. You claim to be a victim of rumors, but you're not a victim, you love it."

He stared at me, as if challenging me to continue. Daring me to say the quiet part out loud. I was happy to oblige. "You love being the suspected murderer, lurking around your hometown, making people uncomfortable. You cultivate it." I waved my hands in the air in front of me, unable to stop. "It's all part of your persona, and if you moved, you'd lose that." I noticed people at neighboring tables were looking at us and I lowered my voice. "I don't want any part of that life, Dad."

That was the last time we spoke. I moved to Paris. Got married and then divorced. When I finally returned to the United States at age twenty-five to attend journalism school in Chicago, I was a new person with a new name, forged from the flames of my father's dysfunction.

* * *

I sit again, determined to make my way through the first full legal pad. Desperate to find something I can revise into an opening chapter. I linger for a moment on the dedication: *For Danny and Poppy—This isn't your story, it's mine. But I hope in the telling you'll be able to shine again, if only for a moment.*

I pick up where I left off, but soon lose the thread. Danny and Poppy flying kites, my father watching them from a blanket.

From there the timeline bounces around. Some pages are about my mother, Lydia, who'd been my father's girlfriend in the months leading up to the murders. Others are about vandalism at the high school. A neighbor's missing cat. I start to skim, trying to make sense of the whole. Suddenly we're back in March at a backyard barbecue. Then with Poppy as she's wandering around with her Super 8 camera. It's like reading someone's account of a complicated dream, with abrupt segues and shifting perspectives. I jot some notes:

Riding down a big hill/fall
Family dinners—Mom terrible cook
Poppy's birthday—got a camera

I latch onto that last idea, thinking it might be interesting to start with that. I flip back through the legal pad until I find the short scene describing the day in early March 1975—a rollerskating party Danny had been allowed to skip but my father had been forced to attend. A second celebration at home with just the family, a meal eaten in the backyard with a fire in the firepit and music. I try to imagine what they might have been listening to. The inside jokes they shared. What they ate. The evening air cool and crisp, requiring sweatshirts, the heat of the fire warming them. Laughter. Singing. Wrapping paper and cake. I begin to see the outlines of a scene so I open my computer and start revising, growing it into what I think he intended it to be. This is the job of a ghostwriter and I'm going to do it with fidelity. It's his book, his rules, and no one will ever know I worked on it.

*   *   *

It's a short chapter—only six pages—but when I'm done, I feel like maybe it captures the time and place, giving readers a feel for Ojai in the '70s and the family dynamic. Before I get in too deep, I need to know that I'm on the right track with this revision, so I drop it in an email and send it off to Neil, cc'ing Nicole, then read through it again.

It's hard to believe this was only five years before I was born. When I think about my father and his siblings, 1975 seems like a different era. But Poppy would have been only nineteen years old when I was born. A fun, young aunt, teaching me how to roller-skate. Braiding my hair. Taking me on fun shopping excursions to Santa Barbara or Ventura, giving my parents a night off.

Who would she have become, if her life hadn't ended at age fourteen? I close my laptop and stare at the four walls surrounding me, the boxes towering nearly to the ceiling in places, letting myself feel the loss of someone I never had a chance to love.

* * *

Back with the manuscript, I start flipping through the pages, trying to get a list of things to discuss with my father for our first session tomorrow morning.

But as I continue to read, my father's handwriting grows sloppy, and in some places veers off the lines and downhill. He goes from trite memories of his childhood to fragments of ideas. Sentences that start but don't finish. There's one page that simply reads *She shouldn't have gone.* Over and over, from top to bottom, that same sentence. *She shouldn't have gone.*

I keep flipping, dread filling me as I realize there's very little I can use in here. There is no story. Occasionally, there are notes jotted in the margins, written in a different color ink, as if my father had gone back and added them later. The kind of thing authors do when they're revising and want to remember to drop in an idea. But these aren't ideas related to anything on the page.

I had to bury Ricky Ricardo quickly.
    The darkest places to hide: storage shed, Poppy's closet, attic, garage
    THAT GODDAMN MOVIE.

And then, scribbled near the bottom of a page near the end of that first legal pad is a sentence that chills me. *I wanted to kill Danny.*

Vincent

June 13, 1975

8:30 p.m.

I watch the flames burn, careful not to let them grow too tall. I don't have a lot of time, and I need to get this done. Lydia is waiting and I don't want her to worry. Or come looking for me, asking why it's taking so long to bring her a sweatshirt.

I'd dug a hole, the way Danny had taught me so many years ago, and tossed the bloody shirt into the bottom of it. Then I'd covered it with trash I'd grabbed on my way out of the high school, the custodians slow to gather it on the last day of the school year. The shirt I'd changed into smelled musty from my PE locker, but at least it was clean. I'd also grabbed a sweatshirt for Lydia, glad I'd been too lazy to clear out my things like Mr. Wallen had asked us to.

I let the heat and smoke burn my eyes, willing them to stay open. Hoping that when I close them later, I'll see the shadow and outline of the flames and not everything else.

I watch a plastic cup warp and burn, the smoke pungent and sharp, letting the flames die down, not wanting the trash on top to completely burn. I want people to see what it was and not look deeper to the ashes of the T-shirt at the bottom.

When they're low enough, I cover it all with dirt, tamping it down with my feet until I can be sure the flames and embers

are dead. I scrape my shoes over the top, disguising the hole—
again, just like Danny taught me—before making my way back
through the oak grove to meet up with Lydia. Coming up with a
story for why I smell like smoke, in case anyone asks.

Chapter 5

I leave the manuscript on the desk and head down to my car, needing to clear my head. I drive aimlessly at first, the winding roads of my father's neighborhood leading me back toward the center of Ojai, letting my mind settle. My father isn't well, and what I read about Lewy body dementia mentioned hallucinations and faulty memories. About people insisting on things that were verifiably not true. I can't be certain my father's scribblings aren't any more than that. Burying Ricky Ricardo? A delusion. The man is losing his mind. And as for that last note—*I wanted to kill Danny*—hyperbole. People say things like that all the time. The piece I'm most intrigued by is the full page of the same sentence, over and over. *She shouldn't have gone.* A rumination. But on what?

My stomach growls and I pull into a parking space a few blocks from Ojai Avenue as my phone buzzes with a text from my real estate agent, Renee, a whip-smart woman with sharp edges and a blunt way of delivering information. Showed the house yesterday. Seemed promising at first, but they ended up deciding not to offer. I think we need to have a serious conversation about reducing the price. Call me. I sit there, the temperature of the car slowly rising as I bounce between two awful truths: I will have to sell my house and I will still owe John Calder money.

I shove my phone down to the bottom of my purse, as if that will protect me from Renee's blunt analysis, and walk toward Nina's Diner, suddenly craving one of their burgers. But like all the rest of the old shops along Ojai Avenue, Nina's is gone, replaced with a gourmet grill and a bohemian coffee shop. My stomach rumbles again, pushing me inside. The interior is airy and light; nothing like the walk-up window of Nina's, where we could order and then sit outside on a sunny day.

I order a burger and some truffle fries, then turn to survey the new space. The tables are filled with tourists eating lunch, the blond wooden floor making the room feel brighter, hanging plants descending from a raised ceiling.

I smile at the waitress as she passes me a brown bag with my food, then make my way outside. I only get a few paces away when I see him across the street. Or at least I think it's him. He's taller now with broad shoulders, but I recognize the way he moves, like the memory of a song I used to know.

I should turn away. Duck into a store until he's gone. But instead I call out. "Jack!"

He turns at the sound of his name, but can't locate anyone he recognizes so I raise my hand in a half wave. "It's me. Olivia."

He squints, then crosses the street, a grin breaking out across his face. "Oh my god," he says. When he's in front of me, he hesitates before pulling me into a tight hug, then releases me, his gaze making me uncomfortable.

I gesture for him to follow me around the side of the building, away from the sidewalk, and we cross the bike path that meanders through downtown, curving in and out of a stand of trees. We sit on a fallen log and face each other. "What happened to Nina's?" I ask.

Jack shrugs and says, "Closed down. I think in 2006? They tried to open up another one near the high school, but that one closed too."

I take a bite of my burger, which isn't nearly as good, and say, "There's nothing left."

"Progress," he says, then tugs on the end of my hair. "You're blond."

My heart does a tiny leap at the sound of his voice, so familiar yet so different. Deeper, riper, the years adding weight to it. He wears a flannel shirt and blue jeans, work boots peeking out beneath. Jack had been my best friend from ages eight onward. He was the only one who never treated me like an exhibit at the zoo, something to be studied from a safe distance—causing a lot of conflict with his father, who'd been Danny's best friend. After I'd gone to boarding school in Switzerland, we'd written letters—hundreds of them. I would tell him how much I hated it there, how much I disliked my entitled classmates. He confided in me about how his father's drinking had spiraled into alcoholism and would report my own father's misdeeds from the American media.

"I've looked for you, you know," he says now, giving a tiny shrug. "Nothing stalkery. Just on social media. But I could never find you."

Eventually, our letters had dwindled. By the time I was graduating from high school, it had been months since we'd written and I felt like it was time to cut all ties with my life in Ojai, including Jack.

"I went to France for college," I say. "After that, I moved to Paris and married a professional skier. That didn't work out," I finish awkwardly.

"I'm sorry."

I wave away his sympathy. "Don't be. We were young. It was a starter marriage, but I kept his last name."

"What is it?" he asks.

"Dumont," I say, waiting to see if he'll recognize the name. Not for my books but for the scandal that now pops up first when you google me.

But he seems oblivious. "Where do you live?" he asks. "What do you do for a living?"

"Los Angeles," I say, my mind slipping past the details of my life there. The home I love that I'm about to lose. The looming threat of bankruptcy if I can't pull off this book on the publisher's timeline. "I'm a ghostwriter—famous people hire me to write their life stories and then we put their name on the book."

He grows curious. "Like who?"

"Lots of people," I say. "A few years ago I worked with Rena Salazar, the professional surfer. She started that literacy foundation in Africa." I offer him some fries, deciding to skip over my most recent book and my collaboration on it so abruptly silenced.

He takes a fry, as I knew he would, and looks impressed. "That sounds amazing. But what brings you back to Ojai?" he asks. "Surely it isn't to see your dad."

I chew, thinking about how I should respond, and I wonder if I should have just kept walking. "Actually, it is," I say.

He looks offended. "If you don't want to tell me, that's fine."

"He's sick," I tell him. "Lewy body dementia."

"I think I heard something about that, though people in town have been heavy on gossip and light on facts."

"As usual."

"Is it bad?" he asks.

"I think so," I admit, setting the fries on the log between us. We eat in silence for a few minutes and I savor his presence.

49

How good it feels to be around someone who really knows me. Understands my family and where I came from.

"How long do you think you'll be here?"

I shake my head. "I can't say for certain." I'm never comfortable when I'm prohibited from disclosing my work on a project. I hate misleading people, and I miss out on a lot of opportunities for impromptu interviews. I much prefer when my presence is known to everyone. But this time, I'm relieved to hide behind the facade of familial duty. "Speaking of dysfunctional parents, how's your dad?" I ask.

"Supposedly retired, though you'd never know it by how often he shows up at the vineyard, offering advice and questioning every decision I make. But he's twenty years sober."

"That's great," I say. Mark Randall had always been a drinker, but as the years went on, things got really bad for Jack.

A cool breeze kicks up and my arms prickle with goose bumps. The eucalyptus trees above us cast a long shadow in the sunlight. Jack straightens his legs and leans back on his elbows.

"So tell me about you," I say.

He holds up his left hand to show a ring. "Married five years now."

"His name?" I ask.

"Matt," he says. "We met at the winery, actually. He applied for a job as sommelier. He didn't get it, but I like to say he got something better."

I smile, crumpling up the empty burger wrapper and shoving it into the empty bag. If anyone deserves happiness, Jack does.

"So I guess you finally came out." I look down at my hands. "I'm sorry I wasn't there for you."

He waves away my apology. "It's fine. Turns out, my mother had long suspected and had done a lot of the heavy lifting for me with my dad. They both adore Matt." He looks at me sideways. "What about you? Anyone special?"

I watch a couple biking past us, letting my eyes trail after the pair, noticing the way they pedal in slow circles, perfectly in sync. I imagine they are me and Tom, in a parallel universe, one where I haven't lied about my past. "Yes," I say, looking back at him again. "His name is Tom and he's an architect."

"Is he here with you? I'd love to meet him."

I look back toward the bike path, but the couple is gone. "He's busy with work, so no," I say. Imagining what it would be like to have the two of them in a room together, sharing their own Olivia stories. And while I wish that could be a reality, I know it won't be. Those two worlds will never collide.

We're silent for a few minutes, and I savor the substance of him next to me, how familiar it feels. "Are you happy, Livy?" he asks.

I stare at the trees above us, thinking. "I'd like to think so," I say.

He checks the time and stands, brushing dirt off the seat of his pants. "I'd better get back. Friday afternoon traffic is horrific."

He reaches down to pull me up and wraps his arms around me. He smells the same—mint and pine—and I inhale it. "We need a proper catch-up," he says. "Can you get away for dinner this Sunday?"

"I think so, but I'd like keep my return quiet," I say, thinking of the book and the stipulation that I not reveal my collaboration on it. Knowing that once it publishes, people might have questions if they knew I was here for an extended period of time. "It's been a long time since I've been an exhibit at the Taylor Family Zoo."

He reaches into his back pocket and pulls out a business card. "Text me at that number. It's my cell."

He reaches out to squeeze my hand, his fingers warm and calloused. I squeeze back, and for the first time since I returned to town, I feel a sense of calm, a belief that everything is going to be okay.

##

Around dinner time, I call Tom.

"Hey there," he says when he answers. "How was your day?"

"Long," I tell him, imagining him in his apartment in Brentwood, splayed out on his couch, his flat-screen TV showing some kind of ball game on mute.

"Let me guess, you're holed up in Oprah's guesthouse, hired to write a tell-all by her personal chef."

I laugh, looking around the crowded space, which is most certainly nowhere near what Oprah's guesthouse must look like. "I'm definitely not in Montecito," I say.

"Okay. You're in San Diego working on a book about the Famous Chicken who has always felt shortchanged by never being the Padres' official mascot."

"Definitely not in San Diego either, though that sounds like an amazing book idea. I'll pitch it to Nicole when I'm done here." I settle back, letting the stress of the day melt away, Tom's voice low in my ear. "What makes you think I'm even in California?" I ask.

"Math," he tells me. "You have to be somewhere within driving distance."

"Maybe I drove to LAX and flew somewhere."

"Not a chance," he counters. "Even without the lawsuit, you're too cheap to pay for airport parking."

I laugh, imagining what it would feel like to tell Tom that I'm in Ojai with my sick father, that it feels complicated and scary. That, perhaps for the first time in my career, I'm afraid I won't be able to do the job I've been asked to do.

"Do you have a scope of the job yet?" he asks. "How long will you be there?"

"Not sure." I glance at the stack of legal pads, wondering what I'll find when I really sit down and look. "I've been told it'll only be a month, but I'm thinking it might be longer." My father and I had agreed to give it a week, but already I know I'm not going to walk away.

We make small talk about his day for a few more minutes before he yawns. "Talk tomorrow?"

"Definitely," I say.

"I love you."

I think about what that means to me, the safety I feel with Tom, and hope that in a few weeks, this will all be behind me. The book will be done and I will be back home again. And eventually, the lie I've fed the world, about my father at least, will be true.

"I love you too," I say.

*   *   *

Later that night, I'm hate-scrolling through Instagram, noting which of my colleagues are releasing new books, wondering which of their subjects would have wanted to work with me, had their editors allowed it, when I hear frantic yelling coming from the house. My father's voice, an urgent jumble of words I can't make out. The time on my phone reads just past midnight. I leap from my bed, throw open the door, and tumble down the stairs of the guesthouse and across the courtyard, my father growing louder as I approach. The window to his room is open and I can see the top of his head as he struggles with the bottom sill.

My heart pounds as I follow the sound upstairs, into his bedroom where I find him wearing a T-shirt and a pair of threadbare pajama bottoms. Alma stands next to him, her hand on his arm trying to soothe him.

"What's going on?" I ask. "Is he okay?"

My father's gaze snaps onto me, his eyes widening as if seeing a ghost. "Oh, Lydia," he says. "I think I lost it."

The air rushes out of me. Gone is my commanding father, replaced by a scared old man I barely recognize. I'm about to remind him of who I am when I catch Alma's expression, cautioning me not to argue with him. "It's okay," I say instead.

Alma steps forward. "Let's get you back to bed, Vince. I've got your medicine right here." She takes an empty water glass from the nightstand and goes into my father's bathroom to fill it up.

He looks at the window again. "I can't figure why it won't work."

"Is there something wrong with it?" I ask.

"Poppy's hiding place. It's supposed to lift up," he says, his voice a whisper. "But now . . . I can't find the opening. It's gone."

Alma returns with the water. Before she can reach him, my father turns toward the window again, running his hand along the base of the sill as if searching for something. "Where did it go?" he asks Alma.

"We'll look more carefully tomorrow, when it's light," Alma says, guiding him away from the window. She wears an oversize nightgown that hits right above her ankles, and I notice her toenails are painted purple. My father hangs on to her, his hair mussed from the pillow. The bed is in disarray, the covers torn off and in a pile on the floor, as if he threw them off in his panic.

"Here," Alma says, holding out her hand, a pill cupped in her palm.

"What's that?" he asks.

"Your medication," she says. "It keeps you safe. It lets you sleep. That feeling you're having right now? The overwhelming fear and panic? The medicine will make it melt away, remember? Now take a deep breath with me, in and out." She models and my father follows along. "Another one," she says. He complies. "Now the pill."

He's jittery, his hand shaking as he plucks it from her hand and drops it in his mouth. She helps him hold the glass of water and he swallows it down. Together, they form a tableau, standing in a pool of light, the black window behind them, latched on to each other's eyes as they wait for the medication to kick in. My legs feel like jelly, the adrenaline still rushing through me, and yet I feel like an interloper. I don't belong here. I don't know how to handle this.

"I just wanted to check on it," my father says to me, his voice sounding calmer. "Make sure it was still there."

I finally find my voice. "Check on what?" I ask. "What did you hide in there?"

He gives me a withering look I know well. As if he can't believe he has to spell it out for me. "The knife, Lydia."

Chapter 6

I find myself back in the guesthouse, the door locked and the lights out, staring out the window toward the house. The lamp in my father's room is on for a little while longer and then that, too, goes dark.

The knife, Lydia.

The knife.

The knife.

The words swirl around inside of me, my emotions wrestling with my intellect. I'd looked at Alma after he'd said those words, expecting to see shock. Fear. But all I saw was a calm steadiness, as if she either hadn't heard him or she didn't care.

While I was in the house, Tom must have called because I have a voicemail from him. *If you're still awake, give me a call. I couldn't sleep and just want to hear your voice one more time.* There's no way I can call him back; I'm too rattled and he'd hear it in my voice and press for answers. I click my phone asleep and turn it upside down on the nightstand, sliding deeper under the covers. But my eyes refuse to close. Afraid of what I'll dream when I do. What stories my subconscious might want to tell me. Less than twenty-four hours after arriving, I've shifted from thinking I knew who my father was to thinking perhaps I didn't know him at all.

* * *

I must have slept because I wake the following morning with a start, my eyes gritty, my neck stiff. I find an email from our editor, Neil, in my in-box. It's short. We can't use this. There's nothing happening here.

I stare at the message, taking a moment to figure out what he's talking about before I remember. The chapter I'd sent yesterday.

I text Nicole, even though it's a Saturday. Neil hates the chapter. I did the best I could, revising a mostly coherent scene. I haven't been through the rest of it yet, but I'm not hopeful of finding anything better.

Her response comes almost immediately. I'm at the gym, but I had my assistant set up a Zoom with the team Monday morning at 7 AM your time. Let's get an idea of their vision for the book so you can do what you do best.

I don't respond because I don't know how to tell her that a bigger revelation, perhaps a memory my father has kept hidden for fifty years, has slipped out and into the open. Taunting me, forcing me to question everything.

* * *

I enter the house, careful not to startle my father eating breakfast at the table. "How are you feeling?" I ask him. Alma is in the kitchen behind us, flipping through a catalog.

He looks at me, his expression blank. "Fine."

I slide onto the chair next to him and Alma brings me a cup of coffee. I take a sip, savoring the heat and the caffeine soon to hit my system. "Can we talk about what happened last night?"

He holds a triangle of toast and stares at it, as if he's not entirely sure what to do with it. Then he takes a tentative bite and says, "I had a bad dream. It happens."

"It wasn't a dream. You were awake."

"Hallucinations are very common," Alma says from behind us. "They happen pretty early in the disease, but it's usually a tipping point toward progression. The best thing to do is to validate him when he's having one and help him move through it."

"Thank you, doctor," my father says, his voice tight with sarcasm.

"This wasn't some fantasy about you being a Broadway singer or seeing bugs that aren't there. This was specific, about something that actually happened."

"I'm not sure there's much to discuss."

"You're kidding, right?" When he doesn't say anything, I press on. "You basically said the knife wasn't where you left it. You were panicked. Like something bad would happen if you couldn't locate it." I lower my voice, aware of Alma behind us. "Were you talking about the murder weapon?"

He pushes his plate away and drops his napkin over the remains of his breakfast. "My doctor has told me that my mind will play tricks on me. I will believe things that are outrageously false."

"I don't know, Dad. This seemed like more than that."

"Olivia," Alma says, her voice carrying a warning.

My father shakes his head, as if ridding it of voices. His fingers pluck the used napkin from the top of his nearly empty plate and he smooths it out, spreading it on his lap again, pulling his food closer and poking at it with his fork. He takes a bite and says, "These eggs are cold."

"You've already finished eating," I tell him. Anxiety blooms inside of me, at how fragile he is. He seemed fine when I arrived yesterday, and I wonder how hard he had to work to hide it from me. How difficult me being here might be on the equilibrium that now seems so precarious.

My father's eyes dart from me to Alma to the door, but before he can say anything, Alma says, "Enough. It was a hallucination. Not real. Your presence is dredging up things for him that are painful. I told you this is a mistake. Your father can't handle it."

But he bristles. "Don't tell me what I can or cannot handle."

Alma looks between the two of us, her stare challenging me to argue. "We have to leave at noon sharp." Then she leaves the room.

I look at my father. "Where are you going on a Saturday?" I ask.

He gives a defeated look. "Life is easier if you don't ask questions."

* * *

"Are you sure you're feeling up to this?" I ask him before we start. We're in our old positions from when I was young—him at his desk, his chair turned away from the windows and facing me, and me in my chair by the door.

He gives a tiny shake of his head. "Evenings are rough," he explains. "It's sort of like sundowner's syndrome. I lose my sense of time and place. But it typically doesn't mean anything. Alma knows what to do."

"It just seemed significant," I say.

"I can assure you, it wasn't."

I have a colleague who once worked on a book about a serial killer. I remember her talking about what it was like to interview him in prison. "Everyone is an unreliable narrator," she'd said. "But someone who has killed another person? They are the ultimate gaslighters. You begin to question everything—even the things you can see to be true."

Could my father be a killer? It's always been a possibility that's lived in my peripheral vision. Shortly after I learned what had happened to Danny and Poppy, I asked him outright. "Did you do it?"

He'd scoffed at me in that arrogant way he had, as if he was above such a ridiculous and juvenile question. "I don't have time for this, Olivia."

He'd been packing for a trip, his assistant, Melinda, downstairs in the kitchen making me a dinner of hot dogs and tomato soup, her overnight bag sitting in the entry. I watched my father fold sweaters and pants, stacking them carefully in his suitcase, and I tried to imagine him with a knife, slashing at the bodies of his brother and sister. The rage that might have pushed him to commit something so violent. I tried a different tack. "I won't tell anyone," I promised. "You can trust me."

He started to laugh as he snapped his suitcase shut, lifting it by its handle. "I'll keep that in mind," he said, brushing past me, his footsteps echoing as he descended the stairs.

I push the memory away. "I started reading the manuscript," I say now. My father looks at me, searching my expression for a hint of what I might have thought but I'm having a hard time meeting his gaze. "There's not a lot I can work with."

I wait for him to get angry or defensive. But he seems to collapse into himself. "I was afraid of that," he says. "This illness, it's deceptive. It tricks you into thinking you have a grasp on reality, on events of the past. You believe them, fully and completely." He sighs. "But then you find out that nothing you believed is real. None of it happened the way you think it did." He sits forward, his expression intense. "I need you to remember the good things. The treasure hunts I used to design for you.

The way everything came together at the end—the clues, the prize. The fun."

I'm confused, and a little worried about this sudden segue, wondering if this is how our conversations will go—on topic for a few minutes and then veering off into some other lane, some other memory that has nothing to do with the memoir. "Dad, we need to stay focused on the book. I tried doing what you asked—I revised a chapter and sent it to your editor. He said it didn't work." I wait to see if he'll be the one to suggest what needs to happen next. When he doesn't, I say, "That's why I need to talk to other people. I have to be able to make sense of this narrative."

He sits back again, resigned. "I don't think we need to do that," he says. "I'm at my best in the mornings and I haven't completely lost the thread yet so I can still tell you what you need to know. To make sense of whatever mess I've created."

"It doesn't work that way," I explain. "A memoir is your recounting of your life, but it's stronger with voices of the others who were there."

Downstairs I can hear Alma in the kitchen, the clatter of pots and pans faint through the closed door.

"I can't let you do that," he says. "No one can know about the book until it's ready to release."

"Why?" I ask. "Early buzz can only help you."

He looks at me, his watery blue eyes latching onto mine. "Because there are things I never told the police. I want to be very mindful of what we say, how we say it, and most importantly when we say it. You have to trust me on this, Olivia."

I stare at him, thinking again of last night. *The knife, Lydia.* Thinking about the jotted notes in the manuscript.

She shouldn't have gone.

I wanted to kill Danny.

Finally I say, "Well, let's start there. Did you hide the murder weapon in Poppy's window?"

He looks as if I've slapped him. "Is this how you work with all your subjects? Corner them at the start and accuse them of murder?"

"You just said—"

"This isn't easy for me. I've spent fifty years staying silent—at my own peril. It's not a matter of what needs to be said, but how the story should be told."

I fight down my impatience, reminding myself that if this were anyone else, I wouldn't have phrased my question that way. Interviewing a subject—especially at the beginning—is a delicate balance of building trust and looking for openings. There are no rules, only instinct. "You're right. I apologize. Why don't you start by telling me about Poppy and Danny. Whatever memories come first."

He inhales through his nose and closes his eyes, reminding me of a musician about to perform. When he opens them again, he says "Danny loved to camp. When he was younger, he took an outdoor survival class and fell in love with the woods. With the solitude of nature." He pauses, thinking. "But he could be scary at times. He'd get this look in his eyes that was terrifying. Like he was working hard not to hurt you."

"Was he always that way?" I ask.

My father gives a faint smile and says, "No, when he was younger, he was vibrant."

"That's a really interesting word. What do you mean?"

"Just what I said. In elementary school, kids were drawn to him, to his energy. It was like he lived on a different plane than the rest of us. They'd do whatever it took to live inside his orbit. But things changed when he was a teenager. He used to read these survival books. You know . . . how to live in the woods eating only plants and bugs."

"Did your family go camping a lot?"

"I can't believe we never had any of these conversations," he says. "I always thought we'd have more time, but . . ." he shrugs. "To answer your question, no. My family didn't camp. My father wasn't an outdoors kind of person. He worked and then he came home and watched the news with a cocktail. My mother would have died if she didn't have access to her hot rollers and a telephone. But Danny loved sleeping out in the grove near our house. He'd take a tent he'd gotten for his birthday and a sleeping bag and set up out there. Sometimes he'd be gone for the whole weekend."

"Your parents let him camp out there alone?"

My father laughs. "It was the '70s. They didn't care, so long as he didn't interfere with their weekly bridge game or Walter Cronkite."

"How old was Danny at this point?"

My father takes a moment to think. "The first time he went out there on his own was when he was about twelve," he says. "Initially, just among the trees in the field behind our house if it was dry enough. Later, he'd venture into the oak grove." The oak grove, an expanse of land just a few blocks from his childhood home. "He did it all the way up until he died. One time I asked him if he'd ever want to live like that, and he told me he thought about it all the time. That living at home felt constricting. He was going to apply to some tiny college up in Oregon, and I think the appeal for him wasn't just the distance from Ojai and from our family, but because it was a place he could still find the outdoor space he needed."

It feels as though my father and I are inside of a bubble. His voice is deep and melodic and I find myself hanging on his words. He's never spoken so candidly about his siblings, and it feels like finally scratching an itch that has plagued me for decades. I want to sink into his words the way I used to when I was little, listening to him spin a tale about Lionel Foolhardy. I want to mute out everyone and everything and just listen to my father tell a good story.

"So Danny was unhappy?" I ask, reminding myself that I'm not the audience, I'm the author.

"I think we all were," my father admits. "In our own way. I'd act out, but Danny would travel inward, to a place no one could reach. You have to understand, our family wasn't an easy one. We had a father who was emotionally unavailable and a mother who was constantly complaining about us to others, often while we were standing right there. Well, not Danny so much. But me? My god, she'd bitch to anyone who would listen about how hard it was to be my mother. The calls from the school, the complaints from other parents, my grades, the clothes I wore. She was the same with Poppy, who in my mind was near perfect. Always moaning about how her hair was the wrong color or the wrong style, how boys wouldn't like her if she didn't wear dresses and skirts." He pauses for a moment. "It was a strange time. We had a lot of freedom, but we also had a lot of rules. Which, of course, we broke."

"Like what?"

"Our parents imposed a curfew of eleven o'clock. No room for negotiation. At 11:00 p.m., the doors were locked, and if you knew what was good for you, you'd be inside." He gives a rueful smile and says, "We could sneak out through our bedroom window, but getting back inside was problematic without a boost. So Danny disabled the lock on the window in the back door. The latch would appear to be locked, but it would lift right up, and from there you could reach inside and unlock the door."

"Didn't you have a key to your own house?"

My father shakes his head. "We never needed one. No one locked their doors during the day."

His eyes latch onto mine, both of us realizing what that could have meant, how events of that day could have turned out differently.

"You said Danny could be scary. Tell me more about that."

My father's voice grows low and he stares down at his hands as he speaks. "I came across him once, in the grove." He pauses, as if gathering the courage to continue. "It was shortly before he died. I was on my way to meet your mother and I heard this sound. A *thump thump thump* and a choking noise, like whoever it was couldn't get enough air."

My father has always been a talented storyteller. He knows how to moderate his voice, how to slow his words down to build tension, and I find myself stilling my body, waiting for him to continue. "It was late afternoon," he continues. "I remember the slightly decomposing smell of dead leaves and damp soil. I think I knew, instinctively, to be quiet. That it was Danny out there, and whatever he was doing . . . I wasn't supposed to be witnessing it."

He's silent for a full minute, and I let him gather himself to tell this next part, my gaze landing briefly on my phone, making sure it's still recording. "I found him digging a hole. His back heaving with effort, his face red with rage. He was stabbing at the ground with that shovel as if he was trying to attack it. Next to him was a bundle of something, wrapped up in a T-shirt. Spots on it were bloody, but from where I stood, concealed behind a tree, I could tell the blood wasn't coming from Danny. I stared hard at that bundle, until my eyes started to water. Waiting to see what it was."

He swipes his eyes, as if they're still burning and I notice how his hand shakes. How he's reliving this moment. Not a hallucination. Not a night terror, but a memory that he needs to get out. "It was the neighbor's cat, who'd gone missing. Poppy had been head of the search committee, rallying all the kids to put up flyers and check everyone's garage." He shakes his head. "When he got the hole deep enough, he tossed the shovel aside and kicked the cat into the hole."

"Did you say anything? Ask him what happened to the cat?"

He looks at me as if I'm insane. "No. I got the hell out of there as fast as I could."

"Maybe he'd found the cat already dead," I suggest. "Killed by a coyote and he was sparing Poppy and the others from finding it."

My father shakes his head, resolute. "Danny killed that cat."

I can't help but feel skeptical. "Are you suggesting Danny was some kind of sociopath?" I ask. "No one, in all these years, has ever said anything like that about him."

My father's gaze is steady. His hands are no longer shaking, as if he's detoxed himself in the retelling. "I know what I saw. I was always the volatile one, but Danny was something else. Something much more dangerous."

I take a moment to imagine the scene. The smells, the shadows in that grove of trees. How my father must have felt; the fear I can still hear in his voice. What's he trying to suggest, that Danny killed Poppy? The question is almost out of my mouth before I pull it back, remembering how angry he got when I'd asked him about the knife. Knowing, instinctively, that it's too soon to ask him a question like that.

And then I take a step back. What he's describing is disturbing, but I have no way of knowing if it's true.

At the beginning of a book, I try not to let my subjects talk too linearly. I'd rather have them bounce around in time because that will reveal the touchstone moments around which the rest of their story will flow, so I decide to leave this line of questioning alone for now. "Talk to me about the aftermath of the murders," I say. "You'd been in the oak grove with Mom and your teacher, emerging into a whole new reality. Tell me about that night."

"To be honest, I don't remember much. We had to stay in a motel since the house was a crime scene. But I was in shock, I think." His expression is distant, trying to return to that time. "Some things are better not to remember."

"I'm going to ask you to try," I say.

He nods, thinking. "We weren't allowed in the house to get anything," he recalls. "So we slept in the clothes we had on. I remember the way the motel manager looked at us when we checked in. With a mix of pity and relief—like he was glad it was us on that side of the counter and not him. When my father tried to pay, he waved the money away. 'No charge,' he'd said."

"Why a motel?" I ask. "Why not stay with friends?"

His honesty surprises me. "Aside from your mother, I didn't really have any. And my mother's friends didn't like me very much. The last thing they wanted to do was to sleep under the same roof as me." He chuckles. "I can't say I blamed them. I was an odd bird and the whispers about the possibility that I'd killed them had already started."

"Did you all share a room?" I can imagine them, huddled into a small motel room, his parents in one bed and him in the other, unable to let their last remaining child out of their sight for a single moment, considering what had just happened.

But he shakes his head. "No, they put me in the room next to theirs. The walls were really thin—they could have heard me burp if they'd wanted to." He sighs. "But my mother's crying drowned everything out." He pauses, remembering. "It seemed like she would never stop crying."

"And you? Were you crying?"

"Siblings define who you are at that age. I'd always been the middle child, measured against Danny and Poppy my entire life. Then suddenly they were gone and all that was left was this vast emptiness. Silence. Except for my mother's crying."

It's not until later, when I'm transcribing this conversation, that I notice he didn't answer my question.

Vincent

Friday, June 13, 1975

11:30 p.m.

I lay on top of the covers in the motel, the cheap scratch of the bedspread poking through my T-shirt. Not the one I'd put on this morning, that I'd worn to school, then later to the carnival, the one that had blood all over it but still smelled like laundry detergent when I'd pulled it off. The one that was now burned to ashes beneath a pile of trash.

The walls of the room are thin and I can hear my mother sobbing next door, the low voice of my father trying to console her, grief thick and heavy in his words. The sound of her rakes across me like sharp nails, making me want to jump out of my skin. I wish she would just be quiet for one blessed minute.

Would you kids be quiet for one blessed minute?

That won't be a problem any longer.

My eyes are dry as I stare at the ceiling, speckled and bumpy, a slash of light from the streetlamp outside casting a stripe across it. The adrenaline of the evening still pumps through me, my heart rate refusing to fall despite the fact that it's been hours. My head pounds with every heartbeat in the spot where Danny had slammed it into the wall, a lump I can feel just under my hairline.

I imagine the police, still swarming all over our house, the bodies of my brother and sister now removed in a silent ambulance—no flashing lights or loud siren, just a slow acceleration down the cul-de-sac, no need to hurry. I can see in my mind the giant pools of blood left behind—Danny's in the hallway and Poppy's in her room. I doubt it will ever come out, though I hope we'll never live there again.

The police will be looking for evidence. Trying to figure out who could have committed such a horrific crime—the brutal murder of two kids—a stabbing so much more personal than a gunshot. More barbaric than poison. They will find clues, but they will never see the truth.

This morning, I'd woken up the weird middle child—the volatile, moody one everyone is just a little bit afraid of. And less than twenty-four hours later, I'm the only one left. The one my parents already can't bear to look at, a sharp reminder of who else is no longer here.

My mother's crying softens through the wall and I breathe a little easier, hoping she'll stop soon. But then it ratchets up again, a loud wail that must have everyone in the motel knowing that we're here. Thinking about us and what's happened.

I roll onto my side. I can't think of Poppy, about what she must have been thinking in her final moments. It's easier to think about Danny, how hard he'd fought. How I was almost the one who'd died in that hallway.

The truth I can never say aloud is that I'm not sad about Danny. I'm glad he's dead.

Chapter 7

After my father leaves for his appointment, I jump in my car, deciding to do a little location research.

First I drive by the motel where they'd stayed for the three days the house had been a crime scene. My father had named it in our conversation and I'd remembered it from my childhood. The Starlight Motel out on Highway 150 had been bright yellow with blue trim and had a neon sign that flashed on and off. But when I circle by now, it's a Radisson. I sit in the parking lot and stare at the beige building, trying to imagine what rooms they might have had.

From there, I head toward my father's old house on Van Buren. As I drive west, the houses grow smaller, poorer cousins of the estates on the east end. Dirt front yards, aluminum window frames, and older-model cars in driveways: this is where Ojai's working class lives. No Airbnbs over here. No city transplants living out their retirements in a quaint country town with world-class restaurants and trendy boutiques that cater to the tourists who keep Ojai running. The people who live over here are the ones who work at the resort. Who teach at the schools. Who wait on customers in those fancy restaurants and boutiques.

Another right, then another left, and I'm heading down the quiet road, many of the driveways empty of cars on this beautiful Saturday afternoon. And there it is, the house that still looms large in my memory.

I park and take in the familiar features. The porch that spans the front of it, covered with a shingled roof propped up with four posts. Two concrete steps that lead up to the front door. The windows that flank it are uncovered and I think again of my father's night terror. His certainty that the knife hadn't been where he'd left it in Poppy's hiding spot, and I feel a flutter of nerves, wondering if I'd be able to convince whoever lives there now to let me in and look.

I get out of my car and head up the front path as an older man exits the house next door, carrying a basket of gardening tools. "If you're looking for Frieda, her nephew moved her into a home a few months ago," he calls to me.

"Oh, that's too bad," I say, improvising. "Was she ill?"

He shakes his head, studying me. "Just old."

"Any idea what they're going to do with the house?" I ask.

His smile fades and he sets his gardening tools down. "Are you a reporter?"

I feign confusion and say, "No. Why? Who owns it?"

I close the distance between us and take in his features, placing him around my father's age, give or take a few years, though he looks much healthier than my father, with tanned skin and muscular legs. "There's a management company that handles the property," he tells me. "Markham and Sons. You should direct your questions to them."

A phone rings from inside his house. He glances toward his open front door and says, "I'd better get that." He looks back at me as if he's unsure whether he should leave me unsupervised.

He finally turns and closes the door behind him, leaving his gardening tools on the steps. I'm about to approach my father's old house again, but the curtains next door twitch and I see the neighbor watching me. I give a friendly wave and head back to my car, navigating slowly out of the cul-de-sac and around the corner, where I park and google the number for the management company he mentioned.

A woman's voice answers my call. "Markham and Sons Management Company, can I help you?"

"Yes, I'm interested in the house at 554 Van Buren."

Her tone turns abrupt. "I'm sorry, we can't help you with that."

"I thought your company handles that property."

"We do, but that house is not for rent."

"But it's vacant," I tell her.

"That may be, but the owner isn't interested in renting it at this time. We have other properties available if you like."

"Who is the owner?" I ask.

Her voice grows chilly. "Like I said, that property isn't available. Please let us know if you'd like to see something else."

Then the line disconnects. I sit, staring at my phone. A woman walking her dog passes, glancing at me and then continuing.

As a journalist, I used to have access to all kinds of databases and sources I could call, but it's been a long time since I moved in that world. I could spend the day figuring out how to pull a property title, or I could find a new source.

I pick up my phone to text my real estate agent, Renee, but when I open the thread, I realize I didn't call her after that last text she sent about reducing the price of the house.

Sorry I never responded to this. I'm up in Ojai and would love your help on something. I'm interested in a property here, but I'm having a hard time figuring out who owns it. It's not on the market, but it's vacant. Is there any way you could you look it up for me? And I'll seriously consider reducing the price. I promise.

I type the address into a separate text, then stare at my phone, hoping to see the three dots showing that she's responding. But after five minutes of silence, I drop my phone into the console and head back to my father's house.

* * *

I decide to take the long way back, letting my memory spool out—not just of my time living in Ojai, but the first year I lived abroad. I remember feeling cut off, lonely for the routines of home, the sound of my father in his office writing, or of his voice on the phone. I missed everything—even the things I claimed to have hated. My father's drinking. His late nights. His frequent trips. I realized how much I missed the possibility of his presence when his presence was now thousands of miles away, out of reach. Other parents would come and visit their kids, but my father only attended one parents' weekend the entire time I was away at school.

It was November of my first year and I'd begged him to come. My father had seemed more like himself on our calls—he was working on a new book he was excited about. He seemed sharper, responding to my questions and asking some of his own. No long pauses where I'd wonder if the call got dropped or if he'd fallen asleep. Instead he seemed excited to see me. I imagined having him there—his old self, the one that knew how to tell a great story. Who made anyone he spoke to feel special.

He'd arrived late Friday night and we'd made plans to meet at the dean's coffee reception the following morning. I'd stood in the entry to the Alumni House, the last student waiting for a parent to arrive. Wondering what version of my father would be showing up. Or if he'd show up at all.

When he finally arrived, he seemed hurried. "Let's get this over with," he'd said.

I trailed after him. "What do you mean?"

"I set up a meeting with one of my foreign publishers while I'm here. Just a quick meet and greet."

I halted. "On parents' weekend?"

He turned to face me. "This school isn't going to pay for itself."

"I never even wanted to come here." I hated how petulant I sounded, and I knew it wouldn't go over well with him.

He sighed, exasperated. "Not this again, Olivia."

I followed him into the reception, watching him grab a cup of coffee from a table set up by the back wall. We stood there, not talking, and I noticed how his cup rattled against the saucer. My father must have noticed too because he ditched the saucer on a nearby table.

One of my teachers approached us. "Mr. Taylor, a pleasure to meet you. My name is Francesca Williamson, Olivia's English teacher and advisor. You have quite an extraordinary daughter."

"Thank you. I'm glad to hear she's settling in."

Ms. Williamson took a step closer to us and said, "She's more than just settling in. Olivia is the founding member of a new student group, the Women's Empowerment Club. So far we have about twenty members."

My father rolled his eyes. "Oh for god's sake."

Ms. Williamson looked startled. "Excuse me?"

"I sent her here to get the best education money can buy. Not to start some feminist club that won't accomplish anything other than to make a lot of noise and cause a lot of trouble."

"I disagree," Ms. Williamson said. "So far the club has given a voice to many young women about issues they care about.

Equity in student government. Making sure female authors have representation on class syllabi."

"Jesus," my father muttered, setting his coffee cup down and looking toward the exit. His voice grew louder, catching the attention of several people around us, silencing their conversations. "When history repeats itself, only the fool stands around and watches it happen."

"Please don't do this," I whispered

"Do what?" he said. "I want you to focus on getting the education that I'm paying tens of thousands of dollars for you to receive, not become the next Gloria Steinem." At this point I could see the sweat blooming on his forehead. The panic rising in him—a caged animal looking for an escape.

More people were looking at us now and I could feel my face burning. The silent judgment of Ms. Williamson, who I'd desperately wished would excuse herself so that she wouldn't have to bear witness to my father's unraveling. "Why can't you just behave?" he asked. "Do what you're supposed to do—go to school. Do your homework. Listen to the adults. Why do you always have to be agitating toward something? Making waves. Noise."

He wasn't making any sense, although that wasn't new for me. "All I wanted was to have more current authors on my reading lists," I said, though my voice was low, barely above a whisper.

"I need to go, but we can discuss this more at dinner," he said. "I made reservations at the hotel; I assume you can get there on your own?"

"No," I said. "I need you to pick me up."

But he was already turning away from us.

"Students can't leave campus unless an adult signs them out or it's a school-sanctioned trip into town," Ms. Williamson explained.

"Call Melinda. She'll sort it out," he said over his shoulder.

"In California?" I called after him. Melinda could make pretty much anything happen, but I doubted she could sign me out of my boarding school thousands of miles away.

He pushed through the doors and was gone. Around us, conversations resumed and I suddenly noticed how the other parents were with their children. A mother straightening a collar. Brushing hair off a forehead. A father's hand on a shoulder.

"I think I'll go back to my room," I said to Ms. Williamson.

Thankfully, she let me go.

* * *

Renee gets back to me later that night. I'm sorry but I've been called out of town for a family emergency. I've got another agent in the office handling all my clients, though to be honest, you won't get much more interest on the property until you drop the price.

My thumbs hesitate over the keypad of my phone, wondering if I should fire her or press her for what I need. She didn't even bother to include the name of the agent covering for her. But another option comes to me—my friend, Allison, who works for an escrow company. I'm sure it would be no problem for her to look up the property and get me what I need.

I type out the text quickly. Doing some research on a potential project and need to track down the owner of a house in Ojai. I drop the address into the message and then hit Send, hoping for a quick answer so I can get into that house and search Poppy's hiding place myself.

Chapter 8

On Sunday evening, I leave the lights on in the guesthouse and skirt around the side of the garage to my car, not wanting to answer any questions about where I'm going or who I'll be seeing. Once I'm on the highway, I relax my grip on the steering wheel, reminding myself I'm forty-four, not fourteen, and make my way to Jack and Matt's house.

When I arrive, Jack peers out the window and two seconds later he's standing in the open doorway of their cottage on the grounds of the winery, tucked between a small hill and the vast vineyards beyond.

"I would have brought wine but . . ." I gesture toward the vineyard.

He ushers me inside and says, "I'm so glad you came. I was half-worried you'd cancel."

I pretend to be offended, but a spark of shame flares inside of me because I spent the better part of the afternoon trying to figure out how to do just that. Allison had texted me back: On an island in Fiji with limited cell service. Okay if I do this when I return in two weeks?

I'd sent her a thumbs-up, swallowing down my frustration. Trying to figure out a faster way to get what I needed. But there wasn't one.

I step into the cozy cabin with colorful art on the walls, a shabby-chic decor that belies the dusty environment outside.

Matt emerges from the kitchen, the smell of garlic and butter clinging to him, a dish towel tucked into his belt.

He's about my height and lean, like a runner, with sandy-brown hair that flops in an artful way I can tell costs money to maintain. After the introductions, I hesitate, wondering what Jack has told him about me and about my family. What kind of context he's given for this long-lost friend suddenly appearing back in town after so many years away. But Matt's wide smile melts away all my reservations. "Olivia, you're exactly how I've always imagined you," he says, letting me know, in just those few words, that no explanation is necessary.

*   *   *

We eat crusty French bread with giant plates of chicken parmesan. Jack and Matt banter in a way that includes rather than isolates, and I feel a warm glow pooling deep inside of me, human contact nourishing me more than the food. After the meal, Jack props his chin on his fist and says, "Tell me about the marriage."

I laugh. "Craig. The infamous French downhill skier."

"How did you meet him?" Matt asks.

"It's not very interesting," I warn. "My roommate in Paris was Craig's sister's best friend. He was handsome and reckless and the kind of guy any twenty-year-old would fall in love with."

"What happened?" Jack asks.

I take a sip of wine, an expensive red Matt filched from the winery. "We were young," I tell them.

"Nope, sorry," Jack says, sitting back in his chair. "We need the real story, not the sanitized version you'd tell my mom." Matt nods in agreement.

"There really isn't one," I insist. "He traveled a lot. Partied a lot. Cheated a lot." Jack winces and I hurry to explain. "Honestly, it was a marriage in name only. I stayed long enough to get French citizenship and then we went our separate ways."

"A marriage of convenience," Matt says.

I nod, but I can see understanding bloom on Jack's face. What it might have meant to me, to shed my old name. My old identity. To return to the United States as someone new.

"So what brings you back to Ojai?" Matt asks.

"I'm here to help my dad," I say. "He's got Lewy body."

Matt touches my hand. "Oh, that's rough. I'm sure he's glad you're here."

Jack nearly chokes on his wine but Matt ignores him. "How long are you planning to stay?"

"I'm not sure."

"Jack tells me you have a partner in Los Angeles?"

Cool air floats in through an open window, low music playing from hidden speakers, a full stomach and the buzz of alcohol making me feel relaxed. "His name is Tom and he's an architect. We met when he designed my writing studio." Matt and Jack are quiet and it feels good to talk about Tom. To bring him into this space with me. "We've been together a couple years, and it's one of those relationships that just clicked, right from the beginning. He doesn't mind my chaotic writing schedule, and I don't mind when he becomes consumed with a new project.

"We have this way of always knowing where the other one is. Not just where in the world, but in our minds. Our hearts." As I speak, I feel the widening distance between us. How much fear and pain I'm carrying, while he believes I'm somewhere simply working on a book.

I notice Jack and Matt share a quick glance and I recognize the gesture as something Tom and I do as well. A quick, silent connection. A confirmation that we are of the same mind. But I don't want to grow morose so I turn toward a painting on the wall and say, "Is this original? I love it."

Another glance passes between them and I pretend that I don't miss the ghost of the person I love, sitting at my shoulder, getting to know my childhood best friend and, in the process, getting to know me.

* * *

As I'm leaving, Matt says, "Tom should come up one weekend. We'd love to meet him."

I search in my purse for my car keys so I don't have to look at them when I lie. "I wish he could, but he's pretty busy on a big project right now."

We say our goodbyes and Jack walks me to my car. "Tom doesn't know about your father, does he?"

I sigh and look up at the night sky, at the same wild riot of stars I can see from my deck at home, and I wonder where Tom is. What story he's telling himself about the book I'm working on, certain it's nothing close to the truth. "I don't want to be here, dealing with this. And I certainly don't want to drag him into it."

"You can't hide from who you are."

"It's worked well so far," I say.

Jack looks down at me, his gaze skeptical. "Has it?"

Later that night, when I'm in bed, the lights dark, I scroll through my phone looking at pictures of Tom and me. I trace the progression of our relationship—early photos of the construction of the studio, Tom in his white button-down shirt, plans tucked beneath one arm, smiling next to the framing. He'd always arrive at the end of the day, and I'd begun to expect his white truck to come bouncing down my long driveway around three o'clock. I'd have coffee ready and we'd chat about our respective work—he'd discuss a renovation he was doing in Malibu and I'd talk about the book I was working on—the connection between us instant and powerful.

I flip to another image, a close-up of his face, laughing at something I'd said. I'd fallen for his eyes first—a velvety brown that would hold me in place. I loved the way he listened to me talk, as if the world had stopped and I was all that was left.

Another photo, one where we'd grabbed a drink at a dive restaurant near the beach, the wind tousling his brown hair, reminding me of how he looks in the mornings, his eyes still heavy with sleep.

I should call him—he'd texted during dinner, checking in—but I know what he'll ask. *How is it going? Are you meeting interesting people?* So many questions that will lead to things I can't talk about.

But the pull of hearing his voice is too great.

"Things are not going well," I tell him when he answers. "This project is so much more complicated than I originally thought."

"In what way?" he asks.

I wiggle myself deeper under the covers and roll onto my side, trying to figure out how to explain the problem without telling him anything of substance. "My subject is . . . unreliable," I say.

"Can't you just write what they want you to write and be done?"

"It's not that simple," I explain. "I can't write things that are outright fabrications. I'd get slaughtered and I can't afford another hit to my reputation. The problem is, I can't figure out what's true and what's not. And tomorrow morning I've got a Zoom with the publisher to basically tell them that."

Tom blows out hard. "Tell me what you need from me. Solutions? Distraction?"

I close my eyes and say, "Distraction. Definitely."

So he launches into a description of his newest client—a woman with too much money and too much time on her hands. I try to laugh in all the right places, but he must sense my disconnect because he says, "I think it's time to let you sleep."

After we say goodbye, I click my phone asleep and roll onto my side, staring at the moon through my window. I know that I haven't given Tom the chance to show up for me. He wouldn't care who my father is or what he'd allegedly done. I could tell him, he would still love me, and we could move on. Jack's words from earlier tonight run through my mind again. *You can't hide from who you are.*

But shedding my past felt like stripping off an old prison jumper and stepping into the kind of freedom I'd always dreamed of. And really, telling Tom the truth at this point would only hurt him. I have no intention of maintaining a relationship with my father once the book is done. I'll try to write what my father wants me to write, it'll be his name on the cover, and I can go back to letting Tom and the rest of the world believe that my parents were who I said they were.

Chapter 9

Monday morning at seven sharp, I find the Zoom link Nicole's assistant sent over. I've been working on an outline of the scene my father described, of coming across Danny digging a hole for that cat. Capturing his voice isn't hard; I know how my father likes to tell a story—slowly, rolling out the surprises one delicious twist at a time.

But I also have another scene drafted, in a separate document. Of my father's night terror, every detail I can remember from the moment I heard him scream to the vibrant purple shade of Alma's toenail polish. I don't plan on showing that to anyone, but I needed to get it down. Needed to know it was there because I still don't know if I'm writing a book *with* my father, or if I'm going to have to write one *about* him.

It's not just the way my father seems to shift between reality and fantasy, like stepping through a veil. Last night I woke up to see the outline of him standing in his window, illuminated from behind so that he's just a silhouette. Staring across the courtyard and into the window in the guesthouse door. Unlike that first night, he's perfectly still, perfectly quiet. Almost as if his body is there but his mind is somewhere else. Tonight I plan to dig an old sheet out of the linen closet and tape it over the window so if he does it again, I won't know.

Nicole's face appears on the screen as she lets me into the meeting first. "This is going to be tricky," she says. "We don't want them to think you're not up to the task of writing this book. We just need you to have more leeway in writing it."

"I have to be able to interview other people about what happened from their perspective," I tell her. "If I can't, we won't have much of a book."

"Got it," she says.

A new window opens and I'm surprised to see an entire conference room full of people, an older man sitting at the head of a long table. He has salt-and-pepper hair and wears readers and a button-down shirt. As he starts to talk, it takes him a moment to realize he's still on mute.

He presses a button on a remote and says, "Sorry about that. Nice to finally meet you, Olivia. I'm Neil Grayson, Vincent's editor." He gestures toward the others sitting around the table—three women and one man. "You're on our big-screen TV in the conference room and I've gathered the sales and marketing teams here with me." He quickly runs through their names and they wave. "And I've got Sloane Valerian, the publisher of Monarch, on speakerphone."

A disembodied voice says, "Hello, Olivia and Nicole. So glad we could all gather and regroup. I apologize for not zooming in, but I'm in the car on the way to the airport."

I pick up my phone and text Nicole: Jesus.

She texts back: This is good.

Another face pops on the screen—a young man with a stylishly rumpled appearance that probably requires several hours of prep to achieve. He unmutes himself and says, "Sorry I'm late. I'm Lance Cameron, Mr. Taylor's literary agent."

Lance Cameron is the son of my father's former literary agent, Arthur, who passed away several years ago, leaving his eponymous agency in his son's hands. Since then, there have been rumors of lawsuits about financial discrepancies and established authors jumping to other agencies, but unfortunately, my father isn't one of them.

Nicole takes charge. "Thank you, everyone, for taking time out of your busy schedules to meet this morning. The goal of this conversation is to let Olivia catch us up on Mr. Taylor's project, as well as explain some of the unique challenges she's facing. We thought it would be easier if we could talk instead of doing it over email. I'm going to turn it over to Olivia so she can walk us through what she's got so far and what her ideal next steps would be."

"Thanks, Nicole," I say. "It's nice to see you all. As Nicole mentioned, this project presents a unique set of challenges. I've spent the last couple days trying to sort through Mr. Taylor's first draft and conducting some preliminary interviews with him. I'm sure you're aware that he's been diagnosed with Lewy body dementia." Neil nods on the screen. Lance doesn't look up from whatever it is he's looking at, most likely his phone. "Due to this condition," I continue, "we have only about two or three hours per day where he's lucid enough to work. The remaining time has been spent trying to untangle what he's written."

Neil chimes in. "I know you're a pro at this, Olivia. In fact, I loved the book you did on Magdalena Ruiz. You captured her voice perfectly."

I offer a polite smile. "Thank you." Magdalena Ruiz, senator from Arizona and a rising star in the Democratic Conference. I'd spent four months with her during her reelection campaign, learning everything there was to know about her. Interviewing her parents. Her campaign manager. Her best friend from high school. Shadowing her at town halls and donor events. Sitting with her late at night, eating pizza and drinking beer. Magdalena had the kind of energy that was magnetic. Easy to capture on the page. "Vincent Taylor is a different beast," I continue. "We're asking him to recount events from nearly fifty years ago. Under the best of circumstances, memory can be tricky."

Nicole cuts in. "Olivia's job was to come in and revise an existing manuscript. We think that objective needs to be revisited."

"The chapter I sent was a straight revision of what he's given me to work with," I say. "I've scanned a few pages of the original, and I'd like to send it to you so you can see for yourselves."

I click away from the Zoom meeting and over to my email where I've attached the PDF. "I'm sorry, Sloane. I don't have your email, but I'm sure someone on your team can forward it to you."

"Thanks," Sloane says.

I jump back to the meeting and hear the ping of Neil's email. "Give us a second to take a look," he says.

I watch as Neil pulls up the email on his iPad, and a few people gather around him to read. I'm hoping they'll see how far gone my father is, that they'll realize I need more time to start the book over and begin again. I'm about to say that when the woman to the left of Neil speaks, unaware they're still unmuted.

"I told you this was a mistake. It's a vanity project. And honestly, no one cares anymore."

"We should have gone with Calder," her male counterpart says. The name rips through me and I try not to react. "Maybe we should send him a few pages of this and see what he can do with it."

I search my mind for the name Neil gave during introductions. *Tyler Blakewood.*

Neil looks up at them. "Vincent insisted on Olivia. My hands were tied," he says.

"It's your call, Neil," the disembodied voice of Sloane, the publisher, says. "If you want to pull the plug, I'll back you up."

"Sorry to interrupt, guys, but you're not on mute," Nicole finally informs them.

Neil scrambles to cover as everyone finds their seats again. "As you can hear, we have concerns. But I'm willing to let you run with this a bit longer. What do you need?"

I shove my hands beneath my legs to stop them from trembling. Nicole looks supportive on the screen, her expression urging me to push through. Publishing is a business, and their objective is to produce a book and make as much money from it if possible. If they can't, I shouldn't be offended if they decide to walk away. "His memories are there, but as you can see, I can't use what he's written. This is no longer a revision project, but a brand-new book that has to be written from the beginning. That's going to take time and it's going to require that I be allowed to speak to other people who have memories of Mr. Taylor as a child. Who can fill in the blanks he's either unable, or unwilling, to share with me."

"We might be able to give you more time," Neil says. "But I'll have to defer to Lance on the rest."

Lance looks up. "Mr. Taylor was quite clear that he doesn't want people in town to know about the book. He doesn't feel they will give him fair representation and thus speaking to them would be more of a liability than a help."

"If I may ask," I start, trying to regain my equilibrium. "I'm still trying to figure out what he wants this memoir to be. Was there a proposal? A pitch? What did he give you that compelled you to buy it? Maybe if I could see that, I'd have a better sense of direction."

"I pitched the book on Mr. Taylor's behalf," Lance says. "With the fiftieth anniversary of the murders approaching and with his own declining health, Mr. Taylor wanted to write a dark and atmospheric book that would explain exactly how both Danny and Poppy died. That he was ready to end his five decades of silence and tell the truth."

Neil smiles. "How could we say no to that?"

Dark and atmospheric I can do. To the group I say, "That helps. Yesterday, he shared a story about coming across Danny in the woods, burying the neighbor's cat." I go on to describe the scene, delivering it with the same level of drama my father had told it to me. "It was as if the details were seared into his memory," I tell them. "The fear and dread he so clearly felt at discovering his brother had done something so disturbing."

"That's exactly what we want," Neil says. "Draft that chapter and let's talk again."

My phone buzzes with a text from Nicole: Stay on the zoom after everyone leaves.

To the group, Nicole says, "So to recap, Olivia will start the book over, and you will give her more time. Can we say September instead of June?"

Neil looks sideways at his colleagues and for a moment I'm certain he'll insist on the original June deadline. That I'm going to have to produce an entire book on a timeline that's next to impossible. "The best we can do is July," he says, "and I'll need to see the chapters as they're being written, just to stay on top of the direction the book is taking."

I'm caught off guard by the request, one he might make of a much younger, less experienced writer and not someone who has done this dozens of times, to great acclaim.

This is the consequence of speaking out as a woman. We are labeled *hysterical, emotional, unreliable,* and finally, *incompetent.* I consider refusing, telling him I won't work that way. But I don't think I have room to argue, since they're just as inclined to cancel the whole thing. I should never have sent him that revised chapter. But if I hadn't, I would have spent weeks revising a book they wouldn't accept. "Sure," I tell him, knowing I'll regret it.

"Let's let Olivia get back to work," Nicole interjects. "We can regroup in a couple weeks. I'll have my assistant reach out with potential dates."

"Thank you, everyone," Neil says.

Then they're gone and it's just me and Nicole. "Are you okay?" she asks.

I give a shuddering laugh. "I think so. Mostly I'm relieved they responded so positively to the new chapter. It's a compelling scene," I say, thinking again of my other chapter, of my father ranting about the missing knife. Believing I was my mother. I wonder what Nicole and the team at Monarch would think of that, but I shake the thought away and continue. "I'd like to figure out if it actually happened or if it's just a figment of his declining memory. What do you think would happen if I spoke to people on background?" I ask.

She looks sympathetic. "As your agent, I'd have to advise against that. You know the rules as well as I do."

"If they cancel the book, do I have to pay back the first chunk of the advance?"

Nicole looks uncomfortable. "That depends," she says. "If you're in breach of contract, or you are unable to perform to their standards, then yes. But if they pull the book themselves, then no. Try not to worry about that and just go out and do what you do best. We bought you a little more time, so hopefully you can work your magic." She checks her watch. "I've got to jump to another meeting, but call me later if you want to talk more."

Chapter 10

"What should we talk about today?" my father asks when we sit down later that morning for our session. He looks energized, ready to work.

"I'm working on that scene with Danny and the cat," I tell him. "I spoke with the team at Monarch early this morning and they're very excited for more chapters like that."

My father nods. "One time Danny locked Poppy in the garage. Threatened to beat me up if I let her out. It used to make me so angry, how everyone—even your mother—used to think he was so fantastic."

There's a thread of bitterness in his voice, the remnants of a younger brother trying—and failing—to measure up. But I'm wary of letting this memoir turn into one of petty grievances and sibling rivalries. I want to get to the core of my family. Figure out who each of them really was—separate from each other, but also because of each other.

"Typically, I ask to speak to your closest friends and then mine them for information about you and about that time. Then you and I dig into the same topics and I craft a narrative around the memories that everyone shares. Weaving the consistencies into a book, revisiting the inconsistencies until we can all agree on what likely happened. But obviously, I'm not allowed to do any of that." If my father catches the resentment in my voice, he ignores it. "Instead, I'll need to rely on what you remember and hope I can suss out what's true and what's part of your disease."

"I understand your frustration," he says. "But this is why it's so important to get this book done now, when I can still remember the more important moments." He leans forward, animated. "I'm going to give you the same advice I give all young authors I mentor. *You can't protect your characters.*"

I look up. "This is your memoir, Dad, and you're not mentoring me," I remind him. "I'm also not a fiction writer."

"Of course you're a fiction writer. You always have been."

"What are you talking about?"

"Don't you remember?" he asks. "The stories you used to write? They were quite good for someone your age."

"I never wrote any stories. Is this one of your delusions?"

He brushes my words away, annoyed. Then he stands and leaves the room. I wait, wondering if I should follow him.

He returns holding a large box with a fitted lid. The kind you'd put a large toy in and wrap with a giant red bow. He lifts the top and rummages around inside until he finds what he's looking for, pulling out a sheaf of papers clipped together with a butterfly clip and handing them to me. On them, I can see the scrawl of cursive across the wide-lined pages.

He gestures toward the packet. "My favorite story in there is the one where Lionel Foolhardy goes to summer camp. I can't believe you don't remember writing these."

"You were the one who invented Lionel Foolhardy, not me."

He shakes his head. "Lionel was one hundred percent your creation."

I flip through the pages, memories floating back. How I'd sit with my father while he worked, with my own notebook, drafting story after story. Lionel goes to summer camp. Lionel volunteers at the local animal shelter. How we'd stop at three for a drink—him his first whiskey of the day, and me a Shirley Temple with a maraschino cherry. We'd talk about plot problems and character arcs. "I'd forgotten," I say.

But I'm unsettled. As a ghostwriter, I know better than most how easy it is to tell ourselves a story until we believe it's true, no amount of evidence to the contrary convincing us otherwise. I spent my entire adult life believing my father created Lionel Foolhardy as a way to entertain me. And yet, a parallel universe has existed where I was his creator. I was the one who penned those stories and made Lionel a fixture of my childhood. If I can't remember something so basic about my own life, what hope do I have to untangle the fractured pieces of my father's memory?

"What else do you have in there?" I ask.

He hands me the box and I balance it on my knees, peering inside. At first it looks like a jumble of junk, no different from the boxes out back, but I start to recognize pieces of my childhood—the bracelet I wove for him when I was seven and went to summer camp, the brightly colored thread now faded. A small box that might have once contained jewelry rattles when I shake it. When I open it, I find all of my baby teeth inside. I see report cards from elementary school. Several drawings, and a few notes written in a clumsy childhood hand. *I love you, Daddy.*

"I can't believe you kept all this stuff."

He looks offended. "I can't believe you think I'd throw it away." His voice is quiet when he speaks again. "I saw you, you know."

Confused, I look up.

"At that conference in New York," he clarifies. "I saw you in the lobby. I looked for you later, but I was told you'd checked out early."

"An emergency at home," I say.

"Of course," he says, and I can tell he knows I'm lying.

I replace the lid and set the box on the floor, imagining him taking it down every now and then, flipping through mementos that suddenly end when I turned fourteen and left for school, never to return again. How perhaps he'd planned to fill the box with more memories that had never come. His belief that I would return home. Come over for dinners and the holidays. And how painful it must have been when I didn't.

I'd assumed the years of womanizing and drug and alcohol abuse were a coping mechanism for the trauma he'd suffered as a child. But now I see that it was perhaps a father, trying to forget that he was alone in the world. Immersing himself in the easiest ways to forget.

I swallow hard, not wanting him to see my emotion. "You do have a tendency to fill a box with junk," I say.

He looks embarrassed. "I've been meaning to deal with those boxes for years but . . ." He trails off, perhaps unwilling to admit aloud that now he's not in any condition to be making decisions about what's trash and what's not. "I know you're only here to write this book," he continues. "And please say no if I'm overstepping. But Alma's hands are full with all of my appointments, medications, and managing the house. Plus, there are probably some valuable things buried in there among the trash that might be worth some money—correspondence with other authors, old annotated manuscripts we might be able to auction off. Alma wouldn't recognize their value, but you would. Maybe, if you need a break from working on the memoir, you could sort through them?" He gives me a wry smile. "No dead hamsters. I promise."

I laugh and say, "To this day, I still hesitate before opening a box."

"Like I said," he continues, "feel free to say no. You don't have any obligation other than the book. Assuming you've decided to stay on," he finishes.

I think back to our initial conversation, knowing there was never a question of me accepting this job. "I don't make it a habit to walk away from hard projects," I tell him, leaving out how very precarious my financial situation actually is. "And looking through the boxes in the guesthouse might help, given the fact that I'm not allowed to interview anyone." I wait to see if he'll respond, but he just gives a curt nod and I push on. "They extended our deadline to July," I say. "But that's still only four months. My number one job is to make you sympathetic to the reader. They need to want to spend 300-plus pages with you— either because they like you, or because you're telling them something they want to know."

"I think likable is off the table."

I dip my head in silent agreement. "They have to believe the information they're getting is new, but they also need to feel your vulnerability in the retelling."

He nods and I check to make sure my voice recorder is on, then pick up the legal pad I brought with me, flipping around until I get to the page I want. "You have a full page here, with just one single sentence on it, over and over again. *She shouldn't have gone. She shouldn't have gone.*" I start to hold it out to him, but then remember he can't read it anyway so I set it on the table next to me.

"No, let me look at it," he says.

I pass it over and he stares at the page, running his fingers lightly over the words, slowly nodding to himself. "'She shouldn't have gone'?" he repeats. "That's what it says?

95

"Yes."

He looks out the window, the light illuminating his profile. "I'm a fool," he says, almost to himself. "I thought you could come in here, we'd spend a few weeks chatting, and you could take what I'd already written and clean it up."

"Writing a memoir is challenging, even under normal circumstances. It requires you to face painful memories that have sometimes been buried for years. It's a commitment to telling the truth, even if it's hard." I point to the pad and say, "So tell me about that page. Who is it referring to?"

I expect him to tell me it's about Poppy, hitchhiking into Ventura alone. That the fault was hers for luring a killer back to Ojai and destroying my father's family. Or perhaps he'll tell me that she shouldn't have gone back to the house the night of the carnival.

But he surprises me. "I'm pretty sure it's about your mother."

"I'm not following."

"There was a party. A bonfire. Everyone was going, but I was grounded. I was a bit insecure at sixteen, with my first girlfriend. I wanted her to stay back with me and, in the way of young boys everywhere, didn't know how to simply ask for what I wanted." He gives a quiet chuckle. "So I left it up to her, and she took me at face value. Went to the party with Danny and Poppy."

I point to the page, filled with the same phrase over and over again, and say, "Are you sure that's what this is about? This seems more . . ." I hunt for the words. "Unhinged. Ominous."

"I can't tell you why I wrote it over and over. But I can say with a fair amount of confidence that it was about that bonfire. About a boy who got caught ditching sixth period and was grounded for it, who wanted his girlfriend to choose hanging out with him over going to a party."

I sigh and say, "Okay." My panic is slowly rising. I've maneuvered myself into an impossible corner. I have one solid chapter about Danny, and another one I have no intention of showing anyone. I was hoping this page would lead me to another scene I could write. But instead, it's teenage angst. I feel like I'm riding shotgun with a man who has lost control of the car and there isn't anything I can do but wait for us to crash.

Vincent

March 8, 1975

I sit at my desk, the heat of the desk lamp burning my skin. I was supposed to be doing homework. Supposed to be *using my time wisely*, as my father suggested when he'd grounded me. But really, I'm supposed to be at the bonfire with Danny and Poppy.

Lydia.

My stomach does a funny flop, as it always does when I think about her. So beautiful. So funny and graceful. It's only been three weeks and I'm still astonished she'd chosen me. From somewhere inside of me, I hear Danny's taunting voice. *She only chose you because I'd already rejected her.*

From the living room, Lawrence Welk's voice floats down the hall. I get up and wander into the kitchen, opening the refrigerator and staring into it, my mind stuck an hour earlier. On Lydia's disappointed expression when I told her I couldn't go to the bonfire. And how it had shifted when Danny – who'd originally called the bonfire a stupid waste of time – suddenly changed his mind and decided to go after all, inviting Lydia to hitch a ride with him and Poppy. "No sense in you being grounded as well, just because my brother is stupid enough to ditch sixth period and get caught."

I saw right away what Danny was doing, but Poppy had been thrilled by his change of heart, jumping around, making a racket. "Would you kids be quiet for one blessed minute?" our mother had shouted from the kitchen.

I'd hoped Lydia would say no. To volunteer to stay behind with me. We could have spent the evening pretending to do homework, waiting for my parents to go to bed so we could watch Saturday night television and make out on the couch.

For a second, I thought she was going to. *No thanks, I'll keep Vince company.* But instead she'd turned to me and asked, "Do you mind?"

Everyone had been looking at me. Lydia, waiting for me to say, *Sure, no problem.* But I saw the way Poppy's hands froze, her gaze rising from her new Super 8 camera—barely a week old and already she was rarely without it—where she'd been loading a fresh roll of film. I noticed the way Danny's eyes had danced in anticipation, waiting for me to have one of my famous explosions.

My father's voice startles me from my thoughts. "Shut the refrigerator door. Do you think I'm made of money?"

I turn from the open refrigerator to see him standing in the doorway of the kitchen, an empty beer can in his hand. "And quit your moping." He tosses the can into the trash and exits again.

I let go of the fridge handle and the door eases closed. The window over the sink is black, and I imagine the bright light of the bonfire, the high school kids gathering, parking their cars along the side of the highway and walking, some carrying beer, others concealing joints in their pockets. That the party is at Mr. Stewart's house is another thing that's worrying me.

Lydia is obsessed with running track and won't stop talking about the private coaching sessions he's giving her for free. *Mr. Stewart says I need to do extra training sessions on the weekends.* Or *Mr. Stewart says I've shaved an eighth of a second from my split times.* Whatever split times are.

All the other kids are obsessed with him as well; the cool, young PE teacher everyone hopes to get. The one kids can relate to. Talk to. Walking around campus in his shorts and T-shirt, kids following him like an entourage. It's all I can do not to throw up.

Even Danny had been enamored for a while. When he was twelve, he'd joined Mr. Stewart's outdoor survival class that went into the woods on the weekends, learning how to dig a hole to shit in, or how to skin a rat to roast over an open fire. "You should look into doing Mr. Stewart's survival class," my father had suggested earlier this year, after I'd gotten into trouble at school yet again. "Channel some of that energy into the outdoors."

"I'd rather eat glass," I'd countered.

"No one is stopping you," Danny said.

I'd lunged at him, but he'd leapt out of reach at the last minute, glanced at our mother whose back was toward us, and given me the finger before slamming through the back door.

"Vincent, honey, moping in the kitchen isn't going to make this any easier," my mother calls from the living room. "Why don't you do something productive? Maybe write a book report."

I glance out the window toward the neighboring yard. The one that will soon belong to Mr. Stewart. This bonfire is to celebrate one last night at his old house, out on Route 33, before he moves to town. Into the house right next door. Poppy is over the moon, but the last thing I want is a teacher for a neighbor. I get enough of them at school.

I open the fridge again, grab a Coke and make my way back to my room. I set the unopened soda on my desk and flip through Danny's albums. Pink Floyd. The Grateful Dead. Led Zeppelin.

I pull Danny's favorite Hendrix album from its sleeve and put it on the turntable, setting the needle to "Foxy Lady" and dial the volume up to eight. Looking for something that will take my mind off of the image of the three of them leaving me behind.

"Keep an eye on Lydia," I'd said to Poppy.

She'd looked back, teasing. "You want me to spy on her for you?" She held her camera up. "I'm sure she'd love me to follow her around. *Smile for the camera, Lydia! Vince wants to make sure you're behaving.*"

"That's not what I meant," I'd said. But in fact, that was exactly what I'd wanted. Proof that Lydia was mine. And that everyone at the party knew it.

Danny was driving and Lydia had followed him to the car, sliding into the front seat. Poppy got into the back and aimed her camera at me, standing on the porch. But before she could get any footage of the loser who'd had to stay behind, I turned and walked inside. Not wanting the camera to catch the expression I knew was on my face. The one that's still there, as Hendrix wails about a woman who had to belong only to him.

It's jealousy. Fury. Rage.

Take your pick.

Chapter 11

I have my father's old photo albums open on the dining room table—the ones Jack and I used to pore over, trying to imagine Poppy and Danny into existence—when my father comes downstairs looking for me. I'd finished the chapter about Danny and the dead cat and sent it off to Neil yesterday. I've been checking my email obsessively ever since, hoping to get word that I'm on the right track.

"Aren't we working today?" my father asks. Then he looks worried. "What day is it?"

"Tuesday," I tell him. "I thought we'd have more room down here."

He hesitates when he sees what I have in front of me.

Most people have a set of stories—tried and true anecdotes they return to again and again. Moments—big or small, happy or sad—that have rooted inside of them, for whatever reason. I've found that it's best to let them talk themselves out before I begin shifting the lens to either the left or the right. To the spaces around those landmarks.

He sits in his usual chair and I slide mine closer to his, pulling one of the albums with me and opening it to the first page, showing a photograph of Danny standing in front of an army-green tent. He looks to be about twelve and he's grinning, holding a hunting knife.

My father leans closer, studying the image. "I'd forgotten how bright his smile was. How much energy he had."

He turns the page and we see Poppy, perched on her bed, posters of Olivia Newton-John and Donny Osmond on the wall behind her. "Looks like Poppy had all the typical preteen obsessions everyone else had in the '70s," I say.

My father laughs and I feel him loosening up. "Our mother bought those for her. Poppy hated them and tore them down the first chance she got. At the end her walls were covered with collages of Betty Friedan. Shirley Chisholm. Gloria Steinem. Those were Poppy's heroes." He looks at me, his eyes shining with mischief. "She even had a *Roe v Wade* poster but our mother made her get rid of it. Said it was immoral. At first, I thought Poppy put those posters up as a way to bait our mother, but the reality was, she was a budding activist."

"She started young."

"She was incredibly bright, skipping the second grade. My mother hated the fact that she was only thirteen when she started high school, but Poppy was unstoppable. In middle school, she put together a petition to allow girls to do wood shop." He grins at the memory. "She won that one, but then she started another one, arguing that if it was a requirement for girls to take home ec, it should also be a requirement for boys. She believed they should also know how to cook, clean, and do laundry. But Mr. Leahy, the principal, shot that one down. Which led her to write a letter to the board of education asking why district leadership was predominantly male."

He looks back down at the image of a younger Poppy, surrounded by teen pop idols she didn't worship. When Jack and I had looked through this album, we imagined her lying on her bed daydreaming about Donny Osmond. Instead, it turns out she was daydreaming about equal rights and fair household labor distribution.

My father looks back up at me and says, "You remind me a lot of her."

"You don't really know me." The comment leaps out, reminding us both of the baggage that sits between us.

My father isn't fazed. He says, "I know your work. Where the rest of the world hears your subject's voice on the page, I hear yours. Poppy would have loved your books. She would have admired your ferocious commitment to elevating female and marginalized voices."

I think about all I've lost in that regard. How certain I'd been of my position, believing I could say what I thought, like any of my male counterparts, and be safe. When in reality, I'd spoken the truth and been erased for it. Forced to lower myself to Calder's level, selling myself to the highest bidder. "I don't seem to have much of a voice at all these days," I say.

"You're a survivor," he says. "Remember, no regrets, no looking back."

I roll my eyes at the familiar line. One he would trot out anytime I felt sad about my mother, or about something mean someone had said to me at school. *No regrets, no looking back, Olivia.* It didn't work then and it doesn't work now. My father will never understand a world that doesn't bend to his will.

I turn the page, to a picture of Danny with his best friend, Mark. Jack's father. They're clowning around on skateboards, channeling their best Tony Alva and Jay Adams. "If Poppy was a feminist, what was Danny?"

"When he was younger, he was spirited. Funny."

"And later?"

"He was fun, until he wasn't."

"Give me an example," I say. "The first one that comes to mind."

My father thinks for a moment. "One time he got the idea to build a trailer for his bike. We had some wood and Poppy's old tricycle, and his plan was to tow us with a rope."

"How old were you?"

My father blows out hard. "Maybe twelve? Thirteen? Anyway, Poppy and I were enthusiastic apprentices, and we spent all weekend building it. There was one wheel on the front of the box, two on the back and an old pillow inside for cushioning."

My father pushes the nearest photo album away and spreads his palms flat on the table, remembering. "When it was done, we took it over to the high school parking lot to try it out. Poppy was begging to be first, but Danny said it should be me." He gives a hollow laugh. "That should have been my first clue. But like a dummy, I hopped in and Danny started pedaling. The plan was to circle the lot to see how it held up. Then give Poppy a turn."

"But that's not what happened?" I ask.

My father shakes his head. "Danny did one slow circle and I thought he'd stop. But he kept going. Standing up on his pedals to go faster. I realized pretty quick that there was no way for me to steer—or to get out. I started to yell at him to slow down, the wheels literally rattling my teeth. I could hear Poppy screaming as well, but he started heading toward this ramp that led down into a lower lot. It didn't seem very steep when you were on foot, but kids used to like to skateboard down it. I was terrified." My father pauses, remembering. "Later, he claimed he couldn't hear me. Then he said he thought I was yelling because it was fun."

"What happened?"

"About halfway down, the whole thing tipped over. I flew out, splitting my chin open on the cement." He tips his head back and points to a thin scar. "Eight stitches, and our mother was furious."

"Did Danny get into trouble?"

"No. Both Poppy and I knew that if we told on him, he'd do something even worse, so we said it was an accident."

"Did he do that often? Hurt you? Threaten you?"

My father gives a tiny shrug. "All the time. But he had this way of making it sound like he was just playing around, deriding us for not being able to take a joke. He'd lure us in with smiles and promises of fun, and then"—my father snaps his fingers—"he'd just shift. Without warning."

I sit with that image for a moment, my mind puzzling through different scenarios with Danny as the perpetrator and not my father, as I'd always believed. I stare at Danny's grinning face, wondering if what my father says is true. I think again of his story about Danny and the dead cat, the question I'd had to swallow, lest it set my father off. The idea that Danny could have somehow been involved in the murder of Poppy, instead of the tragic hero everyone made him out to be. But my father's gaze seems far away, latched onto something I can't see, so I save that idea until I have more to back it up. More substance with which to push. A couple of anecdotes aren't enough.

Finally, I flip to the last page of the album. After April 1975, there are no more Taylor family photos. I point to the single picture, tucked behind a plastic sleeve that's losing its adhesive cling. It's an image of my father and Danny in their room. My father has his back to the camera, balanced on a chair, hanging a Pink Floyd *Wish You Were Here* poster. He's reaching up to attach the fourth corner and you can see his muscles straining, his skinny arms poking out of his short-sleeved shirt. Danny sits on the bed, staring directly into the camera, a chemistry textbook propped up on his knees. He's not smiling, as if the person taking the picture is interrupting him and he's just waiting for them to leave again.

"This photograph has always haunted me," I tell my father now. "Likely the last photograph taken of Danny. The way he's looking at the camera, it's almost like he knows he's only got weeks left to live."

My father is silent, staring at the image. Finally he says, "I'd forgotten about that concert. Your mother and I went together, early on in our relationship."

It takes me a moment to figure out that he's talking about the Pink Floyd poster. "That must have been fun," I say, frustrated to be moving away from Danny and back to my mother.

He smiles. "It was. We hitchhiked; rode our bikes out a ways and ditched them in the bushes."

"Did kids hitchhike a lot when you were young?" I ask, thinking of Poppy. I'd always assumed she was brave to have hitchhiked alone, but maybe it was more common than I thought.

"It was the only way we could get into Ventura, which in our minds was where all the fun was."

"Who gave you and Mom a ride to the concert? Anyone you knew?"

He cuts his gaze sideways, his tone offhand, and my internal radar pings. "I have no memory of getting there or getting back. But I remember the sense of freedom. Of being in a huge venue, holding hands with your mother. Of feeling like it was the beginning of something good."

I wait for him to acknowledge that with hindsight, he can now see that it was actually the beginning of the end, but he doesn't.

Vincent

April 26, 1975

It seems as if everyone from our high school is in Ventura to see Pink Floyd. I stand on a grassy slope, anxious for Lydia to get back from the bathroom. The opening act will be wrapping up soon and I don't want her to miss anything.

So far, the evening hasn't gone as I'd hoped. It had started with the ride from Mr. Stewart. When I'd seen his flashy Mustang barreling down the highway, I'd stepped back from the edge of the road, not wanting to get caught hitchhiking. But Lydia seemed to know something I didn't.

"He's a teacher," I said, pulling her back.

Lydia had shaken me off. "He's cool."

"How do you know?"

She smiled and stepped forward, thumb out.

The ride had been even more awkward, with Mr. Stewart's girlfriend, Amelia, making comments about how great it was that Mr. Stewart had bought the house next door. That we were now neighbors. I'd shrugged, wondering why everyone thought it was so wonderful to live next door to a teacher.

Then Mr. Stewart had started in on Lydia's running. How talented she was. How she could get a scholarship to college if she trained hard enough. I'd felt a tightening in my chest, a small knot of tension at the idea of Lydia leaving, exiting the small world we were building together and entering something bigger than I could ever offer.

People around me begin to clap, chanting for Pink Floyd to take the stage. I shove my hands into my pockets and decide to make the trek over to where they've set up a line of out-houses. If Lydia is going to miss the opening, then we'll miss it together.

I'm descending into the area near the parking lot, the scent of pot, incense, and patchouli oil giving way to the ammonia stench of outhouses, when I see her burst through the door of one of the toilets, as if something inside is chasing her. She runs around behind it, disappearing from view.

I hesitate, wondering if I should follow or if she'd be annoyed with me. I don't have an instinct for girls the way Danny does. In fact, up until a few months ago, I'd been certain the only reason Lydia was friends with me at all was so that she could be closer to Danny.

But it had been me she'd chosen. And now, on Saturday nights, she comes over and we sit together on the couch, some-times with her head in my lap so I can play with her hair, and we watch Mary Tyler Moore. Bob Newhart. Carol Burnett.

I'm just about to cross the crowded area and press through the snaking lines when Lydia emerges from where she'd disap-peared, Mr. Stewart alongside her, his hand on her lower back. I halt, sinking back into the crowd so they won't see me spying.

Mr. Stewart turns Lydia so she's facing him, and I wish I could read lips. To know what they're talking about. People move around them, a stream heading back to the concert, where recorded music plays while Pink Floyd sets up. The concert will be starting any moment, and Lydia is too engrossed in a conver-sation with Mr. Stewart to even notice.

She's mine, I want to shout down to him, and I wonder if I will ever be settled. If I will ever be the kind of person who will feel secure with what I have, instead of always feeling like I'm about thirty seconds away from losing everything.

Rage beats through me, the blood rushing through my limbs, pounding beneath my skin. If I say something, I'll fuck it all up. So I turn and head back to where I'd been, where she'd left me when she promised she'd be back in a second, just a quick trip to the bathroom so she didn't have to miss any of the concert. I step around clumps of people laughing and smoking, over trash and discarded beer cans, trying to estimate where I'd been. Not wanting her to know that I'd followed her again.

My mind touches on the bonfire last month. That nagging feeling of anxiety that plagued me all night, imagining her there, laughing and partying without me. So much of Lydia doesn't make sense. She's nothing like Poppy, who will tell you exactly what she's thinking, even when you'd rather not know. Lydia is a puzzle I can't quite solve. One I'm not sure I'm meant to be solving. It's hard not to wonder why she's with me. Hard not to notice the questioning glances at school, the snickers and whispers behind hands. The silence that follows me wherever I go.

A few minutes later, Lydia appears, her eyes a little watery and her hand shaking a bit as she takes mine. It's clammy and sweaty at the same time, and I wonder if I should ask if she's okay, or if I should just pretend I know nothing.

She smiles, tentative. "Hey," she says.

And in that one word I get a whiff of vomit. That's the second time today she's thrown up, and I wonder if she's sick. Worried that maybe we shouldn't have gone so far from home.

"Are you okay?" I ask.

"The smell in that outhouse . . . it got to me. I got sick behind."

She looks away, unable to meet my eyes.

I squeeze her hand, relieved. Suddenly understanding Mr. Stewart's concern. Glad that for once, I hadn't rushed in with assumptions and anger. "Come on," I say. "Let's see if we can get closer."

Chapter 12

"I know you can't tell me about the job, but how are you spending your time when you're not working?" Tom asks.

My father has a standing physical therapy session every Thursday at eleven, so we'd stopped early and I'd gone out on another research tour. I'd called Tom from the car on my way back from the cemetery where Danny, Poppy, and my grandparents are buried. Their gravestones were modest, lined up in a row:

Edmund Frederick Taylor
    Beloved father and husband
    January 19, 1937–November 15, 1978
Patricia Sampson Taylor
    Devoted mother and wife
    July 27, 1941–December 4, 1980
Patricia "Poppy" Marie Taylor
    Forever in our hearts
    March 3, 1961–June 13, 1975
Daniel Edmund Taylor
    Gone but never forgotten
    February 26, 1958–June 13, 1975

I imagined my father coming here to visit his family and wondered what it had felt like to be the only one left. And what it will feel like when that's me.

"I'm never not working," I tell Tom as I check the driveway for my father's car. Making sure he and Alma are still gone before I disconnect my phone from the car and make my way around the house toward the courtyard and the guesthouse.

He sighs.

"What's wrong?" I ask, tossing my keys onto the nightstand and settling at the desk.

"I don't know," he says. "Our last few conversations have been weird."

"Weird how?" I'm running through the week since I arrived. We've talked every day, usually right before I fall asleep, and everything seemed fine to me.

"I don't know," he continues. "I know this job is hard. I know you're struggling. But I feel like there's something else you're not telling me."

I laugh. "There's a lot I'm not telling you."

"No," he says. "This isn't about the job. It's an evasiveness. A distance." He's quiet for a moment before finally saying, "I don't know. I'm probably imagining it."

"I'm fine. We're fine," I tell him, hoping he can hear the certainty in my voice and not the guilt over how much I've been concealing.

But after we get off the phone, I'm worried too. That he's intuited my stress and wondered if it was something other than the job troubles me. Tom once told me his radar is tuned differently than most people's. He picks up on signals the rest of us ignore. I've always thought it was wonderful that he could read me so well. But now it's become a liability and I will need to be extra careful when we talk. To give him my full attention so that he doesn't start asking questions that I don't want to answer.

*   *   *

Later that evening, Alma tells me my father needs my help with something.

I head upstairs to find him sitting at his desk, staring out the window. "What is it you need?"

He turns to look at me. "I was hoping you might be willing to take a swing through my email just to make sure there isn't anything important I'm missing."

"Oh. Sure," I say. He stands, letting me sit at his desk, the leather chair swiveling under my weight.

I click over to his email and ask, "Password?"

"It should already be logged in," he tells me.

I point to the screen and say, "It's asking me for a password." When he hesitates, I say, "You don't have to tell me, but I can't look at your in-box without it."

"Rebecca," he says, his voice quiet. As if he's embarrassed to say the word too loud.

I look at him. "Mom's middle name is your password?"

"Have you ever been in love?" my father asks, and I think again of Tom. Of how in tune he is with me, and an ache passes through me.

"Why hang on to a woman who left you? It's been decades," I say, trying to move the subject away from my love life.

"You can't erase the past by not thinking about it." My father gives a hollow laugh. "Believe me, I've tried. Your mother was the best thing that ever happened to me. Better than any of my books or awards."

I snort and look back at the computer screen. "She left you to raise her daughter alone."

"My daughter too," he reminds me, his voice quiet.

I type in my mother's middle name and find hundreds of messages waiting for him in his in-box. "What do you want me to do in here?" I ask.

"Clean it out," he says. "Make sure there isn't something buried in there that I need to deal with."

I scroll through emails from the *New York Times* and *Washington Post*. Solicitations from local politicians asking for donations. Tons of junk mail from retailers. "The Gap?" I ask.

He shrugs. "I like their T-shirts."

On the second page, I find something that might need a response. "They want you to be a keynote speaker at Southwest-Lit." A big literary conference held in New Mexico every fall.

"Email them back. Tell them I'm not available."

I hesitate. "Do you want me to identify myself as writing on your behalf?"

"Of course not. Just pretend to be me."

"How about *Thank you for the honor, however I have other obligations that preclude me from attending.*"

He nods his approval, so I type it, then hit Send.

"There are still several more pages, but it's mostly junk. Do you want me to delete them or mark them as read?"

"I don't give a shit, Olivia," he sighs. I turn back to the computer and say, "Let me just ..." but the rest of my sentence evaporates. On the screen in front of me, buried about halfway down, is a name that makes my stomach turn to lead.

John Calder.

* * *

It's past midnight when I log into my father's email on my own computer. All evening, I'd wrestled with the idea of whether I should read it, or if I should just let it go. But I can't shake the discomfort of the two of them talking. Colluding. My father never mentioned he knew Calder, but there was an email in his in-box telling me otherwise.

The subject line simply says, Question. When I open the message, it's short.

Just following up on this.

I notice that John has responded to an older email he sent and I scroll down to read it.

A friend at Monarch tells me you're writing a memoir. I'd love to pitch for it if you're open to it. Please let me know.

I look at the date—March 12. The day after that first catastrophic Zoom with the Monarch team, when someone mentioned how they should have pitched Calder instead. I stretch back into my memory for the name. Tyler Blakewood.

Before I can change my mind, I click respond.

Tell me what you have in mind.

Then I hit Send.

* * *

Unable to sleep after that, I stare at the ceiling, turning over how to talk to Tom about this because he's always been the person I turn to. He'd come with me to the Calder trial, sat behind me while the judge read his verdict, and then taken me to get drunk afterward. He'd counseled me, consoled me, listened to me, and even when he hadn't agreed with my decisions—he'd advised strongly against that social media rant—he was always on my side.

I sit up and grab my phone, my fingers hesitating over the blank text screen, unsure of what to say. Of how to stay vague without unraveling all the lies I've told.

Instead, I grab my laptop and open it, transcribing a conversation with my father earlier today, zeroing in on a small exchange I'd wanted to revisit. It was about my parents and it matched what others have always said about my father—that he was jealous. Volatile.

I shove my AirPods into my ears and rewind the recording back to the beginning of the segment, trying not to think about why John Calder is pitching for a book that is already under contract. Whether Monarch is letting me fail first before pulling the project from me. Which would likely force me to pay back my advance.

My voice resonates in my ears and I push my worry away, focusing on work I know I can do better than John Calder.

Vincent: I used to sit on your mother's porch, waiting for her to get home from track practice. I'd tell myself I just wanted to see her, but I was insecure. I wanted to make sure she'd been where she said she'd been.

Olivia: Did you do that often?

VT: Often enough.

O: And was she? Where she'd said she'd been?

VT: My mother had something she'd say whenever Poppy got too nosy. Sometimes, when you go looking for something, you might not like what you find.

O: That doesn't answer the question.

VT: Sometimes your mother lied to me. Mostly because she didn't want to upset me or make me jealous about things that didn't matter, like her workouts with Mr. Stewart, which seemed to take up all her free time and energy.

O: Did you argue a lot?

VT: Not any more or less than other sixteen-year-olds flush with young love.

O: So was your mother right? Did you find something you didn't like?

VT: <Quiet. Contemplating.> Probably. I don't remember.

O: I need you to try. The memoir has to open you up so others can see your vulnerabilities. It's how readers will know you're telling the truth.

VT: You're the liar, Lydia, not me.

The recording ends there, but I can still feel the shock, the shift from conversation to anger. The pain of hearing him spit her name at me, a warning.

But I'm also struck by the image of my father, sneaking out to check up on his girlfriend. Not trusting her. Following her. Obsessing over where she said she had been, and checking to make sure that was true.

Vincent

May 2, 1975

It's long past dark when Mr. Stewart's car pulls up at the curb. From the front porch, I can see Lydia in the passenger seat, the lights from the dashboard illuminating her features. I pull myself into a tighter ball, trying not to move. I don't want to talk to Mr. Stewart; I want to talk to Lydia.

When she reaches the porch, Mr. Stewart's car pulls away, the rumble of his engine fading. Lydia is digging in her purse for her keys when I emerge from where I've been hiding.

"Where have you been?" I hate how angry my voice sounds. How hurt. But I feel like I'm losing her. She's pulling away, and in my panic all I know how to do is hold on tighter.

Lydia jumps at the sound of my voice. "You scared me. How long have you been here?"

"Where have you been?" I ask again.

She looks over her shoulder, as if Mr. Stewart might still be there to tell her what to say. "Training," she says.

I gesture at her blue jeans and close fitting top. "Wearing that?"

"My gear is in my duffel bag. I must have left it in his car."

She's lying. I can see it in her expression. I step closer, fighting to keep my tone conversational. "I can go get it for you. It'll be no trouble for me to go home, walk next door, and ask him for it."

Lydia closes her eyes. "Vince," she says. "Can we just go inside? I'm exhausted and it's cold out here."

I step aside, allowing her to unlock the door. We enter the dark living room, with its faded brown couch and black-and-white television, magazines strewn over the coffee table, the scent of her mother's perfume still lingering in the air. In the corner is a dining room table positioned under a dusty chandelier, and Lydia flips the switch on, illuminating the surface with a couple empty wineglasses and some unopened mail. At the center is a note that Lydia reads, then hands to me. *Hope you had a good training session with Mr. Stewart. I left some tuna casserole on the counter for you. Don't wait up for me. Love, Mom*

"She also believed you were studying with Dawn when really you were with me in Ventura seeing Pink Floyd. Your mother isn't exactly a lie detector."

"And you are?" she asks.

"I know when something doesn't add up. I know you weren't at the track because I went there looking for you."

Lydia rolls her eyes. "We went to the city college so I could run on a real track, not that dusty circle we have at the high school."

I've seen Lydia after a hard workout, many times. She's always flushed, energized. Not weak and hollowed out, as if her stomach hurts. Tonight she looks pale. Sick. "What are you not telling me?" I finally ask. "Did Mr. Stewart do something to you?"

"God no!" she shouts. "He's the only adult who ever gave a shit about me. He's the only one around here who believes I can grow up to be something more than a whore like my mother."

"I believe in you," I say. Hurt that I have to say it out loud.

"You want me to stay here after high school. Marry you. Have kids." She chokes on the words, perhaps the idea too repulsive to consider. "I want to go places. Be someone. Mr. Stewart is helping me do that."

"I'll have to think of a way to thank Mr. Stewart," I say. Then I turn and walk through the still-open door, not bothering to close it behind me.

Down the steps in three strides, across the tiny patch of grass in four. I'm grateful for the dark so no one can see me swallowing back tears. See my clenched fists, my nails digging into the palms of my hands, tiny half-moons that will still be visible in the morning.

I cut across the yard at the corner, fighting the urge to look back, to see if she's following me. Or at the very least standing in the doorway, watching me go. I break into a slow jog, only wanting to be home until I remember who my new neighbor is.

I'm losing her to Mr. Stewart. Fucking hell.

At least it's not Danny.

Chapter 13

It's been nearly a week since I'd emailed Calder from my father's account, but now that I've entered into a dialogue with him, I'm unable to step away. How often do you have the chance to speak with someone you despise under the pretense of being someone else?

I'd woken the following morning to a response from him.

I can do for you what I did for Mac Murray.

However I was only interested in one thing—how Calder came to be pitching for a book no one was supposed to know about. How did you hear about the project? I asked.

The response came within two minutes. I have sources in high places. I'm perfectly positioned, not just to write the book, but to market it as well. Like you, my name is synonymous with blockbuster. We would be a formidable team.

I'd responded. Why are you pitching for a book that's already under contract?

I tried to imagine how he would respond. What he might say about me, about my ability as a ghostwriter. Perhaps slamming my reputation and legal troubles in the process.

But he hadn't responded, and I've spent the last several days reading and rereading the exchange, wondering exactly what I want from it. Questioning my own motives and wondering if this is a distraction I can afford.

Voices float through the open window as Alma and my father return from whatever appointment he's had. I head downstairs and into the house, where I find Alma in the kitchen, pulling food for dinner from the refrigerator.

"Is he upstairs?" I ask.

"Yes, but I wouldn't disturb him right now. These occupational therapy sessions tire him out."

"I just have a quick question."

I've spent all afternoon trying to make sense of a small scene in my father's handwritten manuscript about an argument Danny had had with Poppy, who'd been spying on him. Following him around, filming. All of our conversations over the past few days have been about Danny and his conflicts with my father. But this is the first mention of an argument between Danny and Poppy.

Alma takes a step toward me and says, "I have to ask that you save it until tomorrow morning."

The idea of sitting around the guesthouse waiting until the morning is crazy. I ignore her and jog up the stairs.

I find him in his office, staring out the window. He turns when I enter, his expression startled. "When did you arrive?" he asks.

I falter. "A couple weeks ago," I say. "Remember?"

"Why? You said you'd never come back here."

"You hired me to write your memoir," I remind him.

He shakes his head. "You can't write a book, Lydia. You need to leave," he hisses. "You can't be here." He turns toward the doorway. "Alma!" he yells, panic threading through is voice.

Alma arrives, wiping her hands on a dish towel.

"He thinks I'm my mother again," I tell her.

"Go downstairs. I'll handle it."

As I exit, I hear him say, "Did you know she was coming? She knows about the book. Did you tell her?"

Alma says, "Shh, Vincent. That's Olivia, your daughter. She's the one helping you with the book, not Lydia. Lydia lives in Bakersfield, remember?"

Alma finds me ten minutes later.

"You can't ambush him like that. He's easily confused in the afternoons. Sometimes paranoid. He forgets things, and that scares him and he covers it up with anger."

"I'm familiar with that, at least," I say, remembering the times when I would hear my father railing at someone on the phone—his agent, his publicist, a reporter.

Alma shakes her head. "This is different."

"The manuscript," I explain. "It's not exactly cohesive, and when I have questions, I don't have time to wait for an appointment to get answers."

Alma's expression is steely. "I think I'm going to have to set some boundaries," she says.

"I have a job to do—" I start, but she interrupts me.

"So do I," she says, her voice rising. "You need to understand what is happening to him. Lewy bodies are growing on his brain, which is manifesting in a number of ways. Right now, he mostly understands that his hallucinations aren't real. We've been controlling them with meds, but as you can see, that's not going to work indefinitely." She looks toward the stairs and I imagine my father up there, waiting out the confusion. Waiting for his brain to start working properly again. Alma continues. "If you push him too hard, if you press him about things that he can't remember, he could grow violent and hurt himself. Or you. And if that happens, there won't be a book at all."

"Are you afraid of him?" I ask.

She brushes off my words. "Not like that. But I need you to listen to me. When I say *no*, that needs to be respected, for your own safety as well as his."

She holds my gaze, challenging me to argue. But I don't. Because even though my father thinks he's the one in control, he isn't. Alma runs this show.

*   *   *

Dismissed, I return to the guesthouse, at loose ends until tomorrow. If I'm not writing, I need to be moving. I look toward the door when it occurs to me—the boxes my father wants me to sort through and the possibility there might be something useful in one of them.

I flip the lid of the one closest to me, peering in to find it jumbled with old take-out menus and several packages of plastic straws. I set it aside as trash and keep looking.

I plow through ten boxes, each one filled by a man with hoarding tendencies, before finding something different in a box near the bottom of a stack next to the bathroom. Old Pee-chee folders from the '70s. An old ERA button, the back side pocked with rust. I open one of the folders and find a typewritten report on Shirley Chisholm, Poppy's name in the top right corner, dated 1974. It's riddled with typos, and as I skim it, it becomes clear Poppy was never going to be a secretary. I tuck the report back into the folder and hold it, wondering about the girl who'd written it. Who'd likely gone to the library to research it, reading newspaper articles about the first Black woman to run for president in 1972. I feel a smile creeping across my face, admiring my aunt's passion. Wondering what her teacher thought about her choice of subject.

I look at the exterior of the box, searching for a label, but it's blank. Whoever packed it hadn't given much thought to making sure it could be found again. As I lift it, something slides along the bottom and I remove the rest of the Pee-chee folders to find a round film canister. The metal is rusty around the seams and a pulse of adrenaline flashes through me as I imagine my aunt and uncle appearing on screen. Hearing their voices for the first time.

I try to pry it open with my nails, but it's rusted closed so I grab an old butter knife from the kitchenette and set to work, chipping the rust away and wiggling the rim until it loosens and finally scrapes off.

But inside isn't a reel of film. It's a diary. The old kind with a tiny lock, the key likely long gone. I trace the edges of the cover with my finger, a mottled pink with red hearts running around the border. My pulse accelerates as I realize what I'm holding. This is exactly what I need—Poppy's own words. Poppy's secrets. I use a paper clip to pry it open.

The first page has been cut out, the rough edges poking out of the spine. After that is a blank page, but when I turn to the next one, my throat clenches.

May 6, 1975

I heard a rumor today. That Lydia was pregnant and now . . . she's not.

Poppy

May 6, 1975

I dig through my closet, tossing out shoes and dirty laundry, looking for that diary my mother bought me a couple years ago for my birthday. The one she thought I'd record all my secrets in, so that while I was at school, she could read them. As if I'd ever be that stupid.

Instead, I'd written a fake entry. *Today, Margot and I bought some pot from Tommy Snyder and went into the oak grove to get high. It's really growing on me, how happy and silly I feel. It makes it much easier to eat my mom's terrible cooking.*

Two days later, my mother had confronted me, her face blotchy from crying. "Are you getting *high*?"

"Where'd you get an idea like that?" I'd asked. "From my diary? The one that's supposed to be private?" I'd waited for understanding to dawn on her. To realize her mistake, that I'd tricked her into admitting that she snooped through my things. Then I said, "Stop trying to pry into my life, Mom." And I'd walked away.

I figure now that a couple years have passed, my mother has forgotten about that diary.

I finally find it—wedged next to an old Malibu Barbie my mother bought me for Christmas several years ago—and open to that first entry. Taking my scissors, I roughly cut out that page. Then I write a new entry, thinking back on the conversation Margot and I just had.

* * *

"I heard Lydia had an abortion."

Margot had whispered the word and I hopped off my bed, peeking out to make sure my mother hadn't heard it. She blew her top whenever someone mentioned the word *abortion*, swearing up and down she would disown any child of hers who got one. Which meant me.

I closed the door and hurried back to the bed. "What?" I asked. "Where did you hear that?"

"A couple of girls were talking about it in the bathroom at school. They didn't know I was in there."

"That's impossible," I said, though the truth was, I wasn't exactly sure how it all worked. My mother had dropped a box of sanitary napkins onto my bed when I got my period and said, *Don't get pregnant. It'll ruin your life.* Which wasn't exactly informative.

"My mother says it only takes one time," Margot said, shooting me a warning look, as if I ought to take heed of her mother's wisdom. As if I were the one who needed to be careful. "What do we really know about Lydia?" she continued, picking at a chipped piece of pink nail polish. She peeled the rest of it off and dropped it in the tiny white trash can next to my desk, the appliqué daisies on the outside bright and childish compared to what we were discussing.

"I know she dated Dave Gunderson for like a second last fall. And then Pete Mayhew around the holidays. And then Vince,"

I said. It seemed like a lot of guys to me, but I had only turned fourteen in March. What did I know about boyfriends?

"I meant her family," Margot said, giving me a meaningful look. "Her mother isn't exactly normal."

My gaze bounced around my room, clothes hastily shoved into my closet, the sheer curtains covering my windows filtering the light, softening the pink walls I'd hoped to paint a more grown-up color this summer. I tried not to think about my own mother, how *not* normal she was when no one else was around. How she drank too much, then cried in her room. Some days she wouldn't even get out of bed. But she always put on some lipstick and a bright smile whenever we had people over, as if she could paper over the cracks that everyone could see.

"I like Lydia's mom," I said. But the truth was, I'd only ever spoken to her once, when she came by to pick Lydia up. She'd given me her pretty smile and said, *What a cute little thing you are!* Which normally would have annoyed me, but coming from her, felt like a present bought just for me.

"My mom says she sleeps around," Margot said, shaking her head in the same disapproving way her own mother did. "She called her a 'man eater.'"

We both giggled at the phrase. "Maybe it's not true," I said, meaning that someone like Lydia probably knew how to not get pregnant. And yet.

Margot hesitated, as if she didn't want to tell me the next part. "They also said it wasn't Vince's."

I felt my body grow cold and I fought to keep my voice steady. To not show Margot how much that part worried me. "Did they say whose it was?" I asked, not wanting to know. But needing to understand.

"No."

"If you had to guess," I pressed. I glanced at the closed door, listening for sounds of my mother. Pretending to dust so she could eavesdrop, hoping to hear about my secret crushes or problems with friends.

"Maybe she got back together with Pete or Dave," Margot suggested.

I shook my head. "Pete is dating Ginnie from the pep squad now and everyone knows she's got him on a short leash. She even waits outside the boy's bathroom for him to pee." Margot snort laughed and I continued. "Lydia doesn't do anything except hang out here, run track, and go to school." I looked up at her and said, "Wait. Who's her lab partner in biology?"

Margot wrinkled her nose in disgust. "Charlie Carson and he's a nose picker. No way."

We fell into silence, each of us running through possibilities but coming up blank.

"Do you think Vince knows?" Margot asked.

I shook my head. Things were bad now, but they'd get a lot worse if he found out. "They fight about stuff, but I think I'd know if it was about a baby and an abortion."

*   *   *

I sit in my room now, listening to the sounds of my family—my mother in the kitchen, making dinner; the thump of bass from Danny's music—and reread the single sentence I'd written—*I heard a rumor today. That Lydia was pregnant and now . . . she's not*—trying to imagine how this will play out. What this information will do to Vince, who already seems on edge.

Chapter 14

I sit on the floor next to the empty box, my mind racing. I count back from the date of the entry—May 6—and do some math. I suppose it's possible my mother had gotten pregnant before she'd started dating my father in February of that year, but it would have been tight. It would have required her to wait a dangerously long time to get the abortion if so, and I know that wasn't likely.

There's so much about my parents I don't understand. So much about them I don't know if I'll ever be able to unravel. What my mother saw in my father. Why she stayed with him when everyone else was certain he'd killed Danny and Poppy. I flip to the next entry, dated May 8.

Something's on that film that Vince doesn't want me to see. March #1, Clip #3

I turn the page, hoping for a longer entry, but Poppy seems to have decided the diary might not be a safe place to write anything down. I make my way through the rest of her entries quickly.

May 10: I don't even know who Vince is anymore. May #1, Clip #7.

One entry is just dialogue.

> May 14:
> It's like you're not even into me anymore.
> If I wasn't into you, I wouldn't be here. Why are you so angry at me all the time?
> All of a sudden it feels like you're pulling back from me.
> I'm at your house every day after school! How is that pulling back?
> Poppy tells me that every time you come over and I'm not here, you ask if Danny is home.

Next to that last part, Poppy had written in giant block letters *NOT TRUE*.

I flip the page.

> May 20: I think Margot and I are right about the father of L's baby.
> May 30: Vince/Danny fight. Did he learn the truth about Lydia??? Everything feels different now. May #4, Clip #9

I'm turning the pages faster now, but there are only three more entries.

> June 4: One of them is going to kill the other one.
> June 7: Amazing day fighting for Equal Rights. Can't wait to send the film in. Can't wait to leave here forever.

And the last one, which chills me. Written just three days before she died.

June 10: Oh my god oh my god oh my god. I feel sick. No one will believe me and now I've lost the proof. I need to tell someone, but Danny will kill me if I tell.

I reread that last sentence again. *Danny will kill me if I tell.*

Could the stories my father has been telling me about Danny be true? I flip back to the beginning and read it all again, noting references to the movies she filmed. Clips she cited. Links to these entries that would show me what she wanted me to see. I push myself to standing and start digging through the rest of the boxes. I need to find those film reels.

* * *

Two hours later, I've emptied every box, touched every single item—old bills mixed in with letters from famous authors mixed in with galleys and old manuscript drafts. But there are no reels of film. Tom had called during my search and I'd let it go to voicemail, feeling as if I'm on the edge of figuring something out, and I don't want my mind pulled away until I can grab it.

I head back downstairs and into the house where I find my father watching television. "Hey, Dad," I say, hoping he's more lucid, though I wonder what he might reveal if he thinks I'm my mother. What questions I might ask that would lead him to tell me more.

I settle on the couch next to him and we stare at a show about penguins in Antarctica. "Since when have you started watching nature documentaries?" I ask. "What happened to *Law & Order*? *48 Hours* mysteries?"

"Alma says I can't watch regular television anymore. It confuses me and I have bad dreams."

I look around for her, but she must be upstairs. "What ever happened to Poppy's home movies?"

"No clue," he says. "She'd get them processed, but I never saw any of them."

"Did the police take them?" I ask.

"I know they were interested in finding them, but I don't think they ever did."

"Maybe she gave them to Margot?" A spark of hope blooms inside of me, an excuse to reach out to Poppy's best friend.

"Margot said no," my father says. "The police looked for them for a little while, but I got the sense they didn't try very hard."

"Well, they can't have just vanished. They have to be somewhere."

My father looks at me and says, "I think she tossed them all."

"Why?"

"She and Danny had a huge fight, a few days before they died. I think she filmed something she wasn't supposed to see and she got rid of them."

Danny will kill me if I tell.

"What was their fight about?"

"I don't know," he says. "She wouldn't tell me."

"So she just threw all her movies away," I say. "Three months worth of them."

"That's my theory."

I think again of his night terror, of the hiding place he was searching for. His fear that the knife he'd hidden had somehow gone missing.

"Did anyone check the hiding place inside her window?"

134

He looks shocked. "How do you know about that?"

"You told me."

He shakes his head as if to clear away shadows. "That was a pretty small space. Reels of film wouldn't fit in there."

We return our attention to the documentary. Father penguins caring for their babies while the mothers went off to find food. What an upside-down world we humans live in. I sit with the idea of Poppy throwing all her movies away, but it doesn't fit. She was so meticulous about recording in her diary which film clips were important. She was clearly trying to tell a story.

So many threads are tangled in my mind—my mother's abortion. Danny's temper. Poppy's last diary entry, her fear palpable on the page. I can't figure out how it all fits together. And yet . . . if Poppy was protecting a secret, perhaps she did get rid of her reels? I imagine them decomposing in a garbage dump somewhere. Buried and useless after fifty years of being exposed to the elements.

Just then Alma comes down the stairs, wearing a sweater and rummaging around in her purse. "Oh good, Olivia," she says, standing between us and the television. "My sister just called and needs me to take her and my nephew to the emergency room."

"Is everything okay?" I ask.

"He fell and broke his arm," she says. "I'll need you to feed your father and make sure he has his meds."

She gestures for me to follow and together we make our way into the kitchen, leaving my father alone on the couch with the penguins.

She's got everything lined up on the counter—a plate of lasagna covered in plastic wrap, an empty glass, his bottled protein drink next to it, and a multicompartmented pill dispenser with times and days of the week on the various lids. "Put the lasagna into the microwave for two minutes, covered," she tells me. "He likes his protein drink in a glass, no straw. He needs to take these three pills *before* he eats, and these other two *after* his meal, but make sure he finishes his protein drink first. I shouldn't be more than an hour. My brother-in-law can pick them up if it's going to be longer."

Together we walk back into the living room. "Vincent, Olivia is going to get your dinner ready and give you your evening meds. I'll be back long before it's time to go upstairs for bed. Make sure you eat your food or your stomach will get upset."

My father stares at her as if he can't believe his life has come to this. "If I finish my vegetables and promise to do my home-work later, can Olivia and I do a craft after dinner?"

I stifle a laugh but Alma ignores him. "I'll be back soon," she says.

I heat his dinner according to Alma's strict instructions, give my father the first three pills, and sit across from him, watching him eat, the slow motion of his fork as it travels from plate to mouth to plate again. The regular sips of his protein drink. I've got the last two pills ready to go as soon as he's done.

He sets his fork down on his plate and wipes his mouth with his napkin. "Do you remember the treasure hunt I did for you with the book?"

There had been a lot of hunts over the years, but unlike with the poor hamster, most of the time I'd find something fun on the other end. The jean jacket I'd been begging for. Once I found a new bike leaning against the fig tree in the back corner of the property. Other times they were smaller things—barrettes. Music boxes. A glitter wand.

I shake my head and point to his plate. "Alma will kill me if you don't finish that. And I don't know what you're talking about."

"That book you were obsessed with. I think you read it at least ten times." He searches his memory for a title, but grows frustrated. "The one with the kids and the game. I left you clues in it."

A memory clicks into place. Of me, in the fifth grade, sitting alone on a bench, my book resting open on my knees, and looking across the yard to the field where Jack played soccer with some of the other boys in our class. Two girls passing by me, arms linked, neither of them giving me a glance as they headed toward the bathroom where a group of them liked to congregate to try on lip gloss and gossip about clothes—Benetton sweaters. LA Gear sneakers. Guess jeans. Adjusting scrunchies in their hair or piling them on their wrists. Another reason I usually asked permission to go during class.

Sometimes my teacher would let me read in the classroom during lunch recess, but that day she'd had a meeting so I was stuck on the bench in the shade, my otherness poking at me. I opened my book—*The Egypt Game*—and started to read.

I was just sinking back into the story, the playground around me fading away when I turned the page and noticed a note penciled into the margin right next to the page number, in my father's handwriting. *The date of your birthday holds the first clue.* I stared at the words, my mind turning over the idea of another treasure hunt. It had been a while since the last one; he'd been so busy with his new book and with the move from our apartment and into the giant house on the east side of town, a Spanish compound with a wall surrounding it, cutting us off from the world.

I flipped back toward the beginning of the book and found page 8, where the word *meet* was circled, and another clue written in the margin. *The last two digits of our phone number.*

I found page 29, the word *in* circled. In the margin: *my birthday.*

The yard became a background noise to my hunt, deciphering his message, paging forward and backward in the book until I had the whole message memorized.

Meet in front of school at three.

"It was *The Egypt Game,*" I tell him now. "I was eleven."

He nods, growing animated, and picks his fork up again. "I'd just gotten back from a trip and I wanted to do something special for you. I remember coming up with the idea on the plane ride back. You always got so mopey when I'd travel and I wanted to get you excited about something." He chews, looking at me, waiting for me to pick up the thread. To agree with him about how much fun that treasure hunt had been.

I stare at him, wondering how he could possibly think that was a happy memory for me. I remember how I'd held that clue close to me all afternoon. How I'd hoped my father had sensed my loneliness and planned one of his grand adventures for the two of us.

But with my father, it was always good to keep my expectations low. His success had changed him, his new money not only buying us a new house, but a flashy new Mercedes for himself. Hiring Melinda, who sat in a small office under the stairs managing my father's calendar and telling me he was too busy to eat dinner with me. Dropping a McDonald's hamburger on the table, still in the bag, and letting me eat it on the couch while I watched *90210*, not even noticing when I switched over to *Twin Peaks.*

"'Meet in front of the school at three,'" I say now, my voice low and robotic.

But my father doesn't notice. "Yes! That was the clue." He finishes his food and pushes his plate aside, pleased that he's remembered something.

But it's like he's remembering something from a story he's told himself so many times, it's crystalized into something that never happened. Eliminating all that came before and after.

"I remember waiting impatiently for school to let out," I tell him. "I spent the afternoon imaging how you must have snuck into my room after I'd gone to sleep to pencil those clues into the margins, knowing I'd find them the following day. Planning a fun afternoon just the two of us." I wait, wondering if he'll remember, or if I'll have to tell him the story again. Remind him of the many ways his memory is failing him, forcing me to relive another one of his disappointments. "Finish your protein drink, take your pills, and let's finish your documentary," I say.

He stares at me and I can tell that he really doesn't remember. Finally he says, "Tell me the rest of it."

I shake my head and gather his plate and fork, crumpling his napkin on top of it. "It doesn't matter, Dad. It was a long time ago."

"Tell me, Olivia." His voice is commanding and I freeze—old habits dying hard—sinking back down into my chair again.

"When the bell rang, I lost my nerve," I tell him. "All afternoon I'd been imagining what we'd do. Where we'd go. Ice cream and a drive-in movie. Or a trip to Santa Barbara for dinner at a fancy restaurant. But as all the kids rushed out around me, I couldn't picture you out there with the rest of the parents, milling around waiting."

"I showed up," he says, his tone slightly unsure. As if even he couldn't count on his former self to do the right thing.

"I saw your car parked down the street, that silver Mercedes you bought, remember?" He nods, and I continue. "I remember feeling excited. Hopeful. Thrilled that you'd come for me. Imagining your laughing face, happy that I'd cracked the code, assembled the clues you left for me in the margins of my book." I stop talking, remembering that moment, how a bright, white joy seemed to carry me down the sidewalk, the sun glinting off the windshield of my father's new car. "It was a fun afternoon," I finish, standing again. Carrying his dishes into the kitchen and setting them in the sink. Filling a glass with water and bringing it back to him where he's still seated, staring at me.

I gesture toward his pills and slide the water toward him, but he ignores them. "You're lying," he says.

"I'm not," I insist, looking past him and into the living room where the penguin documentary is paused on the screen.

"Why won't you just tell me?" he asks.

"Because it doesn't matter," I say back, my voice rising. "It's just one example of many where you let me down."

"But I showed up," he insists. "I was there, you just said so."

I shake my head, incredulous that he can latch on to such a small detail—the fact that I was picked up that day—and spin it into a narrative where he comes out looking like a loving father. "No, Dad. You didn't. When I opened the car door, it wasn't you behind the wheel. It was Melinda. You'd sent her to take me on a shopping spree."

I can see the moment he remembers, and I wonder what's playing through his mind. Perhaps a last-minute conference call with his editor that he felt was more important that I was. Or his first drink of the afternoon stretching into two or three, taking school pickup off the table. "Is that such a bad thing?" he asks. "Surely Melinda was a better person to take you shopping for clothes than I was."

Even now he can't own it. He can't see how heartbreaking it was for me to open that car door and see the person he'd essentially hired to parent me so that he didn't have to. "Sure, Dad. You're probably right," I tell him. Knowing there's no use trying to explain it to him. Knowing he'll never fully understand what I needed from him.

Just then, Alma returns, dropping her purse on the floor. "A fractured wrist and a red cast," she announces. My father and I turn to face her, torn from our conversation and forced back into the present. "Did he eat everything?"

"Plate's in the sink," I tell her. "Protein shake consumed, meds done." I grab my phone from the table where I'd left it and head toward the back door. As I'm closing it behind me, my father says, "I'm glad you remember."

Poppy

May 8, 1975

Every year on my birthday, my father gives a toast. "When Poppy was born, she was beauty and grace and light. And she continues to be that, all her beautiful days."

But my father doesn't see me for who I am. In his mind, I'm his baby, his little girl. Smiles and laughter and *light*. But light casts shadows. And it's always been the shadows that interest me the most. The idea that certain things thrive there, that the dark is where secrets live, and I want to understand them. To seek them out. To peer into people's darkest places and bring the truth out into the open.

For my fourteenth birthday, I asked for a Super 8 camera. I told my parents it was so we could record family memories—birthdays, holidays, special events. My mother was skeptical. My father was amused.

But film won't lie the way memories do. I want a record of things that happen so people can't brush off my feelings and tell me I'm overreacting, or I don't understand.

I want to document my brothers fighting. *All boys love to rough and tumble.*

My mother's drinking. *Everyone has wine at the end of the day.*

But I know better. I know it's not normal. If I can film it, people will see what I see and they will believe me.

I sit now with my father's old projector and a bedsheet covering a wall of boxes in the garage—one of the only dark spaces in the house. I've loaded my first reel and turned the lights off. The sheet isn't smooth, warping the images as they flicker in front of me. My birthday party in early March, just a couple minutes of me spinning in a circle, catching my parents at the picnic table outside, Vince on the back steps and Danny by the fire.

I hate that there isn't any sound, but I couldn't afford it.

Ned, the owner of the camera shop, had seen how disappointed I was and tried to cheer me up. "Don't worry," he'd said. "You can get more for your money if you go without sound." He winked. "Besides, when you can't hear the words people use to distract you, you focus on what they're doing instead. The truth lives in people's actions, their unguarded moments, not in the lies they tell."

Turns out, Ned was right.

It's easy to see the way my mother wobbles when she stands to dance with my father, her wineglass nearly empty. The wistful way Vince looks when he thinks no one is watching him. An unguarded laugh from Danny makes me realize how long it's been since I've seen him so relaxed. So happy.

The party cuts away and I'm wandering through the house. Vincent and Lydia on the couch. I lean closer to the screen so I can study the way his hand strokes her arm. How she leans in to him, soaking up his attention.

Behind me, I hear someone enter the garage. I glance over my shoulder to see Vince, drinking a soda. "My first reel," I tell him.

He comes closer. "Cool."

Together we watch as the scene shifts again. The bonfire party at Mr. Stewart's old house. The tall flames spiraling high into the night, sparks caught on film, bright dots of light melting into the dark. The camera zooms out to show groups of kids dancing, sitting on lawn chairs and in the dirt, the shadows of trees behind them. I can still hear the music—Grateful Dead. Eric Clapton. The Who. A kid I don't know grabs a laughing girl around the waist and pulls her toward him.

Behind me, Vince steps closer. "Turn it off," he says, his voice a low warning. He moves closer to the sheet, staring at it.

"What?" I ask. "Why?"

He turns to me, his cheeks growing flushed. "I said, TURN IT OFF." He grabs the bedsheet and yanks it down, the images vanishing against the brown boxes behind them.

I cut the projector. "It was just a party, Vince. There will be others."

Vince drops the bedsheet on the floor, and I move to pick it up before it can get dirty. But he stops me. Shoves me toward the wall, then tries to pull the reel off the projector.

"What are you doing?" I shout, grabbing the projector before it can topple over. I get a sharp elbow into my chest as he tries to push me away. "Vince, what's your problem?" But my gaze cuts toward the film, wondering what he'd seen that had set him off.

Our mother opens the door to the garage and says, "What's going on in here?"

We leap apart, but I keep my hands on the projector, protecting it.

Vince pushes past me, past our mother still standing in the doorway, and disappears.

My mother stares at me a beat and then points at the sheet, still on the floor. "That better not have a speck of dirt on it." Then she, too, disappears.

I slowly unroll the film from the projector and place it back in the canister I'd carefully labeled March #1, my hands shaking, my chest aching where Vince had elbowed me, and a thump of worry passes through me, knowing he would have destroyed this reel if my mother hadn't interrupted. I think of the arguments he and Lydia have been having. The whispered ones they think no one can hear, and the louder ones they have when they think no one else is around. What I know about Lydia that Vince doesn't. I think again of the images of my family, their unguarded moments caught on film to be studied later. And I wonder what else I might be able to see when I go back and really look.

Chapter 15

The following morning, I find my father drinking coffee in the courtyard, his face tilted toward the sun. "Good morning," he says. "Did you sleep well?"

"Well enough," I say. "You?"

He shrugs and looks at me. "Every night is an adventure these days."

I swipe the hair off my forehead.. "I was planning on going to the library this morning to look up the news coverage of the murders. If you won't let me talk to anyone, maybe I can make sense of things using those as a framework."

A hummingbird hovers next to the lemon tree, and we both watch it dart in and out of the branches before lifting into the air and vanishing over the garden wall. "I might have something that will help," he says.

He enters the house, says something to Alma, and the two of them disappear up the stairs. The courtyard is quiet, not even the sound of traffic passing by, and I'm reminded of my own house in Topanga, the way the chaos of the world seems removed. I feel a homesickness rise up inside of me—for Tom, for my space, my life in Los Angeles that I'm on the verge of losing. To a time before I owed John Calder close to $500,000 and my attorney another $200,000. Before my father decided he needed to share his secrets, yanking my childhood questions out of the past and into the present.

He returns carrying a folder and Alma resumes her cooking. "I'm not sure what's in there," he says, passing it over. "It's been a long time since I've looked." He glances toward the house. "Alma will have breakfast in about a half hour if you're interested."

"That's okay. I have some groceries upstairs. I think I'll just fix a small snack and dive into these. Okay if we skip our session this morning?" I hold up the folder. "This will help me with background."

He studies me and I wait to see if he'll challenge me. But he just nods and turns away, sliding the glass door closed behind him.

*   *   *

Upstairs I'm about to settle in to read when I see a notification of a new email from John Calder on my father's account, finally picking up our exchange.

I slide the file folder to the side and read his response. Some on the team aren't happy with Olivia Dumont. To be honest, I was surprised to hear you chose her without opening it up to others to pitch. I'm not sure she can do what you need to be done.

My mind flies back to that first Zoom with Monarch. *We should have gone with Calder.* Heat fills my chest, to see my name spoken so easily by a man who has trashed my reputation and my life so effortlessly. I'm tempted to email Nicole, to tell her there's a leak somewhere and Calder is trying to take this job from me, when I realize I'd have to explain how I know and reveal what I've done.

What exactly do you think I need done? I type. I should end the email there, but I can't help but add one more sentence. Why do you think Ms. Dumont can't do this job?

I wait for his reply, and when it doesn't come after five minutes, I close my laptop, my mind running a loop. If I allow myself to be sidetracked by this, I'm certain I won't be able to focus the way I need to, and then Calder will be right.

I push away from the desk and head downstairs, through the courtyard and into the orchard. The air is crisp, my feet silent on the soft earth, and I make my way through the trees at a brisk pace, trying to clear my mind. Calder doesn't matter. He can't take this job from me unless I let him.

* * *

An hour later, I'm back at my desk, but I leave my laptop closed and flip open the file folder my father gave me. There are several newspaper clippings, faded with age. The first one is dated June 14, 1975, and the headline reads: *Tragedy During Ojai Summer Carnival*. It's relatively short, but has a photograph of the house, police tape wrapped around the perimeter of the property.

> Mr. and Mrs. Edmund Taylor returned home Friday evening to a heartbreaking tragedy in their home—the bodies of two of their three children brutally slain by an unknown assailant. Both children were declared dead at the scene by authorities who responded to the call placed at 9:17 p.m. According to officers, one child, age 17, was found deceased in the hallway. The other, age 14, was found deceased in a bedroom. Due to their ages, names have not been released to the public. Police will not comment on whether there were any signs of struggle inside the home, citing an ongoing investigation. A third Taylor sibling, age 16 was not home at the time of the slayings and is now the Taylors' sole surviving child.

I imagine my grandparents waking up to this article in the local paper. Someone—perhaps my grandmother—had taken the time to clip it out and save it, tucking it away somewhere out of sight.

The second article is from the funeral. *Taylor Family Lays Children to Rest as Entire Community Turns Out.* There isn't much to the article other than quotes from Danny and Poppy's friends, teachers, neighbors. No comment from the family. But there's a photograph of them exiting the church. My grandparents, clinging to each other as they make their way down the steps, my father thin and pale in a black suit behind them, my mother just a shadow next to him. I stare at them, how young they were, my mother's dress seeming to envelop her whole.

The next article features school photographs of Danny and Poppy dated July 14, 1975. *More Questions than Answers in Ojai Summer Carnival Slayings.* This one is longer, containing the coroner's time of death—7:00 p.m. for Poppy, 7:20 for Danny. Witness statements had him leaving the carnival an hour earlier, but it was unclear whether he'd walked in on an attack already in progress, or shortly after.

> Police are focusing on looking for anyone who saw Poppy exit an unknown car the weekend prior, reporting that she'd hitchhiked into Ventura and back again. "We ask anyone with information about the make and model of that car to please come forward." The lead investigator says the person who gave Poppy a ride isn't a suspect. "We just want to speak with them, to eliminate them so we can focus our energy elsewhere."

But friends close to the deceased children tell a different story. That Vincent Taylor, 16 and the sole surviving child of the Taylor family, knows more than he's saying. They speculate that Danny had been the intended victim as opposed to Poppy, citing ongoing conflict between the two brothers. Police will not comment other than to say that all members of the Taylor family have been questioned and all have verified alibis during the time of the murders.

The last article, from September of that year, is just a few paragraphs, the news cycle relegating the killings to a back page. The headline reads: *First Day of School Vigil to Remember Danny and Poppy Taylor.* The article basically rehashes what's already been reported. No leads. No suspects. Devastated family and friends seeking answers. With one notable observation: *Vincent Taylor, now a junior, was not in attendance at the vigil, though many claimed he was present at school that day.*

I wonder where the other articles are. The one that I remember being passed around the playground when I was ten. I grab my keys and my purse, sidestepping the house where I can see my father seated at the table alone. If he hears me, he doesn't look up.

* * *

I ask the librarian to pull issues of the Ojai paper from June 1985 and June 1995, and I start in the obvious place, June 13, 1985. I flip through each page, scanning for something related to the anniversary, but it's a pretty bare edition. I pull out the film and plug in June 12, and that's when I see it, on the front page below the fold: *Ten Years Later and Still No Answers.*

This one is less about the murders and more about Danny and Poppy. Speculation that my father had something to do with the murders is more obvious, with Poppy's best friend, Margot, leading the charge.

Twenty-five, and recently returned to Ojai after attending UCLA, Ms. Gibson is still emotional when recounting the events of that day. When asked if she thought Vincent would harm his brother, Ms. Gibson says, "I have no doubt."

Vincent Taylor, now twenty-six, is married to his girlfriend from that time, Lydia Greene. The two have a daughter, age five. Mr. Taylor attended city college in Ventura, then returned to Ojai and is working at a local grocery store stocking shelves while he pursues a writing career. He declined to comment for this piece, but we were able to speak briefly to his wife, Lydia, who said, "We were in the oak grove with our teacher, Mr. Stewart. The police eliminated Vince as a suspect in 1975."

Memories of reading this article with Jack come back to me. I'd forgotten most of it, but one line from my mother stood out then, and I read it again now. "*I would never allow my daughter to live in a house with someone who'd done something so horrific. That should tell you everything you need to know.*"

I pause, trying—and failing—to picture my mother saying these words. But I can't even conjure her face, let alone remember her saying anything like this about me.

There are still more questions than answers in this decade-old tragedy, but what people find most surprising is Mr. Taylor's lack of interest in pursuing the case. Police say the investigation is still active. However, after the death of his parents several years ago, Mr. Taylor has done nothing to keep the case in the public eye, and in fact goes out of his way to avoid speaking about it.

He may have an alibi, but he still has a lot of questions to answer.

I'd been living abroad when the 1995 retrospective was published, but it's essentially the same as the others—a rehashing of my father's misdeeds, his refusal to speak to reporters, but in this one, Margot and Mark reveal that they'd both been called in to a grand jury for questioning in 1993 and that my father seemed to be the target of their inquiry. The reason, according to the article, has something to do with malpractice on the part of the coroner who worked Poppy and Danny's case.

Dr. Nelson, who had been the county coroner for ten years at the time of the Taylor siblings' death, was removed from his post in 1990 after a whistleblower revealed that he often performed autopsies while under the influence. As a result, several convictions tied to his tenure have been overturned. This calls into question the time of death he gave for Danny and Poppy and ultimately could negate the alibi Vincent Taylor has been leaning on for so long.

I stare at the screen, thinking again of the story my father is telling me, spinning Danny as dangerous. Of Poppy's diary hidden deep inside my duffel bag with references to films long gone. Wondering if somehow the information my father claims he never told police has something to do with the alibi.

I press the button to print the article and collect my things to go home.

* * *

"When is it okay to break an agreement you've made?" I'd called Tom as soon as I got in my car.

"Never," he says.

His answer doesn't surprise me, but I need him to give me a different one. "But what if you're stuck?" I ask. "Like, you can't honor one agreement without breaking another."

"You figure out how to honor both, to the best of your ability." He doesn't even hesitate. There is no gray area for Tom. Only honor and truth and openness. "It may not be perfect, but that's sometimes the best you can do."

I wish I lived in a world like Tom's. Where there are no secrets. No fictional backstories. No complicated traumas that make people behave in unexpected ways.

When I get back to my father's house, I find Alma gathering their things, preparing to leave for his physical therapy appointment. My father sits on the couch, waiting, his hands clasped like an obedient child.

"Did you know there was a grand jury in 1993? That the coroner who did Poppy and Danny's autopsy was using drugs?" I ask.

He looks up at me and I'm relieved to see his gaze clear. "My attorney had heard rumblings, but they quickly determined they didn't have enough evidence to move forward."

I wait for him to continue, but of course, he doesn't. Apparently that's all he's got to say on the subject of his near-indictment.

153

"Why didn't you push for the investigation to continue after your parents died?"

He lifts one shoulder, a half shrug, and says, "All I wanted to do was forget. Your mother and I . . . we were traumatized. I'm certain it was at the root of all her problems later. Mine as well. We probably never should have gotten married. I think there's a term for it now—trauma bonding." He sighs. "My thinking at the time was that nothing would bring them back. My parents believed it was the man who'd given Poppy that ride home the weekend before. Who'd come back for the carnival, followed her to the house, and Danny got in the way. And that person was long gone."

I cut my gaze toward Alma and lower my voice. "Here's what I'm wondering." I pause, trying to find a way to word my question so that he doesn't feel attacked. "In all the articles I read, no one—and I mean no one—ever mentioned Danny as unstable or volatile. The only place I've ever heard that is from you."

"Because no one outside of the family ever saw it," he says. "And you're the first person I've ever told."

I think about how convenient it is that there isn't anyone left of his family to corroborate this for him. It's time for me to finally ask him about what he thinks Danny did to their sister. But what he says next sucks all the air from my lungs and renders my question obsolete. "Danny was a lot of things to me— hero and abuser—but I could never figure out how to suggest he could have been a killer."

Chapter 16

I've read and re-read Poppy's last entry.

> June 10: Oh my god oh my god oh my god. I feel sick. No one will believe me and now I've lost the proof. I need to tell someone, but Danny will kill me if I tell.

This, plus the stories my father has told me over the last two weeks paint an ominous portrait of Danny, and yet, Danny as the killer doesn't make sense. If Danny killed Poppy, then who killed Danny? My father? It's possible he's building up to confessing just that; however the idea feels too simple to me. And while I'm not comfortable presenting his stories as fact, the only thing I can do right now is write them down and try to see through them to whatever might be lurking below.

I spend several afternoons at the Ojai library, immersing myself in that era. I read through old issues of the *Ojai Valley News*. But I'm not only interested in articles about the murders. I read about city council meetings. About the sports teams at Nordhoff High. Ojai Valley School and Thacher, the local boarding schools. I read about new businesses. Local gossip. The weather. Politics at the time.

And I write. AirPods shoved into my ears, I listen to the hits of 1975. Aerosmith. Queen. The Eagles. Laptop open, trying to time travel back to Ojai, the summer of 1975. I lose myself, my own problems falling away. It's a relief to shed my life and dip into another era.

I also spend hours in the grove behind my father's old house, now the Ojai Meadows Preserve. When my father was young, this was nothing more than fifty acres filled with weeds, tall grasses, and small clusters of eucalyptus trees. But now, they've turned it into a nature preserve with walking trails, native oak trees, and a pond. I also explore the trails in the nearby oak grove where Danny used to camp alone. Where he'd buried the neighbor's cat. Trying to imagine my parents, Poppy, and Danny, living in this stretch of land, using it as their backyard.

And between the conversations with my father, the time in the library doing background, and getting a sense of the setting, I look into the coroner. The man who'd possibly gotten the time of death wrong. Digging into that developing story in 1993 has been a distraction, but not a waste of time. I think about questions I might ask. The coroner himself is unfortunately deceased, but I have a list of names. The DA at the time of the inquest. The lead detective on the case, looking for links to people from my former life as a journalist. Any old favors I can call in to get confirmation that the coroner had been high the night of Poppy and Danny's autopsies.

I'm in my element. This is a job I know how to do, and one that I'm exceptionally good at. I've managed to keep myself busy enough not to return to my father's in-box, to see if Calder has responded, telling myself it doesn't matter what he thinks or what he wants.

Ghostwriter is often a term men like Calder push back on. They fight to have their name on the cover alongside the subject of the book. However, I'm happy to disappear, letting my subject's voice shine through. I love to inhabit their lives, their minds—and with everyone I start off easy. *Tell me what you remember about that year. Tell me about your parents. Your siblings. What your school years were like.* I build trust.

The work I'm doing with my father is a collaboration, like all the others I've done—the Olympic ice skater I spent three months shadowing on tour. Watching him rehearse in the mornings, perform in the evenings, then talking for several hours late into the night. Writing the book on a tour bus. In airports. Eating fast food and mainlining black coffee to make my deadline. Or the world-famous country star who'd lost her ability to sing, but who now spearheads funding for major medical research.

I force myself to forget that this particular job is personal. I try to stay objective, open to the stories my father is slowly unraveling for me—three siblings who loved each other and what happened when one of them suddenly became dangerous.

* * *

Near the end of my third week in Ojai, I'm back at Jack and Matt's, drinking wine and talking about anything and everything other than why I'm still in town. Jack hasn't pressed me again, though sometimes I can tell he wants to ask me a question about how exactly I'm helping my father when he's got a perfectly capable caretaker in Alma. He doesn't ask whether my father and I have arrived at some kind of mutual acceptance and forgiveness. He simply lets me be here, which is a gift.

"Tell Kamala that I want to see her in the Oval Office someday," Matt says, setting down an artful charcuterie board on the table in front of us. He loves that I'm on texting terms with famous people.

"I don't know Kamala, but I pitched AOC once for a book." I take a cracker and break it in half. "I didn't get it."

Matt, with his loose jeans and floppy hair, is exactly who I imagined Jack would fall in love with. Whip-smart, sarcastic, and soft-hearted, he's the opposite of Jack's cowboy persona. He wears designer loafers without socks. He uses hair products.

Matt slides onto the bench next to me at their dining room table, nudging my shoulder. "How's your dad doing?" he asks.

"He has his good days and bad days," I tell him. "Alma has a lot of rules that supposedly keep him from getting too confused. But I'm not sure how well they're working because a couple times, he's mistaken me for my mother."

"Jack told me she left when you were young," Matt says. "Will you tell her he's sick?"

My gaze locks with Jack's before I say, "I doubt it." If this were any other book, I wouldn't hesitate to seek out the ex-wife of my subject. In fact, she would be the first person I'd want to talk with. To question her about her memory of that time. But my mother's name sits on my list alongside Margot Gibson's and Mark Randall's like a bomb waiting to detonate.

"What was your mom like?" Matt asks.

Jack starts to speak, undoubtedly to tell Matt that my mother has always been a topic I don't like to discuss, but I wave him off. Here, in Ojai, I can't lie about my family. It's not possible for me to tell people the stories I've created about two loving parents, how hard it was on my mom when my dad died, how she struggled to learn how to pay the bills and manage the house on her own. How she worked to hide her illness from me so I could finish college. And how devastated I was to lose her. Ojai exists as a bubble in my life. Everything and everyone who knows the truth lives inside of it, and I'm not afraid of speaking about it here. Confident I can keep it contained.

"I don't remember much about her," I say. "When I was young, I used to imagine I had one of those PTA moms who would bring in cupcakes for my birthday. Who would work at the book fair. In middle school I imagined her as a shop owner—maybe jewelry she made herself, or a bakery—and I would sit behind the counter and everyone would comment on what a good assistant I was. Then my mother would say, *"I couldn't do any of this without Olivia!"* Matt's gaze softens and Jack grows still, their silence allowing me to continue. I don't let myself imagine what Tom would say if he were here, listening to this story. In this moment, he seems light years away from who I am and what I'm working on. Almost as if I've imagined him altogether. "And later, when my father started actively drinking, I used to fantasize about my mother coming to get me. The two of us living in a small apartment or on a houseboat in Ventura. Heating up frozen dinners and eating them at a tiny table. Watching TV on the couch, just the two of us. Not a lot of money, but security. Consistency."

For years, my mother was a dark hole into which I poured hours of wondering. Imagining. Dreaming. After I went abroad for high school, I tried not to think about her at all, other than to lay the blame for my father's addictions and my subsequent exile squarely at her feet. It was because of her that I'd been sent away to boarding school, my father claiming I was too old for a babysitter but too young to be left home alone while he traveled. It was her fault that she was unable to withstand the rumors about my father, about what had happened in 1975. If both my father and I could deal with the whispers that swirled around us, why couldn't she?

"A mother is supposed to love and protect you," I say. "Mine chose to abandon me, and it's something I've never been able to forgive her for doing."

"There," Jack says, his voice just above a whisper. Meant only for me to hear. "Was that so hard?"

I know he's referring to my honesty, how willingly I spoke about my mother. A quiet criticism of who I am when I'm not being myself.

Chapter 17

The snacks I'd bought myself when I first arrived have finally run out. Though Jack sent me home last night with leftovers, I'd rather save them for dinner so I'm raiding my father's pantry, grateful for the break. I find a package of Doritos, rip them open, and lean against the counter, savoring the quiet of the main house. As soon as I eat something, I plan on checking my father's email again to see if John Calder has gotten back to him. Or whether he will at all. The last two times I checked, there hadn't been anything. Just more emails from the Gap.

I'm reaching into the bag for another handful of chips when my phone rings. It's my friend Allison, finally getting back to me. I look around, desperate for something to wipe my hands on before settling on my pants, and brace myself.

"Allison," I say, my voice hollow and breathless.

"Sorry I'm just now getting back to you," she says when I answer. "Fiji was amazing. What's the deal with this Ojai property?"

"Just research on a potential project," I say. "I want to track down the owner."

I've been back to the house several times, sneaking in through the preserve when the neighbor's car is gone. I've peered in windows, dug around in the garden, and tried to orient myself with the floor plan from the outside, matching what I can see with photographs from my father's albums. I feel a rush now at the idea that I might be able to track down the owner and get in.

"This particular house was pretty locked down," Allison says. "My supervisor says he sees this with homes owned by entertainment industry folks who almost exclusively purchase their homes through an LLC. This one was no different. I was able to get the name of the LLC and from there you can go to the secretary of state's website and see what pops up. But it'll probably be another entity."

I look out the window to the orchard in the distance. "What's the name of the LLC?"

"I'm emailing it to you as we speak."

"Thanks so much for digging into this for me. I really appreciate it."

"Happy to help," she says. "Look, I've got to run. Catch up when you're back in town?"

"Definitely," I tell her.

We disconnect and I check my email, the Doritos forgotten on the counter next to me. At the top is the message, as promised. I open it and scan past the boilerplate language to the name of the entity that owns the property.

Lionel Foolhardy, LLC.

Motherfucker.

Chapter 18

I approach my father's childhood home from the back, following a path through the preserve that leads to a small grove of trees, a mixture of oak and eucalyptus. Beyond it is my father's backyard, a long expanse of unfenced land that meets the edge of the preserve.

Above me, a canopy hangs, the sky only a patchwork behind the layer of green. Birds call, insects buzz, and a squirrel watches me from a nearby tree.

I imagine my father, skinny and awkward, walking alongside my mother and their teacher, looking for a quiet place to hash out their argument. The smell of eucalyptus in the evening air as the sun's heat faded away. Maybe the faint sound of music from the carnival, laughter and voices a background to their conversation.

I hear a car pull into the neighbor's driveway and I watch him get out, tugging a gym bag over his shoulder. Apprehension grips me and I wonder if I should have talked to my father first. Confronted him with what I've learned and demanded access to the house. I'm pretty sure an interview with the local police will violate my contract in some way. His front door closes and I wait a few minutes more before approaching my father's back door.

It's the kind you find on a service porch, with a window on the top half. I jiggle the knob but it holds firm. Peering through the window, I can make out the kitchen to my left, the central hallway straight ahead, and the door to what I believe is Poppy's room on my right. I press my hands against the cheap aluminum frame of the window and push up. At first, nothing happens, which is what I expected. Surely someone at some point would have noticed the lock had been disabled.

But how often does anyone check whether their windows are really latched? I think back to my own, trying to remember. You flip the lock, watch it engage, and walk away. I give the frame a few sharp taps, the noise louder than I want, and I glance to my right again to see if the neighbor heard anything. But all is quiet. When I wiggle the window again, it's looser. Dark, damp dust, compacted over years along the bottom edge, loosens and the right side lifts enough for me to get my fingers under it and jimmy it so that it's open a few inches. I glance over my shoulder again before reaching inside and turning the knob. Just as my father said he and Danny used to do.

I stand with my back pressed against the closed door, listening. For footsteps outside, a voice calling, demanding to know who I am and what I'm doing. But all I hear is the distant buzz of a plane and the sound of birds.

The house smells dusty, the air stale after being closed up for so long. I enter the kitchen, which still has the original dark cabinets. A dingy white refrigerator is in the space where the old one used to be, but the range appears to be the same harvest-gold one that was in the photographs.

I try to imagine my grandmother in this spot, watching her three kids eating breakfast on that last day, not knowing it would be the final time they would sit there together.

I look out the window over the sink, a straight view toward the preserve in the distance. Had the killer—perhaps Danny?— stood here, waiting for Poppy? I imagine him, watching her run toward the house, entering the unlocked back door and going straight to her bedroom, where she'd been trapped.

A swinging door leads to the dining room, and connected to that is the living room. It's smaller than I imagined. The fireplace is outlined in red brick with a floating mantel over it, a barrel ceiling arching overhead. A central hallway leads to the back of the house and the three bedrooms.

Brown carpet covers the floor, outlines where heavy furniture once sat still visible. I feel like I'm on a broken-down movie set. Just the background remains, empty spaces where my father and his family once lived their lives.

I walk down the hallway, which is dark, so I flip a switch and a single fixture overhead illuminates the space in a dim light. I gather my courage and move toward the end of it. Danny had been found, right about where I stand now. I crouch down and brush my fingers over the surface of the carpet, wondering about the young boy who died here, who'd never had the chance to grow up. Live on his own. Get married and have children. For many years, I imagined that he'd been terrified, forced to listen to his sister suffer in the next room, knowing he was powerless to help her. But these past few weeks with my father have me imagining it differently. Seeing Danny in a more sinister light based on my father's stories. And I wonder if Danny hadn't been running toward Poppy, but away from her. Leaving her to bleed out and finish what he'd started.

If I lift a corner of the carpet, I'd likely see the black stain of blood. Perhaps now only a faint shadow, but surely it would still be there. It had been several hours before the bodies were found. How much blood would that be, seeping into the wood?

In the kitchen, the refrigerator motor clicks off and I'm left with silence that feels heavy with fear and regret. I glance over my shoulder, shaking off the chill that's come over me. I don't believe in ghosts, but if I did, I'm certain they'd be here.

I stand again and peek into the primary bedroom, which is small and only has a sliding-door closet on one end. In our conversations, my father has talked about his parents some. They showed up for award ceremonies and when the school needed them to intervene, but there were no heart-to-heart conversations about feelings or dreams. No conflict-resolution discussions between the three siblings. Just a *get over it and get on with it* mentality.

Much like my own childhood. *No regrets, no looking back.*

Next I stand in the doorway of the middle bedroom. The one once shared by my father and Danny. Twin beds on that wall over there, across from two windows overlooking the side yard and the neighbor's house. I wonder what it had been like for my father to live in this room for three years after the murders. To go to bed every night next to the empty bed of his brother, who'd been slaughtered just fifteen feet away. My father told me that his mother refused to get rid of Danny's bed, insisting it remain, with the same sheets that had been on it the day Danny died.

Finally I move into Poppy's room. In the photographs, the walls were pink with a rosebud-trim wallpaper. But now they're just a dingy white, scuffed in places, the ugly brown carpet showing me where a desk once sat, a discarded and outdated modem still on the floor in the corner. Afternoon sunlight slants through the windows, splashing bright light onto the carpet near the closet.

I think back to my father's night terror, the way he threw open his bedroom window, convinced that he was somewhere else instead, desperate to find a knife he'd hidden there. It's ridiculous, but I have to look, to see for myself that it was just a delusion.

I start with the window on the left, opening the sash and inspecting the sill below, tapping on the wooden frame. Gripping it in the same way my father had, trying to wiggle something loose. Then I slide my hands up the sides, all the way to the bottom of the window. I trace the corners, looking for a place where my fingernails can find purchase, but the seam is solid.

I lower and lock it again, then move to the other one. I start to pull up the sash, but it sticks. I have to wiggle it as I did the back door window, one inch at a time on each side, and notice water damage around the edges. When it's finally open, I trace my fingers again along the center, gripping the wood to see if it moves. It feels solid enough, but when I look at the seam in the corner, there's a tiny hole, no bigger than the circumference of a paper clip. I try to fit my fingernail into it, but it's too small, so I retrace my steps to the back door where I'd dropped my purse and carry it into Poppy's room, searching the bottom detritus of pens, notebooks, and an old gallon-sized baggie, searching for a paper clip.

I find one and unfold it partway so that it looks like an inverted L. Then I slip the tip into the hole, feeling the wood release.

The sill lifts out in one piece, about two feet long and four inches wide. I use the flashlight on my phone and shine it into the opening. The space where there should have been insulation is empty, just the exterior frame about a palm's width away from the interior drywall. I imagine Poppy pulling it out, piece by piece, maybe using a sock or a glove to protect her fingers from the whatever material they used when the house was built, dropping them outside the window to be collected later. Hiding her most private things in here—magazines she wasn't supposed to read, notes from a boy she liked. The diary, encased in its metal canister.

The space is pitch-black and riddled with cobwebs but the narrow beam of my flashlight catches on something metallic tucked deep inside. I reach my arm down, trying to angle my body to get maximum stretch, and my fingers brush over a serrated edge. I'm on my tiptoes now, my mind racing ahead to what I might do if I pull out a knife. Confront my father with it, or go straight to the police?

My fingers finally gain purchase on the object and I can tell right away by the weight and shape that it's not a knife. I pull out a button about four inches in diameter, its edges rough with rust, that reads *Pro Roe 1973*.

All the decisions I might have been faced with evaporate into the air around me. Of course, Poppy had hidden this button in her window, away from her mother's judgmental eyes. I spin it around in my palm, imagining Poppy as the young activist my father had described, then slide the button into my purse, glad to have an artifact that I can keep. One without a confusing narrative like her diary. Just a simple button, proclaiming something that mattered to her. That matters to me as well.

I stand in the middle of the room and stretch my mind back fifty years and feel Poppy's presence here. Not a ghost, but the vibrations of a young girl gone too soon. This was her sanctuary. And even though it looks like a generic spare bedroom in a run-down house, my mind is layering over the space with the images I saw in the photo album. Her bed over there, against the wall. Her desk under the windows. Clothes scattered across the floor leading to her closet.

I wander over to it and slide the doors open. Plain white walls. An empty clothes rod. It's not a walk-in, but deep enough for a small child to hide in if she wanted to. I crawl inside and lean against the back, looking out into the room. Which is when I see the words written on the interior wall not visible from the outside. Faint scratches of an old marker, written in the distinctive hand of my father.

Someday soon, you'll be dead.

Chapter 19

I reel backward, hitting my head on the wall behind me, then reach up and fumble with the cord on the closet light, but it doesn't turn on. "Shit," I mutter, my trembling fingers needing several tries to tap the flashlight icon on my phone.

I stare at the sentence, my mind scrambling to make sense of what I'm seeing. Thinking back to every conversation I've had with my father about Poppy, trying to dig out anything that would indicate conflict between the two of them. There were many stories, but nothing that would point toward my father deciding to write something like this on the wall of his younger sister's closet.

A low dread begins to churn inside of me as I think about all the times I've seen my father lose his temper. The anger that would overtake him, the yelling. The rage. Especially after he started drinking and doing drugs. When I was younger, he wasn't like that. I'd always assumed his temper had developed due to fame and substance abuse. That his true self was the one I remembered from when I was a little girl. But maybe it's the other way around. Maybe, during that brief time of my childhood when I'd worshipped him, his true self had been buried deep inside, waiting to come out again.

I scoot out of the closet and stand in the center of the room, my heart pounding. Reconciling myself with the very real possibility that, as a teenager, my father had done something horrific and gotten away with it.

And now he's trapped me into cementing his lies.

* * *

I call Jack. "Can you meet me?" My voice is barely above a whisper.

"This sounds serious," he says. "Hold on a second." While I wait, I try to think of an explanation, a reason my father would write those words on the wall of his little sister's closet. A threat? A joke? Jack comes back on the line. "I'm all yours. Where do you want to meet?"

"The preserve."

When Jack arrives, I lead him toward my father's old house. Perhaps the same route Poppy might have taken fifty years ago. The shadows are long, afternoon sun barely tipping over the hills in the distance. We walk quietly until we get to the edge of the property when I put a hand on Jack's arm to keep him from going forward.

"Why are we here?" he asks.

I ignore his question, keeping my eyes trained on the neighbor's house. Making sure he isn't gardening again or sitting on his back porch. Then I gesture for Jack to follow me. We sprint through the yard and up the back steps where I twist the knob on the door that I'd left unlocked.

"What are you doing?" Jack hisses.

I step inside and gesture for him to follow. When I close the door, I turn to face him. His gaze darts from the door to the hallway where Danny died, and back to me. "I really don't want to get arrested," he says.

"Don't worry, my father still owns this house," I tell him.

His fear morphs into a look of disbelief. "Shut up," he whispers.

"There's more," I say, leading him down the hall and into Poppy's room. I pull out my phone and shine the flashlight on the inner wall. He leans in and I watch him, his eyes widening as the meaning becomes clear. "Oh my god," he says.

We stare at each other for a beat and then he must realize where we are because he says, "This was her room, wasn't it?"

I sink down onto the scratchy brown carpet and Jack does the same. We sit, facing each other, and I can still see the young boy I once trusted more than anyone. I can't do this by myself. I can't keep the secret of the book, the secrets my father so clearly doesn't want me to discover, even though he's tasked me with writing a book about them. I can't tell Tom, but I can tell Jack. Tears well in my eyes and I cover my face, allowing myself to cry.

"Hey," Jack says, scooting closer, wrapping his arms around me. He holds me until I can catch my breath. Until I've made a decision.

"I'm not here because my father is sick," I tell him, wiping my cheeks and nose on my sleeve.

"No shit."

I give myself a moment to gather my thoughts, knowing what it will cost me to reveal this, but knowing I need my only friend to help me sort through everything I've learned. Jack already knows the worst parts of my past; I don't have to explain my secrets to him, or give him context. "My father hired me to ghostwrite his memoir," I tell him. "He wants to write about what happened."

Jack is quiet as he absorbs the information and I continue, telling him about the incoherent draft of my father's book, his refusal to allow me to work the way I usually do. I tell Jack about how hard he's been working to convince me that Danny was dangerous. Working toward something—a reason? Justification for what he's planning to reveal? I tell him about finding Poppy's diary and her concern about my mother's pregnancy and abortion. And then I swallow hard, forcing myself to say it out loud. "Do you think my father killed them?"

"We don't even know when that was written."

I shake my head, still trying to absorb that the man I'd once idolized might have done this to his brother and sister.

"What about the alibi?" Jack continues. "You can't look at that one sentence, assign meaning to it and ignore everything else."

"Poppy was too scared to write anything down in her diary. But if she told my father about the abortion and that the baby wasn't his, he would have been enraged."

Jack shakes his head. "Take a breath and think. How would you handle this if it wasn't your father—your family—you were writing about? What would you do next?"

I don't have to think very long. "I'd try to figure out why the DA thought he had enough evidence to bring a grand jury together to look at things in 1993. And whether that coroner got the time of death wrong."

"Okay then," Jack says.

"If my father finds out I violated the contract," I tell him, "I'll lose the job. The only person I'm allowed to talk about it with is him. And I think he set it up that way on purpose. To keep me from figuring out the story he's been telling me is a lie."

We sit there, on the floor of Poppy's room until Jack finally says, "No offense, but this place gives me the creeps. How about we go back to my place? Matt and I can get you nice and drunk."

"Hold on," I say, pulling my phone out of my pocket again. I crawl back into the closet, kneeling this time so that I can capture the words with my camera. I take three pictures, making sure I have a good shot, before sitting back on my haunches.

That's when the floorboard beneath my left foot wobbles. I rise up and shift my weight back, and it wobbles again. I dig my fingers into the edge of the rug and pull it back. Hardwood floorboards are directly beneath, the carpet nails still sharp around the perimeter.

I fold it over and kneel on it, pressing down on the floorboards until I find the one that's loose. Lifting it up, I shine my flashlight into the crevice, revealing several round film reel canisters.

I start pulling them out, one at a time, stacking them on the rug as Jack watches, dumbfounded. All of them labeled in a young girl's hand.

March 1975
April 1975
May 1975
June 1975

Poppy's missing home movies.

Chapter 20

There are ten film reels in all. Three from March, two from April, four from May, and one from June. Such a short period of time. And such a consequential one.

I spool out one of the reels—the one labeled *March #1* in Poppy's familiar handwriting—and hold the film up to the light. Jack leans in, our heads touching as we each try to see what's on it. Tiny shapes move across it—people I can't quite recognize, rooms and locations all unfamiliar—1975 alive and waiting for me to discover.

He looks at me, grinning. "I think you have your next steps."

People's recollections are tinted with their own biases. Their beliefs, layered over the top, sometimes rendering a completely different meaning. Red becomes purple. Yellow becomes green. I'd always believed my father had invented Lionel Foolhardy, until he'd presented me with evidence to the contrary. There's a reason historians rely so heavily on primary sources. Because human memory is flawed.

Up until this moment, all I've had to work with was my father's broken memory and Poppy's cryptic diary. But now I have the film that will unlock everything.

* * *

"I've got ten Super 8 reels I need transferred to digital." I've driven straight to Ventura with the movies. Jack had given me a rain check on that drink and made me promise to tell him if there was anything earth-shattering on the film.

The man behind the counter nods and says, "Let's have a look."

I pull them out of my bag and stack them in front of me, and he opens one of the reels, peering at a few inches of film. "These are pretty old," he says.

"My aunt shot them when she was a young girl in 1975," I tell him. "We just found them."

"You won't have any sound on these," he says, tracing a finger along the edge. "There's a gold band that runs along the base that recorded sound." He spools out a few more inches of film. "This one doesn't have that." He wraps it back up again and slides on the lid. "I can put these on a flash drive or I can email you a link."

"A link would be great. How soon can you get them done?"

He slides all ten reels to the side and consults a notebook open next to the register. "I have a couple jobs ahead of this one, but definitely by end of the day."

I smile. "Perfect. Thank you."

*   *   *

When I get back to my father's, he waylays me in the living room. "Olivia," he says. He's sitting at the dining room table. "Where have you been?"

I push down a wave of anger, thinking of the words he wrote on the wall of his dead sister's closet, of the home movies I've just found. The house that he still owns, that he neglected to tell me about. The lies and half-truths he's been feeding me, the information he's conveniently forgotten. I freeze, suddenly terrified he can read my mind, that he will somehow know what I've learned about him. "The library," I tell him. "Fact checking."

He taps the table in front of my old seat and says, "Let's get some work done."

I can't. There's no way I can sit across from him and listen to him tell me more stories. More lies. "I've got a splitting headache," I tell him. "And a call with my agent."

He stares at me a beat and I wonder if he can see the lie. When I was young, I used to wonder if he had special powers, always seeming to know when I wasn't telling the truth. But finally he nods and says, "There's Advil and Tylenol in the upstairs bathroom if you need it."

I grip my phone, thinking of the photo on it—the words on Poppy's wall. *Someday soon, you'll be dead.* "Thanks," I say, and then push past him, out into the courtyard, taking the stairs two at a time and standing, breathless, my back against the closed door of the guesthouse.

Jack's question comes back to me. *How would you handle this if it wasn't your father, your family, you were writing about? What would you do next?*

* * *

My shoulders ache from several hours spent hunched over my father's notepads when the films drop into my in-box. Ten links with names that match what was written on the outside of the film canisters. I download the first one on the list, labeled March #2, tapping my fingers on the desk, impatient.

A flickering black screen flashes for a few seconds and then I'm seeing my father's neighborhood as it was in 1975. The film is color, but it's faded with age, giving everything an antique patina. The neighbor's house is vacant, a For Sale sign in front of it. I think about who might have lived there at the time of the murders, and how long they remained afterward.

The camera pans from left to right, taking in the street with its 1970s-era cars—old-school Fords, a shiny Volkswagen Bug, and a Camaro—the tree across the street smaller but recognizable. The grass in the front yard of the house looks healthier than the crabgrass that lives there now, and I imagine my grandfather tending it on weekends. Mowing it, fertilizing it, watering it. Or maybe that was a job for my father or Danny. A chore they had to complete before they could play with their friends on a Saturday.

I'm hungry for a glimpse of Poppy. To see her smile and laugh, even if I can't hear her voice any longer. But she's behind the camera. She turns and walks in through the front door of the house. And there, on the couch watching television, are my parents. Teenage Vincent is skinny—all elbows and knees poking out of a T-shirt and shorts. But it's my mother I can't take my eyes from. I pause the film to study her.

She has the lean legs of a runner, and I remember my father mentioning once that she'd been good enough to get a scholarship to college to run track, but that life had different plans.

I press Play again and see my father say something to Poppy behind the camera, and my mother laughs, her face cracking open into a wide grin that lights her up. I ache to hear her. To have her smile at me that way.

Poppy shifts away from them and walks through the dining room, where their mother is working on a puzzle and drinking from a mug. She has a scarf tied around her head, and she looks up at her daughter and smiles, then gestures her away, camera shy.

I never knew my grandmother. She died a few months after I was born. Aside from that one photo in the newspaper from the funeral, there are no pictures of her from the time after Poppy and Danny died, and few from before. To see her smiling and laughing, the graceful way she shoos her daughter away, the long fingernails on her hands painted a pale pink. I wish I could reach into the movie and grab her, tell her what was to come in just a few months' time, beg her to stay home, not to go into Ventura to see that movie. The events of June 13 killed her as well, it just took longer for her to die.

But this is who she was. Her true self, the woman who raised my father, who raised three children for a short while. And it breaks my heart all over again to know what's ahead for her.

The screen goes dark for a split second, then lights up again with a different scene. Poppy has the camera pressed up against a door, open just a crack. Through it, I can see Danny—so young, so handsome—lying on his bed reading a book. The camera zooms in on him, tipping the door open a little bit more. The motion must catch his attention because he looks up, straight into the camera. His eyes are a piercing blue, set against the black of his hair, and I can see why he was so popular. My body tenses, thinking of the stories my father has told me. About how angry Danny would get when someone came into their room uninvited. How he used to rage against Poppy following him everywhere with her camera.

But on the screen, Danny sits up, grins, and throws the book at Poppy, who peels away right before it hits her. I rewind and watch it again, looking for hints of the person my father has described. An ominous flicker beneath Danny's smile. A flash of temper suppressed. But I don't see any evidence of that person at all.

I watch different scenes from their home—their father smoking a cigarette on the back porch, then a panoramic view of Poppy's bedroom cluttered with stuffed animals. And there are the collages my father told me about—images of ERA activists at marches and rallies. A giant *Equal Rights* poster next to her desk.

Poppy approaches her bed and the view from the camera turns around, facing the door, lowering as she sits. My father again comes into view, poking his head into the room, making faces. Saying something else that makes my mother, lurking behind him in the hallway, laugh. It's surreal to see expressions and emotions bloom across their faces as opposed to the static smiles in photographs. To see their gestures, the way they move. It's hard to fathom that these moments still exist while the rest of the world has moved on.

But I still haven't seen Poppy. Every now and then I get a glimpse of a hand, shooting out to direct someone. But here, there is nothing of her at all. Just her world, her life, viewed through her eyes.

This reel ends, a series of jumbled moments, much like my father's manuscript. I quickly download the next attachment and start to watch. But this one, from May, is different. It takes me a while to figure out that it's the high school gym. In the film, a man wearing coveralls is on a ladder, methodically scrubbing away spray-painted words—*fuck you*—from the wall. Poppy keeps the camera on him for several seconds, then zooms in on the floor beneath the ladder, panning right and then left. I lean closer to my laptop, trying to see what she's seeing, but it's too pixelated.

The next clip is of a burned-out shell of an equipment shed, the blackened interior revealing the paraphernalia of a 1970s PE curriculum. Melted plastic hockey sticks poking out of a metal trash can. The blackened edges of what I think were red handballs, soccer balls, and basketballs.

Poppy pulls away from the shed and she's walking down a narrow alleyway between two buildings. Then the camera tilts to one side, as if being pulled away from her face, and turns off. When it's on again, we're somewhere else. It's night, and Poppy is filming out her bedroom window, the camera poking through her curtains. I recognize the shadow of my teenage father sneaking across the backyard. Poppy zooms in to show him disappearing into a nearby grove of trees.

The rest of this reel is more of that. My father alone, surreptitious. Once, he sees her filming him and he approaches the camera. I watch, fascinated to see my father's younger face up close. So many familiar landmarks—the hairline that dips in the center of his forehead, the way his ears stick out. But his cheeks are fuller. His eyes aren't so sunken. As he grows closer, Poppy keeps the camera trained on him. He's angry. He reaches out, grabs the camera, and I see a flash of sky. A flash of Poppy's hand, her hair, and then the picture goes dark.

Not exactly how my father has described things to me. I get out my own notebook and Poppy's diary, ready to match the clips with Poppy's entries, hoping I can follow the trail of clues she's left me. And so, I go back to the beginning.

May 6, 1975
I heard a rumor today. That Lydia was pregnant and now . . . she's not.

And then the next one:

Something's on that film that Vince doesn't want me to see. March #1, Clip #3.

I label my notebook with the entry and the clip, then download it from the list of attachments, fast forwarding until I get to the third clip. It's a party. Kids gathered around a bonfire, flames dancing into the dark sky. Poppy's camera pans in close to the flames, then eases out, the frame growing larger, pulling in more figures: shadowy couples making out, three girls dancing in a circle, their arms held above their heads. My imagination fills in the soundtrack—maybe Fleetwood Mac or Led Zeppelin—the high-pitched laughter of the girls, the low voices of boys growing into men. It's shadowy and dark, and I pause the frame every few seconds, trying to see what Poppy wants me to see. But it's just kids at a party. On the far left side of the screen, the figure of a man I can't quite make out—an older brother? Someone's dad?—is picking up empty soda cans and dropping them into a garbage bag. People I don't recognize, teenagers mugging for Poppy's camera.

I rewind and watch again. The same dancing girls. The same flames reaching toward the sky. The same man cleaning up. I make a note to see if I can find an old yearbook, to match some of these faces with names and then go backwards, trying to figure out if any of them were relevant at the time. Whether any of them knew my mother. Perhaps one of them was the father of her baby. There aren't any more references to the clips on the March reels, so I skip ahead to the next reference in May.

May 10: I don't even know who he is anymore. May #1, Clip #7.

I'm barely two seconds in when I sit forward in my chair, a zip of recognition passing through me. Because it feels familiar, as if I've seen it before. The camera pans through the wooded area near my father's house, and Poppy seems to be walking slowly. In the distance, I can make out a figure, hunched over a shovel. Digging. My mind fills in the gaps, just the way my father described this scene to me. The sound of the leaves crunching, the smell of damp soil, the steady thump of the shovel. This is what I've needed. Corroboration of my father's stories. Confirmation that he's been telling me the truth. He hadn't mentioned that Poppy had been with him when he'd come across Danny burying the neighbor's cat. Or perhaps my father had swiped the camera and filmed this himself.

Either way, I stare at the screen, watching it unfold, exactly as he described it. The camera zooms in as close as possible, and I can make out the bloody bundle that must have been the cat. But it's the boy who catches my attention. That has me slamming my thumb down on the space bar to pause the video.

Because it's not Danny burying the cat.

It's my father.

Poppy

May 10, 1975

I move through the trees of the oak grove, shadows cascading around me, the late afternoon sun too low to poke through the branches that arc overhead. I'm still angry about what Margot said. *I mean, it's hard, but it happens. Maybe he'll come back. Missing cats often turn up after a week or so—hungry, but okay.*

I pause by a large stump, sounds other than my footsteps breaking through my thoughts. Beneath the usual noise of the grove—the wind brushing the tops of the trees, the chirp and fluttering of birds and critters—is a dull *thunk-thunk-thunk* coming from somewhere just beyond me. I glance toward the high school, knowing in a few weeks it will be overrun with people setting up for the summer carnival, but it's too early now.

I turn toward the noise and start slowly, creeping from tree to tree, keeping my camera low, allowing me to film and still see where I'm going. I'm not afraid—I've spent enough time in here to know exactly where I am, how to get out quickly if I need to—but that doesn't mean I shouldn't be careful.

I pause again to listen. Beneath the steady noise there's something ragged, like heavy breathing.

I'm about ten yards away when I see him. Vincent, his back to me, digging a hole in the ground next to one of the large boulders that make up the Rocks—a place kids like to go to get high or drunk. I creep forward, careful not to make a sound, zooming the camera in as close as it'll go.

His shovel strokes are steady; however it sounds like he's crying. Above us, a patch of blue sky is dusted with late afternoon light, shimmering down upon the boulder crusted with moss. Next to the hole is what looks like a bundle of rags. "Vince?" I say, keeping my voice low, not wanting to startle him.

He spins around, fear clear in his expression. Tear tracks trace down his cheeks, cutting a dusty path toward his chin. He wipes his nose on his sleeve and says, "You don't want to be here."

"What's going on?" I ask, lowering the camera and turning it off. "What are you doing?"

Vincent glances down at the bundle on the ground next to him and nudges it with his foot into the hole. "Go home, Poppy." I feel a sadness descend. He seems so unreachable lately—angry and volatile—and I wonder if he knows about Lydia.

I step closer, until I'm standing in front of him and my gaze travels toward the hole. Something has been wrapped inside Vince's yellow Grateful Dead T-shirt now splotched red. A white paw, crusted with blood hangs out of the side. Vincent kicks the rest of it into the hole when he catches me looking.

A sick fear churns inside of me, and I look over my shoulder, as if expecting someone to catch us here. "Is that . . ." I trail off, unable to finish my sentence. I'd stapled the signs on telephone poles and handed them out in town. I feel the air rush out of me, my legs suddenly weak. I know, without having to be told, what has happened to Mr. Stewart's cat.

I stare at Vincent, our eyes locked in on each other, neither of us speaking. He lunges forward suddenly, as if to grab me, but instead he gives me a hard shove and I fly backward, hitting the ground hard. I hold my camera against my chest, protecting it from the fall. "Get the fuck out of here!" he yells. He steps forward as if he's going to hit me, and I scurry sideways on my backside, my feet scrambling for purchase. I stumble more as I stand, backing away from him, tears making my vision blurry. "What is wrong with you?" I ask.

His chest heaves, his fists clench. I've only ever seen this expression on his face when he's looking at Danny.

"For the last time, go home."

I walk backwards, unable to take my eyes off my brother, the hole, the dead cat inside. It isn't until I bump into a tree that I turn and run.

Chapter 21

I close my laptop and sit, my mind reeling through options—confront my father? Call the publisher and explain that I can't do this job because the subject is actively trying to mislead me? But a quieter thought breaks through the chaos, reminding me that it's possible my father's illness has made it so that he really believes it was Danny who killed and buried the cat. One truth remains—I cannot write this book without talking to other people. It's not just my own principles as a ghostwriter. I've seen what can happen when a book isn't fact-checked. When it comes out later that events have been embellished or made up completely. It tanks the book and destroys the ghostwriter's credibility. I'm already on the verge of becoming obsolete; I can't afford a mistake like that.

And then another thought slams into me. I'm going to have to pull the chapter I've already submitted, describing Danny burying the cat. This is why I don't like sending chapters before a book is done. Things change, memories shift, and I can't afford to look like I've lost control of this project.

I'm considering calling Nicole, not just to tell her I need to pull that chapter, but to ask again what I'd asked after that first Zoom with Monarch—what would happen if I spoke to people about the book on background—when I freeze, an idea blooming inside of me. A way for me to get what I need.

I open my laptop again, this time searching for a copy of the contract, reading through the terms, my pulse quickening as I see the loophole.

As a ghostwriter, it's never my name on the cover, never my photo on the book jacket. Olivia Dumont is simply the name on the contract and one of the many people thanked in the acknowledgments.

But to the people in Ojai, the ones I grew up with, the ones who knew my parents—and Danny and Poppy—Olivia Dumont doesn't exist. To them, I'm Olivia Taylor. And the contract doesn't say anything about an estranged daughter coming home at the end of her father's life, looking for answers. Tom had been right. A solution has appeared that will allow me to satisfy everyone.

I stand and start to pace, dialing his number. Hoping he'll pick up so I can tell him. Not the specifics of what I've figured out, just that he was right. The room is stuffy so I open the door, hoping for some air to blow through, though I'm still seeing my father's scrawny teenage back, digging the hole. Burying that dead cat.

"I figured it out," I tell him. Everything will now fall into place. I can talk to the people I need to, write the memoir based on their recollections alongside my father's, and no one will be the wiser. And then I can go home.

"Hold on," he says. "I need to go somewhere quieter." The noise behind him sounds like jackhammering and I picture him on a job site, with his button-down shirt tucked into his Levi's and work boots peeking out the bottom. With a thunk of a car door, the sound disappears and he says, "Now say again?"

I walk back to the desk where I still have my contract pulled up and say, "I found a loophole that will allow me to adhere to all of the agreements I've made—with my subject as well as with the publisher." Relief rushes through me, that I might be able to pull this off.

From the base of the stairs, Alma calls up through the open door. "Olivia, your father would like a word." I freeze, praying

Tom didn't hear what she just said. But I can tell from the sharp inhalation on the other end of the phone that I'm not that lucky.

"Your father?" he says, his voice carrying the low timbre it gets when he's angry.

I sink down onto the bed. Alma appears at the top of the stairs to speak again, but I hold my hand up, silencing her. She shrugs and disappears. "I can explain," I say, my mind quickly sifting through my options, which are few.

"You told me your father is dead," he says.

I consider doubling down on the lie, of trying to create a godfather figure of some sort, but I know how much worse that would make things. "I know that's what I told you," I say. "The truth is complicated, and not something I've shared with anyone." I consider telling him my father is dying, that I've been called home to help, but bringing that up now feels like a flimsy attempt to garner sympathy.

"So you lied to me." In those words, in that tone, I hear the betrayal, sharp and painful. The one thing Tom has always insisted on, I've violated. It doesn't matter that I told him the lie before I knew how much I would grow to love him. I can see now that it won't matter to him that it's a story I tell everyone, that I'm not deceiving him alone. "And so the book?" he asks. "Is that also a lie? All the struggles you've been having with it, stringing me along making me think you're working when you're . . . what? Visiting your father who actually didn't die of a heart attack in the mid-nineties?"

"That's not what this is," I start, but he interrupts me.

"I think this is where I say goodbye." His voice is calm, but sad.

"Wait, what?" I ask, panic coursing through me. "Tom."

I think of how I was able to tell Jack about the job. About my father. How I spoke about my mother with him and Matt. And now, I'm completely logjammed. "I am working on a book. That's true." Here is my chance to tell him. About my father. The murders. The book that I just figured out how I can actually write.

But the phone beeps in my ear. Tom has already hung up.

I dial his number, but he sends it straight to voicemail. I wait a few minutes, then try again. Voicemail. I text him. Please, let's talk about this. I start to bargain with the universe. *If he takes my call, I'll tell him everything.* All of it. My father, his career, and the mystery around the deaths of Poppy and Danny. I will violate the contract and tell Tom why I'm here and what I'm working on. I text him again. I'll tell you what you want to know. Everything. Please. I stare at my phone, waiting for a response, which comes almost immediately.

I told you at the beginning that lying is a nonstarter for me. You lied about your family. You lied about a job. I can't be with someone I don't trust.

I spend the next two days alternately crying, begging Tom to take my calls through texts and voicemails, and sleeping. I don't eat. I don't write. I tell Alma to let my father know I have to take care of some personal business and that I can't be disturbed.

But a fifth email from Nicole on day three demanding a check-in finally pulls me out. Regardless of my personal life, I have to finish this job or John Calder will finish it for me.

I stare at Tom's last message, feeling as if I'm standing on a deserted island, watching the rescue boat depart without me. Knowing no matter how long I scream and wave my arms, it's too late. It's not turning back for me.

Chapter 22

Margot Gibson was Poppy's best friend. The one Poppy was supposed to meet at the Tilt-A-Whirl after a quick trip home to grab her sweater. The one who'd waited a half hour and then figured she'd misunderstood. The one who'd spent the rest of the carnival looking for her best friend among the crowds, until news had finally filtered back to her about what had happened. Where Poppy had been found.

Honestly, it's a miracle Margot didn't go to the house and find them herself. Or worse, become a third victim.

I'd looked up the basics about her. Public records searches and social media show that she's owned Ojai Valley Books since 2016 after retiring from her job as a paralegal for a local attorney. When I was younger, I used to see her every now and then, my kid-radar picking up on the whispers of the adults. *Poppy's best friend. Such a tragedy.* But she'd never spoken to me or acted as if she knew who I was.

I find the bookstore on the eastern stretch of Ojai Avenue in what used to be a video rental store, gold lettering over the plate-glass windows framing a colorful display of books.

Inside, the shelves are painted a light blue and line three walls. The fourth is taken up by a long counter and a small alcove where I imagine they set up chairs for author events. Lower, free-standing shelves are arranged throughout the shop, creating a thoughtful maze that carries shoppers deeper into the store.

"Be right out," a voice calls from the back.

I use the time alone to look around, my gaze scanning past the cookbooks and self-help section to the nonfiction shelves, automatically finding several of my own books. Projects I'd poured my heart and soul into, passion for each subject taking over my life for a period of weeks or months. A time when my father was relegated to a dark corner of my past, not someone front and center, demanding once again to be dealt with. A time when I didn't owe a misogynist hundreds of thousands of dollars for speaking the truth. A time when I was simply falling in love with the architect designing my studio, before I knew what my mistakes would cost me.

A voice from behind me says, "Can I help you find anything in particular?" She's standing behind the counter, looking at me over the top of a pair of black-framed readers.

I walk toward her. "I'm Olivia Taylor," I say. It's the first time in over twenty years I've said it aloud, and the name rattles around inside my ear.

She takes a step back, as if unsure whether to talk to me or not.

I hold my hands up and say, "I'm not here for anything other than to learn about my aunt Poppy." I wait to see if she'll retreat, but the mention of her friend pins her in place. "I'm sure you've heard through the grapevine, but my father is ill. I don't know how much time he has left, but there are things I'd like to know before he dies. What happened to Poppy and Danny is one of them."

Approaching someone cold is what I used to have to do as a journalist. We were taught that when people might be unwilling to meet, it's better to seek them out. Ask a few questions and see what you get. But I vowed when I transitioned into ghostwriting that I'd never do that again. Ambush someone, asking about their most painful moments. Pressing them to talk about things they don't want to remember. And yet, here I am, doing it again. "I know this is hard for you and I really don't want to cause you any more pain." I look at her, beseeching. "I've read everything there is to read about what happened. Every retrospective. Every piece ever written, from every angle. You've been interviewed in all of them." I shrug. "I just figured you'd be willing to answer some of my questions as well."

"Does your father know you're here?"

I'm glad to be able to answer truthfully. "He absolutely does not, and I have no intention of telling him."

She nods once, and gestures toward two chairs in the alcove.

I sit in one and set my computer bag on the floor next to me. "What can you tell me about Poppy?" I ask.

Margot sighs. "She was sunshine personified, and when you were around her, you felt like anything was possible."

My heart breaks to think about the kind of aunt Poppy might have been to me. The kinds of things we might have done together, had she been given the chance to grow up. "How long were you friends with her?" I ask.

"Since the third grade. Poppy had skipped second grade and didn't have many friends in our class yet. We sat next to each other at lunch one day and were inseparable from that moment onward, until the day she died."

"I read that the police focused their energy looking for a mysterious car that had given Poppy a ride the weekend before. Can you tell me more about that?"

Margot rolls her eyes. "Not that again."

"You don't think that was worth looking into?"

"Maybe," she admits. "But not exclusively."

"Why was Poppy hitchhiking?" I ask.

"There was an ERA rally in Ventura. We were both going to go, but I had to visit my aunt instead," Margot says. "I assumed she would skip as well, but turns out she went anyway."

"Bold, for a fourteen-year-old to hitchhike alone," I say, thinking of that stretch of highway. Of how deserted it must have felt in 1975 before Ojai became a vacation destination for the wealthy.

"That was how it was in 1975, but that was also Poppy," Margot says. "Her parents had a double standard that used to drive her crazy. *Why should my brothers get to hitchhike wherever they want to go but not me?* she'd ask. *I refuse to accept there are things I can't do simply because I'm a woman.*" Margot smiles a sad smile that makes her whole face wilt.

My fingers itch to take notes or, at the very least, record the conversation on my phone. But I hold my focus on Margot. "What did she say about it afterward?"

"She got a ride into town from a woman with a kid. But on the way back she said it was some guy. Kind of creepy, so she said she had him drop her at the high school so he wouldn't know where she lived. The police latched on to that. Said that he must have seen them setting up for the carnival, or perhaps Poppy said something about it and he returned the following week looking for her."

"Not a terrible theory," I say.

"A complete dead end," Margot insists. "Especially when there was so much going on inside that house to look at instead."

This is what I've been hungry for. It's why ghostwriters always find people close to their subject and spend hours interviewing them. Because there are always things people will censor about themselves. "Tell me more about that," I say. "What were the weeks leading up to the murders like for her?"

Margot grows thoughtful, thinking back nearly fifty years. "She was troubled by something," she says. "She wasn't herself. Distracted. Unwilling to do things she normally would enjoy doing. A couple days before the murders, Mr. Stewart hosted his annual end-of-year party for all the kids and she didn't want to attend, which was unlike her. I had to beg her to go with me, and then she proceeded to drink too much and caused a scene." She pauses, as if trying to remember the specifics. "That entire last week . . ." Margot's voice fades for a moment. "She wouldn't tell me what was bothering her, which was also unlike her. We told each other everything."

"Do you have any guesses? You were closer to her than anyone," I say.

"Things between Danny and Vince were escalating. There seemed to be something new every day. She didn't talk about it much, but I got the sense that Poppy was scared of Vince."

Again, it seems my father has flipped the script, and my decision to speak to people who were there feels like the right one. "What specifically was scaring her?"

Margot hesitates, as if making a decision, and then says, "A week or so before she died, Poppy told me your father pulled a knife on Danny. Pressed it against Danny's chest."

I wanted to kill Danny. The note from the margin of my father's manuscript floats through my mind.

"She was rattled," Margot continues. "Scared. She said things were getting physical between her brothers, but that Vince was the one instigating. Coming after Danny." Margot looks at me, her expression willing me to see things the way she sees them. To see the threat she so clearly sees.

"So you think Danny was his target and Poppy got in the way?"

"I'm certain of it," she says. "I think your father would have killed him a hundred times over, if given the chance."

I wanted to kill Danny. A confession?

"Why?" I ask.

"I never could figure that out. Danny was fun. Handsome. Poppy worshipped him." She gives me an embarrassed smile. "So did I for a while."

I choose my words carefully. "My father never spoke much about Poppy or Danny, or about that time. But the things he's been telling me recently lead me to believe Danny was the dangerous one. That Poppy was scared of him and my father was too."

Margot thinks for a moment, then says, "Poppy was growing scared of both of them. Danny could sometimes be cruel, but Vince was truly frightening."

I sit with that for a moment, thinking again of how tricky memory can be. Of how our brains will lead us toward a story that fits into our own worldview, and no amount of evidence can convince us otherwise. I lean forward in my chair. "I've always wondered, why didn't you go back to the house and look for Poppy?"

Margot looks sad. "I don't know. I've thought a lot about that over the years, because it's certainly something I would have done. But Poppy had been so troubled that week. It wasn't very cold that night so I figured she just used the excuse of a sweater to get some space."

"In one of the interviews, you communicated skepticism about my parents' alibi. Do you still feel that way?"

Margot sighs. "I think when you have a county coroner who is abusing drugs while doing autopsies, it's not a big leap to question the time of death. Mark Randall overheard your father making plans to meet Poppy at the house. And after that conversation, that's where Poppy went."

"Wait. What?" I ask. This is new information and it unsettles me, how easily my father's narrative is unraveling, and what could have happened if I'd accepted it at face value and published it. "But no one saw my father go to the house. Or leave it, correct?" I ask. "According to my parents and their teacher, they were all in the oak grove."

Margot shakes her head, as if I'm not understanding. "Vince would never have stood Poppy up."

"Who would my father have prioritized?" I press. "He's supposedly in a huge fight with a girl that he worships. If she's demanding they go somewhere to hash things out, is he really going to make her wait while he goes to talk to his sister?"

Margot looks out the front window at the people passing by the store—some carrying shopping bags, others just window-shopping on a beautiful spring day in Ojai, and I wonder what she's really seeing. Perhaps two young girls from long ago, arms linked, laughing and sharing secrets. Believing they'd have decades more of them to share. "You can know something in your bones and not have any concrete evidence to prove that it's true," she says, looking back at me. "I believe your father was in the grove with Mr. Stewart and Lydia. But I also think he killed Danny and Poppy. Which means it was the coroner who got it wrong." Margot looks down at her hands. "Your father killed them," Margot continues. "I don't know why—there could have been any number of reasons. He was a messed-up kid. But if I could prove it, he'd be in jail."

I decide to switch gears. "I heard there were rumors that my mother had an abortion and that the baby wasn't my father's. Do you think it's possible Poppy found out who it was and told him?"

Margot gives me a weak smile. "It would definitely explain her behavior that last week," she says.

"Who do you think the father was?" I ask.

"Poppy and I spent a lot of time theorizing about that, but I really don't want to speculate." She shakes her head, at a loss. "Honestly, I'm not even sure if Lydia was ever pregnant. It was a rumor and nothing more. You know how kids are."

"But what if it was true?" I press.

"Lydia spent all her time either at the track or with Vince. Near the end, I think Poppy was beginning to suspect Lydia's coach, Mr. Stewart. Your father was certainly jealous of that relationship. But then Poppy died and the idea that Lydia might have had an abortion just . . . didn't matter anymore. No one cared."

Heat creeps up my neck, and I think again of the diary. *I think Margot and I are right about the father of L's baby.* "Her track coach?" I ask. "The same one who gave them the alibi?"

"Mr. Stewart, yes. But looking back at it now, the idea seems absurd." She shakes her head. "We were teenage girls. We loved a good scandal and Ojai was pretty boring."

I'm not so sure she's right, but I leave it for now. "I found Poppy's home movies," I say.

Margot's expression sharpens. "Where were they?"

"Under the floorboards in her closet."

Margot gives a hollow laugh. "Poppy loved her hiding places." Then she looks at me. "Was there anything interesting on them?"

"I'm still trying to sort them out. She seemed interested in the vandalism at the school. Graffiti and a burned-out shed?" .

"We thought that was Vince, targeting Mr. Stewart." She shrugs. "We were filling in the blanks as best we could, but we never did figure out who was behind it." I think again of the first diary entry: *Something's on that film that Vince doesn't want me to see.* And then directing me to the bonfire clip.

I pull my computer out of my bag and balance it on my knees, angling it so she can see the screen. I've cued it up to the bonfire. "What can you tell me about this night?" I ask.

Margot leans toward the screen, a tiny smile on her face. I watch her, looking for a hint of surprise or shock—to see if she can see what Poppy had seen.

When it's over, she says, "We used to go to parties like that all the time." She chuckles. "I don't recall that particular one."

"Can you watch it again?" I ask. "I'm curious to see if there's anything off about it because I also came across Poppy's diary." Margot's eyes latch onto me. "It's cryptic," I explain. "There's nothing in there other than references to her movies, and she seemed to think this clip was important."

Margot obliges and I play the clip again. When it's over, she says, "I don't see anything. It's just a party."

I sigh, another dead end. "I found another clip I think you'll like," I tell her, pulling up Poppy's first reel in March, filled with family and friends. She's holding the camera and spinning in a circle. You can see flashes of a table, with crumpled wrapping paper and the empty box of the Super 8 camera, her parents leaning against each other, watching her. Then there's Danny at the firepit, feeding logs into the flames, and my father, sitting on the back steps, the house lit up behind him in the twilight, all of them wearing party hats. Around and around, we see them in flashes, smiling at her. Laughing at something someone has said. At one point, her parents are up and dancing to a song lost to time.

"That was her birthday," Margot says, looking at me and giving me a sad smile. "The last one, in March. She was heartbroken when that camera got lost."

I pause the video. "When was that?" I ask, thinking of the last entry in her diary. *I've lost the proof.*

"The week she died. She was devastated."

"What happened to it?"

Margot shakes her head. "When I asked her, she just said, *I don't want to talk about it.*"

"Did that strike you as strange?"

"When something like this happens, you look at every incident, every small moment, trying to see the connections. To link events into a sequence that makes sense. But her camera meant everything to her, so I could understand why she'd be upset and not want to talk about it."

I nod and press Play again, but my mind is somewhere else. Wondering how she could have lost the thing my father claims was in her hands every waking moment.

The party disappears, and I fast forward to a clip near the end. A younger Margot is on the screen, doing cartwheels in the backyard. Danny enters the scene, messing up Poppy's shot. You can see her hand slice out from behind the camera, waving him out of the way.

Margot leans forward, her expression softening, allowing her mind to travel back to a time when her friend was still alive, filled with potential. She reaches out to pause the video and points to a bracelet on Poppy's wrist, a thin gold chain with a hook clasp. "I bought that for her birthday. She was wearing it the night she died," she says, her voice just above a whisper. "I still have it; her mother gave it to me to keep." Margot's words shimmer with the pain and trauma she's carried all these years. She'd only been fifteen when she watched her best friend walk away, a last moment squandered. What kind of fiction has she told herself over the years about what she could have done differently? How many nights has she lain awake, going over it again and again, yearning to go back in time and insist Poppy remain with her?

I unpause to finish the clip. A cat streaks across the frame and Margot says, "There's Ricky Ricardo. Poor thing."

"What?" I say, my tone sharp.

She looks at me, surprised. "He was Mr. Stewart's cat. He went missing and Poppy was captain of the search committee. Posting flyers, going door to door. Asking to look in people's garages and storage sheds."

I think again of the notes in my father's manuscript. *I had to bury Ricky Ricardo quickly.* Not a delusion, a memory. Which means perhaps the other margin notes are true as well.

"Did they ever find him?"

Margot shakes her head. "I don't think so. Probably a coyote or something got to him. Poppy searched for about a week, but then gave up."

Poppy

May 16, 1975

"Girls, I'm off to run some errands," my mother says as she enters the kitchen. She eyes the open bag of potato chips on the table between me and Margot and sighs. "Maybe you could have some carrot sticks instead?" she suggests. "You'll be glad you did when you're my age."

She doesn't stick around long enough to hear me mutter, "You mean when I'm old and pickled with alcohol?"

But Margot laughs and takes another chip from the bag. "So who do you think did it?" she asks.

We'd been talking about the graffiti that appeared this morning in the school gym.

But I'm sidetracked again when I hear my mother say, "Hello, Lydia."

Margot's eyes lock with mine.

"Is Vince home yet?" Lydia asks.

"He's supposed to be, but you know Vince. Feel free to come in and wait. There are some Diet Rite sodas in the fridge and the girls are in the kitchen."

"Thanks, Mrs. Taylor."

"Did you just come from track practice?" we hear my mother ask. Lydia says something I can't make out and then my mother says, "Well, lucky thing you have some time to tidy up. Feel free to borrow my lipstick if you like. It's in the top drawer of the bathroom."

I roll my eyes and Margot stifles a giggle. The front door closes, and Lydia wanders in.

"Hi," Margot says, offering her a bright smile. I kick her under the table.

Lydia glances at us. "Hey," she says.

When she turns to open the fridge, I gesture for Margot to follow my lead. "All I know is that the graffiti was already there in first period because Lana Simpson has PE first period and she said Mr. Stewart canceled their volleyball game and made them run laps instead. He wouldn't even let them inside the gym."

"So someone must have broken in either early this morning or late last night, because when I was there for basketball practice yesterday evening, everything was normal," Margot says.

"What are you talking about?" Lydia asks.

I turn to her and say, "Someone broke into the gym at school and wrote *Fuck You* on the wall right by the PE offices."

Lydia pulls the tab from her can and tosses it in the trash, taking a sip of my mother's favorite no-calorie soda. I watch her, trying to see if this news surprises her.

"Were you training with Mr. Stewart this afternoon?" Margot asks her, her tone overly friendly. Almost suggestive.

Lydia looks at her, wary. "Yeah," she says.

"Did he mention the graffiti to you?"

"Why would he?" Lydia says to her. "He gives me laps to run and I run them. We don't really talk."

"Uh-huh," Margot says, taking another chip. She holds the bag out to Lydia. "Want some?"

Lydia shakes her head and takes another sip of soda.

"So who do you think did it?" Margot asks me, her question performative. We both know Vince did it, and we're pretty sure we know why.

"Who knows?" I say. "Could have been anyone, really. Vince once told me that some of the kids in his class used to pry open the side door—you know, the one by the bike racks—and get drunk in there."

Margot wrinkles her nose. "Gross. That place smells like an old shoe." Then she glances toward the hallway, where Jimi Hendrix is blasting from Danny's room. "Do you think Danny ever did that?"

"Nah, he prefers the oak grove. Always has."

Lydia coughs, tears forming in her eyes, and I look at her. "Are you okay?"

"Bubbles," she says.

Just then, the door of Danny's room opens and he comes out, wearing a pair of shorts and no shirt. Jimi Hendrix's guitar blasts from his stereo and Margot and I stop talking.

Danny walks past us, grabs the bag of chips off the table, and shovels a handful into his mouth, winking at Margot, who blushes. She's so obvious.

He barely glances at Lydia, still standing by the doorway, silent. He opens the fridge, pulls out one of our father's beers, pulls the tab and drops it on the counter, where our mother is sure to find it, and strolls back toward his room again, the music fading as he closes the door.

"Why go through the effort of breaking into the gym when they could have just written it on the outside?" Margot says, picking up the thread of our conversation.

"Placing it inside, next to the PE office, feels personal," I agree, watching Lydia. For the first time in a while I really look at her, noticing how hollowed out she seems. She's lost a ton of weight, and she didn't have much to lose to begin with. My mother is always complaining about dark circles under her eyes, but Lydia actually has them. She certainly looks like someone who's had an abortion.

"Poor Mr. Stewart," Margot says. "To have to clean that up."

"Don't be dumb," I say, turning to her. "It's Frank who will have to do that."

Frank, the beloved custodian, who loves to joke with the students, who is always happy to unlock a classroom so they can retrieve a forgotten item after hours.

Lydia pushes off the counter and goes back to the living room where we hear the TV turn on and the click of the dial changing the channel, finally stopping on *Let's Make a Deal*.

Margot looks at me, her eyes wide, as if an idea has just occurred to her. "Did you notice how fast she left the room when Mr. Stewart's name came up? What if her baby was Mr. Stewart's?"

"No way. He's a teacher."

"A young, hot one," she counters.

"Still," I say. And yet, the night Lydia and Vince went to see Pink Floyd, I'd followed them. Down the highway, ditching their bikes in the bushes. I remember the confident way Lydia had stepped into the road when Mr. Stewart's car had appeared, as if she already knew Mr. Stewart would be happy to drive them to Ventura, no questions asked. The way Vince had pulled her back, his hand rough on her arm. The way they'd had a hurried argument before she shook him off and jogged to the waiting car, forcing Vince to either follow or get left behind.

"I heard he's only twenty-nine," Margot says.

"That's still old," I say, trying to imagine how that would even work. Like, were they kissing in the equipment shed? Behind the gym after track practice?

"It may seem old now," Margot says. "But when she's forty, he'll only be fifty-four. That's not a big deal at all. My aunt Joan married a man who was sixty." She shivers. "Watching them kiss at the wedding was so gross."

But I'm only listening with half an ear, my mind turning over the fights Vince and Lydia have been having. How he doesn't like how much time she was spending training. Asking why she always gets a ride back to our house from Mr. Stewart. Vince is the only one who doesn't think it's cool that Mr. Stewart lives next door. Well, Danny doesn't, but Danny doesn't think anything is cool except him and Mark.

"Well, anyway, she looks awful," Margot whispers.

I get up and peek around the corner of the kitchen, through the dining room and into the living room where Lydia sits on the couch, gripping her Diet Rite in both hands, staring at the television. On the screen, Monty Hall asks a man dressed as Little Bo Peep if he wants to keep the $500 behind door number one or trade it for what's concealed behind door number two.

I return to the table and roll the bag of chips closed. "Remind me never to have sex," I say.

*　*　*

It happens again just a few days later. Someone had kicked in the door of the equipment shed, slashed all the balls with a knife, dragged a trash can inside and set it on fire. This time, I hear about it at the beginning of second period. Two girls, whispering their theories to each other as we wait for our English teacher, Mr. Connelly, to return from his cigarette break and start the class.

"It happened around eleven last night," one of them says. "A neighbor saw smoke coming up from over the school and called the fire department."

I'd been doodling a giant sun with rays poking out from the baseball pictured on my Pee-Chee folder, and I freeze, unease pulsing through me. I'd filmed Vince sneaking out of the house last night around ten thirty.

I turn to the girls who were talking about the fire and say, "Who do they think did it?"

The other one, a girl named Frances, snaps her gum and says, "They definitely think it's a kid. I mean, this plus that graffiti the other day. It's obvious they've got a problem with one of the PE teachers."

There are only three of them—Mr. Stewart, who is by far the most popular. Then there's Mr. Wallen, an ex-military guy who'd fought in Korea and who makes his students chant cadences when they run laps. And Ms. Kantor, who everyone knows is gay, but no one cares because she teaches PE so it makes sense.

I pick up my pen again and begin shading in the rays of the sun I'd drawn, my mind worrying about Vince's rising temper. What he'd done to Ricky Ricardo. And now this. But why go all the way to the high school to target Mr. Stewart when he could just go next door to his house? Take a rock and break a couple windows. Or slash the tires of his car. There are lots of ways Vince could make a statement if he wanted to.

Like killing his cat.

The bell rings, bringing Mr. Connelly with it, the smell of Tareyton cigarettes and Old Spice cologne wafting after him. He claps his hands together and says, "Okay, everyone. Pens out. We're writing an essay on *Othello*."

Groans erupt from around the room and I pull a few sheets of loose-leaf paper out of my binder, trying hard to push away the image of Vince sneaking across our dark yard last night, or the possibility that Margot was right about the father of Lydia's baby.

Chapter 23

Three days after my conversation with Margot, I'm sitting on a Zoom call again with Nicole and the team at Monarch. I'm supposed to meet Mark Randall, Danny's best friend, at the country club in an hour, and I'm anxious I might be late.

To be honest, I'm glad to be busy, filling my days with interviews, research, and meetings and my evenings at Jack and Matt's. Anything to avoid the silence of my phone. Tom has always been a touchstone for me at the end of the day, no matter where I am in the world. But now it's just this suffocating quiet.

Neil's face comes onto the screen and he's smiling. "Olivia, we've all had a chance to read the new chapter and we wanted to tell you we loved it."

Nicole grins, but I fight a tightening in my chest. "I'm really glad to hear that," I say. "But I'm actually going to have to pull that chapter."

A shadow passes across Neil's face, and I push on, hoping my explanation will be compelling enough for him to want to see the revision. "I've come across some information that renders that chapter incorrect, as it was told to me by Mr. Taylor," I say. "In his retelling, it was Danny who'd killed the neighbor's cat and buried it. But I've recently discovered that it was Mr. Taylor himself who'd done that."

A murmur passes through the team, their faces showing intrigue, shock, excitement. "I can rewrite it pretty easily," I continue. "The scene itself happened as he described it to me."

Neil finally speaks, his voice tight. "What's your source material for the change?" he asks.

"Poppy was an aspiring filmmaker. Mr. Taylor told me about how she'd gotten a Super 8 camera for her last birthday and spent those final months filming everything and everyone," I tell them. "He still has some of her old reels."

"There are movies?" Neil asks, his tone lifting. Hungry.

"A few, yes," I tell him. "But there's no sound."

Excitement ripples through the room. I hear the words *exclusive web content. Tie-ins.*

I hurry to explain. "On one of the reels is a clip of young Vincent with a shovel, burying a dead cat." Neil's eyes nearly sparkle at the idea of something so dark and sinister at his fingertips. "But that's not the story he's told me," I continue. "It's been tricky, navigating his memories without upsetting him. He seems to truly believe that it was Danny who buried the cat, and I have to be careful not to push him too hard. But there is definitive proof that it was Vincent."

"Would you be able to send the movies to us?" Neil asks.

"I'll ask Mr. Taylor," I tell them. "This was his sister, remember. His brother. He wasn't aware of the existence of these reels either, so I want to be respectful."

But the truth is, I'm the one who is hesitating. I'm not too eager to share them until I'm certain what they reveal.

"Go ahead and rewrite that chapter and send it over," Neil says, before signing off.

When they're gone, Nicole asks, "If he didn't know about the film reels, how did you come across them?"

I realize my mistake and quickly formulate a lie, substituting the diary for the films. "He gave me some boxes to look through. Stuff packed up from the house long ago that he never had the heart to throw away. Most of it was junk, but some of Poppy's things were in one of them—old folders, schoolwork, and these movies."

"Wow," she says. "That's a lucky break."

All these years, I've thought the story I told people about my family was harmless. But now I can see that I'm no different from my father, omitting everything that feels painful or complicated. I'm beginning to realize that once you lie about your past, you wall yourself off from the present. From the people who care about you. And now that I'm tasked with tunneling through my father's lies—hardened and calcified by time—I wonder who will stick around to tunnel through my walls and find me.

Not Tom.

* * *

Mark Randall looks older, his gray hair cropped close to his head, and he wears khaki pants and a light-green collared shirt. But he still maintains an air of authority and I feel as if he's caught me doing something I'm not supposed to be doing.

"Thanks for meeting with me," I say. We're sitting in the restaurant of the local country club, a large, airy room that overlooks the golf course, filled with dark wood and vintage photographs of golfers on the wall.

"I'm not sure what you're hoping I can tell you," he says.

"I'm guessing you've heard that my father is sick, that he's nearing the end of his life." He nods and I continue. "I have questions about those months leading up to the murders. I want to know what really happened to my family." I bow my head and look at my hands in my lap, wishing again I could take notes or record the conversation. But that's what a writer would do, not a daughter seeking answers.

A server comes and takes our drink order—iced tea for me, a sparkling water for him. I remember that Jack said his dad has been sober for nearly twenty years, and I wonder how sharp his memories of that day are, or whether they've been softened and marinated by years of alcohol abuse.

"What does he have?" he asks.

"Lewy body dementia," I tell him. "Basically, he's losing control of his mind and his body."

Mark winces. "I'd like to say I'm sorry, but I'm not." He looks out the giant plate-glass window and onto the course. In the distance, a foursome finishes up and loads their bags into their white golf cart.

The server returns with our drinks, and we each smile our thanks, dismissing her.

"Tell me about Danny," I say. "Did he have a lot of girlfriends? Margot tells me she had quite a crush on him."

Mark laughs and says, "Margot was a cute kid. But yeah, most of the girls had a crush on Danny at one point or another."

"Anyone lucky enough to date him?"

"Here and there. Now and then," Mark says, and I wonder what that means. "Nobody serious."

"Why are you so convinced my father was the one who killed them?"

Mark takes a drink and says, "That night at the carnival, I was in the haunted house and saw your father and Poppy arguing. She needed to tell him something, but she didn't want to talk about it there, so they made a plan to meet back at their place in ten minutes." Mark looks at me, trying to gauge whether I can see what he's suggesting. Then he says, "If your father was in the oak grove with your mother and Mr. Stewart, how could he be meeting Poppy?"

"Maybe he didn't show up," I say.

"Or maybe that junkie coroner got the time of death wrong."

"Margot told me the same thing. But I read there was a grand jury and that the coroner was cleared."

Mark looks at me, his gaze steady and sure. "Grand juries get things wrong all the time."

"I understand that my father and Danny were fighting a lot in those final days," I say.

Mark gives a hollow laugh. "That's an understatement."

"Enough for him to kill Danny? And then kill his sister?" I look at him, trying to see things from his perspective. Trying to travel back in time through his eyes to that day in 1975.

"I'll put it this way. We were all taught never to hurt a girl. But from the looks of what I walked into at the haunted house, Vince had no such concern. He had his sister shoved up against a wall. She looked terrified. He looked like a psycho."

"What were they fighting about?" I ask. Thinking about the abortion. Poppy and Margot's suspicions about Mr. Stewart. Could Mark have overheard Poppy telling my father and walked up just as my father was reacting to the news? But then why would Poppy agree to meet him back at the house?

"No clue. But that was Vince. Always going off about something. Danny told me Vince had come after him with a knife for no reason, just a few days earlier. Completely lost his shit on him." Mark shakes his head. "It's my fault Danny went back to that house. I told him about their fight, and . . ." He trails off, remembering. "He got real quiet. Then he told me he had something to do and he'd be right back."

I think about everything Margot told me and about my father's night terror, searching for a missing knife in a place no one would ever think to look for it. Of how he told me Poppy had been following Danny, describing Danny as volatile and dangerous, and yet Poppy's home movies show the opposite. They're filled with clips of my father. Not just of him sneaking out, but charging at Poppy as she filmed, anger on his face, spit flying from his mouth. There was even a clip of my parents, silently fighting in the backyard. My mother, scared and withdrawn, my father pushing into her space. Causing her to step back further.

I pull out my phone and open up the photo of the graffiti I found on Poppy's closet wall. *Someday soon, you'll be dead.* "I think my father wrote that inside Poppy's closet."

Mark nods. "Yeah, I totally believe he'd say that to her."

"So your theory is that Poppy was the target, that my father was angry with her, hurt her, and Danny got in the middle of it?"

"Your father was angry at everyone. But yeah. If things got physical back at the house and Danny walked in on that, there's no way Danny wouldn't have intervened," Mark says.

"Did you tell the police?" I ask.

"Of course I did," he says. "But I was a kid. They didn't give a shit about what I had to say. And Vince had that alibi, so what I told them went nowhere." Mark taps the table in front of him with his finger, as if trying to drill his words into me. "I know what I saw. I know what I heard. Your father went back to that house angry at his sister, and my best friend died trying to protect her."

His voice is laced with emotion, of unshed tears and nearly fifty years of frustration.

"Maybe my father changed his mind," I say. "Or got side-tracked by that argument with my mother."

Mark gives me a hard stare and says, "You asked me what I thought. That's what I think."

"What about that teacher, Mr. Stewart?" I ask, thinking of the abortion rumors. Of teenage Margot and Poppy suspecting the baby might have been his. "I hear my father was pretty jealous of the time my mother spent with him. Was he right to be worried?"

Mark shakes his head and takes a sip of his drink. "Nah. Mr. Stewart wasn't that kind of a guy. Sure, he pushed boundaries. He'd be crucified in today's world, but he had a girlfriend." He looks thoughtful, trying to grab the name. "Amanda? Amelia? I can't remember. Believe me, girls tried to get together with him but they all got nowhere."

"Why would he get crucified now?"

Mark shrugs. "He was a young guy who understood what it was like to be a teenager in a small town. He'd buy beer and keep it in the fridge on his back porch. He knew Danny and I would sneak over and steal it, but he didn't care. He used to sell a little weed now and then, but only to the older kids. And he'd throw a big party the final week of school," Mark says. "There must have been at least a hundred kids there that last year." He gives a hollow laugh. "Different times."

He takes another drink, emptying his glass, then slides it onto the table, away from him. Signaling the end of our conversation. He tosses a couple dollars next to his empty glass and says, "You did the right thing to come home—for yourself, not for your father. It's an awful thing to go through life feeling as if there had been more to say to someone." He pauses, as if considering his next words. "But I'm not sure you going around asking questions about what happened in 1975 is a good idea. Danny's gone. Poppy is gone. You should just leave them where they are and move on. Very rarely do people like what they find when they go digging into the past."

"My grandmother used to say something like that," I tell him, remembering what my father had shared with me.

"Your grandmother was a piece of work, but that's a different conversation for another day." He checks the time. "I need to get on the course. My tee time is in five minutes."

He exits the restaurant without looking back.

Chapter 24

"Tell me about the vandalism happening at the school."

I'd made extensive notes from my conversations with both Mark and Margot, noting places where their theories overlapped and where they differed. Each of them seemed to believe a different sibling had been the target. Neither of them mentioned Danny as a threat. Certainly not a killer. My father is the only person claiming that.

"Vandalism? Where did you hear about that?" My father asks now, looking surprised.

We're holed up in his office again and I've decided to keep the existence of the diary and films to myself for now.

Over the last several days, I'd watched and rewatched several clips of Poppy's movies documenting this vandalism, but she'd made no mention of them in her diary. Why film them if they weren't important? Then I'd gone back to the library and scoured the newspapers for the month of May, looking for any reference to them.

"There were several mentions about it in the paper," I tell him now. "The police were looking into it. One student was quoted as saying they thought Mr. Stewart was the target. Did they ever figure out who was doing it?"

My father looks annoyed. "Why are we talking about vandalism that happened fifty years ago? We have a book to write. It's not related."

I decide to humor him. "Probably not, but I'd like to learn more about it for context. After all, you didn't live in a vacuum. Life was happening all around you and I'd like to capture it." My father gives a reluctant nod, so I continue. "What kind of vandalism was it? The papers were light on the details. Just something in the gym and then later an equipment shed?"

I think again of those clips—the man on the ladder, the burned-out shed, a broken lock dangling on its hook, the interior blackened by flames. Was Poppy just wanting to document something that surely would have been a big topic of conversation among the kids? Or was there more?

"It was just those two incidents," my father says. "Obviously, people thought I was the one who was doing it, but they blamed me for everything." Then he leans forward. "Danny didn't like Mr. Stewart either, but no one ever talks about that."

"So you think Danny was the one who vandalized the school?" Not once did Poppy capture Danny sneaking out at night. But there are several clips of my father, creeping across the yard, Poppy filming him from an interior window as he disappears into the field behind her house. And there are two such clips, on either side of the vandalism ones. I think again of the story of the cat. How my father had layered over his memory with something different. Could this be the same?

"All I can say," my father tells me, "is that after Poppy and Danny died, the vandalism stopped."

"Or maybe the person who'd been doing it didn't want to be out alone at night anymore," I suggest. "I can imagine everyone must have been on edge in the days and weeks afterward."

He shakes his head. "It was Danny. He'd been growing secretive. His temper would flip like a switch. One night, he attacked me out of nowhere. We were in our room after dinner. I can still remember what we were listening to on the hi-fi—Joni Mitchell." He leans back in his chair and crosses his legs, settling in for a story. "Our mother had been in the kitchen doing the dishes, our father was in the living room with the paper and his nightly gin and tonic. And I was trying to pick up my side of the room. My mother had threatened to ground me if I didn't clean up. So I was bending over to grab some dirty clothes and Danny suddenly comes flying at me, tackling me into the hallway. Thank god I went through the doorway and not into the wall."

He shakes his head, like he still can't believe it. Slowing his words down, recounting it carefully. "Our father had to pull him off me." He shudders. "It was terrifying. I didn't feel safe around him anymore, so I ended up sleeping in Poppy's room after that." His expression softens. "Pretty much up until the day she died."

I keep my eyes trained on my notes, but my posture has stiffened. Because I recognize this scene. Poppy filmed it and referenced it in her diary: *May 30: Vince/Danny fight. Did he learn the truth??? Everything feels different now. May #4, Clip #9.*

And the story my father just told me isn't how it happened.

Poppy

May 30, 1975

I sit in my room, my camera still on my lap, my mind playing out the fight between my brothers. The way Vince had torn into Danny. The sound of their bodies as they hit the wall, their grunts. The spit that flew out of their mouths, the twisted rage on their faces. What Danny had said to Vince that started the fight, his voice floating through the thin wall that separates our rooms. All of it swirls around inside of me. The way Vince lunged at me when he caught me filming them. As if I was the next person he wanted to destroy.

It's quiet now, but not resolved. Not even close. That wasn't a fight over space in their room, or Vince listening to one of Danny's records without permission. It had been vicious. Relentless.

A knock on my door startles me, making me glad I'd wedged my chair beneath the knob.

"Let me in, Poppy." Vince's voice is low.

I scurry to hide my camera, burying it under a pile of sweaters in my closet before sliding the door closed.

Vince enters, carrying his pillow and blanket, and drops it all onto the floor. "I can't sleep in there with him."

"What happened?"

Vince shakes his head and doesn't answer.

"Is this about Lydia?" I ask.

His gaze shoots up at me, eyes narrowed. "What makes you think that?"

I hold my hands up in front of me, as if I have nothing to hide. I saw what he'd done to Danny and I want no part of it. "No reason," I say. "But I can't think of anything else that would make you that mad." There's no way I'm going to tell him I know about Lydia's abortion. Or that it wasn't his baby.

Vince settles onto the floor, his back against the wall, and closes his eyes.

"If you want to talk about it, you can," I say.

"Shut up, Poppy."

"This is my room. I don't have to shut up if I don't want to."

He ignores me, too tired to respond. I stare at him, wondering how long he plans to sleep on my floor. I think again of Ricky Ricardo and wonder what he might do to me.

Next door, Danny has put on his new Aerosmith record, setting the needle on the sixth track, "Sweet Emotion." We listen to the quiet way it starts, to the escalation of the guitar. Suddenly the volume shoots up when Steven Tyler sings the line about a girlfriend who's a liar.,.

"I hate him," Vince says. "I wish he was dead."

Chapter 25

I see the email by accident. It's been three weeks since I last checked, distracted with all I've uncovered—from the writing on the wall and the discovery of the movies to my conversations with Margot and Mark. I've been in the zone and have relegated Calder to the back of my mind. But after I close a couple tabs, my father's in-box appears and there is Calder's response.

> Olivia Dumont is a hack. Her brand of feel-good story is a fad the industry is already tired of reading.

I've had enough. I don't know what I thought I'd learn. I already know that someone within Monarch has told him about the book; I already know he hates women like me. I don't need to engage with him anymore.

I type: The book is under contract and I'm happy with its progress. I'm afraid that's where we need to leave things.

I hit Send, and then, before I can change my mind, I log out and close the window. Then I head into the empty house, up the stairs to my father's computer, and toggle the screen awake again. I click over to his email and click on settings, requesting a new password. After I enter the old one, the computer suggests a very long and complicated string of letters and I quickly accept it, knowing it'll be saved on his computer but that there's no way I could ever remember it.

It's done. I'm done. I check the time and head toward my car. I've got a long drive to Ventura.

##

An hour later, I'm situated in a coffee shop on Laurel Street, waiting to see a man who'd been a deputy DA at the time of the grand jury in 1993. The lead prosecutor, the DA himself, died about five years ago, but Charles Monahan had been his second chair. I'd stayed up nearly all night reading everything I could get my hands on about the coroner. Which of his cases had been overturned. What evidence they had to exclude. Anything that would help me see whether something had been overlooked.

My father is clearly lying to me, which makes me wonder if he didn't kill them both after all. I feel as though an anvil has been lodged in my chest. A desire for answers weighing heavy on top of the sickening sense that once I know something, I can never unknow it. And the fear that whatever I learn next might change everything I believe to be true.

After he lied to me about that fight with Danny, I've been avoiding my father, once again putting him off with excuses I'm sure he can see through. Claiming to have rewrites on the drafted chapters I've submitted so far. "Best for me to nail down what Neil wants now before we move on," I told him. My thoughts are tangled around one question: To whom—or what—do I owe my loyalty? To my father? To Danny and Poppy? Or to my own floundering career?

Now I sit near the back wall, watching the door, and wave when I see Charles enter.

"Ms. Taylor?" he says when he approaches.

I stand and shake his hand. "Thanks so much for meeting with me, Mr. Monahan," I tell him.

"Please, call me Charlie."

I slide the coffee I'd bought for him across the table and he takes an appreciative sip. "So you have some questions about your aunt and uncle's case."

"I have questions about my father's alibi," I tell him. "My father is ill and I feel like the opportunity for answers is shrinking."

Charlie nods and takes a sip of his coffee. "That's understandable, but I'm not really sure there's anything I can tell you."

"Can you tell me why a grand jury was convened? What evidence was there?"

Charlie sighs and looks across the crowded coffee shop. "Mainly, we called the grand jury because of what was going on with the coroner who did the autopsies of your aunt and uncle. If you've read anything about the case, I'm sure you know he had a problem with drugs around that time." Charlie shakes his head. "But your father's alibi held up and there were multiple witnesses who testified that the coroner wasn't using drugs in June of 1975."

"If you had that information, why call a grand jury at all?"

"The DA had to cross the *t*'s and dot the *i*'s. We figured it was better to let the system make the decision, not us." Charlie thinks for a moment, then says, "I don't know if this will help you or make things worse, but in my opinion the grand jury got this one right." He must see the shock on my face because he hurries to clarify. "I know it's not a popular opinion. A lot of people want to believe your father is guilty because that makes for a better story. But all I can tell you is that in this situation, I believe the system worked. We didn't prove our case, and if we can't do that, then the grand jury shouldn't indict."

I'm stunned. "Really?" I say.

He nods. "The media loves to talk about all the ways the system is broken. Poppy and Danny's friends have a lot of theories about what was happening in 1975 and a lot of really valid concerns, but our only job was to examine the evidence in front of us. To present it in the most honest and compelling way for the grand jury. We did that. And they found it insufficient because at the time, it was. The purpose of reasonable doubt isn't to prove anything; it's to introduce questions. To show that there might have been another route of investigation. Reasonable doubt is like a bell—once rung, you can't unring it." He's quiet for a moment, thinking. "The law can be a fluid thing," he says. "Hard to pin down. We try to make it concrete, to apply it fairly, but it's challenging even under the best of circumstances." He looks up again. "I was never 100 percent on bringing the case to the grand jury. Not at the time. We didn't have enough evidence."

"Like what?"

"The murder weapon, for starters." My mind flicks again to my father's night terror. To Poppy's hiding place, thankfully empty. Charlie continues. "But also, what we did have was completely circumstantial. The time of death, plus the testimony about the coroner which confirmed your father's alibi, convinced them not to indict."

I feel a glimmer of something—Hope? Relief?—that my father isn't completely unknown to me. "So you believe it was the man who picked her up hitchhiking?"

Charlie looks out the window next to us into a crowded parking lot and, beyond it, a busy car wash. "No," he says. "But unfortunately, that's all we've got."

"What about DNA? Technology has come a long way since 1975. Perhaps the evidence you still have could turn up something new."

"Maybe," he says, though I can tell he doesn't believe it.

I think of the story Margot told me, how my father had once pulled a knife on Danny. Surely she'd told Charlie the same story. And yet it didn't seem to matter.

Charlie takes a final sip of coffee, setting his empty cup on the table between us. "This case was never going to make it into a courtroom." He levels his gaze at me, and I see the years of toil, working in the public sector, never making the kind of money that his fellow law-school friends probably made, fighting for justice in a system that most will say isn't perfect, and many would argue is irretrievably broken. "A civil case could have been filed, but there wasn't anyone left to file it. Your father's parents had died years before, and he was the only one left."

"Did you ever meet them?" I ask.

"No. We had their statements at the time of the murders, but that's all we had," Charlie says. "Both had maintained your father's innocence until the very end, though their voices were muted. They'd been devastated by the loss. I don't know if they really believed Vince didn't do it, or if they just couldn't bear to lose their last child."

"What about the lead detective on the case in 1975? Any way I could speak to him?"

"Clint McGinnis died back in 2000." He fiddles with his empty cup, turning in a slow circle on the table. "You're going to find that most of the people who were around that day—firsthand witnesses, people who knew Poppy and Danny, or people involved in the original case—are gone."

"Do you think he'd be indicted if the case moved forward today?"

Charlie gives a hollow laugh. "You're forgetting, we still don't have a murder weapon. But regardless, I doubt it. The time of death plus your father's alibi clears him. Your mother and the teacher they were with have never wavered. He didn't do it."

We sit in silence for a few minutes, and when it's clear he isn't going to say more, I say. "Thanks for coming out to meet me today," I tell him. "You've been incredibly helpful."

He stands and we shake hands again. "You're welcome. I'm very sorry for your loss, and I wish I had answers about what happened to your aunt and uncle. But what we know clears your father, and I hope that helps."

* * *

I text Jack when I get back to my car. I need to meet with you, can you get away?

I sit there, my mind turning over my conversation with Charlie. His belief that the time of death was correct. More troubling was how easy it had been for me to believe my father had killed Poppy and Danny. A sixteen-year-old boy.

Finally Jack texts back. Meet at our spot in thirty minutes?

I send a thumbs-up and head toward the highway.

Our spot is in the Valley View Preserve, nearly two hundred acres of protected land. Jack and I used to meet at a fallen tree a few yards off the trail, where we'd sit and talk for hours, hiding out from our respective families. I find a parking spot near the Pratt Trailhead and make the quick trek, checking over my shoulder before veering off at the giant oak tree with the branches that swoop low across the path.

I find Jack already there, waiting for me. "How did it go?" he asks. When he sees my expression, he says, "I'm guessing not well."

I sit on the log next to him and pick up a twig, breaking it into pieces in my hand. "I'm more confused than ever." I give him a brief outline of what Charlie to me.

"This is a good thing."

I look up at him. "You can't be serious. I have a book to write, and no one can tell me anything I can verify."

"Stay open to all possibilities. Let the story lead you."

I roll my eyes. "You've been living in Ojai too long. Did you use crystals or do a sound bath to come up with that one?

"I actually got it from an interview you gave a few years ago. I found it on YouTube."

I stare at him, then scatter the broken pieces of twig onto the ground below me.

"I know you have a job to do, but don't lose sight of the fact that your dad is dying," he continues. "He asked for your help and you came. No matter what happens with the book or what happened in 1975, you'll always have that—the knowledge that you showed up when he needed you."

"He never showed up for me."

Jack gives me a sympathetic look. "Relationships aren't transactional."

Tom used to say something similar, but I brush away that ghost. Glad at least I won't have to worry about explaining any of this to him. "I still have so many questions," I say. "Nothing he's told me matches up with the films or with Poppy's diary."

He nudges my shoulder with his. "Maybe it's time to ask him about them."

I shake my head and look up at the sky peeking through the branches of the trees. A blue jay flies from one branch to another, calling out to a friend. Then I look back at Jack. "Over the years, Margot and your dad have never wavered in their belief that my father is guilty."

Jack sighs. "Margot was young. Think about a teenager's brain. Layer over that the trauma of what happened to her best friend."

"And your dad?"

"Danny was a hero to him," Jack says. "Best friends, the way you and I were. How much is memory and how much is emotion?" He scratches his work boot in the dirt and says, "Have you thought about talking to your mom?"

"Very funny," I say.

"I think you know the truth," he says. "But you've built so many walls, you can't see it anymore."

I look at him, understanding crashing over me. "You never thought he was guilty."

Jack looks into the trees beyond us, choosing his words carefully. "I could never reconcile the man I knew with a killer." He shakes his head. "How could the guy who used to insist on ice cream sundaes for breakfast, who taught me how to tie a necktie, be the same person who murdered his siblings?" His voice grows quieter. "Your dad was a mess, but he always seemed to know when I needed him to get his shit together and step in. It's like he intuited when my own father was struggling and just quietly gave me what I needed."

I don't know what I'm feeling, a mixture of confusion, maybe a little betrayal, a lot of regret. "You never told me that."

"It wasn't my place. Maybe if you hadn't been halfway around the world, we could have had a conversation about it. But I wasn't going to argue with you through letters."

"You thinking my dad was innocent must have gone over well with your own father."

Jack gives me a sad smile. "I never said anything to him either. What would be the point?"

"What did you think when my father started partying his way through the nineties?"

"I think everyone copes with trauma and grief in different ways."

"And what about what he wrote on the closet wall?" I ask.

"We have no context. We don't know when those words were written in Poppy's closet, or even if he wrote it."

"He wrote it," I say, my voice coming out louder than I intend so I soften it. "He also told me Danny killed the neighbor's cat, but it was him on the film, burying it."

"We have no way of knowing how that cat died. All we know is that your father buried it." He must see the skeptical expression on my face because he says, "Let's say, for argument's sake, you find out your father killed his brother and sister. What happens next?"

I think about it, about a path forward in the legal system. "Nothing," I finally say. "There wouldn't be any justice for Poppy or Danny. There's no way he would be considered competent to stand trial."

"Think about his life," Jack says. "The years of substance abuse. The loss of everyone who mattered to him. He lives alone in that big house with only angry Alma for company. What kind of life is that?"

"If he did it, he should have gone to jail," I say. "Spent the rest of his life behind bars."

Jack laughs, but he's not really smiling. "You're kidding, right? He's a rich, white man. I highly doubt it would have been the rest of his life." In a quieter voice, he continues. "Now let's say you find out he didn't do it. He's irrefutably innocent. Then what?"

This is what's been nagging at me ever since I left the coffee shop. The weight that's been hanging around my neck, threatening to choke me. "Then he spent decades being the villain in other people's stories. And I went along with it."

"But you're here now."

I watch a chipmunk scurry across the brush in front of us and disappear under another log. "Everything he's told me is a half-truth. He's been spinning Danny as this cruel, dangerous person when the truth is something totally different."

Jack's voice is gentle. "Then you need to ask yourself why this is the story he wants to tell."

Poppy

June 1, 1975

About a week ago, before his huge fight with Danny, Vince had started another treasure hunt with me, perhaps an attempt to get me to forget about how angry he was when I came across him burying Ricky Ricardo in the oak grove. Normally I'd have been excited to start a new one, but this time the theme was *dark places* and every clue has felt like a trap. A reason to get me alone in a dark place where anything might happen. I couldn't stop thinking about that hole. About poor Ricky Ricardo in a dark place of his own, dead and buried where no one will find him. The way Vince had turned on me, shoving me to the ground. The fights he's been having with Lydia. The way he'd attacked Danny just two days ago. *Dark places.* We did metaphors this year in English, and I couldn't help but wonder if this is one.

* * *

But our treasure hunts haven't always been this way. They started two years ago on my twelfth birthday. My mother had gotten me that stupid diary. Danny got me some sparkly barrettes, and Vince made me a treasure hunt.

Where do you go when your head is both wet and aching?

You don't have to go to the best room in the house to find the top place overall.

A princess would have noticed this weeks ago.

Clues leading me around the house, to the hall closet, the attic, and finally under my bed where a pair of wristbands—the same ones Chris Evert wore—were hidden.

After that, treasure hunts became our thing. Not just for birthdays, but for everyday things as well. Prizes might be a package of Kit Kats Vince wanted to give me from his Halloween bag. A baseball I found at the playground, scuffed with use. A snow cone in the freezer. It's how we communicated with each other, little notes and messages tucked into a binder, or a pair of shoes, or between my pillow and my bedsheet. Eventually, the game shifted to its current version with spoken clues. Vince poking his head into my room and saying, *"Sugar and spice, and everything nice, but Danny will never eat this,"* which would have me jumping up from my homework and racing toward the pantry where I'd find a clue wrapped around the peanut butter jar.

Which is why it's confusing for me to be playing the game so carefully now. Like walking on broken glass, watching every step, ever vigilant to the invisible shard that will stab you.

* * *

I figured after his fight with Danny, Vince would have dropped the game. Too upset to continue. But tonight he drops another hint while we're at the bathroom sink brushing our teeth.

"This is my favorite time of year," I say, hoping to keep things light and then get out of here. "School's pretty much over, aside from a few tests. The weather is warmer and you can feel summer coming on."

Vince says, "My favorite time of year is when Mom gets out the box of Christmas decorations."

Our eyes meet in the mirror and hold, his eyebrows raised just a fraction of an inch.

I carefully spit and rinse, returning my toothbrush to the cup, and even though I'm in my pajamas, I walk into the kitchen, opening the door that leads to the garage.

But I hesitate. Instead of my father's car, the space is filled with junk my mother can't bear to part with and the Christmas box is all the way on the other side. I'd have to cross the dusty floor, navigate around spiderwebs and I don't even want to think what else. I flip the switch, but the bulb gives a loud pop and then darkness.

"What are you doing?" Danny asks from behind me. He stands at the counter, drinking an Orange Crush.

I try to gauge his mood. If he is in a good one, he might be willing to help. But it's just as likely he would wait until I'm across the garage before closing and locking the door behind me.

So I step back into the kitchen. "I thought I heard a voice in there."

Danny wiggles his fingers in front of me, too close to my face, and says, "Creepy."

Over his shoulder, I see Vince lingering in the hallway, his expression unreadable. I look back and forth between my two older brothers and decide the clue can wait.

The following morning I'm up before either of them to sneak into the garage, pulling down the Christmas box. Taped to one of the red balls we hang on our tree is the clue. *You'll find your prize in the . . .* To discover that last word, I have to find one more clue. The game is drawing to a close.

Chapter 26

"Do you remember the very last treasure hunt I ever made for you?"

My father and I are walking side by side through the orchard, and his question takes me by surprise because the particular hunt my father is referencing is one I remember well. I can't imagine him wanting to remind me of it now.

"How could I forget," I say.

"Tell me what you remember about it," he commands.

I look over at him, to see if he's confused, but his gaze looks sharp. Aware. "What do you mean?" I ask.

"Just tell the story, Olivia. From the beginning."

"I remember it started on a Monday over dinner," I say, pushing my mind back to the summer I was thirteen. "A meal Melinda no doubt ordered over the phone and picked up, leaving the take-out bags on the counter when she left for the day." I glance over at him, to see if he's defensive at the mention of Melinda and how he used to delegate my care to her, but he's watching the ground in front of us as we walk. "You asked if you'd ever told me the story about how you once trapped a raccoon in an outhouse."

I wait for him to say he's never used an outhouse in his life, but he just nods for me to continue. "I was surprised you were bothering to eat with me at all. Most of the time I ate alone in front of the TV. Whatever Melinda decided to pick up for me, while you did god-knows-what upstairs in your office. Drank your dinner, no doubt." We navigate past a tricky knot of roots in silence and I continue. "But that whole week, you came downstairs to tell me these random stories."

I remember that first night so clearly: the carbonara on my plate, the living room cast in shadows, the overhead dining room light the only one on downstairs, save for the light over the stove. At thirteen, I'd started counting the years until I could go away to college. Jack and I talked all the time about UCLA or Berkeley. Somewhere still in California, but far away from the place that made us feel like outsiders.

My father sat across from me, his chicken piccata looking congealed around the edges, lowering his voice in the way he did when he was at the beginning of a story. *Did I ever tell you about the time I trapped a raccoon in an outhouse? I was twelve, and we were staying in a cabin in the woods. It had no indoor plumbing; only an outdoor shower and an outhouse about twenty yards away from the back door.*

"The broad strokes were something about a fancy makeup case your mother used for the trip, while you were relegated to using a paper bag to carry your shampoo and soap in." I glance at him to see if he's remembering it the way I do. The way he dropped the clues of what I was to look for into the conversation. The story within a story.

"Keep going," he says.

"You told me your mother used to keep her toiletry case in the closet under the stairs," I tell him. "Then you picked up your fork and took another bite of chicken, watching me. It took a few seconds for me to get it. To remember that the house you grew up in didn't have a closet under the stairs. Or a second story at all."

Slowly, I pushed my chair away from the table. My father continued to eat, not even bothering to watch me. I moved out of the circle of light and into the dark living room, making my way toward the stairs and the short hallway next to them that led to Melinda's office. On my right was the closet and I opened it. On the floor, directly in the center, was a toiletry bag—a soft-sided one with colorful splashes of teal and orange, arranged to look like abstract fish.

"I carried it back to the table and sat again, setting it next to me, certain you'd probably picked it up on your latest trip, a quick dash through the hotel gift shop on your way out, or more likely at the airport. Then I asked about the raccoon."

"And what did I tell you?"

"You said that was part of the hunt, a story that contained a falsehood I'd recognize."

I guide him to a bench in the middle of the grove, the lemon trees just starting to produce small, yellow-green fruit not yet ready to pick. "The next night it was a story about Chinese food you ate in England on a backpacking trip you took after college."

"I never went to college," he says.

"Exactly. That was my clue to listen closely."

I remember how annoyed I was that he couldn't just give me something. That there always had to be an ordeal. I always had to earn whatever it was he wanted me to have.

From the branches above us, a bird startles and flies away, dropping a feather as it leaves. We watch it float to the ground. "What did I hide for you that time?" he asks.

"A backpack. One of those hiking ones with buckles and zippered pockets cluttering the outside. *School doesn't start for another two months,* I'd told you. You gulped down the rest of your wine and filled your glass again. *You never know,* you'd said."

My father crosses his arms over his chest and I say, "Are you cold? Do you want to go back?"

"I want to hear the rest of this story."

"The last one was about a safari your publicist took. In fact, it had so much detail I was pretty sure it was true. On and on you went, describing the airport, her difficulty fitting her large suitcase onto the small plane. The way everyone—even the pilots—gathered to help her. *Soft-sided suitcases are so much better,* you told me."

That night it was submarine sandwiches from our favorite place in town, the soft bread dripping with vinegar, mayonnaise, and mustard. All I wanted to do was finish my sandwich and clear out. Jack and I liked to watch Thursday night TV together on the phone. Me in my room with the small set on my dresser and Jack in their basement with the big TV his dad used to watch football. We would watch *Mad About You.* Then *Wings* and *Seinfeld.*

"That time it was a new suitcase that you hid in the trunk of your car. I heaved it out and rolled it up the driveway, up the stairs, and back into the living room. A toiletry bag. A fancy backpack, and then a suitcase. When I rolled that suitcase in, you said, *Did you find it?* I was confused. The suitcase was sitting right there. But then you said, *No, not the suitcase, what's in the suitcase.*"

I'd gotten up from the table again and tipped the suitcase on its side, unzipping it slowly, flipping it open to find a glossy brochure. Images of kids, a little older than I was—a handsome boy with brown hair in a science lab, protective goggles over his eyes and a toothpaste-white smile. A blond girl running down a pristine soccer field. Images of brick buildings, clusters of kids walking and laughing. The brochure was in French, so I didn't understand what it was at first.

"Your new school," my father had announced, picking up his sandwich again, a large chunk of salami sliding out the back end of it as he took a bite. He chewed, then said, "You leave in four weeks."

I try now to fight down the tears creeping into my voice, not wanting him to see how much that still hurts. How betrayed I felt. How abandoned. "You just . . . yanked me out of my life without any discussion," I tell him. "Just a series of clues leading me toward the things I'd need to take with me when I left for good." We sit, shoulder to shoulder, the sun no longer high enough to cast shadows, the ground and trees a muted shade of gray.

"I was only trying to make things fun for you," he explains to me now. "The treasure hunts, the clues . . . Poppy used to love them."

"Or perhaps she played them because she didn't want to upset you," I suggest.

"That's not how I remember it." His tone is petulant.

We sit in silence for a few minutes, each of us lost in thought. Again, Jack's words from yesterday come back to me. *You need to ask yourself why this is the story he wants to tell.* With other projects, the narrative has always belonged to someone else. My only job was to shape it into something that will resonate with readers. But this book—about my family, my past—belongs to me as well. Maybe it's my turn to tell a story.

"Do you remember that trip we took to Miami?" I ask.

He thinks for a moment. "I don't remember ever being in Miami with you."

"Technically, you weren't," I tell him. "You spent all of your time either in the hotel bar drinking or trying to score drugs from one of the waiters."

He gives me a quick look. "When was this?"

"My junior year of high school, so 1996? Winter break. I wanted to come home to Ojai and see Jack but you said you needed a change of scenery." I pause for a moment. "When it was time to go home, you told me to meet you in the lobby and we'd take a cab to the airport. You had to *run a quick errand.*"

"Do I want to hear the rest of this?"

"Probably not, but I'm going to tell you anyway. I waited for you for nearly an hour before asking the front desk if they'd seen you. They said you'd already checked out and left."

He doesn't look at me. "I left you there?"

"I was terrified. I managed to track down that waiter and beg him to drive me to the airport." I take a moment, remembering my panic, hot and slick in the back of my throat. The sympathetic, knowing look the front desk clerk gave me. The quiet way she suggested I hunt down my father's *friend*, folding napkins on the outdoor patio. "When I got to the gate, I found you sitting there waiting for the flight, as if nothing was wrong. You were staring straight ahead, sunglasses still on your face. Likely high as a kite. I sat down and really laid into you. Told you what a shitty person you were, what a shitty father. Said I never wanted to take another vacation with you ever again. Not even to come home to Ojai. I informed you that I'd be spending all my breaks either at school or with friends, then I demanded to know what kind of a man did that to their only child. I unraveled years of pain and anger and laid it at your feet. I'm sure the people around us were getting an earful."

"What did I say?" His voice is cautious, as if he doesn't really want to know.

"At first I thought you were livid. *Keep our business behind closed doors, Olivia*, you'd always said to me. But by then I didn't care anymore. I wanted to call you out." I give a shallow laugh. "To answer your question, you didn't say anything. Just that stony silence you'd always have whenever you were too angry to speak. But then I realized you hadn't heard any of it, because behind your sunglasses, you were asleep."

He lets out a sharp snap of breath. "It's a miracle you said yes to this job."

"If I'd had any other options, I wouldn't have."

I wait for him to apologize, to say, *I'm sorry I did that to you I'm sorry for the incompetence and neglect.* But I soon realize he isn't going to. My father never apologizes. Not in the traditional sense. He'll make a gesture—a grand one or a small one, depending on his transgression—but I've never once heard him say he was sorry.

And I realize how many years I've been waiting for that. A small nod of ownership. Of regret. I don't know what I was hoping to get from him in the retelling. Perhaps confirmation that it had happened. Acknowledgment from him that he remembered it too, that I haven't been the only one carrying around these moments, heavy weights still wrapped around my heart.

But my father can't even give me that anymore.

* * *

We make our way back to the house, the sky darkening from purple to black, the orchard lights dotting the path. When we get to the courtyard, I'm about to head upstairs to my room when he turns to look at me. "Every chapter has to have a point. Even if the reader can't yet see it. Every story told must serve two purposes—to allow your reader to know your characters better, and to push the narrative toward the conclusion."

It's early evening, the time of day my father typically starts losing the thread of conversations, when he starts slipping into the past, thinking I'm my mother. Or perhaps this time, a protégé he helped somewhere along the way.

He stares at me a moment, as if waiting for me to confirm that I know what he's talking about. When I don't say anything, he takes a step closer. "Do you understand what I'm telling you?"

Suddenly, I'm back to Jack's questions from yesterday. About why the stories he's been telling me—about a scary older brother and two younger siblings who were growing frightened of him—are the ones my father wants me to write about. His references to the treasure hunts he used to design. The unusual way he'd leave clues for me. A manuscript filled with stories that all point to him.

"I'm not sure," I finally say.

He scrutinizes me, and in his expression I see disappointment. Frustration. As if I'm missing the point altogether. "Then maybe you're not the right person for this job after all."

Chapter 27

I see it all with clarity now. And everything looks different.

This isn't just a memoir. It's a treasure hunt—our last one—and every story is a clue. I'd be impressed if I wasn't so angry. The book is due in July—less than three months from now—and we don't have time for games. And that's when I started to wonder if everything so far has been part of the hunt. The delusions, his inability to read which so conveniently necessitates my presence here. But I discarded that possibility pretty quickly. If that were true, it would require Alma to be a part of it, and she has zero tolerance for games.

My father is an excellent writer, but he's not an actor. The sweat on his forehead and panic in his eyes when he had that first night terror. His anxiety when he thinks I'm my mother. He must know he's revealing things he might not otherwise, that this is the first treasure hunt he's not controlling. That has to be terrifying. And thrilling, for a man who's always looking to raise the stakes.

My father either killed them and wants to admit it, or he didn't and he wants me to figure out who did.

And like so much of my childhood, my father never just comes out and tells me what he wants me to know. He expects me to figure it out on my own.

If he's leaving me clues, it's time I start to tell him what I know.

* * *

"I've been to the house," I say at the start of our next session.

He looks at me now, confused.

"The house on Van Buren. I know you still own it." When he doesn't respond, I say, "Why didn't you just tell me the first day I got here? Why let me skulk around, looking in windows?"

"You have no reason to go there. You're here to write a book, not become Nancy Drew."

"This is another one of your hunts," I say.

But he shakes his head. "Be serious, Olivia."

I brush off his deflection. "I'd like your permission to go there to write," I tell him. "It'll help me get into the time and place and I'd like to not have to break in again to do it."

He gives me a sharp look. "You broke in?" he asks. "How?"

"Through the window on the back door."

A small smile. "Danny and I used to do that."

"I know. You told me," I say.

His surprise seems genuine. "I did?"

"Why did you keep the house?" I ask. "Why not sell it?"

"After the murders, we lived there for a while." He shakes his head, remembering. "It was awful. But my parents couldn't afford to move, and no one would buy it anyway. After I moved out, they were finally able to rent it and move into a small apartment. Neither of them lasted much longer. As you know, my father died of a heart attack in 1978 and my mother died of breast cancer two years later. At that point, selling it seemed foolish. We had a great tenant—a German woman named Frieda who didn't care what had happened there and didn't need anything fancy. It's a miracle she stayed all these years." He gives a small shrug, as if that should explain everything. "Feel free to go there as much as you want," he says. "If anyone asks, tell them you're the new tenant."

I think about the neighbor, the one who seems to keep tabs on the house, and wonder if he'll believe that. He seems the type who would notice no furniture ever arriving. Just a strange woman, entering and exiting with a laptop.

It occurs to me that if I can't get out from under my debt, living in that house might be my only option. I imagine packing up the Topanga house, forwarding my mail, and living inside my father's childhood home. What ghosts might come to me—not just those of my aunt and uncle, but of the person I might have been had none of this happened? What kind of friend could I have been? What kind of partner to Tom? I brush away the thought.

"When I was in the house, I found Poppy's hiding place inside the window." For now I stay quiet about the other space, under the floorboards of her closet. "So your hallucination wasn't really a hallucination. That space exists."

He stiffens. "So what? Poppy knew my secrets. I knew hers."

He's evading. Deflecting. It's time to push him a little bit, Alma's rules be damned. "I want to show you something. See what you remember about it."

I pick up my phone, still recording, and toggle over to my photos, pulling up the picture I took inside Poppy's closet. "'Someday soon, you'll be dead,'" I read aloud to him, holding out the phone so he can see it himself. "When I was at the house, I found this written on the inside of Poppy's closet. It's your handwriting."

I expect him to look scared. Worried. If this is a clue, it's a pretty damning one.

But instead, he laughs.

Poppy

June 3, 1975

Ten more days of school. It's all anyone can talk about. That and the end-of-year carnival at the high school. What rides there will be. Which cute carnies will be returning. What the kids are going to *really* do while their parents think they're at the carnival. I take a bite of roast beef—my mother overcooked it again—and chew, trying to ignore the simmering anger radiating off Vince. The show of indifference from Danny. Trying to shake off the memory of the sound of their bodies hitting the wall. The way Vince seemed to want to kill Danny. And then literally admitting that to me later.

My mother keeps trying to make small talk. Little attempts to draw one of us out. "I heard that the federal government has done away with separate PE classes for boys and girls. Next year, you'll all be in PE together," she says, looking at each of us in turn, hoping we'll chime in with an opinion.

"Gerald Ford is a stooge," my father says to no one. "He's a placeholder, nothing more. Totally useless."

I can't resist. "It's his wife who should be president," I say. "She's the one with the real vision, talking about breast cancer and abortion."

"Poppy," my mother warns.

"Come on, Mom. You can say the words. 'Breast cancer. Abortion.'"

"You're being ridiculous," my father says to me. "A woman will never be president."

"Why not?" I challenge.

"Enough," my mother says, and we all look at her, trembling in her seat, trying to hold a happy expression on her face but failing miserably. "Not at the table."

My father ignores her, holding his knife up to make his point. "At least Ford got one thing right—pardoning Nixon. That would have been a real mess."

"You know what's a real mess," Vince says. All eyes draw to him, mostly because he's barely said two words to anyone other than me since his fight with Danny. "Poppy's closet."

I hesitate, my fork frozen in midair.

"Go on," Vince says, goading me. Not letting me sit there and pretend I didn't hear the clue.

I push my chair back and walk toward my room. Behind me, I hear my mother say, "Do you have to play that game at dinnertime?"

I kick through the scattered clothes and books on my floor and go straight to my closet, sliding the doors open. I push my dresses aside, my gaze traveling across the back for anything he might have hidden there. Then I sift through the jumble of shoes on the floor, scattering them all over the place.

"Come back to the table, Poppy," my mother calls.

I pick up each shoe, feeling around inside it for a piece of paper. I won't let Vince know that my heart isn't in this hunt. That he's starting to scare me. I stand and slip my hand under my sweaters on the shelf, but there's nothing.

"Is it too much to ask that we have a nice meal without people tearing my house apart?" my mother says.

I pull everything out and pile it in the middle of my room. Still nothing.

"Poppy," my father calls, his voice a warning. I have about thirty seconds left before there's real trouble.

I grab my flashlight from under my pillow and shine it around the now empty closet. Into every corner, every crevice. That's when I see it.

Written on the interior wall in marker, my brother has given me the key word that will unlock the puzzle.

Someday soon, you'll be dead.

All thought seems to drain out of me, replaced by fear. His words from the other night—*I wish he was dead*—and now this.

"Poppy!" My father calls. Louder. No longer willing to wait.

I leave the mess and return to the table. Vince stares at me, but says nothing, spearing a piece of asparagus on the end of his fork. I take another bite of mashed potatoes and try to swallow them.

"Well?" Vince says.

I set my fork down.

"It goes with the clue you found in the garage," he tells me when I don't say anything. "You have to put them together."

A request? A threat? I run through the last two lines, plugging in words that rhyme with *dead*. "Someday soon, you'll be dead, you'll find your prize in the . . . bed?" I say, looking at him. Hopeful this game will be over soon.

My mother gasps. "Vincent," she scolds. "What a terrible thing to say to your sister."

"Relax, Mom. It's not a fortune cookie," he says. "It just has to rhyme." To me he says, "Does a bed fit the theme?"

Our mother huffs and takes another sip of wine.

This is the first time a clue hasn't been written on a piece of paper, but rather graffitied onto a wall and I wonder if this is another clue to a different mystery. Whether Vince is trying to tell me something else.

I push the thought away and return to the puzzle at hand. "Someday soon, you'll be dead. You'll find your prize in the . . . shed?"

Vince looks pleased.

There's no way I want to go out to the shed alone. But Vince is staring at me, waiting, and I don't want to let on that I'm scared or do anything to make him angry. So I look at my father. "May I be excused?" I ask, hoping he'll say no. Hoping he'll put an end to our game.

He looks at my plate and says, "Finish your milk."

I drink it slowly, then carry everything to the sink and walk to the back door. It's dark outside, the shed just a faint shadow in the corner of the yard, the vast, empty field pitch-black behind it. It's a tiny structure with only one window, the place where my mother keeps her gardening tools. I walk toward it, glancing over my shoulder to make sure Vince isn't following me.

When I step inside, it takes a moment for my eyes adjust to the dark space and then I see it. The bright-yellow Kodak box. Air rushes out of me as relief floods in. This is typical Vince. Never able to talk about his feelings. Never able to apologize in words, he does things like this instead. He makes these gestures that show you all is okay.

I return to the house, holding it up, triumphant. "My eleventh roll of film, and it has sound!"

Danny rolls his eyes. "Great," he says, rising from the table without asking permission. He carries his plate and cup to the sink and sets them down. "Now she can eavesdrop on us too."

Chapter 28

"It's not what you think," my father says. I click my phone closed, the image of his handwritten threat on the wall of Poppy's closet disappearing.

"And what would that be?" I ask.

"It was part of a complicated game Poppy and I played, our version of a treasure hunt. It could last days or even weeks. There was a written puzzle, divided into pieces. Often a poem, though not always. Once you pieced it all together, it would tell you where your prize was hidden." He's warming up to his subject now. "But the clues to *find* the pieces of the poem were spoken aloud. It required you to listen carefully to every word that person said. Each hunt was always around a theme. For example, if the theme was *red things*, you had to listen for any reference to anything that could be red. If I said something about apples, you might look where the apples were kept and find another piece of the puzzle."

I wait for him to allude to the game we seem to be playing now. A hint that I should be paying attention like Poppy needed to, but there's nothing. "Okay," I finally say. "But why write something so threatening?"

He gives a tiny shake of his head. "I didn't mean anything by it at the time. I was just looking for a word that rhymed with 'shed.'"

"Head. Bed. Sled," I suggest. "There are a lot of words that don't threaten your sister."

"You're reading too much into it," he says.

The suggestion makes me frustrated. Angry. Exhausted. Because that's exactly what he wants me to do. "So what was the theme for this one?"

"*Dark places*, I think." He grins, adjusting his thin frame in his chair. "She turned up a lot of secrets on that one. Danny's pot stash. My father's *Playboy* magazines."

"What about your mother? Did she have any secrets?"

The smile falls off his face, just a little bit. "All her dysfunction lived out in the open."

"What do you mean?"

"We weren't easy kids. She spent most of her days with some kind of a low-grade buzz. Alcohol, mostly. But later, after the murders, pills." A wry smile. "I guess you could say I got my coping skills from her."

I feel the shifting sands of being both a ghostwriter and a daughter. Fighting—and sometimes failing—to maintain an objective distance. Because my own memories are tied up in this tapestry that's slowly appearing before me. Threads connecting my story to this one. It's easy, in a way, to keep the focus on what happened to Poppy and Danny. But that doesn't negate the trauma that came before.

It's time to show him the fight with Danny. The way it really happened, not the version that lives inside his mind. Last night I'd gone back and rewatched the clip and then I wrote the scene. But in it, it's not Danny attacking my father, it's my father attacking Danny. Because I have to write the story I can see on film, not the one he's telling.

I pull out my laptop, clicking through until I find the clip I want to show him. *May #4, Clip #9.* The fight which, according to

Poppy's diary, changed everything. The fight my father described yesterday, proving he's an unreliable narrator.

I press Play, and Poppy's room appears. She's sitting on the bed, her camera pointed toward the open doorway. After a few seconds, she stands and moves over to the door, where she sits on the floor, a straight shot down the hall. Like she's waiting for something.

Danny suddenly lurches out of his room, my teenage father tackling him, their bodies slamming into the wall. He kicks at Danny, spit flying from his mouth, his face turning red. It's obvious my father is the aggressor; every time Danny pulls away, my father attacks from another angle.

After about a minute, their mother enters from the left side of the frame, presumably coming from the kitchen. Black trousers and black flats, you can only see the bottom half of her. She brushes past Poppy's camera, and the first time I watched this, I assumed she was going to intervene. But she steps around her battling sons and into the bedroom at the other end of the hallway, closing the door. Danny and my father are now rolling on the floor, each trying to get the upper hand.

Then their father appears. Still wearing his work clothes, though his tie is gone and his shirt collar unbuttoned. He grabs my father and pulls him back. Danny sits up, rubbing his shoulder where my father must have landed a punch, breathing heavily. My father's gaze hits Poppy's camera head-on and sits there for just a few seconds. And in those seconds you can see such a deep sadness, as if whatever the fight had been about had broken him.

I stop the video. "What were you thinking about in that moment?"

It takes my father a few seconds to return to me. "Where did you get this?" I can tell from his tone he didn't expect me to find her movies. That the game has veered out of his control.

"I found them beneath the floorboards of Poppy's closet," I tell him. "I had them transferred to digital."

"How many did you find?"

"Ten," I tell him.

"Only ten?"

"Why?" I ask. "Were there more?"

His gaze snaps back to mine and he shrugs, saying, "I wouldn't know. Poppy was everywhere with that damn camera. When she wasn't behind it, she was begging people for odd jobs so she could buy more film, or pay to process the rolls she'd already shot." I watch the way he shifts in his chair. The way he tries—and fails—to pluck imaginary lint from his pants. The way his gaze jumps from the computer screen to the window to the door, and then back again.

I tap the screen. "This moment. That look on your face."

My father shakes his head. "I don't remember."

"What was the fight about?" I ask, glancing down at my phone to make sure my voice app is still recording.

"I don't even know when this was filmed . . . How should I know?" His tone is combative.

I glance at the closed door, suddenly worried Ama might interrupt us and put an end to our session. And I can't afford to step away now, not when I'm so close.

When people get defensive, I know I've hit something they'd rather not talk about. But those are the places that will yield the most. Not necessarily as a narrative point, but the feelings and emotions behind why people do—or don't do—something helps me understand their mind better. Helps me get their voice right on the page. I want to know what the fight was about because that might also reveal why he doesn't want to tell me.

"According to the label on the reel, it was filmed at the end of May," I say. "What troubles me is that this is the fight you told me about the other day, but what you described isn't what's on the clip." I soften my voice, hoping I don't scare him off. "It wasn't Danny who attacked you, but the other way around."

My father stares at the screen, his younger self frozen in time, crouched on the floor and looking straight into the camera. His father's hand is gripping Danny's shoulder, and neither of them are fully in the frame. I press Play again, and my father launches off the floor and catapults toward Poppy, placing his hand over the lens. That's the end of the clip and the screen goes dark. I close the lid of my laptop to keep him focused on me. "What didn't you want her to see, or hear?"

Again, he says, "I don't know."

"Dad," I say, feeling impatience taking over. How many ways can he still evade and lie to me? The murderous expression on his face in the clip, the graffiti on the wall of Poppy's closet that he claims was a game, none of it makes any sense without knowing the significance of this moment. The one Poppy said changed everything. "This was just a couple weeks before they were killed. Surely you can remember."

He's shaking his head, a tiny motion, as if trying to rid himself of a memory. Then he looks at me, a facsimile of the expression I saw on the screen. Pain. Regret. "Danny couldn't stand to see me happy. Whatever I had, he either wanted it for himself or he destroyed it." He looks out the window of his office. "It might not surprise you to learn that your mother wasn't interested in me at first. She had a crush on Danny, like everyone else. But she and I were friends. She used to tutor me in math, and we'd often do our homework together at my house. One day, we were at the dining room table studying. I looked up and she was smiling at me like she knew a secret. Then she leaned forward and kissed me."

I can imagine the two of them, the kids I've spent countless hours studying, sitting at the now familiar table where my grandmother would play solitaire and drink tea or coffee from a mug. And I imagine my mother's smile, lighting her up from inside, and what that kiss must have meant to my father. The boy no one liked. Who couldn't fit in anywhere.

"Your mother was my first girlfriend, but she'd dated other people before me. Danny liked to toss these little bombs into my life. Pieces of information he knew would upset me, then stand back and watch me explode." My father's voice is quiet, as if he's reaching back in time, trying to get it just right. "He was the one who told me that your mother had been pregnant. That she'd had an abortion."

He can't look at me, as if he doesn't want to see the judgment on my face. The pain he must still feel is evident in his body language—slumped in his chair, defeated.

But the information sinks in—Poppy's suspicion, Margot's doubt—confirmed as fact. "Was the baby yours?" I ask. Even though I think I already know the answer.

He shakes his head.

"Whose was it?" I ask, my voice gentle. Encouraging. But I feel a tickle of unease, because this was a question Poppy had been following and I wonder where it led her.

"I should know, but I don't. Perhaps at one point I did?" he asks, as if I might hold the answer. "But I don't know if she never told me, or if I've just forgotten. But it wasn't mine."

"When did you find out?"

He looks at me, and I can see the answer on his face before he says it. He points to my laptop and says, "That was the moment I found out. Right there. Right then."

Poppy

June 4, 1975

The knife is an eight-inch butcher knife with a steel blade and a black handle. It's always lived in our kitchen; our mother uses it to chop vegetables, to separate ribs when she makes them for dinner, and our father sharpens it every six months, dragging it across a whetstone, saying *a dull knife is much more dangerous than a sharp one*. When it's my turn to wash dishes, I always hold it for a second, letting the weight of it settle into my bones, imagining how easily it could slice through my palm with one careless slip.

But tonight it's Vince's turn at the sink. Danny stands alongside him, tasked with drying. I'd offered to do it instead, but Danny had declined. A few days ago I'd seen them almost kill each other. Now Danny seems to be deliberately stepping into Vince's space every chance he gets. Goading him with his presence.

For five nights now, Vince has refused to sleep in their room, instead choosing the floor in mine. He's also refused to tell me what the fight was about, thought it was easy enough to piece it together. *It's common knowledge that the guy who takes a girl to get an abortion is usually the father.* Danny's taunting voice floating through the wall. And then bodies slamming into each other. Into the walls. The floor. The crash of a lamp as it fell and their fight tumbled into the hallway.

I'd filmed it, not for any purpose other than because it felt important. The breaking of a final thread between them. Vince swears he'll sleep in my room until Danny leaves for college in a year. The only thing I know for certain is that this house isn't big enough for the both of them any longer.

Danny shifts his weight so that his right side is now touching Vince. I wish I was bold enough to go over there and separate them, the way Mrs. Stadler used to do to unruly boys in the lunch line when I was in the fourth grade. But intervention would only make things worse for me. And I don't want to get anywhere near either of them.

As Vince dips the knife into the soapy water, I see Danny grab his arm as if to steady it, but really I know it was to jostle him. To see if he can get Vince to drop the knife. Vince pulls back sharply, holding his hand up, blood blooming on his palm.

"Whoops," Danny says with a grin.

"You fucking cut me."

This is the way things have been with Danny lately. His jokes now have a mean edge to them. They're easy to smile away when adults are around, but when they aren't, his eyes will glitter with malice as he brushes off our feelings.

Toughen up.

Don't take things so seriously.

What did you think I was going to do to you?

Understanding creeps over me. Up until now, I've been the nosy little sister, spying on Vince. Waiting with my camera to catch him doing something wrong. But that's not what a filmmaker would do. A filmmaker would capture the entire story, from all perspectives. There are other players—Lydia. Danny. Mr. Stewart. And now I have a roll of film that can also record their words.

"Don't be such a wimp," Danny says.

"Don't mess with the guy holding the knife," Vince replies, putting his hand under the running water.

I glance toward the living room, to see where our parents are in case I need to call for help. I'm afraid to move though. Afraid to draw attention to myself.

"Tough guy," Danny says, swatting Vincent with the dish towel. "I heard your girlfriend likes it rough."

"Shut up," Vincent says.

"Lydia," Danny says, as if tasting the name in his mouth.

In one smooth motion, Vince turns on him, the knife still in his hand just an inch from Danny's chest, and I imagine what it might feel like to hold that power, for just a moment.

Danny looks down at the tip of the blade, trembling in Vince's hand, an amused expression on his face. "If you're going to pull a knife on me, you'd better be ready to use it."

He tosses the dish towel on the counter and walks out, leaving Vince staring after him, the hot water still running into the sink, a cloud of steam fogging the window behind it.

Chapter 29

It's common knowledge that the guy who takes a girl to get an abortion is usually the father. That's what my father told me Danny had whispered to him, while Joni Mitchell played in the background. The words that had launched him at his older brother. That had them careening in a tangled mess of limbs and half-landed punches into the hallway. That had been the moment Poppy had captured on film—either intentionally or not. Her diary entry: *May 30: Vince/Danny fight. Did he learn the truth??? Everything feels different now. May #4, Clip #9*

I'd asked my father who took my mother for the abortion, but that part seems lost to him as well.

I've spent the last three days revising the chapter about the fight, inserting my father's perspective, and I finally feel the intoxicating momentum of a book underway, moving toward a completed draft. I've also spent time going through the transcripts of my conversations with my father and the notes I wrote after talking with Mark and Margot. I've watched Poppy's movies so many times I've got them memorized.

Then I created a tentative timeline which I've taped to the wall with some old notecards I found in one of the boxes, faded and yellowing around the edges. In February I have the estimated date my parents started dating, and the bonfire in March. In April I have the Pink Floyd concert. I have the abortion sometime in early May, since Poppy was writing about it on May 6. Counting backward, my mother couldn't have gotten pregnant before she started dating my father. It's obvious she cheated on him—but with who isn't clear.

In the middle of May I have the vandalism at the school, which my father still insists wasn't done by him. And on May 30, I have the fight between my father and Danny, the one that revealed the abortion. Then in June, Margot's story about my father threatening Danny with the murder weapon, which makes sense considering what Danny had told my father just days before.

Then I've got the day of the murders, the timeline mapped out as best I can, based on what my father has been able to remember.

3:00—Finish school
5:00—Go to carnival
6:45 – 8:30—Lydia and Vincent meet with Mr. Stewart in the oak grove
7:00–7:45—Time of death
9:15—Bodies are found

I've met with Mark, Margot, and one of the district attorneys on the case. I've heard their version of events, and aside from my mother, Mr. Stewart is the only one I haven't yet talked to. After my conversation with Margot, I did a Google search for him which didn't turn up much. No social media presence, nothing offering me his address or phone number if I paid a fee, making me wonder if he was even still alive. I pick up my phone to call Jack.

"Mr. Stewart?" Jack asks when I tell him what I want to know. "I never had him, but he had a reputation as kind of an old-school lech. Harmless, but out of touch really."

"I don't know what that means," I say.

"It was subtle. Just a vibe he gave off. A gaze that would linger on a chest or an ass just a little too long."

"Is he still alive?" I ask.

"He bops around the downtown area every weekend in his short shorts and tank tops. For an old guy, he's still in pretty good shape. Goes to the gym out on Highway 150 where all the body builders go."

"Do you happen to know how I could reach him?" I ask.

"Let me put you on hold and call my dad. See if he knows."

I hear a click and the hold music from the winery fills my ear, a soothing classical symphony. After about five minutes, Jack's back on again. "You're not going to believe this," he says. "But Mr. Stewart still lives in his old house."

"You're going to have to tell me more, because that doesn't mean anything to me."

"He lived next door at the time of the murders. Apparently, he still lives there."

The neighbor. The older man who'd tried to chase me off. "I think I've already met him. He doesn't seem much older than our parents."

"He's not. Maybe fifteen years? Less? I think he was about fifty when we were in high school."

I think about what Mark told me. The parties. The beer. The pot. Imagining what it must have been like to live next door to a double murder. To wake up every day knowing what had happened there, and deciding to stay.

*　*　*

Mr. Stewart answers when I knock, his expression morphing into suspicion when he sees me. "What can I do for you?"

"My name is Olivia Taylor," I tell him. I wait to see if the name holds any meaning for him, but he just stares at me, waiting. "I'm Vincent Taylor's daughter." I gesture toward the house next door. "Poppy and Danny Taylor were my aunt and uncle. I was hoping you'd have some time to talk with me about my father's family. Or maybe my mother, Lydia. I hear you were her coach?"

He nods and says, "What is it you want to know?"

I gesture toward the living room behind him and say, "Maybe we could sit down?"

He hesitates, then steps aside to let me enter. The furniture is dated but well cared for and I settle on a brown corduroy couch. A flat-screen TV is mounted on the wall, and two wicker chairs flank the ends of the coffee table. On the wall leading to the kitchen is an assortment of photographs.

He gestures toward the kitchen. "Can I get you something to drink? Some water?"

"Water would be great. Thanks."

While he's gone, I stand and wander over to the wall of pictures. Some are old, of Mr. Stewart and former students at their graduations, smiling in caps and gowns. Others are more recent—Mr. Stewart whale watching. Another one of him with a surfboard.

I'd looked him up in the 1975 yearbook at the library before coming over. Shaggy blondish-brown hair. A wide, white smile. Handsome. Definitely better looking than the other PE teachers. Next to them, Paul Stewart exuded youth. Vitality. Charm. I could see why my father might not have loved how much time my mother had spent with him. I stared at his photograph wondering if there could have been more between them. It wasn't impossible to imagine.

He returns, handing me my water. I sit again on the couch, placing my glass on a coaster. He takes a seat in one of the wicker chairs across from me, waiting.

"I apologize for not telling you who I was the other day," I say. "As you can imagine, I'm careful about sharing my name with strangers. Especially in a town where memory is long. I didn't realize you were the same person who'd been living next door at the time my father's family lived there."

"What happened to them was such a tragedy."

I think of my cell phone, tucked into my purse. I'd set it on record before leaving my car, wanting to capture this conversation. Not caring whether I had permission or not. "When did you move in?"

"I bought the house in March 1975. Back when a teacher could afford property." He shakes his head. "The middle class has vanished."

"Did it bother you to live next door to your students?"

"Not at all," he says. "I loved the Taylor kids. Even your dad. He wasn't much of an athlete, but he had a wicked sense of humor."

"My father told me you and my mother were very close."

Mr. Stewart nods, visibly warming up to the subject. "She was a talented runner. She could have gotten a scholarship to a Division I school if things had been different."

"What do you mean?"

"After the murders, she stopped running. Quit the team and withdrew from everything." He looks at me, his expression softening into one of concern. "She loved your father very much.

But to be honest, it seemed unhealthy. I saw very little of them after that. They spent most of their spare time at her house, understandably. Then the Taylors moved."

"Mark Randall told me about a party you had the week of the murders."

Mr. Stewart gives an uncomfortable chuckle. "I used to have a lot of parties, but that was my end-of-the-year celebration. It was something of a tradition at the time. That was the last year I held one of those." He looks down at his hands, then back up at me. "After the murders, I realized I needed to do a better job of being a role model to my students and athletes, and not a friend. I got hired in 1969 when I was only twenty-three. Barely an adult myself. Danny was in my very first outdoor survival skills class. You know, building shelters. Purifying water. That kind of thing. He loved it."

"Did my parents go to the end-of-year party that last year?" I ask, hoping to pull him away from reminiscing about his teaching and back to the week in question.

"Gosh, I don't remember," he says. "There were a lot of kids there."

"Can you tell me about that day?"

"The day of my party?"

I shake my head and wonder if his confusion is feigned. "The day of the murders."

He blows out hard and looks away. "It was the last day of school," he says. "The kids were wild and the teachers were exhausted. Just trying to make it to three o'clock." He gives a quiet laugh. "I came home after school, went for a run, took a shower. My girlfriend at the time, Amelia, made us an early din-ner. She was going out that night with some friends to a local bar. I was going to do a lap through the carnival, maybe eat a funnel cake, and make it an early evening." His voice is low and melodic, but I could imagine it growing in volume as he yelled directions at my mother on the track. Blowing a whistle. Demanding she push herself harder.

"The carnival was held on the high school field and adjacent parking lot. Not a huge space, but it backed up against what's now the preserve, so you got the sense, walking through, of being delivered into a magical fairyland of rides, music, twinkle lights. I got my funnel cake, joked around with some graduating seniors, and then came across your parents in a heated argument near the back of the venue." He pauses, as if remembering the scene. "Your mother was crying. Your father was standing in front of her and I've never seen him so angry. I don't remember exactly what was said, but he was demanding answers and she was crying too hard to give them."

I think about what I know. About what my father had learned just a week or so prior.

"I offered to help, a listening ear, you know? Teenagers are all the same. What they really want is to be heard. To be understood. I probably said something to your dad like *I know what it's like to be in the doghouse. Is there any way I can help?* But he didn't seem inclined to want me around."

"So how did you end up convincing him?" I know the story well—Mr. Stewart, everyone's favorite teacher, helping my parents mediate their argument in the oak grove while back at the house Danny and Poppy are brutally murdered.

"It was Lydia who finally convinced him," he says. "Your father wasn't my biggest fan. I'd tried to befriend him. Tried to show him I meant no harm, that I wasn't a threat to him or his relationship with Lydia. But he never warmed up to me. Danny?

He would steal my beer and leave the broken tabs all over my back porch. Poppy loved to come play with my cat. But Vince never had any use for me."

The mention of the cat draws a chill through me, but I push forward. "So my mother wanted you to mediate and my father agreed?" I ask.

"Reluctantly, but yes. We decided a walk to the oak grove would be far enough away where we wouldn't be interrupted." He's quiet, thinking. Remembering.

"What was their fight about?"

Mr. Stewart becomes guarded. Unsure. "I think maybe it's best if I let your parents tell you about that," he says.

"Was it about my mother's abortion?" I ask. The mask of friendliness slips from his face, just for a second. "My father remembers a fight he had with Danny, where Danny was antagonizing him," I continue. "Telling him about the abortion and that the person who takes a woman to get one is usually the father. Do you know who took her?"

"I did," he says, defiant. "And I have no regrets. She needed a trusted adult and I was glad to be that for her. But the baby was definitely not mine."

I look at him, trying to gauge his truthfulness and he holds my gaze. "Did you know whose it was?" I ask.

His eyes narrow, as if wondering what I'm suggesting. "I assumed it was Vince's, but I didn't ask and she didn't volunteer."

I think again of the words Poppy was too afraid to write in her diary. The way my father attacked his brother, an idea forming. "Do you think it could have been Danny's?"

But Mr. Stewart shakes his head. "I doubt it," he says. "Your mother didn't care for him very much."

"That's not what I heard."

"Trust me. Danny was horrible to your father. He tormented him constantly, and it bothered Lydia. I tried to tell her that was just how brothers were."

"Perhaps it wasn't consensual," I suggest.

"Honestly, I don't see it. She didn't behave in a way that would ever have led me to believe she'd been assaulted."

I have to bite my tongue to keep myself from asking how, exactly, a woman who'd been assaulted should behave. What clues she was supposed to give that would allow others to pick up on her trauma.

He pinches the bridge of his nose. "I'm sorry, but this is still a very painful topic for me."

"Is there anything else you can tell me about that day?"

He shakes his head. "I wish I had more answers for you. I've gone over it again and again over the years. None of it makes any sense."

"I appreciate you taking the time to talk with me," I say, standing.

He walks me to the front door and opens it. "I used to always tell my students 'Information is power.' It's never wrong to seek the answers you need."

"It must be hard for you to still live here and remember that day."

"It's never far from the surface, but time has a way of healing," he says.

I can't help but think that's not the case for everyone. It hasn't healed Mark Randall. It hasn't healed Margot, or my father.

"I've got one last question for you. Obviously, my father wasn't the killer since he was with you and my mother in the oak grove. So who do you think did it?"

Mr. Stewart gives a small shake of his head and says, "I've been asking myself that for almost fifty years. I can't imagine anyone in Ojai wanting to hurt Poppy. Or Danny, for that matter. I think it was the man who picked Poppy up hitchhiking. The timing of it, the fact that he knew about the carnival. It seems likely that he might have returned to find her."

Poppy

June 7, 1975

I walk down the highway, the early morning sun already warming the back of my neck. The highway is deserted at this time of day on a Saturday, and I'd stashed my bike in the bushes, like Vince and Lydia had done when they went to see Pink Floyd. I'd asked my mother if she would drive me into Ventura so I could go to the ERA rally happening at the city college, but she'd said it would be a waste of time.

"Don't you want to have the same rights as Dad?"

"What does that even mean, Poppy?" She'd been rolling up the cord to the iron, tucking it into the hall closet. "Do I want to worry about paying bills? Getting drafted into the next war?" She shook her head. "I don't think you want that either."

"What about financial independence?" I'd pressed, following her into the kitchen. "What if something happens to Dad? At the very least, you should have your own credit card. You can now, you know."

"I'm perfectly happy with the credit card I have," my mother had said. "The one with your father's name works just fine."

I pushed forward. "What if Dad leaves you for a younger woman? What will you do then?"

My mother laughed. "That's why I have three children," she said, pulling a roast out of the refrigerator and setting it on the counter. "One of you will take care of me." Then she turned to look at me. "Poppy, most women don't have the time or the energy to worry about equal rights. We're too busy."

I'd appealed to Margot next. "Let's hitchhike into Ventura," I'd said. We were sitting on her bed, the smell of her mother's famous chocolate chip cookies drifting under the closed door. "We can get to the rally on our own."

Margot looked unsure. "Is that safe?"

"Fear is a tool of the patriarchy," I'd told her. "It's how our parents control where we go and what we do. The majority of people in this world are good."

This was going to be the new Poppy, who wasn't afraid to do big, scary things. I imagined an interview I'd give, years from now, where I'd be asked about what it was like to be a female correspondent, filming important events and conflicts around the world. "I grew up with two older brothers who wanted to kill each other. War zones don't scare me."

*   *   *

A car passes by me now, a whoosh of heat from the asphalt swirling around my ankles and up my bare legs. I hold out my thumb, hoping I look confident. I have five dimes in my sock, in case I get stuck there and need to call home, and my Super 8 in my backpack.

I hadn't planned to do this alone, but Margot had canceled this morning.

"My mom is making me go with her to visit my aunt Gert in Bakersfield," she'd said. "I'm really sorry. I know you wanted to go."

I feel a reckless sort of excitement—no one would expect me to do this alone, and yet this is exactly what I need. I'm sick of people pushing me around, telling me what to do all the time. I need a break from worrying about Vince and Lydia. About Vince and Danny. I wish I could be an only child like Margot. How simple and quiet it would be. I'd have the space to think about the things that matter. That will affect me as an adult.

Another car passes and I wonder whether I'll spend all day out here, sweating on the hot pavement, waiting for someone to pick me up. I'm young and not unattractive. It shouldn't be this hard.

But that car slows down and rolls to a stop. I jog to catch up to it and see a mother behind the wheel, a toddler bouncing on the back seat. She rolls the passenger window down. "You shouldn't be out here on your own," she says. "It isn't safe for a girl."

"I really appreciate the ride," I say, sliding into the front seat. When the door is closed and she's pulled back onto the highway, I turn to her and say, "Don't you get tired of constantly having to live a lesser life then our male counterparts?" I'd read that line in an article about Gloria Steinem. It wasn't something she'd said herself, but I remember feeling a zap of recognition, of realizing I'd been feeling that way without being able to say it aloud.

The woman rolls her eyes and says, "That's the world we live in."

"It doesn't have to be," I insist. "Women have more power than we think we do."

The woman shakes her head. "You have a lot to learn."

"I'm going to be a part of the solution," I tell her, looking forward, to the empty road in front of us, curving out of sight.

*　*　*

The ride back is different. My legs are sore from standing all day. The woman—her name had been Muriel—had dropped me three miles from the rally site and I'd had to walk there.

But it had been incredible. To be in a crowd of women, all of us chanting—no *demanding*—equal pay and equal rights had been intoxicating. The speakers made me feel as if anything were possible, as if we were standing at the edge of a new era. One that would raise women and girls to equal standing. I'd been moved to tears at one point, thinking how lucky I was to be living in this moment.

But now, as I stand next to the on-ramp of the freeway heading east, all I feel is exhausted. And a little scared. One person had already stopped for me—a man in a black pickup truck, his shaggy beard streaked with gray. I'd waved him on and he'd shrugged, his tires throwing gravel back at me as he sped up and disappeared. I reminded myself that I had five dimes in my sock and could call home. Maybe I'd get lucky and Danny would answer. He could borrow Mark's car and come and save me.

I've just decided to give it twenty more minutes when a station wagon slows to a stop. A middle-aged man with glasses and a pocket protector leans over and rolls down the window. "Where are you headed?"

He's balding in that embarrassing way where men think they can hide it by combing their hair in a different direction. I was hoping for someone like Muriel to stop again. Maybe another rally goer. But I've been standing out here for almost an hour and my mother will go ballistic if I don't get home in time for dinner.

He looks about my father's age and could be someone's dad. "Ojai, if you're going that far."

He nods and says, "I can make that work."

* * *

His name is Craig and he doesn't get creepy until the end. "Where should I drop you, Poppy?"

His gaze lingers a little too long and I can practically feel it crawl over me—my legs, stomach, chest. I look out the window at the empty road, no houses visible in any direction, and realize how alone I am. I think fast. "My dad is picking me up at school."

To my relief, he follows my directions through town, passing my street, and I catch a glimpse of our car in the driveway. We pull into the high school lot where trucks are parked, unloading things for the carnival set to open on Friday.

"You want me to wait with you?" Craig asks. His voice feels slimy and gross. "Some of these carnies aren't safe."

"I'm good," I say, popping open my door.

"I'd love to see you again," he says. He reaches out and brushes a finger over my bare knee and I leap out, slamming the door quickly. A few carnies glance at me as they carry equipment from a flat-bed truck onto the football field.

"Thanks for the ride," I call, my mother's manners drilled into me.

He toots the horn twice. "Maybe I'll come back for the carnival," he calls out his open window. "I'll look for you."

I give a tight-lipped smile and wait until he's turned the corner before bolting toward the line of trees and home.

Chapter 30

After my conversation with Mr. Stewart, I decide to take a walk through the preserve to the high school, imagining Poppy being dropped there after the ERA rally. Thinking about the story Margot had shared about the creepy man who'd driven her home and wondering if the police had it right all along. It's feasible that despite Margot and Mark insisting my father was lying, their feelings are clouded by the conflict my father was having with Danny at the time.

It's deserted today and I take the trail toward the pond, a gorgeous expanse of water that wasn't put in until long after I left Ojai. I try to imagine the meandering paths Poppy and her siblings would have worn down and followed through the weeds and tall grasses. To visualize the trees in a wilder context. But I can't. The conservation group has done a wonderful job of saving this land for local wildlife habitats, and the old acreage now only exists in the memories of people who once lived here and on Poppy's movies.

When I finally return to my car, I notice I have several texts from friends I haven't heard from in months.

You're working again??? Tell me more!
Good for you!
Fuck John Calder.

And one from Nicole, with a link. Call me ASAP.

The link takes me to John Calder's latest social media post. Good news that a certain writer is back to work, since she owes me a lot of money. I look forward to taking a vacation on her advance.

That motherfucker.

I pull away from the curb as my phone rings. Nicole. I turn it off, not wanting to talk until I know exactly how this happened.

When I get back to my father's house, I head straight upstairs to his office. He and Alma are out at another one of his appointments, and I crash into his chair, logging into his computer, the saved password allowing me access to his in-box once again. I see my last message to him—The book is under contract and I'm happy with its progress. I'm afraid that's where we need to leave things. And then Calder's response. I have some ideas about that.

I take take a moment, trying to calm down. To quell the rage that has risen up inside of me. Calder's *idea* is to make it look as though I'm talking about the book so that they'll fire me.

I try out several responses:

Drop dead, asshole. I delete the words.

Please do not contact me again. No.

This is Olivia Dumont. I could sue you for what you're trying to do. Again, I delete the words.

I guess I don't hear the door open downstairs because suddenly, my father is behind me. "What's going on? Why are you sitting at my desk?"

I point to the computer screen. "Calder is trying to pitch you for the book."

I scoot back so he can see the email on the screen before remembering that he can't read it. Calder has been emailing into a black hole, and if I'd never responded, his pitch would have gone nowhere. But that doesn't negate what he's trying to do now.

"How would he have found out?" my father demands. "Did you tell him?"

I hold my hands up, embarrassed to see them shaking. "I haven't told anyone anything about the book," I say, swallowing hard. Knowing that's not true. I've told Jack.

I mentally run through everyone I've interviewed, confirming to myself that none of them could have figured it out. "It wasn't me," I say again. Then I tell him about Tyler Blakewood, the man who thought they should have gone with Calder originally.

"And since you haven't shown any interest, Calder is now trying to get me fired." I read the post aloud, the one that sent a flurry of texts, emails and calls to my phone before I turned it off. "'Good news that a certain writer is back to work, since she owes me a lot of money. I look forward to taking a vacation on her advance.'"

"I'll kill him," my father says. I give him a sharp look and he says, "Calm down. I'm speaking figuratively."

I glance back at Calder's email on the screen. "What should we do? Do you want to respond?"

My father thinks for a moment, an expression I know well blooming across his face. The one he'd get when he was planning something fun. Or diabolical. Or both. "Draft this," he tells me. "*Loved the book you did on Mac Murray. I was sad when he passed away.*" I type the words, wondering where this is going. "*I knew him for years,*" my father continues, "*and considered us close but never knew about the Guatemalan orphanage. What a revelation.*" He thinks a bit more and then says, "Send it."

I do, and look at him, waiting for him to explain. "Mac Murray was a famous filmmaker. Mostly documentaries, but sometimes he'd branch into indies."

"I know who Mac Murray was, Dad."

"Mac was known for a lot of things—his talent behind the camera, but also his partying. We spent a lot of weekends together that I won't go into detail about. However, not a lot of people knew that Mac was also a horrible racist." My father shakes his head. "He put up a good front in public—working in the industry he had to, or risk getting passed over for jobs. But one time, he went on this rant about immigrants flooding into the country, about them taking our jobs. He hated everything and everyone south of the border."

"Nice friends, Dad."

He shrugs off my words. "He had good drugs. But the Guatemalan orphanage Calder wrote about? The trips Mac supposedly made every year?" He shakes his head. "They never happened."

The email pings with Calder's response. "Read it," my father demands.

"*As I said before, I can do the same to rehab your image.*"

My father gives a bark of a laugh. "Rehab my image by making shit up."

"Are you absolutely positive Calder lied in the book?"

My father looks smug. "I'm not the only one who's good at writing fiction." Then he nods toward the computer and says, "Send this to Monarch: *It has come to my attention that Tyler Blakewood has spoken to John Calder about the existence of this book. I expect Mr. Blakewood to be taken off this project immediately.*"

Just as we're finishing up, my phone buzzes with another text, Tom's name appearing on the screen. Something white hot passes through me and I reach out to cover the screen.

"Who's that?" my father asks.

I turn the phone upside down and say, "No one."

He raises an eyebrow. "Doesn't seem like no one to me, based on the way your shoulders flew up into your ears."

I close out his email and put his computer to sleep, then swivel to face him. "Thanks to this job, he's now my ex."

"Explain to me how the book has anything to do with your relationship. That seems a stretch," he says.

"The secrecy," I say. "My inability to tell anyone why I'm here or what I'm working on."

My father shakes his head. "I'll bet dollars to doughnuts you never told your boyfriend who your family even is." He tips his head to one side and says, "Let me guess . . . you're a poor orphan whose parents died tragically. What was it, a plane crash? A car accident?"

I look away. "A heart attack," I mumble. "And cancer."

My father barks a laugh. "Smart. Nothing newsworthy anyone can google." But then he looks at me with sad eyes and says, "You want me to be vulnerable, but you can't even do that yourself."

"I'm not the one who has to write a memoir," I shoot back.

"No, you just have to live your life. And you'll live it alone if you can't figure out how to be honest."

"That's rich, coming from you," I tell him. When he doesn't take the bait, I continue. "Besides, there are worse things. Like being sued by a misogynist and losing my career. Like having to sell my home. Or dying a slow death where you lose control of your body."

I expect my father to agree. He'd never remarried or dated anyone seriously after my mother left, claiming he didn't have time for relationships. But he shakes his head and said, "There's nothing better than being truly seen—truly known by another person. I would like you to have that someday."

He nods toward my phone. "Read the text."

It's another link to Calder's post and a statement. Once again, I don't know what to believe.

I look up at my father. "It's nothing important," I tell him. Solitude is my lot in life. Those seeds were planted by my parents long ago, and it's futile to think I would grow into something different.

"Why did Mom leave?" I ask.

My father looks as surprised as I feel at the question. We'd never discussed it. When I was little, I was too afraid to ask, for fear of upsetting him. And as I got older, I'd convinced myself I didn't care.

"Your mother struggled a lot with depression," he says, his voice resigned. "In fact, she reminded me of my own mother, spending days in bed, unable to get up to do the most basic functions of caring for you. For me."

"Did she drink like your mother?" Because I'd been so young when she left, I doubted any habits like that would have registered with me.

But my father shakes his head and says, "No. Never. She hated feeling out of control."

"What about therapy? Medication? Surely there were solutions other than abandoning her only child."

"She tried medication for a while. But back then, the only ones available left her feeling like a zombie." He looks down at his hands. "Believe me. She was heartbroken to leave. But we both felt it was best."

"I grew up without a mother because you thought it would be best? My whole life, I thought she didn't love me or want me. Do you know what that does to a person?"

He's silent for a moment, but when he speaks again, his voice is quiet. "When you get to be my age, there will be many moments—many decisions—you'll wish you could go back and make again. Choose a different path. That's one of mine."

I stare at him, wondering what good it does me to know that now. To understand that he feels regret without actually having to make amends for any of it.

* * *

Back in the guesthouse, I collapse onto the bed, exhausted from the day. It seems ages ago I sat across from Mr. Stewart and listened to him defend himself about taking my mother for an abortion. About his denial that he was the father. But before I can get to work transcribing the interview and figuring out how it all fits into the narrative of that time, I need to call Nicole.

Even though it's late in New York, she picks up right away. "Jesus, Olivia. Where have you been? We've got a situation here."

"I know," I tell her.

"How in the hell did Calder find out? This isn't good."

I tell her about the email he sent to my father, pitching the book. And the confirmation that Tyler Blakewood had been the leak. "My father and I emailed Neil and Sloane tonight about it."

The words are out of my mouth before I can pull them back. I hear an intake of breath and Nicole says, "Hold up. Your *father*?"

My stomach twists and I close my eyes, wishing I could hang up and pretend this call never happened. I'd love to blame John Calder for the slip, but the truth is, the fault is mine for keeping such a monumental secret from my agent for so long. "I haven't been honest with you about a couple things," I say. Not the best start, but maybe I can get her to understand the complicated history of my relationship with my father and my family history. Maybe I can get her to understand why I haven't told anyone who I am.

So I start talking. Telling her what my father was like when I was young. The treasure hunts. The two of us against the world after my mother left. How I first heard about Danny and Poppy, and my father's slow unraveling over the decades. The rift and my desire to cut him out of my life completely. When I'm done, I say, "I'm sorry I didn't tell you the truth."

She's silent for a moment and I wonder just how angry she is. How badly I've betrayed the trust we've built between us over the years. Finally she says, "I can understand your hesitancy. Your desire to cut ties. But we need to disclose this to Monarch."

I panic. "They can't pull me off the book. This is my family. My story to tell, and to be honest, I don't think my father will talk to anyone else."

"You misunderstand me," she says. "Olivia, this is explosive. The only child of Vincent Taylor, a famous ghostwriter in her own right, returned home to reveal the secrets he's kept for decades. This is marketing gold."

I hadn't really thought that far. Up until now, it had been made clear to me that this would be one of those projects where everyone believed the subject wrote the book himself. My father—at one point—was certainly capable of that. But I can see what Nicole is saying. This collaboration is too good to conceal.

"This is going to be huge, Olivia," Nicole continues. "This is going to make that thing with John Calder seem like a tiny grain of sand in your shoe."

"Speaking of John Calder," I say. Then I tell her about the Mac Murray book. "I'm sure my father would be happy to connect with the Books editor at the *New York Times*. They're old friends."

Nicole laughs. "I think we can quietly arrange that," she says. But then she sighs. "Even though it would be great to see that man get what he deserves, you're still going to have to pay him. Though the good news is that you probably won't have to sell your house to do it."

A flutter of joy passes through me as I imagine calling Renee. Telling her to take the house off the market. And then my mind lands on Tom, and how he will feel when this information goes public. When he reads about it in the paper or on social media, and how he will feel betrayed all over again. "I need my connection to this project to stay quiet until I finish the manuscript," I tell Nicole.

"I don't know, Olivia. The marketing team will need some lead time to change their strategy. To start pitching it right away . . ."

"Please," I tell her, an idea forming in my mind. Of a way to give Tom the entire truth, all at once. In a format I can control. "Let me just get to the end of this story."

Nicole sighs, thinking. "Fine," she says. "But can we say no later than end of May?"

That's only six weeks. It's going to have to be good enough. "I can work with that," I tell her.

"So on that note, tell me how things are going," Nicole asks. "Neil seems pretty happy with the chapters you've sent so far, and I agree, they're good. Very atmospheric. And yet, sort of heartbreaking too."

"The films are really helping set the tone," I tell her. "Not just recounting the events on them, but the glimpses I'm getting of Ojai in 1975. The cars. Clothes. The vibe."

"How many reels are there?" she asks.

"Only ten. They begin shortly after she gets the camera for her birthday in early March, but unfortunately end about a week before the murders. We don't have anything after June 5th. The camera was lost shortly after that."

"What happened to it?" Nicole asks.

I stare at the clutter of boxes that still surround me, the windows dark. "No one knows," I tell her. "She had the camera one day, and the next it was gone."

Poppy

June 10, 1975

I crash through the trees, no longer trying to be quiet, fear hot in my chest. Behind me, I can hear my brother coming after me. The rasp of his breath, a grunt as he leaps over a log in his quest to reach me. To punish me for what I've just seen.

My camera is still in my hand, still filming. When he saw me, I jumped up and took off, terrified of what he would do if he caught me. I fly past the giant eucalyptus we used to call Big Ben and around the stump of a small one that Vince chopped down with a machete when he was eight.

My legs are burning but I don't slow down. The edge of the field is just ahead. If I can make it to our yard, I might be safe. But as I reach the clearing, he slams into me from behind, sending me sprawling forward and landing hard on the ground, causing me to bite my tongue.

"Give it to me," he says, grabbing my arm, my wrist, fighting me off with his other hand. I'm kicking him, trying to land something that will cause him to take a step back, to give me an opening into which I can slip past him. To save myself. To save my camera. But he's bigger than me. Stronger.

I roll onto my back and start kicking him again, but he pins my legs by kneeling on them, pressing me into the ground with his weight. I squirm to get out from under him, but his grip is so tight I feel the blood pounding in my head and wonder if he might cut off my oxygen next. "Get off me," I say, but my voice sounds like it's coming from far away. "Stop it, Danny."

He wrenches my camera from my hand, twisting two of my fingers in the process. Then he stands and hurls it into the trees, a distant crash as it hits one and shatters.

I rise from the ground and start to go into the trees to retrieve it, but he yanks me by the arm toward the house instead. I cast one last look back at the trees, trying to remember the direction it flew, hoping to figure out where it might have landed so I can go back to get it.

Danny shoves me through the back door, down the hall, and into his bedroom, closing the door behind us.

I turn on him, still tasting blood in my mouth, my elbows aching where they hit the ground, my knees stinging. "Danny," I say, thinking of the way he used to laugh—big and loud—and the way it would fill me up, like helium until I felt like I might fly. When was the last time he'd laughed like that?

"Not a fucking word," he hisses.

"How long?" I ask.

"None of your goddamn business."

I take a step toward him.

"Don't look at me that way," he says.

"What way?" I want to reach out. To touch his arm. Show him I'm on his side—even though he destroyed my camera.

"Like that," he says. "You can't tell anyone."

"It's wrong," I say.

We stare at each other, a silent standoff, the magnitude of his secret passing between us. And yet, so many confusing thoughts are swirling around inside of me. Things I believed to be true that aren't. And my camera, smashed somewhere out there in the field behind our house.

"You're bleeding," he says, pointing to my knee. A trickle of blood travels from a cut down my shin. He hands me a tissue and I mop it up.

"If you don't tell someone," I say, "I will."

"If you do, I'll fucking kill you." I can tell by the expression on his face that he means it.

"Danny you have to tell."

"Get out," he says.

I leave, my entire body feeling like one giant bruise. I nearly run into Vince, standing just outside the door and I hesitate, wondering how much he heard.

"What was that all about?" he asks.

I can't look at him. Terrified if I do, I'll tell him everything.

"Nothing," I say.

He grabs my arm and yanks me down the hall, away from Danny. "What did he tell you?" he demands.

"You're hurting me. Stop." But his fingers only squeeze tighter, his expression intent.

"I have a right to know if it was about me," he says.

I yank my arm from his grip, rubbing it. Wishing I were bigger. Stronger, so I could fight back. I'm sick of my brothers pushing me around. "You only wish it was about you," I say, and then I push past him and out the back door again, hoping my camera isn't completely ruined. Determined to put that film somewhere safe until I can convince Danny to tell the truth.

Vincent

June 11, 1975

I'm watching television with Lydia, the two of us sitting side by
side on the couch pretending everything is normal. But inside,
I'm vibrating. I can't eat. For the past week I I haven't been able
to sleep. I want to stand in the middle of the room and scream,
What the fuck did you do? But instead, I sit here, pretending to
watch a stupid game show.

It feels like it's been a year since Danny had whispered, *It's
common knowledge that the guy who takes a girl to get an abortion is usually the father*, and since then I've been at a low sim-
mer. Lashing out at Poppy. My parents. I'm barely able to look
at Lydia.

Suddenly, Poppy bursts through the front door, dumping her
backpack on the floor and heading into the kitchen.

My mother is at the dining room table, playing solitaire and
nursing a mug of what she says is *tea*, but is really wine. "Backpack," she calls, but Poppy ignores her. My mother sighs, flipping over a card, and takes a sip from her mug. "Honestly, I don't
know what's gotten into that girl. Hitchhiking into Ventura? She
could have gotten herself killed."

"She's mad she lost her camera," I say. Even to my own ears,
I sound like a robot. Like I'm playing the part in some big pro-
duction of *Guy Who's Too Chickenshit To Confront His Cheating
Girlfriend.*

My mother looks up from her card game, shocked. "At that rally? Did someone take it from her?"

"No, I think it happened yesterday."

My mother sniffs with disapproval. "I told your father she was too young for something so expensive but he never listens to me."

The front door opens again, and Margot enters, out of breath. "Is Poppy here?"

My mother gestures toward the kitchen wordlessly and Margot disappears, the two girls' voices floating through the open doorway.

"I'm not going," Poppy says.

"You have to," Margot pleads. "Everyone will be there. It's the last week of school and Mr. Stewart invited everyone."

Lydia looks at me. "Are you going to Mr. Stewart's end-of-year party tonight?" Her tone is cautious. As if one wrong word might launch me into a tirade. As if I'm a bomb that has to be handled carefully.

Mr. Stewart had invited all of us this afternoon while he washed his car in the driveway. "Burgers, sodas, a way to close out the school year. Everyone's welcome."

Without looking at Lydia, I say, "Can't. I have to rewrite my term paper for world history or I'll fail the class." I try to keep my tone casual and ask, "Are you going to go?"

She shrugs, looking unsure. As if my question might be a trap. "I might stop by," she says. "I kind of feel like I have to. He's been so nice training me these past few months."

"You don't *have* to do anything," I tell her.

*   *   *

Lydia and I finish the show we're watching, the sky growing dark and the sounds of the party next door growing louder. Music floats in through the open windows and Poppy and Margot have disappeared somewhere. Lydia stands. "I'd better get home. Let you get to that paper."

My mother has abandoned her card game and is now in the kitchen making dinner, the bottle of chardonnay now nearly empty on the counter. The front door swings open and my father greets us, his suit looking limp from the heat of the day. He sets his briefcase down by the door and hangs his hat on the hat stand. "Nice to see you, Lydia."

"Hi, Mr. Taylor."

"Are you staying for dinner, or are you going to the party next door? Looks like every kid in town is over there."

"I need to be getting home," Lydia says. I can feel her glancing at me, though I keep my eyes trained on the floor in front of me. "My mother's expecting me."

"Give her my regards," he says.

Lydia moves in for a hug, but I sidestep around her, opening the door and holding it for her.

"What's the matter with you?" she whispers.

"You should get home," I say.

Pain and confusion flicker across her face, but she tucks her hair behind her ear and descends the stairs slowly, as if hoping I'll call her back. Fat chance. Not after what she's done.

I've been picturing it on a loop in my mind. Lydia walking into the clinic, Mr. Stewart holding her purse while she went into the back. I'm not great at math, but I can add and subtract. And I know she got pregnant after we started dating because I also sat through that mandatory health class last year. The one where Nurse Monahan told us twelve weeks was the cutoff for a safe abortion, but abstinence was the safest choice. The only one Lydia's abstained with is me.

The party next door is in full swing, kids spilling over to the front yard. A pile of skateboards have been abandoned next to the driveway and two senior girls sit on Mr. Stewart's front steps, smoking, while Clapton plays in the background. All the windows are open and I can see a few kids in his living room, lounging on his couch.

Back inside, my father is saying, "Let's go to Ventura on Friday night. Catch a movie and miss the first night madness of the carnival."

I wander into my room and shut the door, sitting at my desk, thinking of the way Danny and Poppy came crashing into the house yesterday. The urgent whispers behind Danny's closed door. The way Poppy could barely look at me afterward, as if she didn't want me to see how pathetic she thought I was.

I stare at my notebook, willing myself to open it. Trying not to imagine Lydia circling the block and returning to Mr. Stewart's party. Cracking open a beer and watching as Mr. Stewart flips burgers on the grill and pretends there isn't something more between them.

Poppy

June 11, 1975

I've never been drunk before. Sure, I've stolen some sips of my father's watered-down gin and tonic when it's my turn to do the dishes. But I've never been spinning, lurching drunk. Until tonight.

Margot had finally convinced me to go to Mr. Stewart's party, and I decided the only way I could get through it was to numb myself with beer. Mr. Stewart wasn't even watching as I opened up the cooler and bypassed the sodas, grabbing a Coors instead. It was gross, but as soon as I finished one, I started another.

I can see now why Danny likes to drink. It gives you a floaty, buzzy feeling that makes all your worries seem far away and blurry. Like you can almost not see them anymore.

I stand in the backyard, off to the side and watch, my hands missing the weight of my camera. The safety I had behind the lens. I can still feel it, twisting out of my fingers, my elbows bruised from where I hit the ground. I'd told Margot I'd lost it, which is technically true because when I went back to get it, it was gone.

There are about fifty kids scattered in groups talking and laughing. Some middle school boys are roughhousing with each other and another one is dancing in a circle, holding his soda high over his head. Mr. Stewart stands at the grill flipping burgers, his hi-fi system blasting "Shining Star" by Earth, Wind & Fire through the open windows.

"The next batch of burgers will be done in five," he calls out to the crowd.

I turn to say something to Margot, but she's disappeared into the house somewhere. I glance again at Mr. Stewart before edging along the side of the yard and heading up the back steps into the kitchen. I stumble at the doorway and catch myself, dropping my nearly empty beer can into the grass before entering. A group of girls are gathered, talking to Mr. Stewart's girlfriend, Amelia, who is arranging cut vegetables on a tray. "Hi there, Poppy," she says, smiling.

I ignore her, trying to walk a straight line through the kitchen and into the living room, where Margot is seated on the couch talking to a boy from my English class. Steve? Sam? I spot an open beer on the coffee table and grab it, slugging down the warm dregs before anyone can stop me. I need to maintain my distance.

Margot gives me a worried look and says, "Check out these photo albums, Poppy. Here's one of Danny when he was in Mr. Stewart's outdoor group."

I step forward and look down, the photograph black and white behind the plastic. A group of boys, some without shirts, stand in front of a tent. Mr. Stewart is in the back, Danny on the end, a half smile on his face. I struggle to focus my eyes, the image wobbling, making me feel seasick.

One of the girls on the couch says, "I wish he'd do a girls' trip into the woods. I wouldn't mind being in a tent with Mr. Stewart."

The others laugh. I look up at the group of them, lounging in Mr. Stewart's living room, feet up on Mr. Stewart's coffee table. One girl smokes a cigarette and blows her smoke out the open window. I give a sharp laugh that sounds more like a sob. "Why are you all here?" I ask, but when I turn to find Margot, I lose my balance. I sit down hard on a chair and close my eyes. But that makes the room spin even more so I open them again.

Margot has disappeared. I look around, peering down the dark hallway that must lead to Mr. Stewart's bedroom. His bathroom. Two closed doors but no Margot.

I push myself to standing and walk over to a wall of photographs. Mr. Stewart in college, wearing a track jersey. Mr. Stewart and Amelia on a beach somewhere. Mr. Stewart and a man I don't recognize, arms slung around each other at the Eiffel Tower.

Margot appears again next to me and says, "I think you should go home."

"I didn't even want to come to this party," I say.

Vince appears on my other side and I reach out to touch his cheek but he pulls back. "This is a dark space, Vince. Did you hide a clue here?" I laugh at my joke, but he doesn't laugh with me. "You shouldn't be here," I tell him.

My words slide into the silence between tracks as Mr. Stewart appears in the doorway "Burgers are ready," he announces.

Then his gaze lands on me. "You okay, Poppy?"

Anger and betrayal swirl around inside of me. I don't want Vince here to see this. He can't know the truth. "Not really," I say, the alcohol making me feel brave. I sway a little bit and Margot steadies my elbow.

The sound of breaking glass and rising laughter floats through the open windows. From the kitchen Amelia calls, "Paul, you'd better get back out there!"

Mr. Stewart ignores her. "I'm worried, Poppy." He gestures toward the closed-off portion of the house. "Do you want to go somewhere private to talk about what's bothering you?"

One of the girls on the couch mutters, "You can take me somewhere private."

The other girls explode into laughter, but Mr. Stewart ignores them, keeping his gaze on me.

"What is it you always say?" I challenge him. "'Information is power.'" I watch him, to see if he hears me. To see if he knows what I know. "What about when you know a secret? Is that power too?"

Our eyes lock for a moment before my stomach heaves and I turn, vomiting into a potted plant.

The girls scatter and Vince says, "I'll take her home."

"I think that's probably best," Mr. Stewart says.

Vince and Margot gather on either side of me and usher me out the front door and down the steps. We walk along the side of our house and ease open the back door, avoiding the living room where my parents are watching TV. They're in their usual spots—our father in his chair, a gin and tonic next to him, our mother on the couch, her stockinged feet curled under her, poking away at her needlepoint, somewhere into her second bottle of wine.

We sneak past the kitchen and into my room. I kick off my shoes and crawl under my covers, not caring about my clothes. Not caring about anything.

"I've got it from here," Vince says to Margot.

She slips out the back door again, no doubt heading home. Vince goes into the kitchen and returns with a glass of water and some aspirin. "Take these," he says.

I turn toward the wall, unable to look at him. Afraid of what I'll say. The room spins and I worry I'll throw up again, so I take deep breaths, trying to focus on one spot.

Vince hovers beside me. "What was that about?" he asks.

I need to sleep. I need to drop into a dark hole and not dream. Not think of anything. I can't find the words to tell Vince the truth, but I can offer him a warning.

"Lydia needs to stay away from Mr. Stewart." I roll over and look at my brother standing over me.

He takes a small step backward, as if my words have hit him and he says, "What do you mean?" He looks scared. Worried. And I wonder if he already knows.

I shake my head but the motion makes me sick so I close my eyes instead.

Chapter 31

I find it in the last legal pad, just one short sentence tucked in near the end.

Danny watched her die.

I feel as though I've been punched. The matter-of-factness of the statement, the words, scrawled in the lower-left margin in black ballpoint pen. So easy to miss if you weren't looking closely.

I'd finally returned to my father's legal pads after several weeks away, slowly making my way through them. Trying to extract nuggets of information I could use—either specific events I could grow into a scene, or pieces of their lives that would make them come to life. The kind of music Danny listened to. The way Poppy liked to sit on the floor to do her homework.

Then I'd decided to collate all the margin notes, assigning meaning where I could.

I had to bury Ricky Ricardo quickly—the neighbor's cat.

The darkest places to hide: storage shed, Poppy's closet, attic, garage—the treasure hunt.

I wanted to kill Danny—the discovery of my mother's abortion.

But this one—*Danny watched her die*—can only mean one thing. My father had been there too.

* * *

"What can you tell me about this line?" I ask the following morning, pulling the last legal pad out of my bag and flipping to the page

I marked with the Post-it. I read it aloud to him. "'Danny watched her die.'" Then I look up at him, waiting.

His face is a mask I can't read. He's not surprised, or angry. Surely he expected me to find the clues eventually, just like I found the clues in my book so long ago.

When he doesn't say anything, I continue. "You've given me a lot to work with. Lots of stories that will help me reshape what you've already written." I speak carefully, not wanting to upset him, knowing how easily that could happen—even before his illness. "Lots of ways to help Danny and Poppy come alive again on the page. But at the start of this, you said there were things you never told the police."

My father stares at me, waiting for me to go on. Perhaps knowing where I'm headed.

"Tell me what you meant by that line."

He shakes his head. "I don't know." But his voice is weak, as if he can't muster enough force to speak at full volume. "I don't remember."

"You keep telling me that Danny had been the one escalating, but that's not what I'm seeing in Poppy's movies." I gesture toward my computer, my voice rising. "A finished draft of this book is due in less than eight weeks and I'm not even close to being done. I can't do my job if you're not honest with me."

Every project has this moment. When I have to push across the abyss—go from the easy stories to the harder ones. The ones that live inside all of us but don't ever come out. "We've talked a lot about the dynamics in the house. The rising tensions between you and Danny in particular." I breathe out slowly. "You brought me here to do a job, and part of that job is asking hard questions. So I'm going to ask you a hard one and I need you to trust me with the truth. And then together, we can decide what to do with it."

He gives a tiny nod.

"Was your alibi a lie? Were you at the house that night?"

"Yes." His voice is quiet. Steady. As if he's been waiting for me to ask that question all this time. He looks at me, his cheeks sunken as if ravaged by grief. "But I wasn't on time. By the time I got there, it was too late."

Vincent

June 13, 1975

6:15 p.m.

I'm making my way through the maze of the haunted house, looking for Poppy. I'd seen her enter just seconds before I had, but she's vanished. A low anxiety has been buzzing inside of me all afternoon. I'd finally confronted Lydia earlier at her house.

"I know what you did." I stood next to the kitchen counter while Lydia cut an apple.

She'd looked up at me, confused, the knife still in her hand. "What do you mean?"

"I know you cheated on me. I know you got pregnant and had an abortion." The words rushed out of me, hot and fast, making my stomach feel hollow.

She'd stared at me, color draining from her cheeks, and I could tell she was considering denying everything. But before she could come up with a story I pushed on. "Don't make it worse by lying."

She set the knife down, the apple forgotten, and covered her face with her hands. I felt frozen, unable to step toward her, unable to walk away. Through her tears, she said, "I love you."

I nearly laughed. "You have a great way of showing it. Who is the father?"

She looked up at me, surprised, as if she couldn't believe I didn't already know.

"I need you to say it."

Just then, her mother came through the front door, the sickly sweet smell of Jean Nate perfume wafting in with her. "Did you get dinner started, Lydia?" she asked, dropping her purse on the dining room table and collapsing into a chair.

Lydia wiped her eyes quickly, put on a bright smile, and said, "I was just about to."

"This isn't over," I'd said as I left.

"Later," she'd promised me.

But first I need to find out what Poppy knows. She'd finally kicked me out of her room yesterday, claiming there wasn't enough space for the both of us, but I could tell it was something else. The way she wouldn't meet my gaze when she spoke, busying herself with folding clothes. Making her bed. Things Poppy never did on her own.

I feel pulled in opposite directions. I need Lydia to tell me the fucking truth. But I also need to know what, exactly, Danny had told Poppy. Why Poppy had said, *You have to tell,* before bursting out of the room she'd been in with Danny and looking at me like she knew something I didn't. What her drunken warning had been about. And I need to know before I talk to Lydia again, because I'm not sure she'll tell me the truth.

Loud music plays from hidden speakers, punctuated with recorded screams, and every turn of the cheaply constructed wooden structure brings some new surprise, its insides partitioned into several narrow paths that wind back and forth in order to give people more opportunities to be scared. A zombie with blood dripping down his chin that pops up from behind a barrel. A straw-stuffed body suspended from a wire, flying down from above, a mummy rising from a coffin, its bandages peeling away to reveal decomposing flesh. In all the years of the carnival, no one has ever thought how stupid it is to have a haunted house at a carnival held in June.

I find a shortcut and tuck myself in a corner near the exit to wait for Poppy, Danny's taunting words still pulsing through me. *It's common knowledge that the guy who takes a girl to get an abortion is usually the father.* That had been what had catapulted me off my bed, hands outstretched, reaching for Danny's neck. Trying to strangle those words out of him, even though they'd been living inside of me since I saw Lydia and Mr. Stewart together at the Pink Floyd concert. The way he put his hand on her lower back, guiding her. The concern on his face. How close they stood to each other, as if they shared a secret. The light from his dashboard illuminating his face when he dropped her off after taking her to some clinic in Ventura or Bakersfield. Had he been apologizing? Telling her it could never happen again? Insisting that it was over between them, or telling her it was just beginning?

Poppy appears and I grab her, pulling her into my corner, blocking her with my body so she can't slip away. "You scared the crap out of me, Vince. What are you doing?"

I tighten my grip on her arm and say, "Tell me what you and Danny were fighting about."

Poppy takes a step toward the exit. "I don't know what you're talking about."

I jerk her back and she winces. "Don't lie to me."

She shakes her head and says, "This isn't your problem."

"It is my problem. It involves me too."

Surprise splashes across her face and then it crumbles, tears filling her eyes. Voices of people entering the haunted house float back to us over the recorded sound of a woman screaming from the speakers every thirty seconds.

I'm done waiting. Done with being the only person who doesn't know the truth. I shove my sister, pinning her against the wall. Her eyes widen, terrified. Somewhere inside of me, I know I don't need to do it this way. I know my sister will tell me what I need to know. But I can no longer separate my rage at what Lydia has done and my frustration that everyone seems to know except me. It has bled out into the world, seeping into every relationship. Every thought. Every moment.

"You're hurting me," she says, her voice cracking over the words.

"Then tell me," I say.

"Meet me back at the house in ten minutes," she says. "We can talk there."

Just then, I notice Mark Randall. I release Poppy and she takes a step away from me, swiping tears from her eyes.

Mark glances at us and says to me, "Leave your sister alone, or I'll tell Danny."

I try to tamp down my anger, not wanting to get sidetracked with Mark. "Mind your own fucking business," I tell him.

Mark shakes his head. "It's your funeral, psycho." Then he pushes through the exit and Poppy and I are alone again.

"Ten minutes," I say to her. Then I, too, pass through the door and out into the open, leaving Poppy behind.

I walk past Margot, no doubt waiting for Poppy to exit, and make my way toward where Lydia stands, her eyes bloodshot. I wish I could cry. Let all my anger, hurt, and humiliation out in one long wail. Instead, it sits like a hot stone inside of me and I'm terrified it will burn me up from the inside out.

"I have to go back to the house for a minute," I tell her.

"What? Why?"

"Apparently, Danny told Poppy about your abortion and I need to go deal with that before the whole town knows."

Lydia reaches out as if to take my hand but I take a step away from her and her hand drops again. "What did he tell her?"

"I assume the same thing he told me," I say, my anger rising up again at the memory. "That Mr. Stewart got you pregnant and then took you for an abortion."

Lydia looks panicked. "He told you that?"

"In so many words, yes."

She closes her eyes as if she's suddenly exhausted. "Just walk me to the rocks. I can explain everything on the way. Please." Her expression is desperate. "Then you can go deal with Poppy."

I look toward the path that leads through the trees and to my house, then back at Lydia, torn. Perhaps it would be better to hear from her first and then go talk to Poppy. After that, maybe I'll be able to figure out how to move forward, either with or without Lydia. "Fine," I say.

Chapter 32

I try not to react to my father's admission, although inside, I'm reeling. Here it is, the piece I've been waiting for, and I don't have time to allow myself to absorb it. I have to keep up a professional facade, to make sure my feelings about what he's just told me, that everything—the fight with my mother, the alibi, all of it—had been a lie. That my father had been in the house when Danny and Poppy had died. And the only way he could have been there was if he'd played some part in their deaths.

I pull out Poppy's diary. When my father sees it, he looks surprised. "Where did you get that?" he asks.

"I found it in one of your boxes." I've marked the page with a Post-it and I flip it open, explaining. "This was why I initially asked you about her films. Because aside from the first entry that talks about Mom's abortion, the rest referenced reels and clips. As if she wanted to show someone what she was figuring out instead writing it down. As if she knew it wasn't safe to do so."

"Give me that," my father says.

I hand it over and he holds it in his hand like an ancient artifact. Gently, he strokes the cover with its faded red hearts running around the perimeter and opens it, his finger tracing the jagged edge of the page she cut out.

"Do you know what was on that page?" I ask.

He shakes his head and flips to the first entry. I can see him trying to decipher the words. To make sense of the shapes that were once his livelihood. But he looks up, defeated.

"Can you read it to me?" he asks.

I nod, and begin. "*I heard a rumor today. That Lydia was pregnant and now . . . she's not.*"

He closes his eyes as I continue. "*Something's on that film that Vince doesn't want me to see. March #1, Clip #3.*"

His eyes open again and he asks, "What's in that clip?"

"I haven't been able to figure it out, but maybe you can tell me."

I pull it up and press Play, setting the computer on the desk so my father can see it. The bonfire. Kids laughing. A man picking up cans. The flames climbing high, sparks vanishing in the night sky. My father leans closer to the screen and I watch him. His jaw flexes but the rest of him is still.

Suddenly his hand darts out, sweeping the computer off his desk and it crashes onto the floor. "Why are you showing me this?" he yells.

I jump to my feet and scramble backward, out of his reach. My computer is still open, the clip still playing, though a corner of the screen is cracked. I scurry around my father to pick it up as he launches into another tirade. "If you had only stayed home, none of this would have happened. But no! You abandoned me."

He's pacing and I clutch my laptop to my chest. "Dad," I tell him. "It's me, Olivia."

"This is your fault, Lydia," he says, stepping closer. "You were the one who made the choice to go to that party." Then he turns to the bookshelves and starts throwing books onto the floor.

Alma enters the room at a run, sees the mess, and turns on me. "Go. Get out."

"I don't know what happened," I tell her.

"It doesn't matter. I need you to leave." To my father she says, "It's okay, Vincent. I'm here. We can figure it out together."

But her words do nothing to calm him down. He picks up a book and throws it at me, missing my head by inches. Even Alma has to step back. Then he turns toward the window, smashing his hand through it.

Alma leaps forward and pulls him back. Blood is pouring from his palm. "Go get a towel," she orders.

I race to the bathroom and return with the towel, and she tries to wrap it around my father's hand, but he's still thrashing. She says, "Call 911. Tell them we need an ambulance for a cognitively impaired patient who requires sedation. Tell them he's punched a window and is bleeding heavily."

When I hesitate, she points toward the door. "Go."

* * *

The paramedics arrive and manage to sedate my father, bandaging his hand to stop the flow of blood. Then they load him onto the ambulance, but when I try to climb aboard, Alma stops me. "It's best if you're not around him right now."

"He's my father," I say.

"You're a trigger," she tells me. "Go back to Los Angeles for a little while. Let him recalibrate. Then we can talk about whether you can finish this book or not."

After the ambulance leaves, I stand in my father's office, surveying the mess. Books are scattered everywhere and I start to pick them up, trying to figure out what was on that clip that upset him so much. Working and reworking in my mind what he said. Blaming my mother for going to the party. Angry with her that she didn't stay behind with him.

When the books are shelved, I sweep up the glass and then return to the guesthouse and start packing my things. I'll have to let Nicole and the team at Monarch know that we've had a setback. That I'm being asked to leave, and I wonder whether John Calder will win. Again.

When I'm done, I rewatch the clip, looking for anything that would have set him off. But I don't see anything. I don't recognize any of the kids in the frame. They're strangers to me, on an endless loop of laughing and dancing. On the left is the man picking up cans. He's definitely older than the rest of the kids, though I only catch a glimpse of the side of his face, and only for a second. I freeze the frame and stare at him. Letting his features layer over ones I've seen before.

Mr. Stewart. This was one of his parties and I wonder what happened that night. Why my father was so angry about it.

Anxiety begins to bloom inside of me at what I know I need to do.

It's time to talk to my mother.

Chapter 33

Highway 150 takes me out of the Ojai Valley and toward Bakersfield, my GPS giving me quiet commands in the early morning light. I'm glad to escape the house, the memory of my father's anger still echoing through the rooms. Glad I don't have to face Alma, who's still sleeping when I leave. She came home late last night and told me my father had gotten nine stitches in his palm and that they were keeping him for observation. "I'll call you in a few days and let you know where things stand," she told me.

I'm grateful for the silence of the car and the empty road in front of me. I need to shift away from my father's condition and start thinking through how to approach my mother, the questions I need to ask.

I have only one solid memory of her. It must have been right before she left, because I was in kindergarten. I'd been invited to a birthday party for a girl in my class. My mother wanted me to wear a purple dress with a sash that tied in the back and black shiny shoes, but I'd wanted to wear my rainbow T-shirt, jean skirt, and a pair of striped socks that I'd gotten for my birthday.

I know from pictures that my mother was tall, with long dark hair that framed her face. But I vividly remember the way it smelled when she'd lean over to kiss me goodnight, like coconut suntan lotion. That day, she sat on the bed next to me and waited for me to stop crying. Then she said, "Olivia, sometimes we all have to do things we don't want to do." Her voice had been heavy, as if she were admitting a sad and painful truth and

I remember being confused by her words. To my five-year-old mind, adults got to do whatever they wanted.

I don't remember the party at all, whether I ended up wearing the purple dress or if I got my way and wore my rainbow outfit. I don't remember whether my mother or father took me, whether they stayed or just dropped me off. It's as if my memory ends with my mother's words, the admission that everyone in life has to accept a certain amount of pain, and it wasn't until I was nearly an adult that I circled back to that memory and began to wonder what things my mother had been forced to do. And how long she had to carry it, waiting until she could break free.

For years, I was chased by questions my father was either unable or unwilling to answer. What kind of mother leaves her child? *A woman who ran out of options*, a voice says in my mind now, and I realize I need more than just information about what happened in 1975. I need to know how it ties in with her departure, because I'm certain the reason I grew up without a mother is directly connected to the murders of Poppy and Danny.

* * *

I park in a modest neighborhood of apartment buildings on a quiet street within walking distance of a main thoroughfare where small businesses cluster between tire chains and fast-food restaurants. I found her by paying $25 to a website that gives you information most people think is private. Current and former addresses, phone numbers, pending lawsuits. My mother's information showed our old apartment in Ojai and this apartment building that thankfully doesn't have a security gate.

Inside the courtyard, there's a fenced pool with metal patio chairs and a No Lifeguard on Duty sign. I find the stairwell and emerge on a balcony that wraps around the courtyard offering a view of the pool below. I find her apartment, my pulse pounding, and I try to concentrate on relaxing my shoulders. Keeping my greeting simple and then seeing what happens after that.

I knock and wait. It's just past eight on a Saturday morning, late enough that she's probably awake, although I don't have anything on which to base that assumption.

When the door swings open, I recognize her immediately. Her hair is grayer, but the style is the same—long sheets of hair brushing past her shoulders, and I imagine a phantom whiff of coconut. Same wide eyes, so familiar it nearly steals my breath. She must recognize me too because she takes an involuntary step back, as if she might close the door. I speak before that can happen.

"Hi, Mom," I say.

"Olivia," she whispers. "Why are you here?"

I know her words are the result of being ambushed, but her question still punches into me. She must see the hurt on my face because she shakes her head and tries again. "Is everything okay?"

"Can we go inside and talk?"

She hesitates for just a second, then steps aside so I can enter. The living room is sparse, an old couch in front of a scarred coffee table, a couple celebrity magazines on top and a television remote to an older model tucked into a cabinet next to a bookshelf. Another chair faces the couch and I choose that and sit.

She finally finds her voice. "How did you know where to find me?"

I ignore her question, taking in her outfit—dark blue jeans and a white shirt, neither of them branded in any way. The clothing of a woman on a budget. The living room leads to a small dining room, where I notice a CVS apron tossed over the back of one of the chairs.

She sits on the couch across from me, perching on the edge as if she might need to exit quickly. I take in her face, the way she's aged. Gone is the laughing girl from Poppy's home movies, replaced by a woman in her mid-sixties, hollowed out by life. By tragedy.

"I need to ask you some questions," I finally say.

"Okay," she says, though her tone is wary.

"I've been in Ojai," I begin. "Staying with Dad."

"I didn't realize the two of you were back in touch," she says.

Her words surprise me. "How did you know that we weren't? Do you and Dad still talk?"

"Not for a long time," she says. "But when you were younger, he'd keep me informed of things."

I need a moment to absorb this fact, that all these years they'd been in contact while I'd been the one cut off. Cut out. I stand and walk toward the bookshelf and scan the titles. Some of Barbara Kingsolver's earlier works, two or three by Danielle Steel. No books by my father. No books by me. On top is a framed photograph of my mother with three other women around her age. I pick it up and study it.

"Those are my friends from the community garden," she explains. "I rent a plot there. Most people grow vegetables, but I like to grow flowers." She's chattering. Filling the silence, hoping to keep things light.

I set the picture down, taking a quick glance at the other frames, noting that there isn't a single photo of the daughter she walked away from. "I'm glad you have friends."

"We also have a book club," she says. "Go to movies. Susan tries to get me to go to church, but I don't have much use for God." She stops talking, perhaps realizing she's veering too close to topics she doesn't want to discuss.

"I imagine not," I say.

"Tell me about yourself," she continues. "Are you married? Do you have kids?" Her voice is tentative, as if she doesn't really want to know what she might have missed—a wedding. Grandchildren.

But her words stab me as well. The life I could have had— would have had—with Tom, if not for the dysfunction and trauma at the core of my family. And as my eyes sweep across the room again—generic prints on the walls, scattered photos of book club friends who most likely return home to an intact family after their night of wine and conversation—I see my own life layered over the top of this one. A life of isolation and loneliness. Of being the friend everyone tries to include out of pity.

"Not married, no kids," I say, returning to my chair and forcing myself to focus. "I live in Los Angeles, but like I said, I've been staying with Dad." I watch her expression, waiting to see if she'll flinch. Look away. She waits for me to continue. "He's been talking about what happened and I have some questions for you."

My mother looks down at her hands, now clasped tight in her lap, and says, "I don't remember much. It was a long time ago."

"I don't really think that's true."

She looks up at me and says, "It was a tragedy. Your father never really recovered from it, though I'm proud of who he's become and the things he's accomplished. I'm definitely appreciative of the money he sends for the apartment."

"Dad pays your rent? For how long?"

"Since I moved out," she says.

"Did he ask you to leave?" I ask.

She shakes her head. "No, I needed to go."

"What does that mean?" I'm losing control of my emotions, but I can't help myself. "I came across an article where you said that you would never allow your daughter to be raised by a killer, but that's exactly what you did."

She looks stricken. "Why would you say that? Your father didn't kill anyone." She glances at the door, perhaps wondering if she should end our conversation.

I push on, not wanting to hear whatever weak excuse she might formulate. Anger that has been lying dormant inside of me bubbles over at this woman who walked away from her daughter and never looked back. "Dad told me the alibi was a lie. The only explanation for why a teacher might lie to the police is if you were sleeping with him."

She stands, her face a blank slate. "I think you should leave."

"Dad's sick," I tell her. "Lewy body dementia. It's similar to Alzheimer's." I see a loosening in her expression, as if the fact that the disease affects the memory is good news. "His memory's not gone yet," I tell her. "But sometimes he slips and thinks I'm you. And he says things."

She sinks back down again, her fingers trembling, and she quickly tucks them between her knees. "That must be hard for you."

"Dad told me about your abortion. That the baby wasn't his. Whose was it?"

My mother covers her face and bends over her knees. I wait, letting her gather herself. When she looks up again, her eyes are wet. It's clear she's devastated, but she also seems resigned. As if she knows what my father is trying to do. "Your father had no right telling you about that."

I take my laptop out of my bag and pull up the bonfire clip. The one that sent my father over the edge. "I showed one of Poppy's old movie clips to Dad last night, and he went crazy. Smashed his hand through a window and had to go to the hospital."

My mother looks startled. "Your father has Poppy's old movies?"

"I found them hidden in Poppy's closet," I tell her. "This one really upset him and I can't figure out why. Maybe you can tell me."

I play the clip for her—the partying kids, the bonfire flames, a young Mr. Stewart picking up cans—but I'm watching my mother. The way she leans closer to the screen, the way her eyes seem to widen at one point, her hand lifting as if to point to something, but dropping into her lap before she can. When it's over, I ask again, "Why did this upset Dad so much? What did he see that I can't?"

She slides her finger across the trackpad, rewinding the video to midway, and I expect her to say something about Mr. Stewart. That my father's rage was because of what he'd done to my mother. But instead, she says, "Look in the background. The camera shifts and you can see us."

The video shows a group of kids sitting cross-legged in the dirt, the flames highlighting their features, making them seem otherworldly and immortal. But instead of looking at them, I'm looking beyond them. At first, it's her legs I recognize—long and lean in a pair of jeans. My mother, sitting on a log in the top right corner of the screen. Leaning toward someone, laughing. Passing a can of beer back and forth. Someone nudges Poppy, or bumps into her, because the camera shifts, and I can see who it is next to my mother. His arm curving around her waist, his head tilted toward hers, the two of them oblivious.

Danny.

I pause the clip and look at my mother. "What happened?"

Her voice is robotic, as if the only way to get through it is to take all of the emotion out of it. "That night, Danny was so nice to me. I started to wonder if Vince had been exaggerating about how awful his brother was. Because to me, he was charming. Funny. I was sixteen . . ." Her voice trails off. "He was so popular. So handsome. He brought me drinks and talked to me all night long. Ignoring his friends, ignoring the other girls who were much prettier and much cooler than I was. After a while, he suggested we find a quiet place to talk more." She looks away, ashamed. "I shouldn't have gone with him. It was my fault."

Her words echo the page my father wrote, the words scrawled again and again. *She shouldn't have gone.* "Did he rape you?" I finally ask, my heart breaking for the young girl that lives, so fresh, in my mind. I think back to all the movies I've studied, now wondering if I'd missed something. Some silent shift, signifying what had been done to her.

She gives a tiny shrug. "When he kissed me, I liked it. It was exciting. But then I remembered about your father. About how much it would destroy him and I pulled away. Danny didn't like that. Said I was a tease." She's lost in the memory, reliving it somewhere in her mind. Then she seems to realize I'm still there, still listening. "You don't need to hear the rest."

"Why didn't you tell someone?" I ask.

She gives me a shrewd look. "That's not how things worked back then. I thought I could forget about it. Danny behaved as if nothing had happened. He barely acknowledged me and I started to wonder if I'd imagined it. But then, I found out I was pregnant. I couldn't tell your father. It would have devastated him." She pauses, then adds, "It did."

"Did Danny ever know it was him who had gotten you pregnant?"

My mother gives a tiny shrug. "No one knows what Danny knew or didn't know. He let your father believe it was Mr. Stewart's baby, which was ridiculous."

"Mr. Stewart took you to get the abortion," I say. "It's not a big leap to assume he was the father. Was there anything going on between the two of you?

My mother shakes her head, unable to look at me. "No."

I'm struggling to make sense of this. Even in the 1970s, even despite Mr. Stewart's righteous claim that he would do it again, it seems like an outrageous risk for a teacher to take. "Help me understand why a teacher would take a student to get an abortion. He could have gotten into a lot of trouble."

My mother looks at me and says, "My mother wasn't the best parent. She liked to say we were more like sisters than mother and daughter. But the truth was, she wasn't even that to me. A sister is someone you can talk to. Confide your problems to. But my mother was only interested in finding a man to take care of her." She pauses here, as if remembering that time. The horrible realization that she was pregnant and the helpless feeling it must have given her. Abortion had been recently legalized but it would have been unlikely a sixteen-year-old girl could have figured out how to access it on her own. "I didn't tell Mr. Stewart I was pregnant. He figured it out. When he offered to help me, I accepted. I was eight weeks pregnant and running out of time.

He drove me to the clinic, pretended to be my older brother and even filled out the paperwork when I couldn't."

"It's one thing to drive a girl to get an abortion," I say. "Quite another to lie to the police in a murder investigation.

"Asking him for the alibi was your father's idea. He used the abortion as leverage to get him to say he was with us."

My voice lowers, though there isn't anyone around who can hear me. "Do you know who killed them?" I ask. "Was it Dad?"

"Poppy had something she needed to tell your father," my mother says. "She was really upset about it. We were both worried that she knew the truth about the baby and what Danny had done to me. She and Danny had been arguing about it and your father wanted to get her to promise she wouldn't tell anyone about the rape or the abortion." She takes a shaking breath and says, "But your father didn't kill Poppy. She was already dead when he got there."

I sit back, trying to absorb what she's just confirmed—that my father was there. "So Danny killed Poppy to keep her from revealing the rape," I say. "But who killed Danny? Dad?"

But my mother doesn't answer the question. "Poppy was tenacious. She'd been following your father for months, filming him with her camera."

"Until she lost it," I say.

My mother doesn't respond, seemingly trapped in a memory. Finally she says, "She didn't lose it. I took it."

"What? Why?"

"I was heading home when I saw Poppy and Danny come tearing out of the grove of trees in the field behind their house, fighting over the camera. I hid behind a tree and watched him tackle her. Wrestle the camera out of her hands, throwing it as far as he could. Then he grabbed her and dragged her into the house before she was able to go get it." Her voice is low, remembering that day. "I was frozen to the spot, terrified Danny would see me and come after me next," she says, swiping a strand of hair off her forehead. "I figured the least I could do was to get Poppy's camera for her. Hold on to it until things calmed down. But shortly after that . . ." She shrugs. "Well, you know what happened."

"What did you end up doing with it?"

She gives me a long, steady look. Then she stands and disappears into her room, returning with a shoebox. She hands it to me and I lift the lid. Inside is an old Super 8 camera, dented on one side, the lens completely gone.

I lift it out and turn it over in my hands, hardly believing she kept it all these years. The compartment where the film is stored is badly damaged, and I look up at my mother. "Is there still film in it?"

"I assume so."

The idea of sitting on that film is unfathomable to me. "Why didn't you turn it over to the police?"

"You think answers will fix everything, but they don't. Mr. Stewart used to always say that information is power. But it's also a burden because once you know something, you can't pretend you don't." She shakes her head. "I kept the camera out of respect for Poppy. But I've never been like her. I don't need to see what's on the film to know why Danny killed her. I thought it was better for everyone to just leave it behind." She looks at me and says, "I'm sure there are things in your past you'd rather not speak of."

Her words yank me out of my own narrow perspective and everything shifts. I've been dropped somewhere new, forced to acknowledge the flaws in my own thinking. That you can make up whatever you want to be the truth and you can live your life as if you've sealed it off forever. But, like a heartbeat behind a wall, the truth is always there, holding you hostage. I'm no different from my parents—refusing to acknowledge or speak about difficult things. And yet, I'm this way because I was raised to be this way. Their weaknesses are my own.

I think of the mother I could have had if she'd been a different kind of person. A stronger person. One who had figured out how to get the help she needed without abandoning her daughter. Who'd be able to teach her daughter how to handle hard conversations instead of avoiding them. "Well, that tracks," I say.

Her expression softens, just a fraction, and then she says, "I'm sorry for the pain I've caused you."

I let her statement hang there, unable to accept or even acknowledge her apology, a handful of words that mean nothing. That won't amount to anything once I say goodbye and walk out the door.

I return to the task at hand. "So Danny killed Poppy to keep her from revealing that he had raped you and gotten you pregnant. And then Dad walked in on it and killed Danny?"

"I'm sure that's the story your father wants to tell. But he walked into something he had no business being in the middle of." She presses her lips together, her hands beginning to shake. "Whatever is on that film is why Danny killed Poppy and why Danny almost killed your father."

Chapter 34

After I leave my mother, I sit in my car trying to absorb what I've just learned. All these years, my mother has held onto evidence that might have given everyone answers. The revelation that Danny had killed Poppy because of something she'd filmed would have shifted everything for my father—from sociopathic murderer to self-defense. It would have shifted everything for me as well. I try to think about what kind of life we could have had, if my mother had only been brave enough to speak up. I'm numb, barely able to feel anything, the revelations still bouncing around inside of me. But I know that won't always be the case. Soon, understanding will seep in and I'll have to deal with the aching loss for what could have been. The rage over what has been stolen from me and from my father.

But I also can't ignore the fact that I've done the same thing. I think of the Olivia I once was, a curious young girl eager to know the truth. And at some point I abandoned her, just as surely as my own parents had abandoned me.

And then I think of the life my mother is living inside the tiny box of that apartment, knowing with certainty that's how I'll end up if I don't do something different.

I need to call Tom. To voice these thoughts out loud, to make them a part of the permanent record before I lose them again to my pride.

I open up my phone to the text Tom sent me two weeks ago. Once again, I don't know what to believe.

I think of my parents, of the connection that still binds them across the years and decades. Each of them alone, yet not. I type, Vincent Taylor is my father. I stare at the words, running them through the lens of my contract, making sure I'm not revealing something I shouldn't. That I am Vincent Taylor's daughter is information anyone could discover if they cared to look. A fact many people already know. I continue. That's all I can tell you right now, but know that nothing I've said about this trip is untrue.

Before I can change my mind, I hit Send. My chest opens up as if filled with a thousand birds escaping, flying into a bright-blue sky.

Then I turn to the shoebox, sitting on the front seat of my car and google local companies that might be able to transfer the film still trapped inside the camera into a format I can watch. I find one that can turn it around in a couple hours, and follow the GPS directions to the store.

Inside is cluttered, with a counter that runs along the back, a fiftysomething man wearing rumpled clothes and readers. "You the one with the Super 8 camera?"

"I am," I say, sliding my mother's shoebox across the counter.

He lifts the lid and pulls out the camera, turning it over in his hands, examining the film compartment. "Not sure what we'll find when I get in there," he says. "Is it okay with you if I break off the cover?"

"Just do whatever you need to do."

"Some of the film might be exposed and damaged."

"I'll have to take that risk," I say. "How long until you can have it done?"

The man looks at his watch and says, "Give me a couple hours. You want a link or an external thumb drive?"

"A link will be fine, but I'd like to have the camera back."

He nods. "Not a problem. I can recommend a company that does camera repairs if you want. I don't think it'd cost too much."

"Maybe. Thank you."

I drive to an Olive Garden and sit at a table near the kitchen, picking at my salad and tearing off pieces of breadsticks, unable to eat. Sick with what I've already learned, anxious about what's left.

A voice in my mind whispers that my mother isn't the villain here. It's Danny. The boy who raped her and got her pregnant. The boy who killed his sister. I can have some sympathy for my mother, sixteen years old and terrified.

My heart breaks for my father. A boy who'd stumbled into a horrific scene and done the only thing he could to save himself.

"You want anything else?" the server asks me, eyeing my barely touched food.

"Just the check, please."

My phone buzzes with an email from the film transfer place and a link to the digital file. I'm tempted to watch it here, but decide to wait until I can be somewhere private. Where I can have the space to see what secret Poppy needed to share with my father, the secret that got her killed.

*   *   *

I return to the shop and the man gives me a funny look as I hand him my credit card. "You know the people on that film?" he asks.

"I'm not sure," I say. "But the camera was my aunt's, back in the seventies."

He shakes his head as he hands me back my credit card but doesn't say anything more. I take the shoebox with the camera back to my car and head toward home.

* * *

When I enter my house, I feel a loosening of my shoulders, my muscles finally unclenching. The air feels stuffy after being closed up for two months and I open the sliding doors to the patio, letting the cool canyon air inside, then look in my freezer for something to eat. I pull out a couple Trader Joe's tamales and put them in the oven, then sit at the dining room table, my laptop in front of me, trying not to think about how different this would feel if Tom were here to greet me with a hug and a hot meal. A back rub after the long drive home.

A quick pass through my bedroom had revealed that he'd been here, clearing out his things. The stack of books that usually sat on his nightstand was gone. So were the shirts he keeps in my closet. His toothbrush. I found his key on the kitchen counter next to the coffee maker. No note. No goodbye. Just an emptiness.

But I refuse to believe this is the end. I have a plan. A way forward, to show Tom that I can be honest with him. That there aren't any more secrets and that I don't want to live a life like my father's. Or my mother's, for that matter.

Her words from this morning come back to me. *Information is power, yes. But it's also a burden because once you know something, you can't pretend you don't.* I stare at the link to Poppy's last film, hesitating. Remembering the strange look the man at the transfer place gave me. Knowing that whatever is on this film will give me answers I might not want.

Poppy

June 13, 1975

6:48 p.m.

I wasn't supposed to die. I know that now, as I fight for air, as my blood pools beneath me and my brother stands over me, terrified.

"I'm sorry," he whispers, tears making his cheeks shiny and wet. In his words I hear everything left unsaid—the lies he told to protect himself, the pain he's carried for so long. His chest heaves with suppressed sobs. "I can't . . . I wish . . ." He can't finish his sentences, and I want to tell him it's okay. We're okay.

They say when you die, your life flashes before your eyes, but I only see pieces of it. My world, as if viewed through the lens of a camera. Moments in time, delivered out of order, like a movie cut and spliced together again.

Christmas lights and hot chocolate.

Roller skates and wind rushing through my hair, the sun warm on my shoulders, adrenaline racing through me like quicksilver.

Spinning spinning spinning in my backyard, until the sky is the ground and the ground is the sky. The soft scratch of grass as I fall. Danny's voice, telling me to get up. To try again. My mother's laughter and the smell of tobacco from my father's cigarette.

My father's birthday toasts—fourteen of them. *When Poppy was born, she was beauty and grace and light. And she continues to be that, all her beautiful days.*

Snippets of memories, fragments of conversations. When you're living it, you can't see how it all fits together, or how it's all going to end. But here, in this space, all your days line up like pearls on a string, each one leading to the next. You get to touch them, live them one last time and finally understand.

Pain radiates outward from where the knife had plunged—such a surprise, how easily it went in. How deep it went and how much it hurt. The blood soaks into the bed beneath me, where I'd fallen, and my hands grip the bedspread, the new one I'd gotten a few weeks ago. Margot and I are supposed to paint my room this summer. Color samples are splashed on the wall by my closet. Creamsicle. Cool Mint. Buttercup. We had just decided last week on buttercup. My senses are heightened, the suffocating smell of my own blood, the bedspread beneath me still scratchy new, yellow rosebuds now soaked in red. My mother will be mad at the mess, but for once I'm not worried.

Danny begins to pace the room, panic taking over. I want to tell him to go for help, to call someone, but I can't draw enough air to do more than a quiet whisper. He grabs at his hair, sound erupting out of him in giant, choking sobs and then collapses in the corner of the room, my blood all over his hands. His arms. My oldest brother, once my biggest hero, his dark hair matted against his sweaty forehead, his skin pasty white. I open my mouth to tell him I forgive him, but I can't. My throat fills with blood and I can't seem to swallow it back down.

He must hear me, because suddenly he's up again, standing over me. "I'm sorry I hurt you," he says.

I wonder, *Which time?* The bruises on my arms are only a couple days old, the mottled purple where he'd grabbed me,

squeezing so tight I could feel the blood pound in my fingertips. The cuts on my elbows and knees from when he'd tackled
me are still fresh. And my camera. I can still see it pinwheeling
through the air, the sound as it smashed against a tree.

Danny had snuck into my room the following night, his
breath hot and laced with alcohol as he whispered into my ear.
"Where's the camera, Poppy?"

He asks me again now. "Where did you hide it?"

I shake my head, just a fraction of an inch left and right, unable
to speak. Then I close my eyes so they don't cut to my window
or toward my closet. Vince will find my diary and my film reels.
Vince will keep looking for my camera and figure it all out.

The pain is increasing with every inhalation and the room
flickers, to another place and time. Me, sitting on the bottom of
a pool holding my breath, listening to Danny call for me from
the deck. I think of the way he used to laugh—big and loud—
and the way it would fill me up, like helium, until I felt like I
might fly. When was the last time he'd laughed like that?

I open my eyes again and he's gone. Had I imagined him?
I'm worried about who will find me. How long it will take for
someone to come, whether they'll be able to help. It won't be my
parents, who won't be back for hours. Will it be Margot, who
will surely come looking for me when I don't show up at the
Tilt-A-Whirl? I hope not.

This is how it ends. It surprises me, how far away everything
feels. The secret I'd been holding, a ticking bomb that detonates
here, before I had the chance to tell anyone.

A sound catches my attention, somewhere in the house. A
door closing. My eyes fly open again, and this time I see Danny
standing in the doorway to my bedroom. Still staring at me, as

if he can't believe what's happening. And I remember why I'm here in the first place.

Vince has arrived. My other brother, just a year younger than Danny. *Irish twins,* our mother used to joke, back when she still found jokes in places other than the inside of a wine bottle. I stare at Danny, waiting to see if he also hears the noise, but he doesn't turn around.

I want to yell, to warn Vince to leave. To get out of the house. But of course, I can't. And so, as the edges of my vision grow blurry, I see Vince creeping up behind Danny, taking in the scene, the bloody mess with me at the center of it. I close my eyes again, unable to watch them destroy each other, once and for all.

Chapter 35

I spend four days at home drafting several new chapters of my father's memoir. Chapters that tell the truth of what happened. I want to have something to share with him when I return to Ojai. And I will be returning, regardless of what Alma wants. I need my father to know that this story doesn't have to end the way he wants it to.

Nearly two months to the day after I made that first trip back to Ojai, I make it again. This time armed with answers.

* * *

I find him in the courtyard, enjoying the early May sunshine, his right hand wrapped in gauze. I approach him tentatively and sit on the bench next to him, resting my laptop on my knees. "How are you feeling?" I ask.

"Better," he says. "That must have scared you."

I wave away his words. "I should have done a better job to prepare you. I had no idea it would upset you so much."

"Of course you didn't," he says.

The entire drive back, I ran through different ways to tell my father what I'd learned. What I suspect actually happened. And how to tell him without sending him back to the hospital.

"I went to see Mom," I tell him.

He closes his eyes and nods. When he opens them again, he looks defeated. "Why can't you just write the book I asked you to write?"

"Because that's not the way I work and I think you knew that, which is why you hired me." Then I touch his arm. "I know you didn't think I was paying attention, but I was. I found everything you left for me."

He gives me a weak smile. "I know."

"Why go through all that, Dad? Why not just tell me what you wanted me to know?"

He's quiet for a moment, and I'm not sure if he's trying to formulate an answer or if he's gone somewhere else in his mind. "I wanted one last hunt with you," he says. "Besides, when you thought I was being deceitful, you felt the information you were discovering was truer than if I'd just come out and told you." He gives me a half shrug and continues. "When I first started showing symptoms, I made a plan. I put the notes in the margins for you to find. I knew what stories I wanted to tell. I just needed you here to listen."

"I have one more clip I need to show you. Are you up for it?"

"I've got some pretty heavy-duty meds in me, so I'm game," he says.

I nod and open my laptop. "That last week, Mom found Poppy's Super 8 camera in the preserve. Danny had broken it because of something she'd recorded on it. The film from that day was still in it and I had it transferred to digital." The video is paused, frozen on the tree trunks of the oak grove near their house. "She meant to give the camera back to Poppy at some point, but then everything happened. This was Poppy's last movie, shot just a few days before she died." I glance at him, trying to gauge his mental state. "I need you to be ready," I warn. "This one has sound. You're going to hear their voices."

A gentle smile floats across my father's face. "The eleventh roll," he whispers.

The beginning of the reel had been scenes from the ERA rally. She'd captured the speakers, the crowds of women, and finally Poppy, who'd turned her camera around on herself, lit up with an energy and passion that had brought tears to my eyes when I'd first seen it. How young she was. How happy. But I've skipped over all of that to the very last clip.

I press Play. At first all you can see are trees and someone walking through them. But this time we can hear the crunch of leaves. Birds singing. The camera finds the edge of Poppy's scuffed tennis shoe, then back up again. A tent comes into focus, and Poppy zooms in on the two figures in front of it. Mr. Stewart, facing Danny.

"What are you doing out here by yourself?" Mr. Stewart asks.

"You're the one who told me how powerful it is to camp alone in the woods," Danny says, his seventeen-year-old voice lower than I expected it to be. Cracking with anger, Or nerves.

"You've been avoiding me since I moved in," Mr. Stewart says, closing the space between them.

"I wonder why."

Mr. Stewart steps even closer, forcing Danny to move back.

"We had a special connection, once upon a time," Mr. Stewart says.

Danny's face quickly becomes a mask and he says, "What do you want, Mr. Stewart?"

"Remember, I said you could call me Paul when it's just the two of us."

"What do you want, *Paul*?" Danny's voice is now a sneer. "Surely I'm too old for you. Are you still taking kids into that equipment shed? Telling them they're special, explaining how to keep big secrets?" He snaps his fingers as if just remembering something. "Oh wait, you can't because I burned it down."

I glance at my father to make sure he's okay. His expression is intent on the screen, watching the scene unfold.

"I got away from you once," Danny says. "And you had to move in next door."

"It doesn't have to be this way, Danny. We're neighbors now. Let's be friendly about it at the very least. After all, it's not like you're blameless," he says. "I know what you did to my cat, and yet I'm able to forgive you."

Mr. Stewart grabs Danny's wrist and pulls Danny toward him. Gripping Danny's hand, he guides it lower, then reaches out with his other to caress Danny's cheek. He leans in to kiss Danny on the lips, which seems to wake Danny up.

Danny shoves Mr. Stewart hard. "Get the fuck off me!"

Mr. Stewart holds his hands up as if he meant no harm, walking backwards with a smile on his face like he'd only been joking. "I hope you'll come to my end-of-year party tomorrow night. It should be fun."

Then he's gone.

Danny crouches down, covering his face with his arms, and sobs. When he finally looks up, he must see his sister, filming. His expression morphs into fear, then rage. He leaps up and Poppy takes off, the camera still rolling.

I stare at my father, watching him watch this moment play out, absorbing what it means. Knowing the ending. There are only a few seconds of film left and I know it by heart now. Flashes of dirt and leaves. Of sky. Of Danny's enraged face. Poppy's feet pounding on the ground, her breathing heavy. A glimpse of Poppy—her hair, her arm, her face at one point, terrified—then the camera pinwheeling through the air, going black.

When it's over I say, "Did Mom know what Mr. Stewart had done to Danny? She spent a lot of time with him. Could he have done it to her as well?"

"No. I'm certain of it." My mother had also been certain, but if she'd been lying to me, I'd have no way to know. "I knew you'd find the movies, but I hadn't anticipated your mother keeping that last reel of film. She never told me she had it." He stares across the courtyard, possibly imagining my mother as a young girl, squirreling away the evidence that would have changed his life. That would have changed mine as well. If he's angry with her, he doesn't show it.

"I talked to Margot and Mark." He gives me a sharp look and I clarify. "I never mentioned the book. I told them I just wanted answers, as Danny and Poppy's niece. They were able to tell me a few things that helped shade in those last weeks. One of the things Margot told me was about Mr. Stewart's end-of-year party and how unusual it was that Poppy didn't want to go."

"She got drunk," he says. "Caused a scene and I had to go get her. She was yelling something at Mr. Stewart about secrets."

"Do you think it's possible that might have tipped off Mr. Stewart about what she knew?"

My father looks at me, astonished. "You think . . . ?"

"I have no proof that Mr. Stewart killed them. This video only proves what he did to Danny. But if Poppy threatened to tell—and from what you told me, she wanted you to meet her at the house so she could tell you something—it's certainly a motive.

And a very good reason why he agreed to lie to the police about where he was at the time of the murders."

My father looks shaken. "All this time, we thought he was alibiing us because we forced him to."

I'm quiet, letting my father piece together what I've shared with him, his gaze forward, yet his mind clearly far away in time. Finally I say, "I'm thinking we should—" but he cuts me off.

"I need a moment," he says, struggling to stand. I move to help him, but he waves me off, walking to the edge of the courtyard where an archway leads into the orchard behind the house. He stands there, his hand braced on one side of it and I watch his shoulders rise and fall.

Behind me, Alma comes to the door. "What's happening?" she asks.

"Dad?" I say, my voice tentative.

"I'm fine," he says, not looking at either of us.

After a second, Alma returns to the kitchen and I wait for my father to gather himself.

When he sits next to me again, I say, "Are you okay?"

"I always thought he did it."

"Mr. Stewart?" I ask.

"No. Danny. I always thought he'd killed Poppy because of the baby. Because he thought Poppy was going to tell." He gives a tiny shake of his head. "I hated him for years, knowing what he'd done to your mother. Believing he'd been the one to kill Poppy. It felt righteous and white-hot and pure." His voice spits that last word. "But now I have to rearrange all of it in my mind. Learn how to think about Danny in a different way. To allow myself to give space to what had been done to him. To what he had to carry for so long." He pauses, gathering himself. "It's not an excuse for what he did to your mother. I'll never forgive him for that. But it gives those actions context. He was just a child."

Then my father does something I've never seen him do. He cries. And I hold his hand and let him.

* * *

When he's gathered himself, I say, "I want to put all of this in the book. We can't prove Mr. Stewart killed them, but we can expose him for what he did to Danny. And likely to other kids as well. It would make sense that he would kill them both to keep them quiet."

My father's expression grows distant. Remembering his brother and sister. Absorbing the secrets they both carried. Adjusting to this new reality, one that finally absolves him. He nods. "Do it. Write it."

"I already did," I say. "Let me read it to you. Tell me if you want any revisions." I flip to the manuscript on my computer and start to read aloud. "'*I walked through the back door, into a silent house. Poppy was supposed to meet me there and at first I assumed I'd arrived before her. But within seconds, I realized that was not the case. The smell of blood—I'll never forget that metallic, cloying scent that seemed to fill my nostrils, forcing me to breathe through my mouth—was overpowering. I saw Danny almost immediately. Dead in the hallway, where he'd landed. Trying—and failing—to reach Poppy, who was crumpled on her bed in a pool of blood.*'"

I read my father the rest. How he'd scurried out the back door again, taking the knife with him. How he hadn't been thinking and then worried it might implicate him. How he and my mother asked Mr. Stewart to alibi them, and their surprise at how easy it had been to convince him.

When I'm done, I look up at my father, relieved to see his approval.

"It's great," he says. "Send it to Neil."

"I do have one lingering question," I say. "You've spent the last fifty years believing Danny killed Poppy. But who did you believe killed Danny?"

"Send the manuscript," he says, as if I hadn't spoken.

"They're going to have the same question," I tell him. "It should be a quick fix."

"I want you to send it now," he insists.

He watches as I attach the chapter and send it off to Monarch, cc'ing Nicole.

Then he says, "Now that's done, I need to tell you what really happened."

Poppy

June 13, 1975

7:00 p.m.

I'm fading in and out of consciousness. I open my eyes in time to see Vince jump Danny from behind. As if from a great distance, I hear their bodies hitting the wall, careening down the hallway. Vince screaming, "What the fuck did you do to her?"

I can't feel my hands or feet, just a dull ache at my core. My mouth doesn't work, my voice nothing more than a whisper. I want to tell them who did this to me before my brothers destroy each other.

More moments flicker through my mind—laughing with Margot at lunch in the fifth grade, my parents dancing to Sinatra in the living room last Christmas. My brothers at the breakfast table—years ago—passing the Sunday comics between them, the sound of cartoons on the television in the background. And later, their fighting. Always the fighting.

I never should have gone to that party. Or had those beers, which hadn't made me feel lighter. They'd made me angrier, amplifying it like the megaphone Mr. Stewart used in PE.

Mr. Stewart.

I'd been looking out the kitchen window waiting for Vince to arrive. Mr. Stewart must have come in through the front door because one minute I was alone and the next, he was standing next to me.

"I think we need to talk. Clear the air," he'd said.

"Get out of my house. My parents will be home any minute."

Mr. Stewart had shaken his head. "I saw them as they were leaving. Going to the movies in Ventura. Your dad told me how much he hated the first night of the carnival. So many people. So much traffic." He peered out the back window and then back at me. "Looks pretty quiet around here though."

As he spoke, my hand had inched to the left on the counter, slowly landing on the knife drying there. When I had a good grip on it, I sprinted from the kitchen, down the hall to my room.

The pain is almost gone now. My brothers tear at each other in the hallway and I hate that my last moments will be spent listening to them fight.

I should have run out the back door. I see that now. Screamed the whole way back to the carnival, telling anyone who would listen who Mr. Stewart really was. What he'd done to Danny. What he'd certainly done to others in that equipment shed.

But I'd run into my room instead. The place I'd always sought refuge, where I'd always been safe. Mr. Stewart crashed in after me. Too big. Too strong. He'd grabbed my wrist and twisted it, angling the knife away from himself and plunging it into my stomach. I felt the blade slip in, sharp and hot, passing through the softest part of me, until all I could see was the handle. Then Mr. Stewart had pushed me back onto the bed, still holding the knife, and it slipped out of me, the spot where it had entered pooling with blood. I'd pressed my hands to the wound, as if I could have held it all in, but there was too much.

"You did this to yourself," he'd said, wiping the handle of the knife with his shirt, then dropping it on the floor. Then he stepped backward, away from the mess. I blinked, and he was gone. I blinked again and it was Danny standing over me, holding the discarded knife in his hand. Crying. Knowing what had happened, what I'd set in motion that he'd tried so hard to prevent.

A loud crash comes from the hallway, pulling me back to the present. Then the sound of a body hitting the floor. Heavy breathing, effort spent. My brothers will never see each other clearly. What a tragedy that Danny cannot see Vince's tender side. Cannot appreciate his dark humor or his sharp wit. And Vince will never see Danny's honor. The sacrifices he's made that allowed us to believe in a world that never existed. Vince will never know Danny's secret because I never had the chance to tell him. And now, without that last roll of film, there won't be anyone left who can tell.

It's quiet now, the fighting stopped. I hear the backdoor open and feel a panic surge through me. Was Mr. Stewart back again? Then an inhalation. A gasp. A cry.

Lydia's voice, shouting, "What did you do to him, Danny?"

I wish I could apologize to her. I'd been so focused on exposing her mistake, her misdeeds, never looking toward the men who'd put her in that position. And now I can never make that right for her.

I don't want to die. And yet, this is exactly how it's supposed to happen.

It's okay.

I'm okay.

Vincent

June 13, 1975

7:45 p.m.

I careen through the trees in the oak grove, crashing through underbrush, over logs, winding my way deeper into the darkness, the sound of the carnival fading. Desperate to leave the reality of what I'd done behind me. My head aches where Danny smashed it against the wall, causing me to black out. Because of that, there's a large swath of time I can't account for. At one point I had to stop and vomit behind a tree. Unsure if it was the stench of blood still lingering on my clothes and in my nose, or if it was the large lump forming on my head.

I need to get to Lydia. Make sure she is where she said she'd be. Together we can figure out what to do next. Who to tell.

I stumble to another tree, grasping it, trying to catch my breath, trying to mute the images that flash through my mind. Entering the house. Seeing Poppy, bloody and motionless on her bed, Danny standing over her. The rage I felt overpowering me. I remember barreling into him, once again fighting with my brother in the hallway, pounding my fists into him, not just for what he'd done to Lydia, but what he'd done to silence Poppy. To keep her from telling me what I already knew. I was sick with fear, knowing I could be next. But then Danny had grabbed my shoulders and slammed my head into the wall and I can't remember anything after that.

I'd woken up next to Danny on his back, clutching his throat, blood pouring out from between his fingers. For the rest of my life, I'll never forget the sound he made—a gurgling wheeze, as if he'd had a leak somewhere and it was filling up with blood.

The knife was on the floor between us where I must have dropped it, and without thinking, I grabbed it and ran out of the house. Through the yard and toward the oak grove. Running away from what I'd seen, what I must have done before I blacked out.

I grip the knife tighter in my fist, unsure what to do with it. It has my fingerprints on it. Danny's blood. Poppy's blood. Everyone will think I'd killed them both. I choke back a sob. No one will believe me if I tell them Poppy had already been dead. That I'd been attacked by Danny and must have killed him in self-defense. I'm Vincent Taylor, the weird, angry middle brother. Everyone will be happy to believe it was me.

I can see Lydia in the distance, her head buried in her arms. Waiting for me. The sound of footsteps catches her attention and she looks up, panicked. She scrambles to stand, pressing herself against the tree and I try to call out, but my voice isn't working. As I approach, she sinks down to the ground again, disbelief and fear on her face. Somewhere in my mind, I must have noticed the blood on her arms. Her shirt. A smudge of it across her forehead. But it doesn't yet register what that means.

Her gaze latches onto the knife in my hand, and I drop it, collapsing next to her, burying my head in my arms, finally allowing myself to fall apart.

She wraps her arms around me and holds on tight, whispering, "I thought you were dead. I thought Danny had killed you too."

And then it all clicks into place. I look up at her, our eyes locking. Understanding passing between us, at what she'd done for me. For us. For Poppy. What we can never reveal. An unspoken promise I will keep for the next fifty years.

Chapter 36

"This is Jessica Schwartz, and you're listening to *Secrets and Lies the podcast where secrets are exposed, lies are revealed and the truth is all that's left*. Today I'm talking with author Olivia Dumont. You may recognize the titles of many of the books she's collaborated on, high-profile celebrities, politicians, scientists, and musicians. You might also remember her from that very public standoff she had with John Calder, who's now in a lot of hot water of his own. But that's not why we're talking to her today. Olivia is also the ghostwriter of Vincent Taylor's memoir, *All Her Beautiful Days*, the blockbuster book that finally answers the questions that have swirled around the bestselling horror author for decades. But what you might not know is that Olivia is also Vincent Taylor's daughter, and to say that she grew up with secrets and lies is an understatement. Welcome to the show, Olivia. Before we get started, I'd like to offer my condolences on the death of your father." Dani's voice is smooth, and as my car rolls to a stop in front of my father's house, I switch over to my earbuds.

After his revelation about who really killed Danny, it was as if the logjam in my father's memory had finally been cleared. He gave me permission to go back to Margot and Mark and interview them again—solidifying dates, times, and events. Making sure we nailed the version we wanted to tell to as many verifiable facts as possible, protecting my mother until it was my mother he'd see during our work sessions instead of me. *You did what you had to do, Lydia*, he'd say to me, over and over again.

Shortly after I finished the draft, I emailed it to Tom with a note. I won't make excuses for myself, but this book will tell you everything you need to know about me and about my family. No matter what happens with us, I want you to know who I really am. After a week of silence, I started to wonder if he'd even bothered to open the email. Perhaps he just deleted it. But then he texted. I had no idea.

From there, we started slowly. Texts at first—cautious apologies that turned into late-night calls. Whispered conversations in the dark, fragments that would float through my dreams.

I never knew . . .
I wasn't able to acknowledge . . .
I wish I could have . . .

And during the day, I worked on revising the book. Frantic hours—sometimes with my father. Later, as his conditioned worsened, alone.

But not alone. Not anymore.

A month after I turned the book in to Monarch, it became clear that taking care of my father at home had become too much for Alma to manage. I visited him at his care facility in Ventura, driving up from Topanga or from Ojai, where I was responsible for cleaning out the house. Boxing up a lifetime that was both tragic and extraordinary. My father was a complicated man with many facets, but together they created someone I wished I'd had more time with. Especially just as I was beginning to understand him better.

"Thank you for having me on the show." My voice sounds odd to me, smoother than I imagine it sounds on a regular day, and I'm appreciative of the quality of the production team. We'd recorded it several weeks after the book was released and I was still in a state of grief, having lost my father in late April. And yet I'd also been energized by my comeback. *All Her Beautiful Days* had released on the fiftieth anniversary of Poppy and Danny's deaths, and just as Nicole had predicted, it has been at the top of the *New York Times* nonfiction list ever since. I've paid off Calder and my attorneys, and Nicole has been busy fielding requests for my next project.

I walk up the front steps of my father's house for the last time and unlock the door, stepping through the threshold and into a mostly empty space, with only about fifteen boxes of my father's things left to take. My footsteps echo on the terra-cotta tiles, swept clean and mopped by the cleaning crew I'd hired. Jack is coming later this morning to take these last boxes to the storage unit I've rented. But that's not why I'm here.

"What was life like, growing up with the famous Vincent Taylor?" Jessica asks. "What kind of baggage did that create for you—not just as a young girl, but also as an adult?"

"It wasn't easy." I listen to my voice tell the story, of how my mother left and what it was like to navigate a world where everyone believed my father to be a murderer. How I'd spent the rest of my childhood abroad, only returning to the United States once I was sure I could live as someone else. "Loving my father was a complicated algorithm. It meant accepting there were things about him I'd never understand. It meant not asking questions I didn't want to know the answers to. It meant accepting possibilities too horrific to contemplate. For a long time, I wasn't able to do that, so I chose not to."

"And yet, you returned to Ojai to help him write his last book," she says.

"It wasn't my first choice of a job, but my options were limited at the time." I hear myself give a small laugh and remember where I was when we recorded this, a dark studio in Hollywood, a producer sitting across from me, separated by a wall of glass. "It was definitely complicated," I admit to Jessica. "At first, he seemed normal. But it soon became clear his mind and memory were failing. He'd get confused and start thinking I was my mother. The more confused he became, the more he revealed. Facets of his life with Poppy and Danny that didn't add up. That required further digging."

After we'd decided on the story we'd tell the public, after we'd finished the book and it was just the two of us, trying to piece the rest of the puzzle together, I'd asked my father, "Do you really think Mr. Stewart killed Poppy?"

"I don't know," he'd said.

"What about Mr. Stewart's cat? Poppy's movies show you burying him, not Danny."

"Danny killed the cat and wrapped it up in one of my T-shirts. He left it next to the shed where my mother would have found it and blamed me." He rubbed his eyes and said, "I hate that Poppy died believing I was the one who killed Ricky Ricardo."

"Could Danny have killed Poppy after all?" I asked him. A question we returned to again and again. Turning it over in our hands like an artifact we were trying to decipher.

And every time, he'd tell me he wanted to believe that he had, because that would justify how things turned out. It allowed him to live with himself, however flawed that life turned out to be.

The last time I asked him that question was November, and at that point, my father had been in the care facility for several months. It was clear he was deteriorating fast. He became argumentative and angry. Accusing me, his care team—even the other patients—of outrageous behavior. It was painful to watch, but I kept showing up, because every now and then he'd be lucid and we'd return again to the events of that day. To the things we still didn't know. "The truth belongs to Danny and Poppy," he'd told me once. "And it lives in the past, where we can no longer reach it."

A few days before my father died, he turned to me, out of the blue, and said, "I should have never sent you away. It was a mistake."

We were sitting in front of the care facility enjoying the first blue sky of April, me on a stone bench, him in a wheelchair next to me. His speech was slower. More labored, which he hated. "It's fine," I said.

He shook his head, a sharp, jerking motion. "No. It was selfish. I was a coward."

"It would have been worse if I'd stayed," I said. "And you were right. It opened a lot of doors for me."

"It was never about that," he said. "I lied."

"What do you mean?"

He looked at me, his expression tired and sagging. "Every day, you were becoming more and more like Poppy. The way you looked. The way you moved. Your laugh. Your . . ." He paused, searching for the word he needed and I waited for him to find it. "Beliefs," he said, looking relieved. "I couldn't bear to watch you age past her. You were a daily reminder of who she never got to become."

347

I placed my hand over his and squeezed. "You did the best you could. No regrets. No looking back, remember?"

He gave a gruff laugh, more of a cough than anything else, and we sat there in a patch of sun, remembering.

That had been the last conversation we'd had.

Jessica's voice pulls me back to the interview. "What was it like to finally learn the truth of what happened? Of the events surrounding that terrible day in 1975?"

"It was shattering," I say. "There's a weight to that kind of knowledge that bears down on you, becoming a part of you."

"I doubt there's anyone on earth who hasn't read the vast coverage of what you learned in your research. Tell us about the moment you realized your father was truly innocent. That Danny and Poppy were victims of a predator who lived next door. Who still lived next door until just a few weeks ago."

I trail my fingers along the railing as I head upstairs. Past my old bedroom, vacuum stripes on the carpet. My father's room looks bright with a fresh coat of paint and polished windows. In my ears, I listen to myself tell the story of my parents, young and in love, grappling with their own enormous secret. Of Poppy, sharp and smart and determined to uncover the truth through filmmaking. And of Danny, shouldering the biggest secret of all, one that eventually destroyed him. I tell the story exactly as my father and I agreed upon. That he and my mother really had been in the oak grove all that time. That Mr. Stewart had been eager to supply an alibi for them, a lie to cover his own lack of one.

But underneath it all lives my mother's secret, the one she's been trying to live with since 1975. One my father and I decided would never surface and why my father allowed the world to believe he'd killed both of his siblings. A man still protecting the young girl he'd once loved so much.

"There isn't any proof that Paul Stewart killed Poppy or Danny," I say. "No physical evidence linking him to the crime scene. A murder weapon that vanished fifty years ago and is unlikely to ever turn up."

My mother had discarded the knife. For a time they'd kept it hidden inside Poppy's windowsill. My father checking on it multiple times a week, making sure it was still there. Until one day it wasn't. Only my mother knows where it went and I have no intention of asking her.

I step into my father's empty office and stand in front of the repaired windows, taking in the view one last time. Thinking of all the books he'd written here. Of all the sleepless nights, turning over events from his childhood. Believing the worst of a brother he'd once loved. The space that was both a sanctuary and a prison.

"Poppy had discovered the truth of what Paul Stewart was doing to kids inside the equipment shed at the high school," I hear myself saying, "and what he'd done to Danny. She'd wanted to meet my father back at the house to tell him, but he didn't get there in time." My voice sounds steady, though my words rip through me, still wishing for a different ending. "One of Danny's friends overheard them arguing about it and told Danny, who knew what she was going to reveal." My voice grows quieter in my ears and I turn away from the view and face the wall of empty bookshelves, waiting for someone else's library. "We're not sure what happened after that, but the result was the death of my aunt and uncle. Two young kids with their whole lives ahead of them."

This is the story I tell Jessica. But my father and I aren't so sure. We can assemble the pieces of the puzzle that we have, but the truth belongs to Poppy. To Danny. And of course, Mr. Stewart.

Jessica's voice pulls me back again. "Several other victims of Paul Stewart—both men and women—have come forward since the memoir was published, with their own stories, spanning from the mid-seventies all the way through 2011. I hear he was indicted?"

"Yes, a couple weeks ago." The police had arrived at Paul Stewart's door with a search warrant, California's laws allowing prosecutors to file multiple cases against him despite the many years and decades that have passed. Within hours, he was taken into custody.

"Does it bother you that he won't be indicted for the murders? That the man who took your aunt and uncle's lives won't pay for that?" Jessica asks.

"Paul Stewart will still go to jail. He'll pay for heinous crimes he committed against people who are still alive to suffer from the effects of those crimes. They're the ones who need justice, more than my aunt and uncle need it."

I stand in the doorway to my father's office and take one last look, at the place where I used to curl up and do my homework, just to be near him. Where I sat once again, not so long ago, and witnessed the beginning of the end of my father's brilliant mind.

Then I turn away, closing the door behind me.

"I'd like to pivot to the house where the murders took place," Jessica says. "Which your family still owned. You recently had it torn down. Why?"

"All my life, this story has lived inside of me. The pieces and the players, the questions. I spent a lot of time inside that house as I finished the memoir. In Poppy's room, seeing what she saw, imagining who she dreamt of becoming. I stood in the spot where Danny died. Sat in the kitchen where they ate as a family." I paused for a moment, then continued, saying the biggest truth I could at the time. "But after the book was done, I needed to close the loop. After the house was demolished, I sold the lot, and now someone is going to build something new there. Which feels like a metaphor for all of us, to build something better on top of the ashes of a painful history."

"That's a lovely way to put it," Jessica says.

Downstairs again, I slide open the French doors and sit on my father's wrought-iron bench to wait. In the distance, I see the motion of the electronic gates slide open and a car coming slowly down the driveway. It rolls to a stop and I rise, making my way around the side of the house just as Tom steps from it, standing uncertainly next to the open car door.

Yesterday, I'd sent him the address and a time, with the words I need to show you where I came from.

And because he's Tom, he came.

Vincent

March 3, 1975

I sit on the back step drawing with a stick in the dirt, the sky turning from pink to purple as the sun sets behind our house, and watch Poppy in the middle of the yard, spinning. She wears a long skirt, one I haven't seen her wear for a while, and she's pinned one of our mother's old scarves to the back of her head—a wispy blue and green piece of fabric so light it nearly floats through the air, tucking it under the paper birthday hat our mother insisted we all wear. As she spins, flashes of her smile blink at me. She holds her new camera in her hands, the Super 8 our father bought for her birthday, despite our mother's protests.

Our parents lean in to each other on the bench of the picnic table, the remnants of Poppy's birthday gifts a scattered mess of empty boxes and crumpled wrapping paper. Danny sits in the chair next to the firepit, feeding wood into it, keeping the flames strong and warm.

I glance at the house next door, the For Sale sign in front sporting a brand-new Sold sticker on top, and wonder who bought it. Perhaps a family with a kid my age, someone who doesn't already have preconceived ideas about who I am. Someone who hasn't heard all the rumors, listened to all the mistakes I've made over the years, trying and failing to fit in.

Poppy pauses to catch her breath. In the dirt at my feet, I sketch a house, a square with a triangle on top. On the radio, the song turns to "You are So Beautiful," by Joe Cocker, and my father stands, pulling my mother up to dance. I imagine dancing to that song with Lydia. My arms around her waist, pulling her close and never letting go. A flare of disbelief, that she'd picked me, explodes inside of me.

Poppy resumes her spinning, the scarf under her hat swelling out like a wedding veil caught in the wind, and I wonder what she'll be like when she gets older, who she might grow into as the years pass. My father's birthday toast echoes through my mind: *When Poppy was born, she was beauty and grace and light. And she continues to be that, all her beautiful days.*

Then I think of the story still tucked in my backpack, to what my English teacher had written at the top. *I might see a budding author in these pages. Keep up the great work.* The first compliment a teacher has ever given me. The idea burns bright inside of me and I imagine a future where things aren't so hard. For the first time, I can see possibility in myself. Trying harder in school. Writing more stories. Maybe even getting paid to do it.

Above us, the first stars are just beginning to appear. The windows behind me cast a warm glow on the ground, patches of light illuminating the rosebushes not yet in bloom. My father gives a bark of laughter and my mother soon follows. I wish I could freeze time. To live inside this moment forever. My family, its best version of itself.

"Vince, come and spin with me," Poppy calls, finally setting down her camera. "You know you want to."

I hesitate, but only for a second. Our parents smile at me and Danny laughs, rolling his eyes as he pokes the fire, sending bright sparks into the air. I drop my stick and go out to join her, grabbing her wrists and leaning back, knowing my sister will always be there to hold me up.

Author's Note

Part of this story takes place in Ojai, California in the 1970s. I've done my best to stay true to the geography and people of that era, though I've had to make some minor changes to serve the story. The most notable change is the annual Ojai summer festival portrayed in these pages. There have been several Ojai carnivals over the decades – The original Ojai Day, which ran from 1917 to 1928, and another one in the 1950s. Nordhoff High School briefly hosted a carnival in the 1990s, until finally Ojai Day was revived at Libby Park in the fall of 1991.

I also altered the geography of the neighborhood and houses surrounding the Ojai Meadows Preserve so as not to resemble any existing neighborhood our houses. My reasons will soon become clear.

Special thanks to Wendy Barker at the Ojai Valley Museum for putting me in touch with local historian and lifelong resident Craig Walker. Craig was instrumental in my understanding of 1970s Ojai, talking to me about the geography of what is now the Ojai Meadows Preserve and downtown areas as well as many of the things kids did in Ojai in the 1970s. Any errors are strictly my own.